Change

of

Plans

KJ

2021

Cover: Em Schreiber

Acknowledgements

I started writing this story in August of 2020. So much global stuff was happening. Melbourne was in the midst of a one-hundred and twenty-four day hard lockdown. One hour outside, face masks anywhere anytime, five-kilometre radius, online shopping compulsory—including groceries, absolutely everything closed, you name it. You'd think it would have been the perfect opportunity to spend time writing. Well, that type of thinking is…hopeful. I actually was hopeful, but realistic because lockdowns cause change. Changes that are abrupt and uncomfortable. So, in that changing environment, I attempted to write. It's funny how life imitates art. While I was attempting to bash out this novel, a many changes in my own life were happening. Change affects us in stages; we are presented with the change and we react, we journey through the change and then we sit in the product of the change. And we react again. Some of us deal with change rather well—or think we do. I'm one of the other sort of people; those who find change remarkably similar to a particularly large and aggressive wave crashing onto the beach where we, immobile, mouth agape, cannot process any part of the situation. Those people. The soggy ones covered in sand and seaweed, sobbing into a conch shell.

You'll come to a bit in the book, about page two, in which Emily states that;

"Her life did not violently veer off towards the trees into the underbrush, collecting nature and God knows what on the windscreen, to come to a halt upside-down in a pond. No. Emily's life did not do that. Plans were not portable in Emily's life. They were large and immovable."

There's a lot of me in Emily, which is why Skye was a lot of fun to write as a counter-balance.

In 'Change of Plans' I wanted to show that sometimes if you find your person, or a big love, then a change of plans can be the only logical outcome, whether you're ready for it or not.

I want to say thank you to the reviewers; the ones who click on the stars through to the ones who write their hearts. You've read one of my books, and given it space in your memories, and that is a gift.

I want to say thank you to the writers, like Sel, and Angela, and Cheyenne, and Rach, and Jude, and Jae, and Melissa, and Lee, and more, who have sent words, memes, GIFs of encouragement in emails, direct messages, and hosted me on their platforms. You've welcomed me into the club and it's embarrassing how much I've rushed about showing off my membership card and lanyard.

My betas Sarah, Sophie, Maggie, Sel, and Sue who reined in my allegorical nonsense, kindly pointed out the truck-sized plot holes, and, knowing me like they do, prefaced their sensible and excellent suggestions with a screenshot or quote from their favourite part of the story so I could still function and type letters into words.

To AC and Em; thank you.

I value every single person who has helped me grow from an invisible human with access to the internet, to "that Australian author who writes in that squirly way like no-one else and has good characters".

Dedication

For Roanne
How many times have we changed our plans, darling? I love being part of this adventure with you.

<u>Coming Home</u> - *Goldie Awards finalist, LesFic Bard Awards finalist*

So many romance books tell the reader how much characters love each other. So few excel at showing you them falling. Honestly, I can't say I remember a book that did it better. This was full of moments. You could feel the adoration. Anytime Abigail observed Sam with Grace was swoon worthy. ~ Bookvark.com

Coming Home is my favourite book of the entire year. I found myself having such an emotional reaction to this story. How could I feel so invested in two fictional characters? Exceptional writing, that's why. ~ KittyKatWordpressCom.wordpress.com

<u>Learning To Swim</u>

More than people falling in love, this book is about finding yourself, loving yourself so that you can then love and be loved. It's about taking charge of your life and taking care of yourself. KJ writes beautifully and even with such a sensitive topic as mental health (since that's what it is), she manages to instil some measure of joy and a lot of optimism. ~ judeinthestars.wordpress.com

<u>Kick Back</u> - *Goldie Awards finalist*

KJ packs a wallop in this book, but is able to tie it all together very nicely. The result is a wonderfully executed novel. ~ The Lesbian Book Blog

The relationship between Cam and Sophia is built beautifully. KJ always writes great dialogues and the MCs have great connection and chemistry. ~ www.bestlesficreviews.com

<u>Art of Magic</u>

KJ's style is so unique. She switches with ease from profane dialogue (which I always love), to these fantastic one liners that are so deep I want to quote them to everyone. From the tone of a contemporary romance to philosophical questions, and artistically rich descriptions, she had my attention from page one. ~ The Lesbian Review

A touch of fantasy, entertaining banter, genuine loyalty and a whole lot of love in all its forms. Brilliant work, K.J! ~ XR - Goodreads

An Unexpected Gift: Christmas In Australia: Five Short Stories

Just a short time after I started reading the first story, I already had a huge smile on my face. KJ's writing honestly is one of the most beautiful ones I know. Every story was a unique and unexpected gift of their own. ~ Conny B - Goodreads

About the author

Best-selling author KJ lives in Melbourne, Australia with her wife, their son, three cats and a dog. Her novel, Coming Home, was a Goldie finalist. Her other best-selling novels include Learning To Swim, Kick Back, Art of Magic, and An Unexpected Gift: Christmas In Australia: Five Short Stories.

Twitter at @propertyofkj
Instagram at kjlesfic
Facebook at https://www.facebook.com/kj.lesfic.7/

I sincerely hope you enjoy reading *Change of Plans*. If you do, I would greatly appreciate a review on your favourite book website. Or even a recommendation in your favourite Facebook lesbian fiction group. Reviews and recommendations are crucial for any author, and even just a line or two can make a huge difference. Thanks!

Synopsis

Emily Fitzsimmons, award-winning architect, creates meticulous plans for every aspect of her life, which is understandable considering her difficult childhood. After all, prudence keeps her safe. Lately, though, too many of those comforting plans are disintegrating and Emily is forced to function spontaneously which has spiked her anxiety so much, she's put her therapist on speed-dial.

Skye Reynolds, bike courier entrepreneur, knows all about exploding plans. That's literally how she lost her job when her company blew up a 40,000-year-old world heritage site. But Skye is not someone who asks for help to reassemble her life blueprints, which is lucky as she nearly always lands on her feet whenever she happily ignores prudence to embark on any new adventure.

When Skye's ad hoc dirt track intersects with Emily's carefully paved freeway, their lives are thrown into disarray, with the added complication of their unexpected attraction. Prudence plays tricks on both of them when they choose to navigate their true paths and explore the direction of their relationship.

Sometimes a change of plans is all you need to see what lies ahead.

Chapter One

It still produced a thrill down Emily's spine when she pushed open the green wrought iron gate to the boutique terrace building that housed *Fitzsimmons Architecture and Design*. The path laid with large black and white Victorian-era outdoor tiles led to the front door; an object that some of the tenants described as old, but Emily thought of as 'reflecting the vast experiences of life'. She paused for a moment at that vastly life-experienced entrance to run her fingers over one of the six shiny brass plaques screwed into the bricks at eye level on the right-hand side. The metal rectangle bore her name, and another little thrill tap-danced along her skin, because here she was at thirty-one years of age with her own business in an industry she loved.

Her smile widened. The plan was still on track.

The red carpet was slightly threadbare in the hallway and needed replacing, but it had that old world charm, so the tenants had asked the landlord to leave it when the renovations had been scheduled last year. In fact, most of the original trimmings, mouldings, and iron fittings had been kept, just spruced up a little, seeing as it was a heritage-listed building. It was part of the reason why Emily had chosen it for her office space. That, and the location. There was nothing like working in a nineteenth-century two-storey terrace house only five kilometres from the centre of the city.

The cream-coloured building had been converted into three large office spaces upstairs and three downstairs, and it was the frosted glass door to the front office on the ground floor that Emily pushed open. It closed quietly behind her as she turned to grin at Jas.

"Morning. That's a new look," she said, taking in her office manager's blue tips of her dip-dyed blonde hair. "I like it."

Jas Conway beamed, flicked her eyes to the computer monitor, pressed a couple of buttons on the keyboard, then turned to give Emily her full attention.

"Morning right back at you, boss. Thanks." She pulled at the ends of a few strands near her jawline. "I figured I'd try something new." The layers and textures floated off to the side. It was a work of art surrounding a face that sparkled with mischief and wit. "It looks great on my profile, as well."

Emily laughed. Jas's boyfriends were the unwitting participants in a catch and release program, which Jas admitted wasn't the most ethical usage of a dating app, but she was generally unapologetic. It made for interesting mid-morning coffee discussions every Monday, and Emily assumed today's would be just as entertaining.

"I've lost count of how many times I've told you not to call me 'boss'," she said through an aggrieved sigh, which Jas brushed off with another huge grin and a shrug.

"Okay. No worries, Oh Mighty Leader, All-Round Excellent Person, and Winner of the Coveted Young Architect of the Year Award," Jas intoned, emphasising her words with a wide-eyed look. "Twice," she added.

Emily laughed. "I'm going to have to live with 'boss', aren't I?"

"Yep," Jas said, then lifted her chin towards Emily's small office inside their large open workspace. The mini office housed a tiny desk with a monitor arranged on top, and a little filing cabinet, which doubled as a storage drawer for her bag and a spare pair of shoes. She generally worked in the main area with Rach Arnell and Dimitri Galanis, her two junior architects—even though Rach was nine years older than her—at the large drafting desks, and at the oversized monitors which displayed their CAD drawings, but every now and then, the office, and more importantly the door to it, was highly valued.

"Your schedule's on your laptop when you plug in, and you've got a video link with the site foreman on the *Cascades* townhouses build at ten."

Emily sighed. The *Cascades* townhouses weren't going completely as she'd envisaged and having to micromanage the interpretation of the plans was becoming very wearing. It was time to send Dimitri on a site visit. Perfect practice for when he decided to start his own firm and had to deal with obtuse foremen.

She placed her laptop bag on the desk, discarded the other into the filing cabinet, accessorised the wall hook with her coat, then straightened to appraise herself in the little mirror attached to the inside of the door. Closely-cropped brown hair that always looked like she'd wandered through a hedge no matter how much effort and product she applied, elfin features, slim body which was perhaps a smidge above average in height, and dark brown, almost black, eyes, that Emily thought too large for her face. She shrugged and muttered a quiet "you'll do" before she slipped into the office chair and opened her computer. A two-tone alert sounded from the depths of the laptop bag perched precariously on the edge of the desk, and she pulled it to safety while scooping out the phone. The text message was brief.

Won't be there tonight. Have back 2 back open houses. X

Emily wrapped both hands around the device and leaned heavily on her elbows. The lock screen photo of thirty-year-old Rebecca Deans demonstrated how very photogenic her girlfriend of fourteen months was. Bec was gorgeous with blue eyes, and long blonde hair that fell in straight lines to her shoulders. In the photo, she was wrapped in Emily's arms, and Emily, in charge of the selfie, was looking adoringly at the side of Bec's face, as Bec stared off into the distance. Emily thought Bec looked contemplative and windblown.

And stunning. It had surprised Emily at first how fast their relationship had begun, as it had only taken a couple of dates, after their initial introduction by a friend, for them to be travelling along the relationship road. Bec had seemed on board with the structured, forward-planned nature of their relationship, and Emily was thrilled with their connection.

Although lately, there'd been a disconnect. Bec's nights in her city apartment had increased to the point where they seemed to only see each other every second or third day—if that—even though Emily had mentioned that it seemed illogical for Bec to travel back to her apartment when her open homes were sometimes only three streets away from Emily's place, so why didn't she stay over? Emily's house, a terrace—she readily admitted that she had a crush on the old buildings of Melbourne—was located on a beautiful tree-lined avenue only six kilometres from the CBD, but night-time open houses and showings, meetings that went on late to fit in, according to Bec, with the daily lives of international clients were now the norm. Bec almost seemed annoyed when Emily pushed, but it was probably tiredness from work. It wasn't like Emily could point the finger, though. Work, work, and more work was really all she'd done since launching out of Uni, clutching her degree, and starting down the road towards 'successful architect please pay attention'. Bec deserved her success as well. She was making a name for herself in the real estate market and if that meant missing many nights together, so be it.

However, even though their organised date nights were being steadily wiped from the surface of the Earth, catching date nights on the fly whenever they were both available was also impossible, because Emily couldn't do spontaneous live-in-the-moment…moments, no matter how much her therapist tried to push. She found it entirely comforting to know that her life was mapped out as a road that ran completely intact towards the horizon, occasionally stopping at a T-junction intersection where she paused, evaluated, analysed, projected and then turned, all planned and perfect, onto a new road. Her life did not violently veer off towards the trees into the underbrush, collecting nature and God knows what on the windscreen, to come to a halt upside-down in a pond. No. Emily's life did not do that. Plans were not portable in Emily's life. They were large and immovable. And Bec was not exactly a paid-up member of the Emily-Needs-To-Plan fan club. Maybe she hadn't ever been? Surely not.

She closed her eyes and breathed deeply. Then sent the reply.

That's okay. I'll call you tonight and we can plan for another time. Good luck with the open houses. Em. XX

Maybe the disconnect had been a bit longer than just 'lately', which made Emily all levels of uncomfortable because that would mean stepping into terrifying unplanned territory.

Tossing the phone to the side of her laptop, she dismissed the cancelled night in and moved on with her day. The video meeting with Julio went reasonably well. A complete surprise, as his emails and voice mails were becoming steadily more clipped and brusque. The offer to send Dimitri over in the afternoon to *Cascades* to help interpret plans, pat backs, nod seriously and deliver a sort of positive masculine hum every now and then was greeted enthusiastically. Emily tapped the red 'end' button and rolled her eyes. Dimitri was a very talented architect, as equally talented as Rach, but sometimes his advantage of being a 'man who spoke man language' helped out enormously. And Emily wasn't immune to playing that card. She sent a quick text to Dimitri to let him know that his manhood was needed and got a laughing emoji in return.

The phone buzzed in her hand, and a glance at the name on the screen brought a smile to her face. Lorraine Hudson. Architect Extraordinaire. Soon-to-be-retired CEO of *Architects Australia* and

Emily's mentor for the first three years of her career. Lorraine was a force of nature; professional, focussed, a mind like a steel trap, and possessor of one of the kindest hearts that Emily knew.

"Hi Lorraine," Emily said, as she relaxed back into her chair. "How are you?"

"Emily! Very well, actually. Imminent retirement does wonders for one's mental health," Lorraine said, her words infused with her cultured Melbourne accent. Emily laughed.

"I'm sure, although I know you'll absolutely miss it."

"Probably, but not immediately. My to-be-read pile beside my bed is tall enough to qualify as your next contract." Emily could picture the subtle purse of the older woman's lips and the cheeky glint in her eyes. Lorraine was kind but very mischievous, and whenever someone called her on it, she always claimed it to be her prerogative because she was old. Apparently, according to Lorraine, when people managed to reach seventy years of age, filters and other tools of tact could be discarded.

"Speaking of contracts, my dear," Lorraine continued, "I'm phoning to congratulate you on signing 45 Anders Road."

Emily grinned. This was fundamentally Lorraine. Not only did she have her finger on the architectural pulse of Melbourne, she always made the effort to contact Emily whenever a new *Fitzsimmons* contract appeared on her radar. It was delightful and produced a warm glow in Emily's chest.

"Thanks. We're finishing a bit earlier today and having drinks in the office to celebrate. Not too many. It's a school night, of course," Emily said, through a quick laugh.

"Of course. Well, just wanted to say congratulations. You're going from strength to strength, and it's wonderful to watch. I have so enjoyed being able to inhabit your work life, Emily. To be involved."

There was a pause, as Emily absorbed the threads of emotion that crept through the phone. Their connection was beyond mentor-mentee. It was more like good friends or like Lorraine was a wise counsel who offered advice as Emily metaphorically journeyed to foreign lands. She giggled to herself at the thought of Lorraine with a cloak and beard, puffing on a pipe.

The sound of shuffling paper came through the speaker. "Now, you received your invitation, I presume," Lorraine said, the wistfulness obliterated. This was the invitation to the *Architects Australia* retirement dinner for Lorraine on the coming Saturday. It was going to be an elaborate event, full of speeches and free alcohol, which was guaranteed to unlock inhibitions. Lorraine would be in her element. People and their plethora of personalities were an endless source of entertainment. It's why Emily, despite their close relationship, had remained somewhat reserved during the mentorship, and in the years since. There was no sense in arming Lorraine with too much personal information. That would be like giving an impish child a collection of brand new toys.

Of course, Lorraine knew about Bec, since Bec operated in the outer circles of Lorraine and Emily's profession, and Bec had no reservations about sharing a great many details of herself with anyone she thought could further her career. It was an aspect of their relationship where Emily and Bec's opinions were very divergent and had caused a few arguments in their fourteen months.

"And how is Rebecca?" The voice was laced with interest. Emily rolled her lips.

"She's fine. Busy, particularly with the market up at the moment," she said, holding Lorraine at bay. The older woman's hum acknowledged the subtle wall that Emily had erected.

"Excellent. Yes, it is looking promising. Now, I must be off. Congratulations, again."

"Thank you." There was hardly a gap between the last syllable and Lorraine hanging up. The smile stayed on Emily's lips, as she looked at the blank screen. Boring was not an adjective she'd ever apply to her mentor.

Nic Hunter, her interior designer, arrived at midday, which ensured that all work stopped, because light, laughter, and exceptional baked goods had appeared in the office. The baked goods were courtesy of Nic's boyfriend, Marco, who was attempting to perfect the ultimate cupcake, and sought feedback from a wide range of sources, including the staff of *Fitzsimmons Architecture and Design*.

"Today, darlings," he declared, standing in the middle of the work space, the cake box perched on an open hand, and size eleven heels planted firmly on the carpet. "We have a vanilla-bean base, with pink fondant layering, and dark chocolate icing, adorned with edible unicorns and rainbows."

Jas clapped, which prompted everyone to join in and Nic beamed. Rach relieved him of the cake box and Nic wandered over to Emily, who was leaning against a drafting board. He flicked a finger up and down.

"Oh yes, Em, the smart casual look is working for you today. Gorgeous blouson-sleeve wool jumper, hon." He lifted his eyebrows and nodded in appreciation. Emily looked down at herself, then wrinkled her forehead and stared blankly at her interior designer.

"Is that what I'm wearing?"

Nic tossed his hands. "Oh, good God, lady. Did you just barge into a shop, point at something and think that'll do?"

Emily opened her mouth, but Nic pointed an elegant finger at her, the red nail polish glinting in the artificial light.

"Do not answer that."

They grinned at each other. Nic and Emily had been friends at Uni, but had lost contact when they'd graduated, and then found each other again at a queer-in-business event in the city two years ago. It was an easy decision to have Nic join the *Fitzsimmons* team, particularly with the star pulling-power he now generated, based on a number of very happy, very rich clients. Nic's drag persona—Nicola Nightshade—was a Saturday night headline act at *Utopia* in the city, and he would regularly come to work, like today, in a gorgeous men's suit, heels, and elaborate eye artistry—the latter simply to try out new designs for his show. Today's was a masterpiece of smokey hot pink with liner along the lid and then something amazing brushed under the outer curve of his brow that made his hazel eyes look like gold. The thinnest line of black outlined, curved, and pulled the colours together to a point beside each eyebrow, so that it looked like he was staring out through the wings of a dragonfly. It was pure genius.

"So, do we get to eat one of these fantabulous creations or just sit around salivating over the cream frosting, while acknowledging how deliciously gorgeous those shoes are?"

The sarcastic teasing from Jas caused everyone to chuckle, including Nic, who executed a tight twirl and waved his hand at the box.

"I expect responses, ratings, and reviews, please. Marco values your opinions, people."

Chapter Two

As far as deliveries went, this one was pretty unusual. A single shoe. A gold stiletto heel to be exact. Skye Reynolds steered her cargo bike onto the footpath outside the block of flats and coasted slowly to a stop at the nearest bike rack. The bulky carrier box mounted behind the front wheel meant that she took up four spaces, but she was never there for long, since time was money as the saying went. In all other aspects, it was a standard bike, except for its weight. Eighty kilograms of cargo, and the bike itself, was tough to manoeuvre, even with her strong arms and shoulders. She'd taken a while to get used to the huge distance between the handlebars and the front wheel, despite her own solid frame and reasonable height. She had started *Quick Cargo* a year ago, but it could have only lasted a week. Dropping the 'I haven't got used to it yet' bike, and staring in open-mouthed helplessness at the box cradling the two-tier wedding cake as it tipped like a slow-motion scene in the *Matrix,* was probably the most alarming experience she'd ever had.

Luckily, her profusion of apologies to both Harold at *Cake At Once* and a rather exasperated wedding planner staved off the expected loss of business, and she'd been able to move on.

Windy days were a killer. Fighting the elements through the wind tunnel that was Graham Street in the city centre up to three times a day usually destroyed Skye's energy levels. But today? Today was perfect. A bit chilly but blue skies, no breeze, and polite traffic. Perfect for a Monday in the first week of June. The weather, the people, the variety of items to deliver ensured that every day was unpredictable. And therefore super enjoyable. That was the cheese at the end of the mouse maze that was the sensible street grid—but not always—system that defined Melbourne city.

She dismounted and pulled the lock and chain from her backpack. Leaving her bike helmet on—it seemed pointless to keep taking it off, plus she'd be exposing seriously awful hat hair to the world—she locked the bike, grabbed the labelled shoebox, and jogged up the building's short path, and into the little foyer. Her blonde ponytail bounced on her shoulders, catching on the rough material of the hi-vis vest she wore over her Lycra top. The bright orange garment was necessary in a city where drivers flung open car doors with blind abandon and made right-hand turns from the left lane. The Lycra top and pants were simply another layer of skin as far as the surface of the road was concerned.

The voice responding to the buzzer had sounded both sleepy, and grumpy, so Skye injected some extra cheer into her smile when she knocked on the second-floor door.

"Yeah?" An unimpressed eyeball peered through the gap created by the security chain.

"My name's Skye. I have a package from Ian at *Club Illusions* for Jennifer Marchetti," Skye said, shifting a little and tilting her head so she was more in line with the woman's eye.

The door slammed shut. There was a scraping of metal on metal, and the door re-opened, with the woman, dressed in a light blue silk robe, beaming into Skye's face.

"You've got my shoe!" she gasped, and thrust out her hands for the box, the action causing the robe to shift and gape, rewarding Skye with an excellent view of the inner curve of both breasts. Skye blinked and quickly averted her gaze. She appreciated breasts as much as the next queer woman, but now was not the time.

"Ah, yes. Are you Jennifer Marchetti?" At the woman's single word affirmation, Skye unclipped the portable electronic signature device from her belt. Then, after listening to a brief, yet convoluted, story about the reason for the single shoe delivery—"Dani's fault"— and how amazing Ian was—"So amazing!"—Skye grinned at a now quite alert and bubbly Jennifer, who suddenly seemed aware of Skye's strong Lycra-clad thighs, and broad shoulders, then wished her a great day and trotted downstairs. These types of random moments absolutely made each day the spontaneous fun that she adored. Even the shoe pick up earlier had been fun.

The nightclub had looked rather stark and forlorn, actually, when she'd completed the pick up an hour before. Ian, the aforementioned amazing, had shrugged his shoulders when he'd registered the job on Skye's e-reader.

"Jennifer's a regular and I try to keep my regulars happy. Solving shoe emergencies qualifies as bringing happiness."

Skye cocked her head. "One shoe?"

"Mm-hmm. Retro Macarena moment. Don't ask." He rolled his tired-looking blue eyes and shook his head.

Skye grinned. "Macarena. Number three on the world's top ten most addictive and dangerous dance routines." Ian laughed and tilted his chin at the exit.

"Thanks, Skye. Call you again if I've got any more lost items of clothing."

She tapped her phone screen when she arrived downstairs at her bike. One shoe returned to a grateful owner. Check. Saving a woman from disaster, even the abandoned shoe kind, was totally Skye's jam. And a behaviour she was trying to eliminate, which was complicated when it felt ingrained into her DNA. Saviour Syndrome. She may as well have worn a cape, because too many times she'd been the strong shoulder to lean on, listening to all sorts of tales and woes from women who were friends of friends, or girlfriends of other friends. And when those women—those *single* women; Skye gestured vaguely at the footpath to emphasise that fact—had later pursued Skye because "Gosh, you're a great listener", she'd leapt in, boots and all, enjoyed their company with total engagement. Only to discover that once the women felt recovered enough from whatever event they'd initially needed Skye's help with, they would thank her and move off. Usually taking a piece of Skye's heart with them. So, from now on it was Operation A.S.S—Abolish Saviour Syndrome. No more complete engagement.

Two jobs had come in while she'd played a walk-on role in the Cinderella story upstairs. Seb Arturo, her co-worker—the only other worker at *Quick Cargo* besides herself—had flagged the job on the north side of the city. Skye knew he was over that way already, so she pulled up the details for the second job. A flower delivery. Skye grinned. They were always a happy occasion, and it was one of the main items that she and Seb handled. Particularly flowers in vases, which was unique for a bike service, but the cargo bicycles were phenomenal. The load rested between the axles, so the juddering was smoothed out and everything sat all stable and happy in the box. It had been difficult to convince the eight independent florists she serviced that her little courier company could handle their fragile products, but a stream of successful deliveries had cracked their hesitation. Same with the cake shops.

Unlocking the bike, rolling it down the slight incline of the footpath onto the road, and setting off towards the florist two kilometres towards the south-side of the city, Skye settled into the push-pull rhythm that allowed for mind-wandering, yet still kept an awareness of traffic. Mind-wandering that included thoughts about her impending homelessness. Skye huffed a sigh. The lease on her current home was up in three weeks, and no amount of frantic searching had found her another place like the one she had. Or even any place at all. It seemed that the rental market had suddenly inflated like an irritated puffer fish, and Skye's budget didn't extend another few hundred dollars a week for a single bedroom dive, just because she needed to live close to the city centre for her work.

At the last open house she'd attended, there had been twenty-three people all vying for the property and the standard whispers to the property agent of "I can offer a hundred more if you bump me up the list" had started before she'd even set foot inside.

Currently, her home was a beautiful, teeny tiny self-contained studio attached to the back of Lorraine Hudson's house. The Lorraine Hudson of *Architects Australia* fame. The Lorraine Hudson who was appointed the first woman chief executive officer of the prestigious organisation and had held the reins for twenty years. Now, here Lorraine was, a week away from retirement, her house on the market, and moving to an extravagant home perched on the hills overlooking the beach on the north coast of Victoria. Skye had gazed at the photos of the structure on Lorraine's phone when the older woman had broken the news of the tenancy finalisation last month.

"It looks amazing, Lorraine," she'd complimented, returning the device as Lorraine settled into the armchair across from the couch. Skye lifted the dainty china teacup and saucer that had been waiting for her on the little side table. The tea-drinking routine existed because despite the presence of a maintenance service, during the two years that Skye had been a tenant, she trimmed the hedges, or replaced tiles, or re-mortared loose brickwork in the house, and Lorraine would invite Skye in for tea.

"Yes. The building is heritage-listed, and I'm so looking forward to maintaining the original elements," Lorraine enthused, the wrinkles on her seventy-year-old face concertinaing into practised smile lines. Then her mouth dropped a little. "Again, I'm incredibly contrite about leaving you in the lurch."

Skye sipped at her black tea. "It's fine. Really. I'm sure something will turn up. And no," she looked at Lorraine over the top of her cup, "I don't need any help." She took in the wide-eyed look of innocence and smiled at how it did nothing to camouflage the nearly permanent cheeky sparkle in the older woman's eyes.

"I simply offered to talk to some people who know people who might know some more people," Lorraine said, sighing in mock exasperation.

Skye laughed and replaced the cup and saucer on the table. "Yeah. I know who your people who know people are, and they probably won't let me rent their studios, if they had one, for the little amount that you charge me."

Lorraine chuckled. "You'll just have to garner a sugar mummy, or whatever the expression is."

Skye coughed. "Um…"

Lorraine laughed gleefully at Skye's expression. "Oh, Skye, dear. I do jest. You're much too independent to tie yourself into that sort of relationship. I'm well aware of that. So, anyway," she gestured airily, "as long as you're sure about finding a place yourself."

Skye lifted her cup, tipped it to drain the last dregs of tea, then replaced it on the saucer. "Absolutely, but thank you. I like to make my own way in the world."

Lorraine had pursed her lips, as if she'd had some thoughts to share about not asking for assistance while making one's way in the world. Skye had ignored the familiar gesture.

Yet, she couldn't ignore the fact that Lorraine's house was to be sold, and Skye's current residential address would become non-existent. In three weeks.

Another wandering driver brought her focus back, and she spotted the street where the florist was located, and flung out her left arm, indicating her intention to the cars behind her. Hopefully, a new place would turn up. It just had to.

Skye dismounted at the little flower shop, locked up her bike, and pushed open the door, the bell above the frame ringing happily for a few seconds. Luke glanced up from his counter, the laminate covered in sprays of tiny flowers and piles of greenery.

"Hey there. You made good time. I only sent the request through half an hour ago."

Skye stretched her arms up, clasping her hands, and tilted her head into each bicep, enjoying the soft pop of her vertebrae. "Yep. Gotta keep my people happy," she replied, a grin planted on her mouth. She leaned on the counter, rubbed a leaf, and brought her fingers to her nose. Eucalyptus. Gorgeous. "Delivery to—"

"*Fitzsimmons Architecture and Design*," Luke said, despite knowing that Skye's phone would have those details. "The lilies in the corner." Skye turned and took in the elaborate arrangement, which was already packed into a secure travel box with plastic cellophane around the flowers to protect them from the wind. She nodded.

"Cool. It's not far, and they'll look just as pretty when they get there."

Luke smiled. "I know, Skye. That's why you're on my speed dial."

With the vase and flowers settled in the cargo box, Skye pushed off from the curb and waved gratefully at the driver who'd stopped to allow her bike to join the traffic. The delivery point —one she'd been to a couple of times before—was a kilometre away, so it seemed only the next minute that she was pushing open the green wrought iron gate to the stunning Victorian terrace that had been converted into office space. The six brass plates at the front door announced a variety of professions, including a lawyer, an accountant, a creative media agency, another lawyer, a consultant—that label sounded exquisitely vague—and the architecture firm she needed. A quick turn brought her through the glass door of *Fitzsimmons*, and she was smiling into the open face of the young woman—Jas—who occupied the tiny reception desk, which was completely dominated by a computer, various stationery items, and a line of eclectic cat figurines. Skye contemplated the blue-tipped hair, then smiled.

"I have a delivery for…" she cradled the vase in one arm and twisted her phone to read the name, "you." She grinned. "You're Jasmine Conway, right?"

The woman's eyes blew wide, and she stood quickly. "That is me. You've delivered here before. Um…" She tipped her head, then thrust out her hands for the flowers. "Skye! That's it. I'm Jasmine. Well, actually it's Jas. I don't normally go by Jasmine unless I'm with my parents or I'm going fancy for a date, which might explain this amazingness, because I really went all out last time, and I'm going to shut up now." She grimaced. "I'm sorry?"

Skye laughed. "No worries. Here you go." She passed over the flowers, her hand clasped around the body of the vase, which dropped slightly in Jas's arms as she took its weight. "Can I get you to sign for them, please?"

A voice, smooth and sassy, travelled across the room, "Well, that's disappointing. I was convinced I'd done the impressing on Saturday night." Skye looked up. An incredibly elegant man uncrossed his legs and rose, brushing non-existent fluff off his jacket, before gliding across to Jas on a pair of impossibly high heels. He peered over her shoulder in an attempt to read the note. She slapped it to her chest and grinned up into his face.

"Too bad, Nic, honey. All mine today," Jas said through a smirk, the gesture including Skye in some sort of solidarity.

Skye laughed. "I've delivered to you before, Nic. Am I an unwitting participant in a competition?"

Nic's smile was dazzling, and the beautiful artistry around his eyes, the wings of colour, which extended from the very beginnings of his eyelashes out to his temples, undulated with the movement of his skin.

"Jas has a trail of admirers like a wedding car has cans, but I get my share of flowers, don't you worry." He cocked his head and stared at Skye. "Either from you or that rather yummy colleague of yours."

"Yummy colleague?" Jas's question was followed by an interested hum, and Skye laughed loudly.

"Seb? Yes, he's delivered here. Only to Nic, though. But I wouldn't know about the yumminess. He's a mate, and definitely not my version of edible." She shrugged, and a knowing smile lifted Nic's lips. Skye registered her accidental innuendo and blushed slightly. Then she gestured at Nic to cover her embarrassment. "By the way, that is utterly amazing eye art."

Nic beamed. "Thank you, lovely. You can deliver here any time." He winked, then strode like a model back to his desk.

Enjoying their banter, Skye lifted her gaze as the little office door opened and a slim woman walked into the space. Emily Fitzsimmons. Skye knew exactly who she was. She'd surreptitiously gathered that piece of information from Jas on her last delivery to the architectural firm. Emily made eye contact and smiled briefly, then wandered across to the only other man in the office, who was leaning over some plans at a standing desk near the window.

Skye's gaze lingered, appreciating Emily's quite short brown hair, which was in such complete disarray that it had to be professionally styled to look like that. Appreciating how that same hair picked up the sunlight so that the dark blonde highlights popped. Appreciating Emily's dark brown eyes and how her pretty face was arranged in that focused, contained expression that Skye had noticed on the other occasions she'd delivered. Imagining how her slim figure would feel against Skye's much more solid body. A delicious tightening, low in her stomach, made itself known and she quickly jerked her head, refocusing on the handheld reader, and ensuring that Jas had signed for the bouquet. Noticing Emily Fitzsimmons was perfectly fine. Drooling all over her hi-vis vest was something else altogether. Time to leave.

"Right. The day is done, folks. We are on for contract celebration drinks," Jas announced into the office space, then she turned to Skye, and grinned at her bouquet. "Thanks for this. Looks like Michael deserves another date night." They nodded in agreement of that fact, and Skye double-tapped Jas's desk.

"Then I guess I'll be seeing you next Monday for Michael's second flower delivery," she said and turned to push through the door. A glance over her shoulder gave Skye the opportunity to catch Emily regarding her with a long look.

Chapter Three

Emily braced her elbow and forearm on the doorframe and leaned forward, stretching the muscles across the front of her shoulder. The tight twinge meant too long at a desk that morning, hunched over plans; both the building and life versions. She swapped arms and repeated the exercise, acknowledging the tension on that side as well. At least she was well-balanced.

She gazed at her team, currently huddled around the small coffee table on caster wheels, where Marco, via Nic, had supplied yet another batch of deliciousness in the form of icing sugar and flour. Two days in a row. He was spoiling her little quirky group. A group she was very fond of. It was a group in which she could smile her brightest, sift away the tension that went with fitting new people into her mental plans, and show more of herself without reservation.

Jas was…well, Jas. Efficient and eclectic. Nic was brilliant and utterly loyal. She couldn't ask for a better friend. Rach's rich, rolling laugh cut through her musings, and she laughed quietly as the stocky forty-year-old architect flipped her middle finger at Jas, obviously in response to a teasing comment. Rach was a late bloomer, having only graduated two years ago. In her shortlist interview, her reply to Emily's gently probing question had been very unfiltered.

"Why now?" Rach had delivered a quick one-shoulder shrug. "Had to get my kids popped out and functioning before I could do what I wanted with my life," she'd answered dead-pan. Emily thought she was marvellous and hired her on the spot. In contrast to Rach's larger-than-life personality, Dimitri was more introverted, and usually pleased to carry on conversations next to people rather than across open spaces. However, he possessed, along with architectural talent, a chameleon-like ability to slip into any social situation and mimic the dialogue, behaviours and expectations necessary for effortless assimilation. It was magical to watch. Emily and Nic stood back and observed him in action last year at the topping-out ceremony for the *Freedom Heights* development. He'd slipped easily into the very elegant, very high-flying cluster of people around Lorraine Hudson, making and taking compliments and small talk, then wandered over to a group of builders, exchanging the glass of champagne for a bottle of craft beer along the way. His body language and gestures had altered infinitesimally, and he'd been absorbed as one of their own. Emily and Nic had grinned with delight. It was why she asked Dimitri to meet with neolithic cavemen masquerading as site managers every now and then.

Emily completed another pair of stretches, then walked to the bar fridge tucked into the corner of the main room. She bent to open the door, stared inside, and groaned. She'd definitely made lunch that morning, organised herself for the day, efficiently planned for the night's meal, kissed Bec good morning and goodbye—that had been a change of plans that Emily still felt conflicted by. Bec had unexpectedly arrived very late last night despite stating that she wasn't going to come over at all, and it worried Emily that a prickle of annoyance zipped through her body when she'd opened the door at midnight. That was a thought for later introspection.

So, probably due to that change of plans, she'd locked the front door, driven to work, and with beautiful finesse, left her lunch on the kitchen bench.

"Crap."

She stalked back into her office, grabbed her coat and bag, and rummaged for her car keys. Then stepped over to the little cupcake-appreciation group.

"I'm ducking back home to get my lunch." She pointed to the cake box. "Save me one."

"Just buy lunch from down the road," Rach said, nodding at her suggestion.

Emily's stomach clenched. It should be easy. Normally it was, because the crazy-planning side of herself usually only made itself known for important life events. But today she couldn't just pop down the road, and she couldn't put her finger on the reason why. Going home to retrieve her lunch, then returning to the office, and eating with her colleagues seemed essential at that very moment. There were ripples in the calm air she liked to exist within. Emily mentally rolled her eyes. Ripples in the air? Really?

"I...uh. It's nothing. I've got to do a couple of other things while I'm out, anyway." She smiled tightly at Rach, who shrugged. Nic gave Emily a considered stare.

"You okay?" he murmured.

"Yep."

Liar.

It was close to two o'clock when she eased her red sedan into the gravel driveway of her terrace house. It was a long building, which was typical of the era, and attached on one side to the next terrace house. The driveway ran along the other side of the house, and stopped at a free-standing single car garage, which Emily didn't use as she had converted it into a studio with a kitchenette, bathroom, and enough open space to indulge in her meditation; Ikebana. The Japanese flower arranging art form had become such an integral part of her life that she couldn't imagine being without it now. Kristen, her therapist, had suggested Ikebana last year when she'd been looking for strategies to compensate for Emily's over-planning, over-scheduling, and overly rigid routines.

"Ikebana."

"Ikebana?" Emily's eyebrows had risen into her choppy hair.

"Japanese flower arranging." The long look that Kristen had delivered was probably supposed to convey all the meaning necessary, but Emily missed it.

"I know what Ikebana is, but why?"

"Because it's all about living in the moment, yet planning ahead," Kristen answered. "You plan your design but as you're working with living things, you stay in the moment and make spontaneous choices based on the organics you have at your disposal. I think you'll find the contemplative nature of it helpful for the more intensive scheduling you engage in, like your latest stress management technique of allocating shoes to certain days."

Emily had been very skeptical. Yet to her amazement, she'd immediately felt comfortable with the craft and, after two months, had converted the garage into her studio. Spontaneity that was planned. Who knew? It certainly seemed to be working. She hadn't given her shoes any permanent weekday allocations in ten months.

She walked up the concrete path and steps to the front door, and she inserted the key, hoping to be in and out and back to the office in under thirty minutes. The sight that met her halted that wish immediately. Bec, her blouse tossed aside, her bra yanked down under her breasts, her fingers tugging her nipples taught, and her skirt rucked up to her waist, was flat on her back on the dining table, which was being used for a much more interesting purpose that the designers had originally envisaged. A tall, well-built woman with a strap-on was thrusting, breasts bouncing with each movement, a repeated single word affirmation grunting through her teeth, and Bec was shouting.

Emily threw her bag to the floor and took a quick step forward.

"Hey! Get off…" The rest of Emily's instruction trailed away as her mind disconnected to properly analyse the situation. Bec wasn't under attack. Nope. Bec was being thoroughly fucked and loving every minute of it.

However, Emily's half-yell had an immediate effect, as both women whipped their heads to the side, and with a loud "What the hell?", tall strap-on woman slid out and began collecting various pieces of clothing from the floor.

"What are you doing?" Emily asked, despite the objective part of her brain delivering a hard stare as if to say, "Really? You're not sure?"

Bec scrambled to sit upright, her legs dangling over the edge of the table. "You're not supposed to be here in the middle of the day," she stated accusatorially.

All the air left Emily's lungs. In fact, everything seemed to lose substance, except perhaps the purple dildo protruding jauntily from the tall woman's pelvis. She seemed to realise the attention it was receiving and tucked it into her pants before continuing to add clothing to her nakedness.

"I don't understand," Emily said. "What's happening?" Her feet were still not interested in making forward movements. It felt much more sensible to ask questions from where she stood near the front door.

"I only met her last night," Bec said, by way of explanation, heaving herself off the table, then adjusting her bra and tugging on her blouse.

The tall woman nodded. "Yeah. We only met last night."

Emily stared at both of them. "That piece of information doesn't enhance this situation." She pointed to the woman now toeing on her shoes. "Get out." Then added, "Please" because she was determined to hold onto her manners even if nobody else was. The woman bundled her remaining belongings, pulled together shreds of dignity from various locations, and marched out the front door without even a backwards glance at Bec.

Which seemed to piss Bec off even more.

"Why are you here? You never change your routine," she stated, her blue eyes flashing, as she fastened the last of her buttons, and smoothed her skirt down, clearly deciding that her panties were lost into the great beyond.

Emily spluttered, the statement galvanising her into action, propelling her feet across the floorboards and right into Bec's space. "I live here. This is my home. And seriously? You're having sex on my dining table," Emily jabbed her finger at the offending piece of furniture, "and it's my fault?"

Bec scoffed and shook her head, her blonde strands shifting about. They held their gaze for another moment.

Emily asked the obvious question. "Why?"

"Why not?" She sneered at Emily. "We don't have random fun. We don't have impromptu anything. Impulsive sex, for example. You never want to fool around in case it messes with the ridiculous locked-in-stone plans inside your head, which rule your life and therefore mine as well."

Emily reeled. "But we do make time. We…we had sex on the weekend." She mentally whipped through a highlights reel. It would qualify as sex. Just.

"Only after you'd made sure that there was nothing pressing on the agenda first. And even then it was perfunctory and pedestrian. I couldn't even get you interested last night."

"It was midnight! And you'd said you weren't coming over, and…" It was all just too much. The structure of her day, her life, was disintegrating.

"Em," Bec flicked her hand at the door, "Theresa was available and panting for it. Sometimes, you just have to live in the moment, you know?" She slid her feet into her high heels.

"No," Emily said quietly. "I don't know."

Bec straightened and contemplated Emily's face, disdain drifting across her own. "And that's the point," she said. She retrieved her bag from the couch, and then, framed by the open front door, declared, "You must have known we were going in different directions, Em, so perhaps this is for the best." Emily's heart clenched. "Maybe it was the Universe giving us a nudge when you decided to break your routine today." She shrugged, like the entire situation was one giant cosmic burp. Emily looked inside herself for anger. Just enough of it to match the situation, but it had disappeared from her emotional toolkit. All she had was disbelief.

"I…I think we should stop seeing each other," Emily whispered, swallowing down the nausea that threatened. Her hands were shaking.

Bec nodded, as if agreeing with a favourable weather forecast, then waved her hand vaguely. "Yes. I'll make a list of my stuff that's here." Her words were so cut and dried that Emily could have used them in one of her more permanent floral displays. Bec turned to the door, then paused as a thought came to her. She looked over her shoulder and said, "Thanks for making my lunch today."

The door closed quietly.

Despite the tsunami of chaos crashing about in her body, Emily managed to hold onto one small detail. She hadn't made lunch for Bec at all.

And it was that realisation that had her stumbling to the couch and sagging into the middle cushion.

"Oh my God," she whispered. Everything was wrong. It was all wrong. She needed to sort out a new plan. She needed to plan the next few weeks as a newly single person. She should start coordinating her dinner menus again. She needed to buy oranges. Oranges must be this week's fruit. Plums for next week. She'd look at the supermarket website to see what was in season. Fruit was reliable. It followed a plan. The next step was to put her wardrobe into order, a schedule of outfits. Tomorrow was Wednesday and she instantly decided that tan boots should only be worn on Wednesdays because that was good, right? Tan boots only on Wednesdays. The red socks? Yes. They would be perfect for Thursdays. Good.

"Oh God," she whispered again, rocking slightly. The far wall held her attention for hundreds of breaths until her phone buzzed from inside her bag, currently a sad heap near the door, and she blinked in confusion. Contemplating that perhaps the person ringing was someone from the office and therefore it was important because right then, it was easier for her mind to disassociate from everything else except work, she hauled herself off the couch and collected the phone, vacantly registering Nic's name as a missed call.

Her interior designer picked up straight away.

"Honey, you've been gone at least two hours. I know that it's disturbingly parental of me to check up on you, but you seemed a bit out of—"

"Bec ate my lunch," Emily said, weakly.

Nic was silent for a moment as if trying to align the random statement with Emily's absence from the office. "Um. Is that a lesbian euphemism, because—"

Emily's sob cut him off.

"Em?"

"Bec cheated on me with a woman wearing a strap-on." She sobbed again. "On my dining table."

Emily could actually hear the mouth gape and blinking eyelids.

"Oh, sweetie. Where are you?"

"I'm here." Then she realised how unhelpful that information was. "I'm at home," she added.

"I'm coming over. I'll move the Grajhi concept meeting to tomorrow." He hummed decisively. "It gives them an extra day to change their minds about their hellish sunken lounge." Emily could hear rustling, as Nic tossed things into a bag, probably looking for car keys. "Hang tight, hon. I'll be there in a tick."

He hung up without waiting for a reply, and Emily stared at the blank screen. Apparently, time was fluid when routines were set ablaze because it seemed mere seconds before Nic was knocking urgently on the door, and then bundling Emily into a hug once he'd stepped inside. Emily rested the side of her face on Nic's chest.

"What am I going to do?"

After a second of absorbing that question, Nic gently pushed Emily away, led her to the couch and eventually, through stops and starts, managed to collect the whole story, not just the day's sudden discovery.

"What if I made her cheat?" Emily picked at the leather stitching on the coaster she'd plucked off the coffee table.

Nic elegantly crossed his legs. "I'm sorry. That's the most idiotic thing I've heard in my life." He glared at Emily's wrinkled brow. "People make choices. Bec's choice was…" He waggled his fingers at the dining table. "You did not make that happen, sweetie."

"Certainly feels that way," Emily muttered, then she sighed heavily. "I really don't get it. I thought we were fine, I guess. I mean, we both work crazy hours, but I've always supported that aspect of Bec's life, and I thought she did for me." She dug her nail into the stitching again. "That's not relevant. It's not about how many hours we work. Bec was able to cheat because I'm so focused on routine. My predictability made me an easy candidate for her opportunity to cheat."

She gasped, frisbeed the coaster onto the table, and entwined her fingers. "Oh! What if she's been cheating all along? It'd be so easy. I mean, I've been like this since…" Emily could feel herself spiralling into an abyss of pointless analysis. Clearly Nic spotted the tide of self-recrimination rushing towards them, so he stood abruptly, hauled Emily upright, and towed her along as he stalked in his heels, like a runway model, out the door, down the driveway and into the studio. He plonked Emily at her crafting table.

"Start," he instructed, waving his arm flamboyantly. "Create something. I can hear the life plans and scheduling flying out of the laser printer in your head. It's disturbing. So, focus on the plants and pointy stabby things. Besides, I need a stunning piece for the Kinnear open home."

Nic stayed for the rest of the afternoon, giving them the opportunity to rehash the whole situation with an occasional flood of tears, and only left when Emily promised not to create a week's timetable for her underwear, then rang her therapist, requested a session, and managed to snag one for the following afternoon. A complete miracle. The next twenty-four hours would be more than enough time to fill the luggage in her mind with darkness, despair, and the overwhelming sense of guilt that had taken up residence in her thoughts. That would thrill her therapist to no end.

***

Kristen was not thrilled. Emily closed her eyes for a moment, as the cushion dipped when she shifted in the chair in the office the next day.

"Emily, I can say categorically that your need to plan was not responsible for Bec's actions. Those actions were entirely her decision. We own our actions," her therapist stated, light blue eyes pinning Emily to the comfortable beige armchair.

Emily rolled her lips together and frowned. "Yes. I know, I know that. Really, I do. Nic said the same thing."

"Nic is a very wise person."

Emily glanced at Kristen. She had been seeing her therapist for four years, and it felt like Kristen knew her so well that she didn't really need to say anything at all. Of course, Kristen would never let Emily get away with that, and so the session travelled in the same direction as every other session.

"Describe your latest sculpture," Kristen instructed right on cue, then sat back in her chair, and crossed her ankle over her knee. Her pant leg crept up and Emily smiled quietly at the black sock with poodles printed on it. Her fifty-year-old therapist was all levels of cool.

Exactly as Kristen had planned, having Emily describe her latest Ikebana sculpture calmed her chaotic thoughts. It probably lowered her blood pressure, as well. Health benefits everywhere.

"I'm thinking of exhibiting it. There's a showcase next month. Or giving it to Nic as part of an open home."

"Excellent." Kristen quirked a smile. "Are you reacting to Bec's actions themselves or are you triggered beyond that?"

Her therapist was brutal with emotional bandaids. Emily inhaled. "Gah," she muttered through clenched teeth and focused her gaze on her thumbnail. "God. Okay, I keep thinking that perhaps my rigidity pushed her into cheating and whatever else, just like Dad's impulsive, spontaneous, awful, lack of planning pushed me into being like this. Like a mirror image of each other." Emily looked up and stared at Kristen, who hummed.

"Okay," she replied.

Emily rolled her eyes. "I know. It's mental."

"You're in the right room," Kristen said, and Emily snorted. "Let's unpack all that. You're saying that because you're an over-planner, it sent Bec into the arms of someone else. Your dad was prone to spontaneous and impulsive actions, which led to you becoming an over-planner. Am I on the right track?"

Emily tilted her head into the back of the chair and stared at the ceiling. "Yes. Completely on the right track."

"Okay," Kristen encouraged.

Emily dropped her head. "It's all I ever seem to talk about when I'm here. You've heard all this," she said through a grimace, but Kristen nodded in encouragement, lifting both eyebrows, and Emily let out a long breath. "Okay. From the time I was born, all the way through until I was twenty, Dad would wake up some mornings and announce that we were…" Emily flicked her gaze about the room. "Off to France," she tossed her hands, "or buying a yacht, or selling up and moving to another state, which wouldn't have been awful, I guess, but it was going to happen *that day*, and so he would withdraw piles of money *that day*, buy plane tickets or whatever—things that couldn't be refunded or were difficult to be refunded—*that day*, despite—" she cut herself off to breathe heavily. "*Despite* not owning passports or anything, and my mother and I would be in this breathtakingly dreadful situation where we wouldn't know what was happening for the next twelve or so hours, or even in the next few days, and then suddenly, he'd decide that no, we weren't flying to the moon or whatever the hell he'd decided the previous day, and we'd hold our breath until the next great explosive announcement. Meanwhile, our money kept dwindling no matter how much he made with his beautiful metal art, and Mum had no idea what to do, and Dad wouldn't get help and it was like walking on eggshells all the time." Emily could feel herself gasping and clung to the arms of the chair. There was silence. Kristen waited, and Emily couldn't help but fill it.

"Bec cheating like that is just like my Dad, you know." Emily gazed sadly at her hands. "She told me that Theresa was an impulsive decision. And look what happened!" Her head snapped up, and her eyes fill with tears. "No forethought, no planning, and everyone gets hurt. It's what happens every time people don't follow plans. I'm angry about it. I hate that it happens to me, and now I need a sex health test after this session just in case dildo chick wasn't Bec's only foray into the world beyond our relationship and I know that makes me sound like a giant whingy-whiney victim and woe is me blah blah blah, but—" Her voice cracked, and she swallowed the rock in her throat.

More silence, and Emily blinked the remaining tears away to stare at Kristen's impassive, sympathetic face.

"Fight back."

"What?" Emily said, pulling her eyebrows together.

"Look." Kristen dropped her foot to the ground and leaned her forearms on her thighs. "Fight back. Not at Bec. Fight back with strategies. You're doing the Ikebana, which is helping enormously, isn't it?"

"Yeah, for my over-planning with the small stuff at least," Emily added a shrug to her response, which made her feel like a petulant teenager, so she sat up straight in the chair. She could sense that Kristen was gearing up for something big. Probably awful.

"I want you to try something a little challenging. Let's go big. Something outside your comfort zone." Kristen's gaze was intense.

Emily mashed her lips together. "I like my comfort zone. I've only just had it redecorated."

Kristen grinned and relaxed back into her chair. "I want you to dip your toe into immersion therapy."

"Oh no." There it was. Emily flung her hands out to ward off the suggestion. "Nope. I can't immerse myself in the exact same thing that I'm sitting here moaning about."

"Yes, you can," Kristen said. "I'm not asking you to become an itinerant fruit picker. I'm suggesting that you try being spontaneous a couple of times." She pointed. "Without planning them."

Emily sighed heavily. "This idea is much too soon after yesterday's awfulness," she groaned. "You know?" She sat up straight. "I started creating a plan for what shoes to wear each day. I regressed, Kristen! I thought I was finished with planning idiotic things. Finished!" She chopped her hand in the air.

"So…you're not able to have a go at immersion therapy?" Kristen asked. Emily stared at her, because again Kristen knew her inside and out. She was daring her to try it.

"Well, of course, I can have a go at it, particularly because I'm aware of what's going to happen. It's not like I'm going to immerse myself in spontaneity without sorting it out ahead of time."

Kristen rolled her lips. "Um…that's not quite how it works."

"I know that. I'm…" Emily gave a sort of growly grunt. "I could do it," she bluffed. "I could. It's not like I'm completely hopeless. I mean, it's only in the big stuff in life that I plan so much. Despite my setback yesterday, I can actually deal with little changes all the time now. I even start a new series without finishing the one I'm watching."

Kristen gave a mock gasp. "No! But that's awful. I can't even do that." She grinned at Emily's glare.

There was another beat of silence, then Kristen rested her elbow on the arm of the chair.

"Bec was part of the big stuff," she stated, matter-of-factly.

"Yes." Emily's voice was flat.

"Did you love her?"

Emily ran her fingertips over her lips. "Yes? Maybe. I…I don't know now. Perhaps not, now that I think about it. Our relationship was okay, though. It was planned out."

"Did she know that?" The intense stare had returned.

"What? That it was planned?" Emily blew out a breath. "Yes, it was one of the accusations she hurled at me when she swanned off with Theresa."

Kristen shook her head. "No, not the planning of events *in* your relationship. The relationship itself. Did she know that it was locked in? Did she want that?"

"I don't think so," Emily said, after a very long pause.

"Mm. Did you ask?"

"No." That question was an open wound.

Kristen tore it open a bit more. "I think that's something we should talk about in our next session."

The muscles in her jaw tightened as Emily visualised that appointment.

"Right," Kristen said, nodding decisively. "So, let's go big. Immersion therapy."

Chapter Four

Despite its flimsy substance, Lycra made Skye feel strong. It was such an utterly ridiculous sensation but that's what it was. A strength. She felt in charge. Of the bike, of her business, of her fate. Simply because she was wearing the artificial fabric version of skin. Weird.

She glanced at her phone clipped securely into its holder on her handlebars. The text that had arrived a minute ago needed to be dealt with, so she veered towards the footpath and rolled up the incline. Her thighs straddled the bike, holding it still, and she read the message in its entirety. Then clenched her fist in celebration.

"Oh, yes!" she exclaimed and shared a grin with the man in his business suit who'd overheard as he hurried past.

Quick Cargo had been accepted into *Rush*, the premier courier race in Melbourne, scheduled to run on a Sunday in five weeks' time. A sanctioned, sponsored race. Not one of the illegal night races where the participants whizzed around the streets at breakneck speeds in a desperate attempt to reach each checkpoint. Road rules were irrelevant in those regular events and the police were always chasing the contestants through the alleys of the CBD. Skye and Seb couldn't bring themselves to enter those, even though it was tempting to compete with other professional urban cyclists. But it was just too dangerous. Sending in the application and the $500 entry fee to *Rush* was all about legitimising her company, particularly because they used cargo bikes.

The bikes were seen by many as a poor second cousin to the fixie bikes ridden by the mainstream couriers. Lacking gears and brakes, fixie bikes were light, simple to operate, and as dangerous as hell. Skye had learned very quickly that to stop a fixie bike meant to stop pedalling. There was no freewheeling on those contraptions. But couriers rode them because they were fast and nimble, and cargo bikes weren't either of those things. But cargo bikes were dependable and safe and delivered much more interesting things than legal documents.

However, she and Seb would be riding their own fixie bikes in *Rush,* as per the rules, because competing for the twenty-five-thousand dollars prize money at the end of the ninety-minutes needed to be a fair contest. *Gowers*, a company which operated a chain of chemists dotted throughout the city, was sponsoring the event, and the winning team also won a year's contract to deliver *Gowers* products and medications all over Melbourne. Skye wanted that contract so badly she could taste it. She slipped her phone back into its holder. The twenty-five thousand would also be helpful she acknowledged with another grin. A whoosh of excitement travelled through her body as she manoeuvred her bike back into the traffic.

With the final delivery of the day—another floral arrangement; this time to a delightful older gentleman who'd blushed furiously but was clearly thrilled—Skye rolled into the mini storage locker she rented in the city. It was not practical to ride such a beast of a bike all the way home when other transport was much more convenient, like her lightweight road bike, which was leaning against the wall of the locker. Seb's slightly accented salutation travelled down the small concreted avenue between the roller doors.

"Hey, Skye. What a day!" He glided to a halt, then planted his foot on the ground, as if pile-driving the cement. Seb was incredibly fit. He had to be, just like Skye, to maintain his job. His impossibly thick, well-defined thighs, which, when combined with his tattoos, strong jawline, and buzzcut black hair made him look like a minor celebrity's bodyguard. In tight shorts. Skye grinned. Seb, and his brilliant smile, flashing dark eyes, and brown complexion due to his Filipino heritage, was a complete marshmallow and one of the nicest people she'd ever met. He was a good person inside and out, and radiated joy like he'd breathed in the sun.

She leaned across her handlebars and bumped his fist.

"It was a great day, mate," she elaborated. "Thanks for taking that extra one this afternoon." Skye dismounted, her solid thighs feeling the slight burn of the eight-hour day.

Seb shrugged, climbed off his bike, and wheeled it into the miniature garage. Skye gazed fondly at her twenty-seven-year-old friend.

"We got into *Rush*," she said and grinned at how fast Seb's head whipped around.

"Seriously? A little company like us?" He couldn't contain his happiness. "We're gonna show them, Skye."

She chuckled, grabbed her road bike and wheeled it out. "Sure hope so."

"Anything on for tonight?" Seb asked over his shoulder as he pulled his water bottle from the carrier.

Skye greedily sucked at her bottle. "Nope. But I have got to find a new place soon. It's crunch time, mate. I'm having a look again tomorrow, so maybe I'll find just the right one."

Seb blinked, hummed, and tilted his head dubiously. Skye breathed heavily. "Or maybe not," she added, sadly.

Seb lived at home with his mother, father and two sisters and despite acknowledging the lack of space in their modest home, had offered, without hesitation, a couch for Skye to sleep on until she found a place.

"You'll be right, Skye. You always land on your feet." He took a step forward, pointed to Skye's sneakers so that she automatically glanced down, then he flicked her chin. Skye growled and grabbed at his shirt but missed as he danced backwards.

"You suck, Sebastian Arturo."

They shared a grin, then Seb pulled his standard bike from the garage, and Skye yanked quickly on the roller-door pull-rope so that gravity could finish the job, then flicked the lock. Her entire business sat in that locker, so security was paramount.

Riding home always felt like a warm-down. Not just for her muscles, but also her mind. Skye let the day's events roll through her head like soft circles in chalk. Then, as she paused at a give-way sign, balanced on her pedals like a praying mantis on a twig, her mind pulled up another image of the considered stare that Emily Fitzsimmons had delivered earlier that week. What was her fascination with the woman? She rolled her eyes and swung around the corner. Emily Fitzsimmons was all levels of beautiful. And had a contained presence that Skye found irresistible. She probably had the world's most gorgeous girlfriend or boyfriend and they lived in a perfect house and—

A child's high-pitched pretend gun noises brought her out of her reverie, so she slowed the bike, doubled back on the street, and cruised past again, releasing the handlebars, and sitting up on the seat. Skye grinned. Rhiannon, the nine-year-old girl, with the light brown hair and hand-me-down clothes, lived in the public housing block on the side road at the very far end of Lorraine's street. She was just visible in the shrubs at the letterbox. The dreadfully sad industrial block fencing and the mundane brickwork of the four basic flats arranged in a cube publicised the government's lack of care in their creation. The shooting noise restarted, and Skye, pedalling and guiding the bike expertly in huge circles, created finger guns, and yelled a volley of 'pew pews' at the shrub, which giggled. Skye laughed as the young girl in the same well-worn jeans and a long-sleeved shirt from yesterday rolled out onto the scraggly grass near the footpath. She was clutching an old Nerf gun held together with duct tape.

"I got you,' she yelled, brandishing the battered plastic.

Skye completed another arc, doubling back again, then stopped, and straddled her bike.

"You did, Rhi. You're getting more stealthy each day."

Rhiannon nodded at that immutable fact, and Skye grinned. "How are you? How's your mum?"

"M'okay. Mum's working," Rhiannon replied, a shrug accenting the answer.

Rhiannon's mum, Yvette, was a cleaner, and worked at two of the public hospitals on their side of the city, splitting her time in a variety of shifts to make ends meet. Skye rarely saw Yvette, but when she did, the friendly, good-hearted woman leaked perpetual exhaustion. Her split shifts meant that she'd often leave Rhiannon home alone purely through necessity, but the very elderly neighbour in the flat above checked in on Rhiannon a couple of times during the afternoon. Or sometimes Rhiannon hung out with Miles, a middle-aged man in a wheelchair who lived in the other ground floor flat.

Skye shook her head sadly. His situation was pretty shit because social services still hadn't installed a proper ramp for his doorway. A friend of Miles had laid some heavy plywood last month just to help out, but it was awfully rickety. The top floor flat at the back had "gross black stuff on the walls" according to Rhiannon, which Skye found out was rampant mould and thankfully no one lived in that one. "Not yet, anyway," Skye muttered, then she eyed Rhiannon.

"Is Mrs. Pandopolous looking after you?" The question received a nod. "Good. Well, I need to get going." Skye flicked her finger towards the end of the street nearly eight hundred metres away. She planted her feet on the pedals and made to push off. "Eat your vegetables," she said, sending a final grin.

Rhiannon laughed and bounced on the spot. "Sure, Skye. I'll see you on Monday afternoon before you see me!"

Skye waved in acknowledgement, checked the traffic and rode off. The daily interaction had started one afternoon when Rhiannon had leapt out from behind the brick letterbox with a remarkably accurate impression of a shouting Ninja, scaring the living daylights out of Skye who was riding past. She'd stopped, taking in the defiant, and proud little person brandishing a Nerf gun like it was her weapon against the world, then grinned and circled back to engage in the best imaginary gun fight of all time. Rhiannon couldn't believe her luck. Normally, she told Skye, people yelled at her, often with some elaborate swearing. To have someone duck and weave and fire back with actual noises was like Christmas arriving early. They'd hit it off straight away. Yvette had worried that Rhiannon was annoying Skye, but through some pleading from her daughter and reassurances from Skye, her fears had been allayed. It was a harmless interaction that the girl looked forward to each weekday afternoon. It crossed Skye's mind that when she found a new place, the daily shoot-outs would cease. The thought sent squirly waves of sadness through her heart.

The tyres crunched lightly on the finely crushed sandy gravel as she halted at her letterbox. The two letters inside were for Lorraine, who obviously hadn't had time to collect them, so with the setting sun creating long shadows ahead of her, Skye leaned her bike at the side of the house, hung her helmet over the handlebars, and knocked on the ornate front door.

A vision in forest green greeted her when the door opened. Lorraine, resplendent in a Helen Mirren-esque evening gown, raised a cheeky eyebrow at Skye's exclamation of praise.

"I will accept that 'wow', thank you, Skye. You do wonders for my self-esteem," she said and moved aside.

"Oh. No, I'm just bringing in your letters. I don't need to come in. You look like you're about to head out, anyway." Skye shuffled her feet on the top step. Lorraine flipped her hand and tsked.

"Goodness, no. Come in. I'm having a pre-dinner drink, while Danica makes some last-minute adjustments to my dress. Despite decades as the boss of it all, being the guest of honour at an *Architects Australia* event requires some liquid fortitude so I thought I'd start twenty-four hours early."

Skye laughed, and stepped inside, dropping the letters on the elegant hall table and her backpack underneath. Lorraine sailed ahead into the lounge and stopped at a woman who radiated competence and efficiency.

"Danica, this is Skye. Skye, Danica," Lorraine waved between them both, and Skye walked over to engulf the smaller woman's hand in her own. It was another reminder of her physicality. Skye was a solid, muscular, tall woman, and even though it still surprised her when women either gave a slightly perplexed blink or leaned into the potential butch experience she represented, Skye understood their reactions. Being in this shape, radiating fitness and health, sporting chiselled lines in all sorts of places, and allowing her blonde hair to grow until it was touching her shoulder blades, created intrigue. It complicated matters because Skye didn't like to label herself. She was just Skye.

"Nice to meet you. Did you make the dress? It's super." Skye cast another admiring glance over Lorraine, who preened.

Danica smiled and bent to continue doing magical things to the hem of the outfit. "I did. Thank you. Lorraine wanted a local designer and luckily, she found me. Having Lorraine wearing one of my creations is going to be so good for my business."

Skye flicked a glance at her landlord, who gave a slow innocent blink, and Skye smiled. So typically Lorraine.

"You know where the tea paraphernalia is, Skye, darling. Make yourself one, or..." She delivered an open palm wave at her crystalline Royal Doulton tumbler on the side table, which held a couple of fingers of neat Irish whiskey, and raised her eyebrows.

"No, but thanks. I'll make some tea." She wandered into the modern white and chrome kitchen, which seemed at odds with the heritage exterior of the house, yet somehow it worked. She set the kettle on its water-boiling journey, collected a cup and saucer, and readied the pot with tea leaves. Lorraine's disdain for tea bags was legendary. The conversation drifted in from the lounge room.

"Tea, Danica?"

"Oh, no thank you, Lorraine. I'm nearly done." There was a pause. "There. You can get changed now."

Skye rescued the kettle just before it began to scream, poured the water into the pot, via the infuser in the opening which contained the three scoops of loose tea—as per Lorraine's strict instructions—and carried the pot and her cup and saucer into the lounge. Danica was collecting her materials and packing the equipment into a large bag, then she zipped it up, and stood. She looked at Skye.

"Lorraine's getting changed," she said to explain the older woman's absence. Skye set the pot and the crockery on the coffee table.

"No worries. It'll allow the tea to steep for a couple of minutes before I pour it. You get better infusion that way."

Danica blinked, and Skye smiled inwardly at what a contradiction she must seem. A tea connoisseur who looked like she'd got lost on the way home from the velodrome.

"Well, it was lovely to meet you, Skye." Danica walked to the front door, where Lorraine, having returned from the bedroom in linen pants and a soft shirt, hugged her, and saw her out. Lorraine strolled back to Skye and frowned.

"Why are you still standing? Sit," she instructed.

"But I'm all gross and swea—"

"Sit!" Lorraine demonstrated the action and pointed to the opposite couch.

Skye sat.

"How was your week?" Lorraine asked, sipping from her drink.

"It was great, actually. We got into *Rush*."

Lorraine breathed out heavily. "Oh, Skye. That is wonderful. There were only so many places. Well done." Then she held her hand against her chest. "I'm still worried. It's terribly dangerous."

Skye laughed and leaned over to pour her cup of tea. "No, it's not. Not *Rush*. Well, it has the same amount of danger as my job any day of the week. The illegal races are stupid, though."

Lorraine hummed. "Yes, well. I'm pleased you're not entering those. I'm rather fond of your particular arrangement of limbs and bones."

Skye laughed into her cup. "Me too." She blew out a breath, and Lorraine caught the wistful nature of it.

"Are you going to let your parents know?" she asked carefully. Skye twisted her lips to the side and delivered a brief, offhand shrug.

"I'll email them. Whether they read it is another matter. You know what they're like. If it doesn't relate to their environmental and humanitarian zealotry in Cambodia or Timbuktu or wherever, then it's not important." She huffed again. "It'd be nice if they could just acknowledge the...I don't know...daily successes. But they won't. The failures get acknowledged but even then I have to," she flicked her fingers up to air-quote, "'sort it out yourself, Skye, because you shouldn't need anyone's help when you live in such a privileged country'." Letting her hands drop, she shook her head. "It doesn't matter."

Lorraine gave her a long look.

Skye glared. "It doesn't matter. Honestly. Getting into *Rush* is another achievement that they won't care about and it's fine. I'm excited about it, and so is Seb. We get to promote the company while doing something we love." She slapped her thigh softly. "It's marketing 101." She gave a wry smile. "Looks like I'm putting the uni degree to good use."

There was a silence.

"You were not responsible for what happened at *Traverse Energy*, you know." Lorraine's voice was measured. "No amount of marketing was going to change the public's perceptions of their abhorrent act on that Aboriginal land."

"I know," Skye muttered, then injected a little more fortitude when she repeated the words a second later. "I know. But...I put everything I had into *Traverse*. Literally, and then they turned around and did..."

Lorraine tutted. "You are not responsible. You've turned *your* life around, Skye. I think you're remarkable. You remind me of me."

Skye laughed, and the older woman's eyes sparkled as she swallowed another mouthful.

Lorraine crossed one leg elegantly over the other. "No, I'm actually serious. I read you straight away, and I was correct. I think it was your determination and openness that helped me make my decision to offer you the studio." They held each other's gaze. "And look at you now. I know a resilient—"

"Bloody-minded and stubborn," Skye jumped in.

"Yes, that too." Amusement coloured Lorraine's voice.

Skye chuckled, looked into her cup, and found it nearly empty. She leaned over to refill it. "I can't thank you enough for doing that. The studio, I mean."

"Piffle. It was my pleasure. Besides, it simply gave me another opportunity to study another person. To find out what their story is. What makes them tick. I'm like...what do you call them?"

"A stalker?"

They laughed.

"No, thank you. I'm like a psychological detective. It fascinates me that humans think they're so intricate and complex and difficult to understand, yet there's more variety in an architectural plan than in a collection of people."

Skye shook her head and let a sad smile lift her lips. "I am going to miss you."

Lorraine studied her. "Apparently, they've invented a contraption called a telephone."

Chapter Five

Thursday and Friday passed with excruciating slowness; each molasses-laden hour giving Emily time to remember and rehash the entire Bec situation. She'd turned up to work both days, absorbing the tentative looks from Jas, Rach, and Dimitri, until she'd quietly given them the abridged version of the recent events. Then she'd absorbed looks of sympathy, which weren't much of an improvement to her state of mind. But they cared and that was lovely. By midday on Friday, Emily made a mental note to have everyone over in the near future for a get-together of some sort just to say thanks. When she was feeling less battered.

Bec texted on Wednesday night, and Emily had stared uncomprehendingly at the message for a good five minutes. Apparently, she wanted to collect her stuff on Thursday evening, so Emily had left the front door unlocked at the designated time and scuttled into her studio to piece together some of the wire-threaded leaves that she'd prepared for her latest instalment. Dealing with Bec was all too stressful and she'd decided not to locate her big girl pants. It was much easier to hide. Metaphorically and literally. So, she'd pulled up the playlist of her favourite artist and buried her heart inside the native grasses and seeds on her table.

Speaking of seeds, Kristen's immersion therapy idea had sprouted inside her brain, and kept jabbing its prickles at her thoughts. The fact that she was even contemplating the concept caused her face to ache. It probably made her seem even more reserved than normal with both her team and with the clients she'd met with that morning. How on earth was she supposed to immerse herself in spontaneity when it was spontaneity—albeit Bec's—that had dropped her into this crappy situation in the first place?

Jas leaned on her doorframe.

"Have you decided what you're wearing for tomorrow night?"

Emily stared at her until she realised what Jas meant. "Oh God, the gala. No. Well, yes, I had it planned because, of course I did. But Bec was my plus one and I can't even—"

Jas threw her hand up like a stop sign.

"Dimitri!" She yelled over her shoulder in such a commanding tone that he appeared as if summoned through the carpet. Both filled the doorway and looked expectantly at Emily, who bunched her shoulders in anxiety.

Jas patted Dimitri's back. "Okay. You're a much nicer person than Rebecca Deans. Better looking if you want my opinion. What are you doing tomorrow night?"

Emily gave an annoyed gasp. "Oh, for the love of—"

Jas thrust out her palm again.

"Nic can't go because he's headlining. I can't go because I have a date," she stated matter-of-factly. "Rach and Darryl have the kiddos, he's working the late shift, and finding a babysitter within twenty-four hours—"

"Wouldn't do it anyway! Babysitters are easy and Lord knows I would give my right tit for a night away from my kids, but I can't stand the thought of getting all tarted up. Sorry, Em!" Rach's voice carried over Jas and Dimitri's heads and into the small office. Emily sighed and pressed her fingertips briefly into her temples.

Dimitri shrugged. "I like getting dressed up," he said, simply, then grinned. Emily repeated her sigh, letting the "Okay" ride along with it, which thrilled Jas because she nodded and clapped, forcing the blue tips of her hair to bounce about, then declared the entire situation as "Awesome!" and marched back into the main office.

Dimitri raised his eyebrows. "So?"

Emily smiled gratefully at the sympathetic face looking back. "Thank you for…just, thank you. Meet you in the foyer at seven?"

***

June in Melbourne was supposed to guarantee winter weather but occasionally mild breezes from Adelaide drifted over the border to spike the temperatures in the city, forcing people to hang up their coats and jackets for a day or two.

However, Emily was entirely grateful for the warmth on Saturday night because it meant that the skin she had showing in her strapless electric-blue cocktail dress wasn't covered in goosebumps like a lizard in a terrarium. Dimitri, in a crisp white shirt, dinner jacket and tailored pants, met her in the foyer of the *Grand* in the centre of the city. His styled, yet floppy, black curls gave away his Hellenic heritage.

"Is it entirely awful of me to say that I'm actually glad that I could take Bec's place tonight?" he said, wrinkling his forehead, his expression hopeful that Emily would understand the subtext of his question. She did.

"Not awful at all." Emily gave his forearm a slight squeeze. "I'm glad you did. You're good company and—bonus," she held up her finger, "you get to network." They shared a smile, then followed the signage to the glitzy ballroom. Tables placed on the dark blue carpet and draped in blindingly-white, linen tablecloths, dotted the room like a monochrome game of Twister. She'd been in this particular ballroom on previous occasions, but still admired the pressed metal ceiling roses that offset the chandeliers, and gold-streaked wallpaper so lush it was tempting to sidle up to an alcove and have a little vertical nap.

The guests were shepherded for cocktails to the enormous outdoor wrap-around terrace that overlooked the river and Dimitri's eyes lit up. Emily chuckled.

"You really don't have to hang out with me. Mingle with the people." She smiled wryly. "I'll see you at dinner, though, because you do have to sit with your boss."

Dimitri paused, tilting his head briefly. "My friend, Em. Not my boss. You've got this." He patted her upper arm.

Determined not to cry, she swallowed forcefully. "Thank you. I'll see you later." Dimitri nodded, looked up, then like a kid in a candy store, made a beeline towards a pair of sustainable design architects who he'd been liaising with on their current project. It's what Bec used to do at any of the functions they attended together. Not that architects and real estate agents really crossed paths in their professions, but that never stopped Bec collecting contacts. Her belief was you never knew who could add another piece of scaffolding to your career, so she'd collect people's information like stamps. Emily wasn't exactly a wallflower, of course, but she liked to spend time talking to a person and engaging in actual dialogue, rather than conducting a conversational fly-by like an RAAF Hornet.

A group from *Melbourne City Planning* welcomed her into their space and Emily sipped on her sparkling grape juice while adding to the trio's commentary of the aesthetic merits of the new *Advance Financial* tower in Sydney. She was in the midst of describing exactly how her team would redesign the foyer of that monstrosity when there was a light touch in the space between her shoulder blades, and she turned to find Lorraine beaming into her face.

"Emily, darling. I'm so glad you could come tonight."

"I wouldn't have missed it, Lorraine. How are you?"

Lorraine gestured with her champagne glass in a vague circle without spilling a drop, which was a testament to experience and skill.

"Rather excellent, thank you. This is all a bit much, though, don't you think?" She looked out at the perhaps one-hundred people enjoying canapés and alcohol.

"Absolutely not! You deserve this. Twenty years at the top, Lorraine, and a trailblazer for women in this field. Everyone's here to celebrate you." Emily smiled. "Besides, I wouldn't be where I am now without your guidance and support."

Lorraine smoothed a hand across the front of her chest, her pink nail polish contrasting with the green of her dress. "Oh, well, thank you. It was and is my pleasure." A look of melancholy passed through her eyes, then she shook herself slightly and looked around in confusion. "Where's Rebecca in all this rabble?"

Emily pursed her lips and pulled them to the side.

"Ah." Not awkward at all. "She...she was otherwise engaged tonight," Emily said eventually. It was probably true.

"That's a shame. It's unlike Rebecca to miss an event like this," Lorraine replied astutely, and then, very subtly, twisted her shoulders so that Emily was forced to shift a little, and like magic, it was just the two of them engaged in conversation. "How is your lovely lady?"

If Emily didn't know any better, she'd swear that Lorraine knew about the split. Which was impossible. But joining dots together was Lorraine's forte, and it looked very much like she'd whipped out a pencil and was having a grand old time creating an accurate picture in her mind.

"Oh, um…" Emily decided that elaborating on how very fine Bec was, what with the dining table, and the purple dildo, would be a little inappropriate. So she went with, "She's great?" It sounded weak and hopeful all at once.

If a pause was an actual piece of dialogue, Lorraine's would have spoken volumes.

"Mm," Lorraine said finally, pinning Emily with a knowing look. Emily felt somewhat like she was being studied, which, seeing as it was Lorraine, was probably true. But even still. Uncomfortable.

The waiters moved about like ants, informing everyone that they needed to transfer to the dining room, and with that Emily found herself escorting Lorraine to the table closest to the small podium, then finding her own seat two tables over.

Dinner was a spirited affair, as the conversations of the other seven guests at her table undulated between pairs, foursomes where leaning across another was essential, and table-wide discussions that consisted mainly of friendly banter and not a little bit of rivalry. Dimitri's sharp wit was greatly appreciated, and his interjections had everyone in stitches.

A variety of speeches peppered the night, including Lorraine's, which was heartfelt, humorous, and contained just enough poignancy to produce a soft, collective sigh of appreciation.

Then that moment occurred when all guests rise and engage in the adult version of musical chairs, and Emily found herself, one table over, involved in a rousing discussion about the merits of conversions and remodelling of terrace houses.

"I am such a supporter of the idea, Peter!" She leaned her forearms on the table and stared earnestly across at the lead architect from *Lowiston*. His bald head bounced the light from the chandeliers as he frowned in disagreement.

"Emily, it's not in keeping with the heritage presentation of the building. There are certain covenants," he countered.

"But that's mostly the facade. My house is a terrace and it's been remodelled inside while keeping true to the time period. I even converted my garage into a self-contained studio and that doesn't impact on the building at all."

"I wasn't aware you had a studio, Emily?" Lorraine's voice seamlessly joined the conversation, and all eyes turned to the guest of honour who'd placed herself to Emily's left. There were shared nods about the table, and then, Emily realised she'd actually been asked a question.

"Yes, I had it done just over a year ago. I use it for—" Chatting with Lorraine Hudson about the direct correlation between garage conversions and cognitive behaviour therapy was never going to happen. "It's quite a delightful space," she finished blandly.

Lorraine's inscrutable expression was hypnotic. There was calculation sparkling in her eyes, and that couldn't be a good thing. Emily had become very close to Lorraine during her three-year mentorship and quickly learned to recognise that glint of interest when Lorraine came upon a business opportunity, new project, or a chance to play in the sandbox of people's lives.

Lorraine adjusted her beautiful dress so she could turn her body square on.

"I didn't realise that we had such a lot in common. Top of your year at University. Successful architect with awards. Studio conversion. I have one as well, you know." She fixed Emily with a piercing gaze, then leaned forward and squeezed her forearm. "Were you aware that I've sold my house and I'm relocating further up the coast?"

The sudden change of direction was dizzying. Emily bunched her eyebrows together. "No, I wasn't. I hope whoever bought your gorgeous place maintains its integrity."

"Oh, I'm sure they will," Lorraine stated, waving her hand about vaguely, then she shook her head solemnly. "But I'm very worried about my gorgeous tenant, Skye. She's been on the hunt for a new place to live since the sale, and finding a little studio is next to impossible in the city." She centred her gaze, and Emily's 'uh oh' radar pinged erratically.

She could literally hear cogs turning inside Lorraine's head. "I'm sorry about that. It sounds diffic—"

"I've just had a wonderful idea!" The older woman exclaimed and clutched at Emily's arm again. "Now, I know I meddle sometimes. All harmless, of course." She trilled a laugh. "But, what if you took on Skye as a tenant in your studio? It would be perfect." She beamed into Emily's face, the skin beside her mouth wrinkled with lines of joy.

Emily tried to convince herself that the noise in her ears was the hubbub of conversations, rather than the rushing of blood around her body as her heart raced away from the starting grid.

"I don't think that's—"

Lorraine tossed her hand and head in the same direction; a gesture which seemed to mean everything and nothing.

"Emily, darling, you have one of the kindest hearts I know. Let me tell you," she leaned in conspiratorially, "Skye's a brilliant tenant. She runs her own bike courier business and has worked hard to make it successful. She's very determined. You'd not only be helping Skye, but you would be," she pressed a hand to her chest, "allaying my fears that a beautiful, hard-working soul like Skye, very much like yourself, continues to be supported in life, just like you were." A beatific smile appeared, and her eyes widened innocently.

Emily blinked. It was like watching a tide rolling in but being forced to remain stationary on the sand. The war between an obligation to her mentor, her innate kindness, the potential invasion of her therapy space, and Lorraine's patent manipulation rampaged about in her brain. The week could not get any more absurd, and a tiny bubble of hysteria grew in her chest, threatening to erupt in a somewhat inappropriate delirious giggle. Then she remembered

Kristen's words on Wednesday. Well, if this wasn't the ultimate of immersions into the shark-infested waters of spontaneity, she didn't know what was. The giggle threatened again. Therapy? She'd need extra sessions to cope with this life change.

"Okay?" Emily said, uncertainly.

Lorraine looked as surprised as Emily felt, although the wily seventy-year-old recovered almost instantly, calling on nearly forty more years of experience in facial rearrangement.

"Oh! Emily, that's excellent. I'm so incredibly pleased. I just know this is going to work out brilliantly for both of you." Another arm grab was employed to add to her enthusiasm.

Emily delivered a sort of muted hum in stunned acknowledgement. Then she gave into Lorraine's excitement and smiled wanly.

"I…I'm glad to help. It's important to pay forward assistance we receive in life, particularly as women."

Lorraine beamed. "Exactly. I read you perfectly the first time I met you. That's definitely how we women should think in business and in life. Now," she leaned back, "rent."

Emily fidgeted. Money. Of course there'd be rent. All sorts of important details seemed to have leaked from her brain. Her eyes widened. Details like her Ikebana. Where on earth was her equipment going to live? Her second bedroom was probably big enough. The third bedroom—more a carpeted nook with a door— would never work. So, the second bedroom it was. But the second bedroom wasn't her studio. Her studio was separate from the house and therefore, when she closed the studio door, it divorced her ridiculous planning compulsion from her life. That was a whole level of psychological analysis right there. She felt like reversing her decision. While her mind circled around the drain-hole of inevitability, she missed Lorraine's question.

"—so she'll continue to pay that amount?"

Emily blinked again. "Sorry? Pardon?"

Lorraine repeated the figure.

"That's…all?" Surely that wasn't the rental payment.

"Oh yes, I settled on the rent amount when Skye moved in. It seemed appropriate, and I really didn't need the extra money. But Skye was too proud not to pay anything."

Emily had never felt so locked into a conversation in her life. Then she asked an obvious question. "How did you meet Skye?"

Lorraine clasped her hands together under her chin, like she was preparing to deliver a particularly amusing anecdote.

"I ran her over." Then she lifted her palm at Emily's appalled expression. "No, no. Not properly. I forgot to use the handbrake when I parked on Graham Street in the city and my car rolled a little, and Skye, the poor dear, was crossing between the back of my car and the Jeep parked behind it. She jumped out of the way, but my car caught her hip and I felt so dreadfully responsible. Well, she simply refused to go to the hospital, insisting that it was only a bump. But, of course, I asked for her phone number to check on her the next day, then took her to dinner as a sort of emotional restitution at least, and I discovered that she's a lovely, upstanding person, so it seemed obvious to offer my studio as her next place to live." There was a pause.

Emily felt like Lorraine's car had run her over as well. What a preposterous situation to be in. A swift river had pulled her in, leaving the kayak on the shore. Yet, despite the fact that Lorraine meddled in people's affairs, she was ultimately a really good person and an excellent judge of character. If she thought that this Skye woman was a shining example of humanity, then that was good enough for her. She took a deep breath.

"Well, I'll try not to run her over as part of her tenancy," Emily said, mainly to allay Lorraine's fears that she'd change her mind. Lorraine's laugh tinkled across the table, as she clutched Emily's arm yet again. "I'll need her phone number," Emily added.

Instantly galvanised, Lorraine seized her purse from the table and pulled out her phone. She poked at the screen with one finger like many of her generation, and Emily heard the alert ping inside her purse.

Lorraine looked up, her lips twitching as the tiniest smile flashed across them. There was more than a hint of knowing and mischief peeking through.

"I really feel that you two will get along quite well." She laced her fingers together on her lap. "Yes." A single nod. "I think you should phone her tomorrow. I know she's becoming concerned about the lack of options available and it is getting close to settlement day on the house. What a wonderful Sunday morning gift that will be for both of you."

If she didn't know any better, Emily could have sworn that Lorraine Hudson had just pulled off a major accomplishment and for the life of her, Emily couldn't work out what that accomplishment was.

Chapter Six

Skye tucked her red and white rugby jersey into her dark jeans, tightened her ponytail, and cast another glance at herself in the mirror.

"Stop it. You're fine. It's not like it's a date," she growled and bent to tighten the shoelaces on her fire-engine-red chucks.

It might not be a date, but it was definitely the coolest but weirdest thing that had happened to her in a really long time. The phone call that morning had been memorable.

"Skye speaking?" The unknown number pushed her statement into a question.

"Hi, yes. Hello. My name is Emily Fitzsimmons and—"

Skye sat heavily on the kitchen stool and felt her eyes widen comically.

"Emily Fitzsimmons?"

"Yes."

"Okay." Why the hell was the gorgeous Emily Fitzsimmons calling her on a Sunday morning? Why the hell did the gorgeous Emily Fitzsimmons have her phone number?

"I'm sorry to call you so early, but it seems that promptness is vital. I was given your details by Lorraine Hudson last night as she is under the impression that you're in need of a new place to live." Emily's voice was contained, like she needed to plan every word in a sentence so that the next sentence would then click faultlessly into place. She couldn't possibly do that in normal conversation, Skye thought. Surely not. It would be exhausting. Then her actual words registered.

"Lorraine spoke to you last night?" Skye asked, then a lightbulb went on. "Oh. The retirement gala dinner."

Emily huffed out a quick laugh, which sent shivers up Skye's arms. "Yes. The gala dinner. She mentioned that you needed a place, and because I have a studio available, she is under the impression that planets have aligned and you're to become my tenant."

That voice was unbelievably sexy.

"That's really lovely of—"

"Look, I know this is highly irregular," Emily implored. "But I'd quite like to meet today, if possible, because I need to settle on some decisions, and I know that you probably do, as well." All of a sudden Emily sounded nervous. Urgent. Which was odd.

Deciding to dismiss the moment of weirdness, Skye said, "Absolutely. You're amazing. I've been looking for a new place and it's incredibly cheeky of Lorraine to mention it, but thank you so much."

A sigh—of relief?—then a soft chuckle drifted through the speaker. "Well, don't thank me yet. Perhaps we could meet for coffee at around two? Do you know the *Oak Street Bistro*?"

Skye's heart sank. That was an eight-kilometre ride—not a big deal—but with the rain forecast for the afternoon, she'd arrive at the cafe looking like a drowned rat. Super. Emily spotted the pause.

"Skye? Is it…?" A thought seemed to occur to her. "Oh, I'm sorry. Do you own a car?"

"No, I ride. A pushbike. But—"

"Goodness, I'll come to you. Um…oh! There's a place down from Lorraine's. *The Fat Duck*."

Skye laughed. "I know the one. It's only a ten-minute walk."

"Great. I'll meet you there at two?"

"Absolutely."

"Um…how will I recognise you?"

Skye stared down at the tatty misshapen shirt she used as a pyjama top and her bare legs. "How about…?" She closed her eyes and ran through a mental catalogue of her closet. "I'll be in a pair of black jeans and a red and white rugby shirt. And red sneakers. But I'll have a black coat on when I arrive because cold, right? And I have blonde hair."

There was a pause. "I'm not sure if that's enough detail," Emily said, the barely contained laughter evident in her voice. Skye grinned.

"Well, I don't want to be lost in the really large crowd of people that could arrive at the same time." They shared a laugh. "Thank you again for this. It's like a powerful being decided to rearrange life events, just so this could happen."

"Yes," Emily said wryly. "And her name is Lorraine Hudson. Well, I'll see you at two. Bye."

Skye had sat for another five minutes, grinning like a fool, until her skin registered how cold it was in the studio, forcing her to get up and switch on the heater. Then she'd thrown on some clothes and marched down the driveway to Lorraine's front door.

"You've got a really strange idea of how *not* to help a person," Skye said, as she strode into the lounge. Lorraine, dressed in eye-watering lime green yoga pants and a yellow crop top, closed the door and eased her seventy-year-old frame back to the floor. She resumed mirroring the pose currently demonstrated by the buff woman on the television.

"I may have mentioned our mutual admiration of studio conversions," she muttered into her left armpit, as she inverted her body.

Skye blew out a breath. "Lorraine, I feel so ungrateful getting cranky at—"

"Then don't." Lorraine straightened her back and extended her arms gracefully to each side. "We all have our talents and skills, Skye. Mine happens to be architecture and knowing just when to step in to help people who will not help themselves." They held eye contact until finally, Skye laughed.

"You're impossible."

"Yes. Now, when are you meeting the stunning Emily?"

Skye pulled her head back. "The stunning Emily?"

Lorraine rolled her shoulders, wincing as something pinched, then walked over to grasp Skye's hands. "Mm, she is. I see a mutual admiration club forming in the very near future."

***

Skye flicked up the lapels of her coat as she strode along the footpath. The gods had enjoyed their pillow fight that morning and the consequences of their violence filled the sky over Melbourne. Cloudy. Damp. Cold. Blah. The sort of weather that was perfect for curling up with a good book or meeting a beautiful woman at a cafe.

"I'll take option two," Skye murmured happily, and reached back to flick her long ponytail out of the coat's collar. Despite rationalising that this was a meeting between a prospective tenant and landlord, the decision to wear the jeans that hugged her well-defined thighs, and the rugby shirt with the stripes travelling horizontally across the material so they highlighted her shoulders, was completely purposeful. It didn't hurt to make a good impression.

Emily Fitzsimmons. Based on one very brief phone call, and a few moments where a smile had been exchanged, Skye had come to the conclusion that Emily was obviously someone who had it all together. She was a woman who wouldn't need rescuing. Emily would never let her life fall apart when the company she worked for went bankrupt.

Skye growled. "Stop it."

She rounded the corner, then slowed as she reached the first black and white market umbrella in the collection that shaded each table at the coffee shop. Her cafe date—*not a date*—was absent, so Skye figured she was early. She pulled her phone out of her coat pocket to check the time.

"Synchronised clocks. Always a good start to a business arrangement."

Skye looked up, straight into the dark eyes of her potential landlord, and felt her lips pull into a wide grin. She stuck out her hand.

"Hi. Skye Reynolds."

Emily nodded, as she grasped Skye's hand. "Emily Fitzsimmons. It's lovely to meet you." Then she tilted her head, her eyes narrowed quizzically. "Do I know you?"

Skye withdrew her hand, which was a shame because the sizzle of warmth that had zipped up her arm when Emily's skin had touched hers was something she'd be happy to experience many times again. Forever, even.

Instead, she tucked her hand into her coat pocket. "I think so. I've delivered to Nic and Jasmine at your office."

"Oh!" Emily's finger popped out and she snapped it. "Yes." She looked around at the outdoor seating area, obviously trying to decide where to sit. It gave Skye a chance to study Emily. The very short brown-blonde hair in that amazing messy-but-totally-meant-it style was gorgeous. In fact, the whole package was gorgeous. Slim, maybe half a head shorter than Skye, those beautiful dark brown eyes which she now knew contained tiny gold flecks. Smooth skin that Skye wanted to slide her fingertips over. Designer jeans, boots, zipped jacket and colourful scarf. Gorgeous.

"I think it's a bit chilly to sit outside. What do you think?" Emily said, those amazing eyes connecting with Skye's.

"I don't mind. My body seems to run hot, but we can sit inside. That's fine," Skye said, then pushed down the blush as she registered her 'hot body' comment. Emily quirked her lips, nodded and walked through the door of the cafe.

With a flat white coffee settled in front of Emily, and a pot of tea for Skye, they sat back in their seats and contemplated each other. Emily had removed her jacket and scarf to reveal a tight-fitting black ribbed polo neck that left absolutely nothing to Skye's imagination. She didn't need to imagine the pert breasts, the shoulders, the smooth skin on the forearms where the sleeves had been pushed up. It was all right there. She dropped her gaze and reached for the teapot.

"You're quite…athletic," Emily said. "I imagine riding a bike all day requires a lot of strength." The thought that Emily had been checking her out as well tingled Skye's skin.

She sipped her tea. "It does. *Quick Cargo* uses cargo bikes. You know, the ones with the boxes between the front wheel and seat?" Emily nodded. "They're quite heavy, and eight hours of steering those around Melbourne will give anyone a decent workout." Luckily, she resisted flexing her bicep, an utterly cringeworthy gesture and she would've had to crawl under the table to quietly die. "But I played rugby at Uni, so," she flicked a finger up and down at her torso, "this came in handy."

Emily tracked the finger with her eyes, then raised an eyebrow. "I imagine it did," she murmured, then sipped her coffee. "What did you study?"

"Business and marketing." This section of the conversation needed to be nipped in the bud. "Tell me about the studio."

Emily didn't seem to notice the abrupt change in topic or at least chose not to comment on it. She sat back and rested her palms on the table. "Well, it's a studio layout, which means the lounge doubles as the bedroom. There's a kitchen area and a separate bathroom. I can have a small washing machine fitted if you like. There's space for one. Otherwise, it's a trip to the laundromat, which is a pain." Skye chuckled at the grimace on Emily's face. She was obviously not a laundromat devotee.

Emily swallowed a mouthful of her coffee, then continued. "The floors are wood. It's a beautiful material to have under bare feet." She paused again, then smiled. Emily's smiles were the sort where a lot was kept in reserve, as if she were afraid that delivering the entire version would deplete the gesture altogether. Skye wondered what the full version looked like. Probably spectacular. "Um...the space is so airy and light...because there's a bank of windows over the kitchen that looks out onto the garden between the studio and the back of the house."

Skye watched animation flare. The sparkle in Emily's eyes, making the dark brown glow, was mesmerising, and it was clear that she loved her studio. Skye sat back in the chair and remained silent.

"What?" Emily stilled the cup's ascent to her mouth.

"You're really...alive when you're talking about your studio," Skye said, then wrinkled her brow. "Are you sure you want to rent it out? It sounds like you'd keep it for yourself if you could."

Emily's expression was indecipherable, but a hint of agitation flashed across her face. She didn't answer for at least a minute, pressing her lips together. Skye waited, but it seemed like she wasn't going to respond, and it occurred to Skye that perhaps Emily wasn't really enamoured with the whole idea at all. She hadn't imagined the flicker of inner conflict revealed in Emily's eyes.

She pushed her teacup and saucer away and sighed.

"Look, I really appreciate the studio offer but if you're doing this simply out of obligation to Lorraine, it doesn't bode well for a great tenant and landlord relationship." She pushed on the arms of the seat, ready to stand.

"Wait!" Emily's hands were taught, fingers flared from her palms as they faced towards Skye. Their eyes locked. "Wait Skye, please," Emily repeated, and it was only after Skye reclaimed her seat that Emily let out a breath. "I'm sorry for appearing so reluctant. I want to help, so it's not out of obligation. Lorraine inquired and then I offered."

Skye squinted, then grinned. "No, you didn't. Lorraine dug and probed and twisted and you caved."

"No, I—" Emily's mouth snapped shut. "She's persuasive," she muttered.

Skye threw her head back and laughed. "I'm seriously having words with her, because I told her not to meddle. I did not need assistance."

The hand flip caught her attention, and Skye's laughter stopped as she took in Emily's look of frustration.

"I'm not reluctant about you, because you seem nice and quite normal, but reluctance just reared its head then because I'm not good at change. And you'd be a change," Emily muttered into her cup, then frowned and stared at Skye in surprise. Clearly, she hadn't meant to admit that vulnerability.

They held the stare for a moment. "Well, I'm not good at asking for help, and you're helping," Skye said eventually.

"Oh. I guess that makes us even in the not-being-good-at-things stakes."

"Guess so." Skye held her smile back, waiting, and then it was like a tiny wall had been taken down, because suddenly she got to see Emily's smile that she'd held at bay, and Skye's breath caught. Emily was stunning.

Toffee-like tension stretched between them, and Skye could have sworn that a single beam of sunlight broke through the clouds to descend upon their little table near the window.

"I'm clearly suffering a brain spasm," Emily announced after a moment, then leaned her cheek on her clenched fist, and flashed another open smile. "I have no idea if this is the right thing to do, because the spontaneity of it all is daunting, but would you be interested in leasing a studio flat?"

Skye grinned. "From a woman who was manipulated into it by a seventy-year-old?"

"Excuse me? I imagine you've buckled under that powerful force." Emily's raised eyebrows issued a challenge.

"All the damn time," Skye replied, shaking her head sadly.

Emily laughed. "Then answer the question."

"Yes, Emily Fitzsimmons. I would love to be your tenant."

The gaze was delicious and Skye's stomach swooped. She rolled her eyes at herself. The rental agreement would definitely not include mooning over her landlord and she needed to ignore her infatuation with a woman who was a complete stranger. Immediately. Tomorrow. At least before move-in day.

Emily broke eye contact and peered into her cup, then drew in a breath. She looked up and smirked. Skye appreciated the flirty gesture.

"Okay," Emily said, her eyes twinkling. "Well, you don't seem to be a serial killer, and you clearly don't microwave your cups of tea." She held up two fingers. "Both of which are clauses in the tenancy contract, by the way."

The cheeky, slightly teasing tone thrilled Skye, and she rolled her lips together so she wouldn't blurt out something inane like telling Emily how gorgeous she was. She probably knew. Actually, she probably didn't.

It was another thirty minutes of conversation, deep enough for details, but shallow enough for comfort, as they sorted out rent—

"But, that's the same as what I pay Lorraine, and I thought—"

"I'd like to match it. I'll give you the bank account details."

—and made arrangements for a moving-in day, which ended up being the next weekend. And then it was time to leave. After separate payments at the counter, Skye found herself standing outside, tugging her coat around her torso. Emily looked into her face.

"I guess I'll be seeing you next Saturday, then," she said, and another flash of hesitancy whisked through her eyes.

Emily was like a hot-cold switch. It was intriguing, and Skye liked intriguing. Probably because it was Emily who was being all intriguing, but that wasn't the point.

Skye nodded. "Yep. Ten o'clock. Seb will be helping me. He's got his licence so we'll hire a mini truck because I've got slightly more shi—stuff than a car's worth."

Emily blinked. "Great." Then she seemed loathe to depart. "What have you got on for the rest of the afternoon?"

"I need to buy a Nerf gun set. Magnetic bullets, a target, and a rifle," Skye said, tucking her hands into her pockets. The temperature had dropped and the rain that had been threatening was about to throw a tantrum.

"That's...do you have a child?" Emily's eyes were round.

Skye laughed. "Oh no. It's for the kiddo 'round the corner, down the road." She explained the daily interaction with Rhiannon. "I don't want her to get in trouble if she chooses a new victim, so I figured if she had a target that was magnetic, she wouldn't lose the darts, and pedestrians wouldn't lose an eye."

Emily regarded her for a long time. "Mm," she said, which could have meant anything. "I'll see you on Saturday. Text me if you have any questions about..." she shrugged slightly. Elegantly. "Just if you have questions."

The handshake lasted for perhaps a little bit longer than necessary, but Skye assumed the warmth on her skin, which curled low into parts of her body that appreciated the heat was completely one-sided.

Not that she was complaining.

Chapter Seven

Emily stared vacantly at her laptop screen, the preliminary plans for 45 Anders Road a jumble of multicoloured CAD lines and scaled measurements. She'd made the right decision. So why did it feel like she was trying to convince herself of it? Yesterday had been quite a day. Meeting Skye. Interviewing Skye. Taking in all that was Skye. It was entirely unfair that Skye Reynolds was a blonde warrior goddess who looked like she'd just flown in from Themyscira, choosing to eschew the gold and leather armour for a rugby jersey and ridiculously snug jeans. Entirely unfair.

At least she'd held back her appreciation of her new tenant in front of her actual new tenant. If anything, she'd dialled up Business Emily a little. It would have been somewhat awkward if she'd professed her admiration of Skye's shoulders over her cooling coffee.

At least Emily had committed to the whole idea, despite the panic that kept poking uncomfortably in her stomach. She'd nearly pulled out as anxiety reared its head very early Sunday morning, which had prompted a phone call to Kristen's message service.

"Kristen, I'm doing something completely immersive and spontaneous and I needed to ring you to tell you about it even though you won't get this message until after I've done the completely immersive and spontaneous thing."

She'd gone on to explain the tenant and studio situation until the end-of-message beep shrilled in her ear. The edge of the phone had left a line in her palm for a few seconds after she'd ended the call, but at least telling Kristen—or her message service—had made it real and that meant following through and being a responsible adult.

Following through had resulted in lovely, and athletic Skye, with those tiny wrinkles beside her eyes born of sunlight and laughter. Skye, with her wide mouth and bright smile, which illuminated the amber in her eyes. Skye, with the corded muscles in her forearms. Skye, with the comfortable gait, strolling away from the cafe, all beautifully relaxed in her skin, heading off to buy a toy for a kid who pretended to be an assassin each afternoon.

She rolled her eyes. Pathetic. Of course, it didn't hurt to look, but showing any interest in Skye was wrong on so many levels. She was a tenant. It had only been a week since Bec left, although that wasn't really a reason. At all. And the idea that she could be a potential lover? *That* idea was totally silly—

"You're muttering to yourself, and you only do that when a build isn't going well or circumstances in your life aren't lining up like bottles on a wall. What's up?" Nic leaned on the doorframe, his eyebrows raised. Emily inhaled deeply, then, even though she'd already done so that morning, admired Nic's eye make-up; the abstract twists of red and gold over his eyelids to represent banksia flowers were works of art. The man was amazing.

"I love your makeup today," she said, pointing to his face.

"Ooh. That's deflection." He spun on his heel, reached into the main office, grabbed the nearest chair, and wheeled it into Emily's office, then sat and looked at her expectantly. His eyes gleamed, and he waggled his fingertips at her. "Spill."

"No."

"Yes."

"Oh my God, Nic. Come on," Emily moaned, and let her head fall back on her neck. Then after a huff, dropped it back down to stare at her friend. "I did something, which is making me question my sanity."

Nic nodded slowly. "And?"

Emily scrubbed at the desk top with her nails and groaned. "I decided to take on Lorraine Hudson's tenant since Lorraine's sold her house and she mentioned that Skye hadn't found a place yet, and it would be really good of me to pay it forward, what with the assistance I received with my career, and helping out Skye would be doing that. And therefore, I'm setting up my Ikebana space in the second bedroom and Skye is moving into the studio on Saturday." The entire explanation poured from her mouth without pause, so she sucked in a quick breath. And stared at Nic, who blinked, then slowly the corners of his mouth lifted.

Emily pointed in irritation. "No! You do not get to make that face."

"What face?" The smile was now firmly entrenched.

"That face. The one that says that this tenancy will be good for me and I might like the change, even though I hate change, and that she's very good-looking and distracting," Emily said, then glared. "That face."

Nic's right eyebrow slowly lifted, animating the banksia flower. "Hmm. Who knew my face could say all of that?"

Emily thinned her lips. "Smart arse."

"So, a completely unplanned-for tenant, who is arriving in five days. A tenant who is taking your studio space. And who is apparently quite attractive." He smirked, but then frowned. "You've met her, haven't you?"

"Yesterday. She's the flower delivery courier who comes here occasionally. Skye Reynolds."

Nic's grin lit up his features. "Oh! Oh, that Skye. Oh my." Then he folded his hands over his knee and waited. It didn't take long.

"What?" Emily asked, knowing full well what Nic was waiting for.

"You're pretty reserved with people when you first meet them, hon. Mind you, it works fine with clients, but inquiring minds want to know how it went with—what was the phrase you used?" He pursed his lips, placing his index finger against them. "How it went with the very good looking and distracting Skye?

"You are so horrible to me," Emily growled.

Nic grinned. "I love you. Tell me how it went."

"It was very pleasant. We had coffee, well, I did. She had tea. And we talked about the studio and the tenancy, obviously. But other things, too. It was…pleasant." Emily stared him down, then bit her lip as a wicked expression grew on his face.

"Really."

"Yes."

"I'm popping over on Saturday morning. I think I have a floral arrangement to pick up. Perhaps I'll run into Skye as she moves in."

"No, you won't, and you don't, and therefore, you won't." Emily glared at her friend who leaned his cheek on his palm and widened his eyes in innocence. She swallowed. "This makes me sweat so hard, Nic, but I said I'd help out, and it's a nice thing to do and—" Something held her back from sharing the immersion therapy aspect of her decision. "I can do this."

"And bonus…she's not Bec." His gaze was sharp. Then softened to sympathy and understanding.

"And she's not Bec," Emily echoed. "It's not the point, but there is that."

***

It took just over forty-five minutes on Friday night to shift her equipment and materials from the studio to the second bedroom. Emily stood in the doorway, scanning the Tetris maze of plastic boxes and cloth rolls of specialised scissors and cutters piled on the carpet, her twin crafting desks folded and stacked against the wall, and rubbed at her chest. The muscles just under the surface of her skin were tight and all the worries about this impetuous left-hand turn in her planned and organised road came rushing back. But if she embraced the change, didn't that mean her road was back on track? Right. Time for her big girl pants. Immersion therapy. She could do this. Resilience, and all that.

With that enthusiastic pep talk, she thrust wireless bud headphones into her ears, cued French composer Eric Lévi's *Era* project and as the haunting, contemporarily-arranged Gregorian chants erased her concerns, she plunged into the vacant studio, where, for two hours, she cleaned it from top to bottom. In the end, the space contained not a trace of herself.

It was strangely cathartic.

***

The small truck's radio kept drifting off the music station, like an inebriated bar patron attempting to make eye contact. Seb took his hand off the steering wheel and gave the dashboard a smack, miraculously making the appliance work and a 1980s easy listening song filled the cab.

Skye, her foot resting on the dash above the glove box, clenched her bum muscles to brace her body as Seb took the corner into Emily's street a little too quickly. He drove vehicles like he rode a bike. A quick check on her phone confirmed what she remembered.

"It's the dark red brick place up ahead. Number thirty," she said.

Seb slowed to a stop so that the back of the truck covered the driveway.

"Fancy digs," he said under his breath, craning his head to peer out of the windscreen.

"No fancier than Lorraine's. Besides," Skye pushed open the door, and jumped down, "I'm at the back of the place, mate. Not inside there. Come on." She met Seb at the roller door at the rear of the truck.

"Righto. Let's get you in, then." He hurled the door up and leapt inside.

"Hang on. I need the keys, and I should let Emily know I'm here. I can't really march down her driveway like I own the place. I'll be back in a minute."

Skye jogged onto the property, along the path, and up to the black metalwork front door; the colour in keeping with the era of the house. A concession to modern life was attached to the wall, and Skye pressed her finger to the button, hearing the buzz inside.

Skye decided that casual clothing suited Emily when the door opened. Cute sneakers, dark denim jeans, and a cream cable-knit jumper, gave Skye pause and it was a full second or two before she finally looked into those amazing brown-black eyes.

"Hi. My name's Skye Reynolds. I'm your new tenant," she said, a cheeky grin pushing her lips into her cheeks.

Emily laughed, the sound filling the doorway between them. "Good morning, Skye Reynolds, new tenant. I'm Emily Fitzsimmons, new landlord." She raised an eyebrow. "I imagine you'll need keys." They shared a grin.

"Generally helps."

Emily laughed again, and Skye was thrilled. This was a version of Emily that she hadn't seen before. Emily had been reserved, formal, almost brusque on occasion last Sunday. Skye thought she'd even sensed an undercurrent of anxiety every now and then. But this morning, Emily and her laughter were light. And delicious.

Emily dug into her jeans pocket, then brandished a silver keyring which held two keys, and a bright red Lego bicycle.

"I had two keys cut because I figured you had a key buddy." Emily's fingers skimmed Skye's palm as she handed over the set. Skye looked at the tiny bicycle for a moment and felt her heart glow at the sweetness of the gesture. Emily had clearly wanted Skye to feel like the studio was her new home. She looked up and their eyes locked.

"Thanks," she said. "For the studio, and for this." She held up the little bike. "It's cute." The soft pink blush on Emily's cheeks was all sorts of delightful and Skye was an instant fan. "I'll," she pointed her chin back towards the road, "start unloading, then."

"Do you need a hand?"

"Nope. I've got an extra pair of hands in my mate, Seb. Besides, I don't really have a whole lot." They shared another smile, then Skye pivoted and jogged back to Seb, who had been watching the entire interaction.

"I've only delivered to Nic at *Fitzsimmons*. So, that's Emily, hey?" He hummed, squatting on the truck's tailgate, and delivering a long look at Skye.

"What?"

"Nothing." He lifted one corner of his mouth, and Skye smacked his shoulder.

"Don't be a perv. Come on. Pass me a box."

The sofa-bed and the free-standing closet were the bulkiest items to move so they left them to last. Then, after two hours of not just unloading, but carrying, unpacking, and rearranging, Skye rested her hands on her hips and scanned the now full studio. The last two boxes of miscellaneous stuff sat against the wall, but other than that, nearly everything was in place or put away. She really didn't have a lot.

Seb perched on the tan leather ottoman and laughed as Skye wandered over to the sofa-bed and flung herself backwards onto the seat cushions.

"I really appreciate you helping me out tod—"

Her sentence was cut off when there was a knock on the door. The knock belonged to Emily, who was cradling a floral arrangement in a low pot, a small plastic gift bag, and a tentative look on her face.

"Hi. I couldn't see any more movement along the driveway so I thought you may have stopped for a breather or were finished. Either way, it seemed like the perfect opportunity to interrupt," she explained in that careful manner that Skye had noticed on the phone.

"You're not interrupting at all. We actually have finished." She flung out her arm like a game show hostess. "All my worldly treasures."

Emily laughed, and Skye suddenly became aware of how clean and gorgeous Emily was—she smelled like cinnamon—how sweaty and dusty Skye was, and how close together they were standing. She eased away, wishing she'd magically been able to predict Emily's visit and therefore managed a quick shower. Oh well.

Seb stood.

"I'm not one of her worldly treasures, thank God. I'm Seb," he said, his wide friendly grin following his words.

"Good to meet you, Seb. I'm Emily. I live…there." She pointed in the direction of the main house with her chin. Then they stood for a moment until Emily seemed to register the items in her hands. "Oh. These are for you." She smiled into Skye's face, which prodded the butterflies to life in Skye's stomach. "Housewarming gifts of sorts." She thrust out the bag of individually wrapped chocolates. "I don't know if you're allergic to anything, but that chocolate is one of my favourites and it's organic and free of anything likely to require an EpiPen."

Skye grinned, reading the label on the swing tag. She knew all about the artisan chocolatier in the city centre. *Quick Cargo* scored a lot of work from the florist next door, and she'd spent numerous occasions drooling at the displays. "Thanks! I'll eat anything." Then she glared at Seb. "And I'm not sharing."

He clutched his chest and dropped back onto the ottoman. Emily laughed, then handed over the low pot with the floral arrangement.

"I know there's not a lot of space and you probably don't need extraneous items, but I thought you may like this." Her voice softened, and Skye leaned in to catch the syllables, which meant that she also lowered her voice. It felt intimate.

"Thank you," she said, then she looked properly at what her hands were holding, and her eyes widened. The five individual strands of bamboo grass were supported by a green leaf, each one an exact copy, as if the florist had searched the earth to find such perfect foliage. The willow twigs twisted around the leaves, alive like snakes, and the tree peony flowers were given specific allocations of space to balance the structure. The low matte black vase was packed with dark green moss. It was artistic and beautiful. It must have cost Emily a fortune.

"This is amazing! Thank you."

"That's okay. The peonies aren't the exact flowers to use in that particular arrangement, but it was a smaller piece and I wanted to complete it today."

Skye gawked at her, flicked her eyes to Seb, who wore a similarly stunned expression, then she swung back to Emily. "You made this? This is your art?"

There was pride on display in Emily's eyes, and appreciation of Skye's gratitude, but Skye spotted something else. A fleeting moment of vulnerability. Like Emily was sharing a tiny window into herself that not many people saw and for some reason, she was allowing Skye to peek inside. It was another gift beyond the flowers and the chocolates.

"Yes. That's an Ikebana in the Nageirebana style." She delivered a little shrug. "It's one of the more free-form versions. Many are more formal, but take much longer to finalise."

"I love it. Thank you," Skye repeated. Emily inhaled deeply, as if she'd accomplished a difficult task, then looked at Seb.

"Lovely to meet you, Seb, and," she tilted her head at Skye, "I'm glad everything is okay. Let me know if you need anything." She gave a nod, then turned, disappearing out the door, pulling it closed behind her.

Skye blinked, then set the Ikebana and chocolates on the tiny square table near the sofa-bed. She collapsed onto the seat cushion nearest the table, and Seb spoke first.

"Eldamar," he said, reverently.

"What?"

"She's one of the Elven from Eldermar with, you know," he fluttered his hands about his head, "her hair like that and those big eyes. She's an Elven."

Skye rolled her eyes. "Except she's not. No pointy ears."

"True."

"And the lack of immortality."

"That you know of." He thrust out a finger, then frowned.

"And the not walking around with a bow and arrow situation."

"Hmm."

"So, nothing like an elf at all," Skye finished and stared at her friend.

He grinned. "Well, all right. But gosh, she's pretty and kind of like Natalie Portman mixed with Audrey Tatou with that aloof friendliness, except I think she's probably got some deep humour just wai—"

"Please stop objectifying my landlord."

Chapter Eight

Kristen looked like she was in psychologist's heaven when Emily revealed the gift of the little bicycle keyring and how she'd delivered chocolates and created the Ikebena piece. Phrases like 'assuaging her feelings of displacement' and 'compensating for the need to re-route routine' were bandied about during the hour-long session, and Emily had a repetitive strain in her neck from all the nodding she was doing for every single analytical comment.

"Then on Sunday, I found a note on my front door. The envelope was tucked into the metalwork."

"A note?"

"Yes. From Skye. It was to say thank you. Again. Then she ended the note with the astonishing information that flamingoes get their colour from what they eat otherwise they're white or a dull grey," Emily said, her forehead wrinkled in confusion.

Kristen laughed. "Okay. I'll bite. What do they eat?"

"Crustaceans, apparently."

"Okay, so—"

"Oh. Not finished. Then last Thursday, and just on Monday, and now two days later this morning, I got more notes. Same location. Each one wishing me a great day, with the distinct hope that it was stress free, and more random bizarre facts." Emily stared at her therapist. "Did you know that wombat poo is shaped like a cube? See? Neither did I." She raised a finger. "And penguins don't have teeth, Kristen, and some species of shrimp have their heart located in their head." They shared a slow nod.

"Why do you think Skye is leaving these notes?" Kristen steepled her fingers.

"I have no idea. She's like a bike-riding Wikipedia. Is it to make me feel better about renting the studio?"

"That's a theory."

"But she couldn't possibly know why I decided to rent it out. I haven't told a soul."

"Then maybe she's just astute and sensed some anxiety. Perhaps she's simply a quirky, friendly person."

Emily exhaled in one long breath. Maybe Skye *had* picked up on her anxiety. She thought she'd kept it under wraps fairly well at the key handover and the gift-giving. God, the gifts.

What. The. Hell.

Her insides swirled. Assuaging and compensating indeed. But she had wanted to give the gifts, because it felt good to make someone—Skye—comfortable, not to assuage her own anxiety. That was another topic to dissect at a later point.

Eventually Emily shrugged, and Kristen continued. "Do you mind the notes?"

"Not at all. They're sweet, and yes, quirky. I actually look forward to them."

"Do you see Skye in passing?"

"Not really. She's gone early in the morning, because I find the notes when I'm leaving for work, and she's home earlier than I am. I did wave to her yesterday afternoon." Emily allowed the most recent image of Skye to take up residence in her thoughts. She'd spotted movement from the side window of the second bedroom at around six o'clock and stood to watch Skye sit up on the bike seat, stretch her back as she coasted down the driveway, after dashing out for bread and milk, if the evidence of the backpack was any indication. She hadn't changed from work, and the lycra emphasised lines of muscles and the sensual shoulder roll she gave pushed out her small breasts. It was incredible how much the eyes took in at a single glance.

Emily pulled her gaze back to Kristen, who was resting her cheek in her palm and holding a smile at bay. Emily rolled her eyes. "Okay. Fine. That's a big lie."

Kristen laughed and gestured for Emily to elaborate.

"Well, we bumped into each other, sort of in passing, this morning at the front of the driveway. She'd leaned her bike against the front fence, and was adjusting her backpack on her shoulders." Emily paused as she recalled the feeling of competence that radiated from Skye. She imagined that Skye could walk into any room and people's tension would dissipate, they'd breathe deeply and mutter "Oh thank God she's here." And it wasn't just her strong body. It was more than that. It was a presence.

Skye's smile had been wide this morning, breaking through the ubiquitous morning fog of the winter's day. "Hi. Good morning," Skye had said, and Emily couldn't help but return it. She lifted her laptop bag and rested it on top of the cube-shaped brick letterbox.

"Good morning back at you. I haven't seen you to say so, but thank you for my notes." She kept her grin. "They've been fun."

They had looked at each other, and Emily basked in the warm caramel hues.

"You're welcome. I scored a personalised keyring, chocolates and a floral display. The least I could do was let you know that wombat shit is shaped like your letterbox."

Emily couldn't help the loud laugh that fell out of her mouth. Skye beamed and then pointed to the front door. "Today's note."

Emily followed the gesture. "Oh! I missed it." She looked back at Skye. "The other part of the notes is also appreciated, by the way. The 'have a stress free day' message. It's nice."

Skye seemed to take a step or perhaps Emily had swayed forward. Something had happened because suddenly Skye seemed closer, her physicality and strength radiating into Emily's space. A glow, an energy, thawed the chill of the air, and warmed her skin.

Skye's voice was intimate. "I didn't want to presume, but you seemed a bit anxious about this whole rent situation. And I have enough self-esteem to know it's probably not me personally, particularly because I'm not a serial killer." She grinned and Emily chuckled. "But perhaps it's because someone is in your space." Skye waved one hand in the air to encompass the house, the driveway, and the studio further away. "I'm your first tenant, and I guess the notes are about me introducing myself." She paused. "Although, telling you about shrimps' hearts being in their heads was really not—"

"It was perfect. Maybe it's where we should all keep our hearts. Might help us make better decisions." An image of Bec flashed through her mind, and she clenched her jaw. "Yes, you're my first tenant. But I'm hoping you'll stay for a long time."

They stood for another moment in their warm bubble, until Skye tilted her head, and reached for her bike.

"I need to get to work. You have a great day, okay?"

Emily nodded. "You, too." And she stayed perfectly still, watching Skye become smaller and smaller as she skimmed along the asphalt towards the city.

Emily blinked away the rather tingly memory and refocused on her therapist.

"It's nice to see you moving on from your feelings regarding Bec's decision," Kristen said, ignoring Emily's eye-roll that had preceded the retelling of that morning's interaction.

"I think so. I mean, I am. I guess." Emily widened her eyes in frustration. "God, that's unclear. Sorry. I don't know. I feel a certain attraction to Skye, which is complicated. I'd like the tectonic plates of my life to stop shifting a little, that's all."

***

The shifting plates in her equilibrium bothered her on several occasions throughout the rest of the week. Thursday night saw her sitting on the couch googling couriers in Melbourne, scrolling up and down the *Quick Cargo* site, enlarging the photo of Skye decked out in lycra and pride. Grinning into the camera. White teeth flashing. Blonde hair pulled back into an easy ponytail. Strong hands curled around the handlebars of the cargo bike. Finally, Emily had collapsed sideways into the cushions and rolled her eyes so forcefully it was a wonder they were still located in her eye sockets. If she wanted to look at Skye that closely, she could wander some metres down the driveway. But this was clandestine and delicious, which meant that Emily could gaze and sigh without being a complete weirdo.

***

Skye poured the hot water into her tea pot on Friday night. She hoped that Emily appreciated how hilarious it was that Agatha Christie got her own address wrong in her autobiography—the trivia in the note on Wednesday—and how mind-bending it was that penguins have high-velocity poo—that morning's note. Two messages about poo. That might have been too much. Oh well. It was a bit random, but then that was the point. It was meant to be fun, and Emily certainly seemed more and more relaxed each time Skye ran into her.

Just this morning, they had met accidentally at the front gate again, as Emily rolled the empty recycling bin—one of two bins; red for main garbage on Mondays and yellow recycling on Fridays—back into the front yard after the early morning garbage truck had been through the street.

"They're getting earlier every week, I think," Skye said, wheeling her bike to a stop beside Emily's car. Emily tossed a glance over her shoulder, angled the bin onto its little concrete pad, then turned to Skye. She was dressed for work, and Skye took in the red Doc Martin boots, black skinny jeans, chunky jumper and scarf flung haphazardly about her neck. Again, her hair was shuffled about, and Skye wondered why such a thrown-together hairstyle on such a put-together package appealed so much. The juxtaposition was beyond attractive.

"They are," Emily responded, walking over, then waved her finger up and down in front of Skye. "How are you not cold?"

Skye laughed, looking down at her track pants, and zip-up jacket. "I've got my cycle gear on under this. That's enough layers. Besides, I think I told you that I run hot."

Emily was only a metre away, but even in the morning half-light, and the fog, Skye watched as Emily's suddenly hooded eyes regarded her, while a blush rose above the scarf on her neck. Time became very stretchy as they maintained eye contact. Her months-long enjoy-from-a-distance crush on Emily Fitzsimmons had only intensified in the last two weeks and it was doing things to her libido. And sanity.

She shook her head at her blathering from the morning, and inhaled the aroma of the Earl Grey tea leaves infusing in the pot in front of her—an end of week ritual—bracing her arms on the flat surface of the bench, then tossed a glance about the studio.

It had only taken a brief moment to make the space her own. Once Seb had left, she'd puttered about the compact area, shifting around the few pieces of furniture, filling her two bookcases with her eclectic mix of literature, which included autobiographies, mysteries, science fiction, bicycle magazines, marketing textbooks, five years of *Guinness Book of Records*—an excellent source of so much useless trivia—and a large amount of lesbian fiction. She'd made her sofa bed, shaking out the doona and fluffing up the pillows, as they'd been stuffed into boxes.

Again, she let the sweet, floral scent of the tea fill her lungs. It was subtle, like the lighting she'd chosen for the evening. A single lamp lit the room, a soft glow casting large shadows inside the space. Her eyes fell on the Ikebana display gift on the little buffet table that held her small television.

The gifts had confused, thrilled, and reassured her all at once. Moving from Lorraine's place after two years had been really unsettling. It wasn't the idea of change. Skye dealt with change quite well. It had been the odd moment of home-sickness bubbling in her stomach as she'd loaded the last item into the truck on Saturday morning. The melancholic mood lasted right up until Emily had knocked on the door bearing chocolates, flowers, and a smile that advertised the kindness in her eyes. When Emily had leaned against her letterbox the other morning, and bitten her bottom lip when her suggestion that Skye live in the studio for as long as possible, something about Emily's demeanour tugged at Skye's heart. She seemed cautious, yet eager. Interested, yet careful. Fragile, yet competent, which was good because Skye had sworn off rescuing women. No rescuing. It only led to heartbreak.

She peered into the infuser, her shoulder-length blonde hair loose and falling forward. Pouring out the tea, she mused some more. Perhaps Emily had experienced something hurtful. It could explain the sense of caution that Skye felt from her.

"For God's sake, you're now literally fixating. Just stop." She glared at her reflection in the kitchen window, the black of the night creating a mirrored effect in the glass. Beyond her reflection, she knew there was a patch of grass, with small bushes attempting to create a hedge near the fence. In the daylight, the back of Emily's house was completely visible, with her large bedroom window facing the studio kitchen. Tonight, the room was dark, but Skye knew that Emily was home, because a shadow moved about, probably in the ensuite.

"Yep. Thinking about Emily in the shower. That's helpful." Skye sipped the too-hot tea, just to give her mind something else to focus on, and winced in consequence. Then, the backlit outline of her landlord, perhaps wrapped in a towel, which Skye's brain instantly confirmed whether it was true or not, filled the window. She froze, as did Emily. Skye knew they couldn't see each other. It was too dark. But Emily was definitely contemplating the building she'd rented out. Were regrets festering? Skye shifted uncomfortably, and her sudden movement must have been visible in the window, because Emily's body jerked. Her arms stretched wide to grab hold of the curtains, ready to yank them together and close out the world, but the action dislodged the towel, and, in a sort of slow-motion, fell away from her body. Skye absorbed the astonishing vision of Emily attempting to clutch at the towel while forgetting to let go of the curtains, because in her haste, the force of her reaction ripped the curtains and railing off the wall, and the entire frame collapsed, and Emily disappeared from view under the weight of metal, fabric, and most likely acute embarrassment. Skye was positive she heard the shocked squeak through two panes of glass and across six metres of lawn.

"Oh! Shit!" She planted her cup on the counter, sloshing tea over the edge, and took off at a run, out of the studio, very happy that she still had shoes on given the sharp stones on the driveway, and halted at Emily's front door. She thumped on the metal.

"Emily! Are you okay?" Skye yelled, then thumped again, until the sound of a lock paused her hand, and the door tentatively opened. Emily looked flustered, which was hardly surprising, and had obviously thrown on the nearest clothing at hand, because she stood in the doorway wearing fleece track pants, and a t-shirt pulled on in such haste that it was the wrong way around.

"Hi. You saw that. And, wow…that's probably the most mortifying thing I've ever experienced in my life." She bared her teeth in a grimace, then hummed, delivered a sort of double-clenched fist gesture close to her torso, then laid her fists tightly over her chest. Another grimace followed. They stared at each other until Emily shivered in the cold.

"You're just out of the shower," Skye said, then winced. "Please ignore the fact that I know that, but you're also getting cold. I… um…wanted to make sure you're okay."

Emily huffed a self-deprecating sigh. "Ah, God. I'm okay. My bedroom curtains aren't, though." Then she seemed to come to a decision, and stepped back, widening the doorway. "Come in. It is cold, and you've hardly got many clothes on either." She blushed softly, taking in Skye's track pants and t-shirt combination.

"All right. Thanks." Skye stepped inside and was immediately enveloped in the cosy atmosphere of the lounge room. It wasn't just the comfortable furnishings—the leather couch advertised cloud-like softness—but the entire space felt caring, gentle. Emily closed the door behind her.

"Would you like something to—oh, for God's sake!" She grabbed the bottom of her shirt and yanked it away from her torso. "Really? Sorry. Wardrobe malfunction. I'll be back in a moment."

Skye used the next few minutes, which seemed a long time to switch a shirt around, to wander into the lounge properly. All the furniture was exactly right. The bookcases were placed properly. The coffee table was in a location that looked perfect. Care had been taken in this room, and Skye assumed the rest of the house was the same. She shoved her hands into her pockets and rocked her feet sideways—in and out. Emily wasn't returning.

"You okay?" she called, realising that she'd checked on Emily's wellbeing at least three times in the last ten minutes. There was a muffled "Yes" from the end of the hallway. Skye looked up when she heard the floorboards creak near the kitchen. Emily had ruffled her hair so that it was even more accidentally adorable, replaced the shirt with a sweater, and encased her feet in light blue fuzzy slippers. Skye's heart flipped over. She wanted to take the woman into her arms. She wanted to kiss the vulnerability. And…she needed to back away. Skye quickly stepped sideways so that the kitchen bench became a distinct obstacle. Necessary.

"Would you like a drink or something?"

Wondering why Emily hadn't wished her a good night and asked her to leave, Skye nodded. "Thank you. Water?"

"I do have tea, Skye. Water sounds like you're not confident with the state of my beverages," Emily said, tipping her head and quirking a smile.

Skye grinned. "Sure. Tea it is." She slid onto a stool and leaned on the counter. "Do you need a hand putting up your curtains?"

Emily paused, the pantry door half open. "Not tonight. Thank you, though. It can get fixed tomorrow. I'll just make sure I don't turn any lights on when I go to bed, because the world doesn't need to see that performance again." She rolled her eyes.

Skye chuckled. "You should have seen it from my end."

Emily joined in with a small laugh, although it really only touched her lips, leaving the rest of her face unsure of what emotion to express. Skye studied the elfin features, and how her hand gripped the door handle with such ferocity it was surprising that it didn't break. Emily's laughter became brittle, stretching thinly until suddenly it cracked, with that strange cough that connects comedy and tragedy. Then her eyes widened as her breath caught, and tracks of tears appeared, twisting down her cheeks. Then, Emily's shoulders folded in and sobs shook her entire frame. Skye leapt up, and dashed around the counter, automatically bundling Emily into her arms, like she'd done it a thousand times before, and held her while she convulsed against her chest.

Skye hushed white noise across the top of Emily's strands of hair, which fluttered with every exhalation. Eventually, the rhythm of Skye's breathing, or the sound of it—something—slowed Emily's sobs to quiet, shaky hiccups.

"I'm sorry."

Skye felt the words more than heard them. The vibrations travelled through her hand cupping the back of Emily's head.

"Hey," she whispered. "No need to apologise. Whatever it is, I'm glad I was here, even if I didn't really do anything."

Emily drew back, ground the heels of her palms into her eyes, and pulled in a deep breath. She gazed wetly at Skye, who left her hands on Emily's shoulders.

"You are doing something. Thank you." She rolled her eyes. "That's twice tonight I've embarrassed myself in front of you. I'm not sure I can handle any more."

Skye quirked her lips. "You have nothing to be embarrassed about." Her fingers itched to wipe the single tear from under Emily's eye, but all she could hear was the yelling match between her 'don't rescue women' rule and her default empathetic response to people's sadness and pain. So, she left her hands exactly where they were. Probably safer. It wouldn't do to overthink the fact that she'd just held a very vulnerable, very beautiful Emily Fitzsimmons in her arms, and how exactly right it had felt.

"If you point me towards the tea things, I could make one." She ducked her head to catch Emily's eyes. "Or do you want something with a percentage from a higher shelf?"

Humour sparked in Emily's dark liquid brown eyes. "No, I think your original choice of water is actually what I need."

"On it. Come on," Skye said, nodding, and swept up Emily's hand in her own, and led her towards the couch. "I'll bring it in."

After a few random openings of cupboard doors, Skye found two glasses, filled each with water, and set them onto coasters on Emily's rather expensive-looking coffee table. She sat on the couch, turned square-on and caught the minute wobble in Emily's bottom lip. There was such a lot of pain there. Skye flipped her hand over, and placed it gently on the leather seat between them, and waited, giving

Emily the option to either ignore it or grab hold. Emily chose option B, and Skye curled her fingers over the slim hand. A little jolt of electricity shimmered up her arm. Oh. That was nice. And absolutely not the time to dwell on its existence.

"This is not just about soft furnishing malfunctions, is it?" Skye asked.

Emily stared at their joined hands.

"No," she said, her voice small.

"Okay. Well, I'm not—"

"My girlfriend cheated on me and we broke up."

Skye sucked in air through her teeth. "Oh, man." Instantly, she hated the ex-girlfriend. That was the drill for this type of situation. Then she realised that the actual existence of a girlfriend had answered another question; an answer which was filed away for later. Skye's response to the cheating revelation was a hand squeeze, which seemed to be the correct choice, because Emily lifted her head and they shared a look.

"Almost four weeks ago."

"That's recent," Skye said.

"Mm." Emily's eyes roamed Skye's face, then she lowered her gaze to their joined hands. "She said that Theresa was a fling. Maybe she picked her up at an open home. She's a real estate agent. They were doing it on the dining table when I came home to grab my lunch."

Without meaning to, Skye swivelled her head to look at the dining table, or where a dining table would be if there was one, which there wasn't. She looked quizzically at Emily, who shrugged.

"I haven't bought a new one yet. The other one got vanished by my friend, Nic. I came home and it was gone."

"Nic sounds like an excellent friend."

"He is. He's my best friend." Emily leaned forward, picked up her glass and drank deeply, the other hand still firmly inside Skye's grip. Skye smiled to herself. How very right it felt to hold this woman's hand.

That was another fact that Skye chose to ignore.

"I'm sorry that happened to you," she murmured, then sent her hand to join the other, sandwiching Emily's, as new tears created more tracks.

"Me, too. I think tonight's accident might have been the thing that tipped me over. I thought I was doing pretty well with everything, actually." She shook her head. "Bec cheating. The break-up. Then trying out Kristen's suggest—" Emily snapped her mouth shut, and darted her eyes from Skye's face to objects about the room

Skye tilted her head. Bec was obviously the ex. Kristen and her suggestion were a mystery, but that wasn't any of her business. Clearly, something else had happened and Skye wasn't about to pry, because Emily had certainly made herself vulnerable enough as it was.

"I can sympathise, I guess. Not with the cheating aspect, but I've had a couple of relationships end. One when I was still quite in love with her." She smoothed her palm over Emily's knuckles, then wondered if she'd said something wrong, because Emily's mouth turned down, her face becoming even more pale.

"That's the problem," she whispered. "I don't think I loved Bec. Not for a while." Then she delivered a low growl under her breath and looked beseechingly at Skye, her eyebrows wriggly lines above her eyes. "Oh my God, I'm so sorry. Again. You don't need to know th—I'm ridiculously oversharing. Clearly, unstable drapery is a truth serum. I'm...just..." The words stumbled over themselves.

Skye wrinkled her brow. "Don't apologise. I'm a safe person, I promise. But..." she hesitated. "Can I ask why you were together if you didn't love her? I mean, please tell me to get lost if I'm over-stepping any landlord-tenant-hugger-huggee boundaries here."

Emily gave a grunt. It was not quite a laugh; more a granting of permission. "Bec was part of a plan I had in my head."

"I don't follow."

"No, neither did she."

"Um..."

"She and I were introduced by a mutual friend. The start of our relationship was all very orderly and we were great for the first five or six months, but I did this thing that I do. I created a life plan about the two of us being together. There weren't really any details in that plan. There never are. Just a railroad that I personally can't derail from. But!" She pointed vaguely at Skye as if to ensure she was still focused on the conversation. "If something does derail me, the entire plan I have falls to bits and everything is chaos." She squished her lips together and flicked a sideways glance at Skye, who was sitting very still, like movement might scare Emily away. "Anyway, I stayed because I couldn't stop my plan. And I'm aware how unreasonable that was to Bec. I really am. But it doesn't give her an excuse, and I'm still so angry and sad and yet relieved all together. It's a lot."

The words hung in the room.

"Thank you for not judging, Skye. And thank you for being a particularly good listener," Emily said softly.

"Emily, I wouldn't judge. It's not something I do." Skye watched the emotional weather patterns drift through Emily's eyes, then spotted a hesitation and knew they'd reached the moment where Emily could awkwardly ask if Skye wanted another drink, despite not having touched the first one, or suggest politely that Skye leave as soon as possible.

Skye came to a decision first. "I should probably go. Are you going to be okay?"

Emily nodded, adding a frown like she was fortifying herself to march down the hall to her bedroom. "I will. Thank you for checking on me, and listening. Oh, and offering to fix the curtains. I have a basic tool kit with a power drill in the laundry, so I'll get on with it tomorrow."

An image of Emily competently wielding a power tool filled Skye's brain, which happily added completely unnecessary details like Emily wearing a sleeveless top, cut-off jeans, and a smirk. Jesus. Time to go.

"Well, that's good." Skye stood, releasing Emily's hand, instantly missing its warmth, and mentally slapping her brain into submission. Emily stood as well. "I'm actually glad that you're fixing it tomorrow because I don't know how steady I'd be on a ladder tonight. I cycled up Graham Street probably four hundred times today and my thighs are rock hard. I need a hot shower to ease them out."

Emily blinked, and a soft pink tinge dusted her cheeks. Skye had seen the blush before but in the muted light of the table lamps, the effect was quite beautiful. She froze. It was not the time to be thinking of Emily's ethereal beauty. No. Oh boy.

They locked eyes for a moment, then Emily drew closer and delivered a brief hug, pulling away before Skye could react.

"Well, I won't keep you. Thank you again." She delivered the note of gratitude with a singular nod and a quick sigh-huff combination.

Skye recognised the signals and made her way to the door.

"No problem. Goodnight, Emily." She looked back, taking in the too-long sleeves on the sweater, the track pants, the adorable slippers, and the expression on Emily's face, which clearly showed a determination to persevere despite flailing in the absence of order. It seemed well-practised, that expression, like Emily had needed to call on it more than a few times in her life.

"Goodnight, Skye," Emily added a vague hand-flip sort of gesture that could have meant thanks, or have a good night, or resignation, or a combination of all three.

And with that last image, Skye found herself outside, standing on the driveway, her shoulders hunched against the cold. The glow of the streetlight caught the steam from her exhalation, and it occurred to her that Emily's life wasn't as put together as she'd initially assumed. Emily had broken parts of her that needed some glueing. But that wasn't Skye's job. Nope. She congratulated herself on not rescuing a woman tonight. Big pat on the back there. Well done. Her feet crunched on the gravel. Then she pressed her fingers into the skin above her eyebrows.

She might not have rescued Emily but discussing rock hard thighs and hot showers meant that she'd accepted the award for the most lesbian sentence ever. And Emily now had that sentence parked in her ears. Her cringe lasted for the entire length of the driveway.

Chapter Nine

The image of Skye's body, her blonde hair loose about her face, her skin pink from the heat of the shower, her thighs—the rock hard version—and water beading across her breasts and shoulders and flat stomach and strong arms and, well, just all of it really, drifted away as Emily woke the next morning. The tingly response in her body quickly faded as she winced at the memory of the events from last night. She flung her arms out sideways and slapped the mattress, like a mortified starfish.

"What the hell?" she enunciated at the ceiling, her eyes wide in disbelief.

It was the perfect question. The only question.

Remembering that she didn't have curtains, Emily shuffled under the doona until she reached the edge of the bed closest to the bathroom, then dropped over the side, and commando-crawled across the carpet until it was safe to stand up in between her four blazers and the collection of shirts in the walk-in closet.

While she dressed, Emily catalogued the alarming number of personal revelations she'd shared. Cheating girlfriend. Check. Now ex-girlfriend. Check. The fact that she was an ugly crier. Check. There was also the fact that Skye had hugged her. Despite being in the throes of a complete meltdown, she'd still managed to acknowledge how warm, comforting, and how very safe she'd felt in Skye's arms.

However, Skye needed an apology. Emily stared at her uncontrollable hair, ran her hands under the running water, then scrubbed her fingers through the strands. It made absolutely no difference. Actually, Skye didn't need an apology. Emily needed the apology. Emily needed to say sorry because it would make her feel better. That was a nice bit of self-awareness.

She wandered into the kitchen and poked the coffee machine awake, then her eyes fell on yesterday's note, one corner held in place by the fruit bowl. The trivia about penguin poo had made her giggle, along with the stick figure drawing of what Emily assumed was supposed to be a penguin. Each upstroke of Skye's handwriting leapt off the page. It was a joyful, vibrant script, like it was thrilled to exist. She tugged the note loose and added it to the others stuck on the fridge under the Melbourne tram magnet. The notes were very Skye, a statement she felt qualified to make despite knowing her tenant for all of a fortnight. She'd been so tender, Emily acknowledged as she poured her coffee and walked into the laundry, placing the cup on the sink top, and bending to find the toolbox. Skye's voice. It was warm, like caramel, but last night it had also been soft like every syllable had needed special consideration and care. Incredibly comforting. Emily yanked the power drill out from behind the laundry powder and lifted the step ladder from its wall hook. She imagined that Skye was probably a remarkably good advice-giver. Particularly when she charged in on her metaphorical white steed and plucked up distressed maidens.

"Seriously? Are you a teenager?"

Setting the ladder under the window, and the drill on the bed, Emily returned to the laundry to retrieve her coffee, strolling back into the bedroom and contemplating the naked window. Maybe her thoughts would lead to words and then to sentences and she'd work out what to say to Skye the next time she saw her. Meanwhile, there were holes in the wall.

***

Fixing the drapes, along with a breakfast of Vegemite on toast, helped immensely in sentence construction. Emily marched down the driveway to the studio. Of course, it was very likely that Skye was out, or busy, or asleep, or even had a date staying over. Emily froze. Oh. Yes, that would be a very distinct possibility, because of course, Skye would have a date. She was gorgeous and delightful.

"And you've only been single for a month, for Christ's sake," she hissed to herself. "Why are you even thinking about this stuff? This is not like you. Pull it together." Then the little voice inside reminded her that it had actually been about two, no…three months of true single-dom.

Shifting from side to side in indecision, clenching and unclenching her fists, she finally knocked quickly on the door before she chickened out. It felt completely unfamiliar to knock on the door of her studio. She resisted the automatic response to simply turn the handle, instead, she deliberately stepped back, twining her fingers together. It wasn't her studio anymore. It was Skye's home.

It took a moment or two, then the door opened. Skye, also dressed in jeans, and wearing a blue hoodie with a large bike printed on the front with the wheels placed directly and deliberately over her breasts, leaned against the doorframe. Emily dipped her eyes, then jerked them back to look at Skye's happy expression.

"Hi there, Emily Fitzsimmons." Skye's smile grew. Emily had no idea why Skye using her whole name made her want to blush, and swoon, and lean in to kiss those lips that curved up at the corners. No idea.

"Hi." Brilliant. Skye, her long hair framing her face, waited. "Right. So, I'm standing here rather awkwardly because I feel like I owe you an apology," Emily finished.

"You don't."

"Well, I did sob quite elaborately all over your hoodie and then shared…a lot." Emily grimaced.

"True." Skye grinned.

Emily stared at Skye's mouth, her eyes which were bright with laughter, then huffed.

"You're teasing me."

"I am," Skye said, then stepped back and opened the door further. "Come on in. I'm in the middle of doing some paperwork for *Quick Cargo*, and I need a break."

Emily stepped into the studio, looking at her—no, Skye's—space for the first time since move-in day. It was very neat. She had no idea why she thought it wouldn't be. Skye was a neat person.

"Did you get the curtain rail back up?" Skye said over her shoulder.

"Yes. All back together. Thanks." Emily dropped her hands into her pockets. "I like what you've done in here. No more box sculptures," she said, glancing about, then winked at Skye—a gesture which surprised them both. Skye laughed, a pink tinge dusting her cheeks. They held eye contact, and she felt the exact moment when delicious tension filled the air. Emily bit her lip, then darted her gaze about simply to reset her equilibrium. Her eyes fell on a stripped-down bike leaning against the far wall. A lot seemed to be missing. Gear sprocket, brake cables, actual brakes.

"Are you fixing that one?"

Skye chuckled. "Nope. That one's done. It's a fixie." Then her laptop on the kitchen counter beeped, and she quickly walked over to it, leaving Emily none the wiser about what a fixie was and why it didn't need fixing. Whatever it was that had grabbed Skye's attention must have been put back in order, because she looked up.

"Would you like a drink or something?"

"Oh. No. No, thanks," Emily said, and internally yelled at herself at how ridiculous she was being. Skye's proximity made her feel off balance. A nice off-balance. The slightly dizzy version. There was just so much of Skye.

So much gorgeous Skye.

Emily snorted and the woman occupying her thoughts cast her a quizzical look.

"You okay?"

"Absolutely. Yep. Sorry." Emily blinked. She was behaving like a teenager with a crush, which had the potential to be seriously embarrassing. She told her mouth to close itself, but apparently it had a mind of its own, because suddenly her mouth said, "Would you like to go with me to see Nic's act at *Utopia* tonight?"

Skye tilted her head. "Nic, as in best friend Nic?"

The invitation was out there now, so Emily ploughed on. "Yes. Nicola Nightshade. Nic headlines on Saturday nights, and I usually go at least once a month. It's a great show."

Skye hummed in interest, which Emily's mouth took as a hint to continue blathering. "Bec used to go with me. She liked the opportunity to socialise."

There was a silence, then Skye folded her arms and contemplated Emily. "Are you inviting me because I'm a good replacement?"

Emily quietly died inside. She reached out, patting the air apologetically.

"Oh! God, no. I wanted to invite you because I thought you'd like it and I'd enjoy your company. I don't know why I told you about Bec. I'm sorry. That's not—" Skye's hand suddenly held the one she was waving about and halted her stream of nonsense. She looked down at the hand, then back into kind brown eyes.

"It's okay, Emily. I'd love to go. I enjoy your company as well."

Skye's hand was warm, and it felt unfair to have to release it, but she did. Because necessary.

***

The invitation had been so unexpected that Skye had remained stationary for a moment after Emily left and bathed in the happy pleasure that bubbled in her heart. The invitation wasn't a date. It was more an apology, a peace offering maybe, or even a compensatory gift. Who knew? But there'd been a moment. A long, stretchy, thick with potential moment, and Skye knew without a doubt that Emily had noticed it as well. Her blush coupled with the distracted hand gestures, like rubbing her fingers into her hair to shuffle the short strands about, were complete giveaways. Skye laughed to herself. She'd have to tell Emily to avoid playing poker.

Despite the not-a-date status of the invitation, Skye desperately wanted to impress. Analysing the motivation behind that need was uncomfortable and she preferred to ignore its pleas from inside her brain. Instead, an hour before she was supposed to meet Emily at her front door, she rummaged about in her tiny closet, and pulled out her best going out clothing, slipped it on, and studied herself critically in the mirror. The long-sleeved fitted silvery-grey ribbed jersey with a mock turtleneck pretty much yelled at people to notice her shoulders and breasts. So that was a win. The soft leather pants that hugged her legs and slipped easily into her black over-the-knee boots were another win.

In two steps, she was in the bathroom to deal with make-up and hair. She left it loose but squirted mousse into her hands, rubbed her palms together, then shoved her fingers through the strands, so that the entire effect was one of slicked back casual. Skye wasn't overly fussy. It sort of looked like she'd just got out of the shower. A quick swipe about her eyes with black liner finished off the look. Skye nodded. Hopefully, it was an outfit that would produce a positive response.

However, when the front door of the main house opened at half past eight, the glow of the porch light illuminated a vision that took Skye's breath away. Her eyes started at the ground, taking in low black boots, black tights, a black suede mini skirt that Skye itched to slide her hand over, and a fire-engine red jersey top that cupped Emily's shoulders, and accented the lines of her collarbones and neck. Skye was convinced that there was an actual click when her tongue unglued itself from the roof of her mouth.

"Oh, wow," she said finally and looked into Emily's face as the remnants of a blush disappeared from her cheeks.

"You look…that's…those boots…you," Emily stuttered in return, then inhaled deeply. "You look terrific," she managed, then she grabbed her bottom lip with her teeth. It was always entertaining when two people on a not-date were reduced to incoherent, gobsmacked hormones.

Skye smoothed her hands down her thighs, her skin sliding on the leather. "What time is Nic expecting us?" she asked, and it seemed to take an enormous effort for Emily to focus on the question.

"Oh. In the next hour or so. We probably should get going."

***

The air inside Emily's car was charged with electricity during the drive to the multi-storey car park around the corner from *Utopia*. Small talk only added to the sparks. Details such as how Nicola Nightshade had been headlining for a year. Flash. Spark. That Emily was thirty-one years of age. Spark. Flash. Skye couldn't stop glancing to the side to admire the movement of Emily's thigh muscle, encased in those ridiculously sexy tights, every time she pushed in the clutch to change gear. They both seemed acutely aware of each other, and Skye was actually grateful for the deep breath she took as Emily aimed her keys at the car from over her shoulder as they made their way out of the parking structure and strolled along the footpath. Close proximity to Emily was producing butterflies and frissons of excitement and glitter showers throughout her body. A fabulous mardi gras.

The line to get into the club was long, however, Emily simply marched up to the buff bouncer guarding the neon-lit door, flashed a smile, turned her body to include Skye in the unspoken request, and they were waved inside via a raised eyebrow and a head tilt.

Shoulder-shimmying their way through the crowd, Emily paused just before the bar, and Skye found her breasts pressed to Emily's back.

"Sorry," she said, as Emily turned, and suddenly not a single person in the packed club mattered at all. Skye stared into Emily's dark eyes, basking in the intensity of her moment.

Without breaking eye contact, Emily asked, "Do you want something to drink?" At least Skye assumed that was what she said, because the music and the surging buzz of the crowd drowned out her words, even when spoken from thirty centimetres away. She leaned in and tilted her head, so her ear was directed at Emily. Then, as her breath caught in her chest, Skye watched as Emily's hand grasped her shoulder and her lips parted and she leaned into Skye's space.

"Do you want a drink?" The words brushed her cheek and Skye decided that *Utopia's* heating system was malfunctioning because her skin was on fire. She eased back.

"Thanks. Yep. Yep, yep." She sounded like a demented muppet.

Emily smiled, mouthed, "Soft drink?" smiled again at Skye's nod, then turned towards the bar. Skye glared at herself. Not suave. At all. The only possible saving grace was a wish for Emily to be in a similar state. Otherwise, she was broadcasting her attraction in neon flashing lights.

Drinks in hand, they made their way to one of the many bar tables that created a dotted line along the edge of the dance floor. A couple of abandoned drinks had already claimed real estate on top of the table, but there was enough space for theirs.

Stage lights suddenly dipped and swooped, and a deep amplified voice boomed through the club.

"Now, for your aural pleasure…" there was a pause and the crowd erupted. "I said aural, all you naughty people. Please welcome… Nicola Nightshade!"

Lights flashed, as the main room was engulfed in darkness, and a vision in a silver lamé gown with shoulder pads honed to eye-gouging points sashayed out from behind the curtains towards the appreciative crowd. The strands of her blonde wig had been fluffed and rolled around maybe seven plastic handsets from landline telephones, and make-up that had clearly been designed and applied by a true artist shimmered in the glare.

Nicola Nightshade was in the house.

She immediately launched in Lady Gaga's 'Telephone' and when the first eight bars were done and the beat kicked in, everyone not holding a drink, and some that were, undulated and writhed towards the dance floor.

The base thrummed in Skye's chest and, without even a thought, she grabbed Emily's hand to catch her attention.

"This is amazing. She's fantastic," she yelled over the music, and Emily grinned. Then, after a quick breath, Emily looked down at their joined hands, then back into Skye's face. She leaned in.

"Do you want to stay here or go dance?"

The lights cast occasional shadows across Emily's face, and her impossibly dark, impossibly sexy eyes captured the pulsing flashes. Her gaze was focused and the crowd disappeared. Again. Skye let her eyes roam, lingering on the red top that hugged Emily's body. Emily seemed to find Skye just as tempting because every inhalation brought her closer.

Just as Skye was about to choose the dance option, a hand clasped Emily's upper arm, and the moment was lost. They broke apart, both their hands and the connection, and Skye turned towards two women, one a tall dark-haired butch, the other a stunning blonde, who was staring intently at Emily.

"Em! Hi! I thought that was you!" The blonde gushed, and something about her set Skye's alarm bells ringing. She cast a glance at Emily, and even in the darkness of the room, she could see that her face had closed down, her mouth in a straight line. The blonde continued, clutching at the other woman's arm. "You remember Theresa?"

Emily's face blanched so much that it could have been illuminated by the black UV lights currently strobing to the final bars of 'Telephone'.

"Sure," she said, although the word was drowned out.

The blonde, in a **spectacular** display of impropriety, then leaned so that her chest advertised its assets and raised an eyebrow at Skye.

"Hi there." The sensuality slipped easily through the doof-doof of the bass. "I haven't met you before, and I thought I knew all of Em's friends. You're new, and that's surprising. I'm Bec, by the way."

Which explained Emily's reaction. Skye tamped down the instant desire to stretch herself to her full height—five-feet-ten, thanks very much—widen her shoulders and tighten her jaw. She knew she could, and it would certainly be impressive, what with the outfit she was wearing, her hair all slicked back. Quite imposing. But she couldn't. There was a fine line between wanting to step in and rescue Emily, or stand by in support. That was the difference in Skye's life now, and so she decided on the second option.

She was glad she did, because Emily seemed to shake off her shock, and moved closer to Skye's shoulder.

"This is Skye," she said loudly over the ra-ra-ah-ah-ah that Nicola was currently belting out to the ecstatic crowd. The elaborate rendition of 'Bad Romance' felt like the soundtrack for the current situation. Skye stuck out her hand, because good manners never hurt anyone, despite wanting to wring the woman's neck. She studied Bec. She was picture perfect. One of those people who ensured that not a speck of dirt, nor a single bit of lint, or even a tiny crease existed on their clothes. It was an interesting quirk of the real estate profession. It seemed only the beautiful, well-tailored sort could be realtors, as if their entire presence said, "If you like what you see here, wait until you see the house!"

"Well, hello Skye," Bec purred, leaning forward, breasts front and centre, and grasped Skye's hand. She slid her fingers further up Skye's wrist in a flirtatious move that was incredibly obvious and made Skye intensely uncomfortable. She quickly pulled away, and Bec smirked.

"This is Theresa. Emily, you remember Theresa, right?" Breathtakingly graceless. The repeated question to Emily was proper mean girl behaviour, and Skye couldn't help it. She squared her shoulders ever so slightly and ex-rugby player, bike courier, rather tall and athletic Skye Reynolds appeared. Bec raked her eyes up and down the tight top and fitted pants, then looked away as Theresa's facial expression drifted from unadulterated awkwardness to apologetic embarrassment, finally settling on a sort of polite, polished smile.

From the stage, Nicola insisted that everyone work it; move that bitch like crazy.

Then, Emily exhaled loudly, grasped Skye's hand—more firmly than she possibly realised—and smiled brightly at Theresa. "Yes, I do. You and Bec share a penchant for purple, right?" Skye had no idea what Emily was talking about, but clearly Emily's comment hit home, because Theresa blinked, and Bec's smug smile dissolved as she narrowed her eyes.

"Theresa, let's get that drink you promised me," Bec uttered, then spoke to Skye. "If you're the new girlfriend, Skye, you'll need to buy a ten-year planner from *OfficeMax* so you'll know what's going on and what's ahead in your relationship." She turned Theresa towards the bar and then tossed the words, "Just a tip," over her shoulder.

Emily's hand was still wrapped around Skye's. They stood, frozen, and stared at Nicola as she strutted up and down the stage, the silver in her dress twinkling with every sway of her hips, cajoling every patron to join in her celebration of being on the right track because she was born this way.

"Are you okay?" Skye murmured the words right next to Emily's ear.

Emily turned quickly, her face close.

"Do you mind if we go? I'm so sorry." Her eyes were huge, and the skin on her face was stretched with tension.

Skye's hand, the one not caught as an anchor, lifted to flutter near Emily's neck, her ear, the fingertips brushing Emily's cheek. Emily's eyes closed briefly at the touch.

"Of course. No need to be sorry," Skye said and squeezed her hand. "Come on."

Nicola's mellifluous voice trailed after them as they exited *Utopia* and walked silently back to the car. It was only when she'd put the car into gear and had turned onto the main street that Emily spoke.

"I'm sorry you had to witness that," she said softly, staring out of the windscreen.

"Bec was unbelievably rude and please do not apologise for her," Skye said emphatically. Emily tossed a glance her way, chased by a smile.

"Thank you. And thanks for being my knight in armour."

"I...didn't think I was," Skye said.

Emily chuckled quietly. "You puffed up. It was kind of nice. Lovely, actually"

Skye blushed. "Oh. I thought I was being subtle."

"Not really, but it gave me a boost because I got my own little dig in, which was probably the wrong thing to do, but whatever." She sighed. "Bec was right about one thing, though. You are new and you are my friend, and I like how that feels." Another glance.

Skye grinned. "So do I."

The remainder of the drive home was contemplative.

At her front door, Emily smiled, standing inside Skye's space, which was completely unnecessary since there was a veritable ocean of concrete on the porch. Skye enjoyed the tingles on her skin.

"We live on the same property. You don't have to walk me home, you know," Emily said softly.

"Yeah, I do." Skye peered at Emily's washed-out features. "Are you going to be okay?"

With a deep sigh, Emily nodded. "Yes. It's a shame our evening was cut short. Normally I catch up with Nic after the show, but I'll text him. He'll be fine with that. I think I'll just go to bed."

Skye studied her. "I'm sure your friends would have said this already, but Bec cheating on you, then saying stuff like that tonight? That's so callous, and all of it, you know, the stuff before and tonight should have never happened to you." She swallowed and decided the next observation was important to say aloud. "And also—you look really amazing." She quirked a smile. "I thought I should say that, too."

Emily bit her lip, darted her eyes past Skye into the darkness, then brought them back. "Thank you. Would you like to go to *Utopia* again? Maybe next month?"

"Absolutely!" Skye nodded emphatically.

"Would you wear that outfit again?" The faint blush on Emily's cheeks was adorable.

"Also absolutely," Skye said, then, after a beat, drew closer and gently brushed a kiss against Emily's cheek. A friendly kiss. Oh, it really wasn't. The way Emily's eyes darkened said that it was so much more.

"Sleep well," Skye whispered.

Then she strode down the driveway, pausing once to look back when she got to the slight bend near the back of the house. Emily hadn't gone inside. She was standing in the same place, with her hand pressed to her cheek, as if to ensure the kiss didn't fly away. She stared at Skye.

A beat or two passed, then Skye lifted her hand in a gesture of good night or thanks. She'd let Emily decide. Then disappeared around the corner.

Chapter Ten

It would have been marvellous if her brain had developed highly specific amnesia about Saturday night but of course it hadn't. It played out the entire event in technicolour on a never-ending loop. Emily grunted softly in frustration at her desk on Monday. Bec's behaviour on Saturday night had stung. It was callous. Was she jealous of Emily? Was she jealous of Skye being with Emily? Was she trying to make Emily jealous by thrusting Theresa in her face? By Sunday, Emily had felt somewhat sorry for Theresa, who'd been used as a pawn in a petty power play, except then she'd remembered the cheating bit and her pity evaporated. But Emily wished she'd had more vertebrae in her confidence spine on Saturday night. She'd come across as a bit of a doormat and that was frustrating.

Skye had texted on Sunday morning with a breezy hello, a GIF of a meerkat popping its head up out of its burrow, and the question, "How are you today?" It was incredibly sweet and after the required "I'm fine, thanks", they'd slipped into a fun exchange that covered a plethora of topics ranging from bees—

"They sting each other."

"Really? Why?"

"The nightclub bouncer bees at the entrance." Emily had giggled at that text.

—To the fact that koalas have fingerprints. Skye hadn't known that fact and the completely irrational, warm feeling from sharing that piece of trivia stayed with Emily long after their text chat finished.

Then, she'd freaked herself out with all the warmth and fuzziness and hidden away for the majority of Sunday, avoiding Skye and attempting to focus her thoughts on her water lilies. She'd hacked at stems and leaves and eventually her inattention meant that the slim blade knocked the skin on her thumb and blood pooled from the cut.

"Ow! Oh, ow!"

Clutching her thumb with the other hand, she'd stomped into the kitchen, shoved it under running water, then wrapped it in a Bandaid, and marched out of the house, grabbing a thick jacket on the way. The enormous public gardens were located at the end of the street, and Emily pounded around the walking track for a good hour and a half, breathing, muttering, and every now and then gesticulating at the trees as she remembered another detail.

Or thought of another question. Like, what was she doing inviting Skye to *Utopia*?

"Well, enjoying myself, number one," she muttered to the grand oak tree standing proudly at the corner of the park. Skye's outfit had caused an electrical malfunction in her brain. Good God. Leather pants. The hair. All that torso being all strong and…strong…and the kiss…and…

"See? Brain spasm." She flung her arms out and increased her speed. The all-too-quick visceral desire that she had about Skye scared her senseless. She could feel the anxious little voice tapping on her shoulder, asking if she intended to make a long term plan for Skye because it was important to make plans. Plans kept her safe. Her brain was going to spontaneously combust from the amount of energy she expended on this stupid aspect of herself. Bec had certainly twisted that particular knife with her parting comment to Skye.

Emily scowled. She'd never admitted to Bec or anyone, except Kristen, why she had such a need to plan major events in her life. Yes, her father had been Mr. Spontaneous, but there was more to it.

It was probably time to call Kristen again.

Now, here she was on a Monday at work, not doing any work. Her phone buzzed on the desktop, her mum's profile picture filling the screen. Deciding to put her on speakerphone, Emily stabbed at the button.

"Hi, Mum."

"Emily, sweetie. How are you?"

So many possible answers to that question, and all of them entirely inappropriate. Emily knew that if she shared, she'd receive vague, airy-fairy advice on how to solve her problems, and all that did was frustrate her beyond measure. Her mum had gone the complete polar opposite in her own coping strategies for Gareth Fitzsimmons' spontaneity. Jane Fitzsimmons became an advocate for the 'Let things happen-everything will work out-let go-life will sort itself out' club, and it drove Emily nuts. Yet, for Jane Fitzsimmons it worked, and Emily was not one to judge—to people's faces, at least—how someone should wrestle their demons.

"I'm fine thanks, Mum. How are you?"

"I am living in the light, sweetheart. Bees have started to visit my dwarf cherry, and it gives me such a glow."

A snort came from the doorway, and Emily glanced up to see Rach clutching at her mouth, holding her lips together.

"Not a euphemism," Emily mouthed at her colleague, who raised both hands in surrender, then pointed at Emily, mouthed, "Five minutes?", received a nod, then backed out of the office.

"That's great, Mum."

"I know your next question is why I'm calling. If you want to pop in on Sunday week, I should be about. Maybe at the farmer's market for a while, but home sometime after that. I don't know." Her mother lived with her sister, Leanne—Emily's aunt—in one of the new developments in the northern outskirts of the city. It was a decent hour's drive to get there, and a visit was usually scheduled for a Sunday. Well, Emily scheduled it.

"I can come up. I'll bring you another arrangement if you'd like. I guess the one I gave you last time is on its final legs," Emily suggested, doodling on her notepad. A sketch formed under her pen, the lines developing into a design of a new Ikebana.

"Oh! That would be lovely. You must be creating such a lot in that delightful studio of yours. I'm so glad you built it."

"Well, I'm not in it anymore. My Ikebana is in the second bedroom." A deep breath encouraged the next sentence. "I took in a tenant and she's living in the studio now."

There was silence, then…"Really? That's," there was another beat of silence. "That's unlike you, sweetheart." Her mother's voice was tentative.

"Mm. I know. I have no idea what got into me, but there it is. Just as well Skye's a really nice person and a great tenant."

"That's fab, love! I'm so pleased. Perhaps you should bring her when you visit," her mum suggested, and Emily spluttered.

"She's my tenant, Mum. I can't invite her to your place. That's…" she faded off as the hypocrisy hit. Skye had been invited into her house when she'd banged on the door. She'd been invited to *Utopia*. And invited into Emily's personal space. So many invitations. Emily shook her head. "That's not going to happen."

"Well, you can bring Bec if she's not too busy doing something else and can spare some of her time."

Her mother was not a huge fan of Rebecca Deans. Emily figured that if she gave too many details, her mum would be using Bec's photo as a dartboard.

"Bec and I broke up," Emily said, in the lightest, no-worries-everything-is-fine voice she had.

"Oh. I'm sorry, hon. That's a shame." It was the same tone she might use if Emily's favourite coffee mug had been chipped. Not a fan of Bec at all. Emily wasn't sure if she should admonish her mum or wrap her up in an enormous virtual hug. Probably both.

"Look, Mum. I need to get going. Rach wants to chat."

"Of course, sweetie. I'll see you when I do. No need to call. Just turn up." A statement which sent shudders through Emily, and her response was the same as always.

"Thanks, Mum. I'll text you when I leave. Say hi to Aunty Leanne for me."

They rang off, and Emily let out a breath.

"Dwarf cherry?" Rach said from the doorway.

"I can't even." Emily waved her in. "What's up?"

Rach pulled the chair closer to her side of the desk, then changed her mind. "Actually, come on out to the monitor. I want to show you something." She tipped her head towards the door, so Emily stood and followed her out to the large monitor that Rach used for her CAD drawings. It had internet access so on the handheld keyboard Rach tapped a few buttons and replaced the most recent design with the *Heritage Council* website.

She leaned her hip against the desk, turning square to Emily, then placed the keyboard on the surface and pointed to the screen.

"45 Anders Road," she stated. "It's going to be demolished because of the fire last month, and the fact that it's derelict, etcetera, right?"

"Right." Emily wrinkled her brow.

"Well, here's my problem. Our problem, I guess. Some of the other houses on that street have a heritage overlay." Emily raised an eyebrow. That was news. Heritage overlays were used to protect sites that had heritage value. It meant that there were very strict rules set out by the government when it came to renovating a listed home. Let alone demolishing one and rebuilding a modern mansion on the site, like the one the owners had commissioned from *Fitzsimmons*.

"Oh?"

"Uh-huh." She tipped her head at the screen. "All the paperwork from the owners of number 45 looked fine. Nothing mentioned about heritage overlays. All good to go and I've done preliminary designs of the plan." She gave a quick staccato run of her fingernails on the desktop. "But I wasn't sure. Something felt off like when things are too slick, you know?"

Emily raised her eyebrows. "Sort of, but anyway. And?" She suddenly dreaded where this conversation was going and squeezed the pen that was still in her hand.

"Well, I checked with the *Heritage Council* and 45 Anders Road has a big fat heritage overlay on it."

Emily's mouth fell open. "No!"

Rach pressed her thumbs into the start of her eyebrows, then moved the mouse on the screen to click through to the listing on the website. "Yep. See?"

"But…"

"I only found out this morning, and I wanted to do some investigation before I came to you," Rach said, and Emily tipped her head in gratitude. "So I rang the owner, and they professed not to know anything, which is annoying, and I'm leaving it with them because they're supposed to deal with it, but our contract is on hold immediately and indefinitely."

"Of course it is. Bloody hell!" Emily tossed her hands and looked at the ceiling.

"I know. It means that we'll have to rebuild the house in its original form, and not go ahead with the design we're contracted for unless the owners can get the overlay lifted. I doubt they will. There are other houses in the street with overlays, and once a couple has one, they usually all have one."

"Christ! This is a pain because you've done work on it already."

Rach shrugged. "Yeah. I can't do any more on it because the owners will have to decide what they want now. The *Heritage Council* will want the house rebuilt, but the owners are adamant that they want the new design. It's up to them to fight."

"Yes. But meanwhile, we have a lot riding on that contract. We'll get nothing if it goes to court or something ridiculous like that." Emily pursed her lips, then she pointed at Rach. "Thanks for looking into this. It would suck to be hauled over the coals with the *Heritage Council* particularly if it wasn't our fault."

"Exactly," Rach agreed, and they shared a look.

"That'd be some serious reputation damage, boss," Jas added from across the room. Emily rolled the pen in her fingers, then straightened her shoulders, and delivered a nod at both of them.

"Not going to happen. I've worked hard, along with everyone here, to make this place ethical and successful and I'm not deviating from that road any time soon. There's a plan in place for this business." She jerked her thumb at her office. "I'll make some phone calls."

"Hang on. Before you go." Rach clicked through a couple of tabs to bring up the *Browning Federal* website. The property developer was the latest big name buying up contiguous lots of land when the government opened its books or needed an injection of cash. Social housing buildings were usually the only structures on the land that was for sale, and the government ensured that tenants were relocated to newer, cleaner units prior to demolition. Then new *Browning Federal* townhouses would appear within eight to nine months. Winning a *Browning Federal* contract would be an excellent step along the road she had mapped out in her head. And a huge cash injection into the *Fitzsimmons* accounts.

"*Browning Federal*?" Emily asked.

Rach finger-gunned at the screen. "Yup. Check out the industry release that came out this morning." Emily peered at the screen, digesting the key words, then she jerked her head back and widened her eyes at Rach, who nodded. "Yup," she repeated.

"You are like the Where's Wally champion for architectural contracts." Emily grabbed Rach's arm. "We're doing it. I know we're little, but we're doing it. You and Dimitri will work on the design, and we'll collaborate when we need to." She poked herself in the chest. "I," she paused dramatically, "am going to put together a kick-arse pitch. Where's the development location?" Emily squinted at the screen and tilted her head. The street sounded familiar. "Oh. That's near where Lorraine Hudson used to live. I'll have to do a site visit if we win the contract, so I'll do a drive-by of Lorraine's old place so I can let her know how well it's being looked after. Right. Onto kick-arse pitches." They shared a grin, and Emily spun on her heel to walk back to her office.

Once seated, she wriggled her finger on the computer's touchpad, but before she could even get started, Jas's voice caught her attention.

"What happened to your thumb?"

Emily looked up. Jas was standing in the doorway, her arms folded.

"Ikebana accident. I wasn't concentrating." Emily shrugged, and Jas mimicked the action, then wandered over to the chair tucked into the corner. She pulled it out and sat heavily, like she was preparing for a long chat. Emily checked the time. Two o'clock. Yes, okay. Time for afternoon tea. Pitches could wait for a moment.

"Were you at *Utopia* on Saturday night?" Jas crossed her legs, her foot bouncing.

Emily leaned her elbow on her desk. "Yes."

"I didn't see you. I managed to grab a great spot near the front. Patrick," she raised an eyebrow, "my date, was really lovely even though he wasn't sure about the club at first. He didn't look uncomfortable as such, more like he'd unwittingly been dropped into the midst of an ethnographic study."

Emily laughed. "Oh, dear. Well, we stayed near the side. It was a great show and—"

"Hold it there!" Jas's hand flew up. "I heard a 'we', so information is missing from this conversation and it cannot continue until it is found."

"Really, Jas?"

"Yes."

The staring competition began.

Emily caved. "Fine. I invited Skye. Happy?"

"Not in the slightest." Jas bared her teeth in delight. "Keep talking."

Emily sighed. "The whole story?"

Jas made a gesture that clearly meant, "Of course."

"Um. Well, I thought Skye saw me in just a towel on Friday night as I drew my curtains, but I wasn't sure, and I thought maybe her possibly seeing me in said towel was inappropriate, so I yanked a little too hard on the curtains to pull them together and the entire structure came off the wall."

She stared at Jas's face, which was turning red from the effort to stop herself from laughing.

"No. It's not funny."

Jas nodded quickly. "But it is," she gasped, then mashed her lips together. Her hand rolled over to indicate that Emily needed to continue.

"Then Skye came to the front door to check on me because she actually did see me in a towel and drapery and then I sobbed all over her as I fell apart because apparently, I haven't got over Bec being awful and leaving"

Jas instantly sobered. "Oh, hon."

Emily shook her head. "So, I felt dreadful about all of that and my brain decided that asking Skye out was a suitable gift of…something. God knows."

The expression on Jas's face struggled to stay locked on sympathy, because her eyes still sparkled with mirth. "That's…oh my God."

"Yes," Emily agreed.

Jas leaned forward and raised an eyebrow. "Was she hot?"

"Who?"

"Really?"

Emily glared. "I am not answering that."

"So she was," Jas mused, nodding with authority.

Emily glared again. Something held her back from revealing the distressing moment with Bec that led to the early exit. Probably because that was still raw. She also held back the cheek kiss because Jas would be thrilled with that little snippet. No. That kiss was Emily's and she tucked it away.

But she did add one more detail.

"Leather pants," Emily whispered. Jas gaped, then grinned.

"Oh, yes!" She formed a fist and waved it airily in celebration.

Rach called from the main space. "Jas! Delivery!"

Jas sprang up and hustled through the door, and because she was curious—more like desperate to know—Emily followed her. Skye stood at Jas's front desk, her arms holding an enormous bouquet. Vivid irises, the palest of lemon roses, mixed with crisp white miniature gerberas filled the stiff brown paper that had been shaped into a cone.

"Skye! We were just talking about you," Jas enthused and cast a wicked glance at Emily, whose feet took over her brain, and covered the space to the desk.

"Were you? All good things, I hope," Skye said easily, a smile flickering on her lips. Her eyes locked fast to Emily's, whose mouth had curled in response.

Jas looked from one to the other, her grin now a permanent fixture.

"Absolutely. I hear you caught Nicola Nightshade's show on Saturday," Jas stated lightly, then absorbed the piercing look from Emily, and ploughed on. "Are those for me? I hope so. Gorgeous."

Skye seemed to take a moment to register the question, then turned to Jas. "Oh! Yes. Patrick?"

"Oh, yay! I'm glad he didn't freak out about *Utopia*. He's a potential repeat." She took the flowers from Skye's embrace and admired their colours. "Hey, Rach. Check these out," she said loudly, and very deliberately, then wandered over to the large monitor. Emily didn't need to turn her head to confirm that the pair of them would be intently watching the interaction at the front desk.

Emily caught Skye's gaze again. "Hi, by the way. Busy day?" she murmured into the warm brown eyes.

"Hi. Yeah. Pretty busy," Skye replied, swapping the electronic signature machine from one hand to the other.

Emily dropped her hands into her pants pockets. They nodded in unison, soft smiles on their lips.

Emily figured it was the work environment that was affecting their ability to function as competent communicators. But even though they'd barely said a word, their eyes had roamed across faces, torsos and back again.

Finally, Skye wrenched her gaze away. "Jas, could you sign for this, please?"

There was a sigh of resignation, which Emily knew was aimed at her, and Jas appeared, deposited the bouquet on her table, then scribbled a signature on the little screen.

Skye smiled, and Emily stared at her expressive wide mouth.

"Cheers. Best get going then," Skye said, looking squarely at Emily, who blinked. Something to say. Quick.

"Okay," she said. Excellent. Then, "Have a great day." Better. Then, "See you at home," which carried a hint of desperation. But then, "You look good in hi-vis." Oh dear God.

Skye blinked, and Jas coughed violently, then gasped, "Water," and scurried away to the mini-fridge.

"Thanks," Skye said, then winked, her expression revealing how much she'd enjoyed their brief interaction. "Okay, so properly going now. See you later." She pivoted, and Emily admired the chiselled lines in her calves flexing and undulating under her skin as she walked out the door.

"You look good in hi-vis?" Rach and Jas said in unison. Emily's face warmed and she threw a look at her colleagues.

"Well, she does and that is a statement that—," she snapped her mouth shut, and made her way to her office. "I am not having this conversation," she added at the door.

"That's okay. We'll carry on without you." Rach laughed.

Chapter Eleven

Zebra lines of shadows from the buildings stretched across the road on Wednesday, then a blast of air, a whoomp of pressure, from the truck barrelling past much too quickly, and way too close, jerked the bike sideways and Skye tensed her arms to keep it upright. She growled. The recent increase in large vehicle traffic in the city had been noticeable with all the new construction. The government seemed to be selling off all their assets—both residential and commercial—to developers, relocating their residents and workers to locations in the outskirts of the city which were more modern, but cheaper, and far from infrastructure, like public transport. It was illogical, but that seemed to be the philosophy of any department in all governments in pretty much every single country around the world. The thought made Skye pause, as an image of Rhiannon and Yvette came to mind. Their building was older, and the social services department hadn't initiated any major renovations in a while. Would they be another casualty to the whims of a button-pusher sitting in a departmental office, selling off their block of units to the next cashed-up property developer looking to toss up another set of townhouses for the well-off?

She figured an across-town ride after work that afternoon wouldn't hurt, just to say hi to her friendly assassin.

So, it was around five o'clock, with the grey of dusk creeping in, when Skye rolled to a stop outside Rhiannon's place, and kicked the stand down on her road bike, making sure that it was towards the edge of the footpath. Pedestrians tended to mutter and thin their lips when rogue bikes interrupted their introspective progression along the concrete.

Rhiannon spotted Skye immediately.

"You're back!" she yelled, running up to the low fence, and grinning up into Skye's face. Skye stuck out a fist for the nine-year-old to bump.

"Just for a visit. Thought I'd check in on your target practice. See if your skills have improved," she smirked, and Rhiannon narrowed her eyes.

"I'm awesome. That target is so cool. Thanks for getting me that." She brandished the lurid orange and blue plastic blaster. "And this."

Skye grinned. "You've already thanked me, and you're welcome." She looked up at the block of flats, then a small sign attached to a post just inside the fence caught her eye. She shuffled sideways to squint at the tiny writing, much too tiny for a sign explaining the events about to befall the occupants of the dwellings in front of her.

"Oh no," she whispered. The sign, written in ridiculous legalese, detailed the sale of the property, and the eviction and relocation of the tenants in sixty days after which demolition was due to occur. She jerked her head to stare into Rhiannon's face, the pinched expression revealing just how much the sale was going to affect them.

"Mum says our units got sold last week, but she says that social services usually find people like us a newer place to live, so that's good, right?" Her expression transformed into one of hope.

"Rhi," Skye began. Jesus. That meant they had seven weeks left. She blinked, then continued. "I'm sorry. I don't know how it works."

"Well, Mrs. Pandopolous said she's fine 'cause she's gonna live in an old person's place, and she said that they'll feed her mush but that's okay 'cause she gets looked after, and doesn't have to hurt her hands anymore when she turns off the taps." Rhiannon nodded emphatically, like kids do when they've been told by a trusted adult that everything is going to be okay.

Skye sat on the low fence, and Rhiannon dropped onto the bricks beside her. "Has your mum said anything else?" Skye asked quietly.

There was a beat of silence. "No. She's always working, and then she's tired. She did get upset the other night, although it was kind of happy and sad, you know?" Rhiannon tipped her head up and Skye nodded. "Yeah, 'cause Miles is gonna move to a place that he can get his wheelchair into, but Mum said he had to yell at the government on the phone a lot to get that new flat. We heard him sometimes. And then some guy came out to interview him. Mum was mad because the people on the phone made Miles upset because they didn't believe him until the guy came out." She shook her head and kicked the heels of her scuffed sneakers against the wall. "Anyway, Miles can't move for a while. Maybe next month, I think."

Skye breathed slowly. That was cutting it fine. She hated the way society tossed people aside. It was so wrong.

"Oh, there you are," a soft voice came from behind them, and Skye shifted to find Yvette walking down the path from the front door of their flat. She smiled at Skye.

"How are you, Skye? Is the new place working out?" Yvette looked even more exhausted than normal, the lines in her face like permanent creases.

"Yeah, it is. Are you off work today?"

A quick head-tilt and shrug preceded the explanation. "I had to cancel a shift because social services were doing a tenancy inspection and we have to be here when they come." She sighed, resigned to the whims and inflexibility of the government department.

Skye frowned. "That's," she glanced at Rhiannon, "tough." Then she pointed to the sign. "That's also tough."

Yvette laughed mirthlessly. "Yep. Life of a government housing tenant, unfortunately. You never know when the carpet's going to be yanked out from under, yeah?" The question was clearly rhetorical.

"Have they sorted you out?" Skye held her breath.

"Not exactly. They reckon there's a place over in Kingston, but I just can't take it."

Skye's stomach clenched. She knew why and Yvette supplied the explanation.

"It's way over the other side of Melbourne. I'd have to give up my job at both of the hospitals because I'd be paying so much in bus fares, and then there's the massive increase in travel time which means I'd never get to my shifts." A resigned shrug. "But with unemployment like it is at the moment, I'm not confident of getting another job at all." She dropped a hand onto Rhiannon's shoulder.

"And babysitting or childcare for kiddo here is impossible to organise at the drop of a hat. I've been lucky with Lydia and Miles."

"I don't know what to say," Skye said sadly, and Yvette blew out a breath.

"It'll work out. I'll keep knocking on the department's door and being a bit of a squeaky wheel." They shared a smile at the mixed idioms. "I'm an optimist, Skye. You have to be sometimes. Just gotta have faith."

Rhiannon jumped off the fence, having obviously decided that she'd had enough of listening to adults being philosophical and depressing, and turned to Skye.

"Do you want to have a go?" she asked, thrusting the gun at Skye's torso.

"Sure. I've got a bit of time." She grinned at Yvette, who smiled, gave a wave to accompany her "Thanks, Skye," and "Don't be out here too long, honey," then she wandered back up the path.

Skye spent another half an hour learning the intricate manoeuvres required to fire magnetic foam darts at a target, much to Rhiannon's delight. It was pathetic that a high score on a plastic target felt more of a success than any she could hope to have in trying to solve Yvette's problem. The situation seemed insurmountable. And wrong.

Finally she was on her way home, heart heavy, the chrome on her bike flashing in the street lights as she cycled through each illuminated lily-pad cast onto the bitumen.

***

On Saturday morning, Skye heard the muttering over the crunch of the gravel under her feet. Certain words were emphasised and as she rounded the corner of the house to take in the front yard, she saw that the emphasised words were accompanied by a weed being simultaneously ripped from the ground.

Emily, in worn cargo pants, sneakers, a paint-splattered sweater, and an adorable red beanie with a pom-pom perched on top, which bobbled with every violent weed removal, looked up when she caught sight of Skye. She sat back on her heels.

"Hi."

"Hey there, angry weed-killing lady." Skye pointed to the casualty pile next to Emily's feet. "Working out some issues?"

Emily laughed. "This is my frustration outlet. I tend to mutter when I'm annoyed about things, according to Nic, so I thought I'd come out and vent at the dandelions and bindis." She grinned at Skye. "They're good listeners until they're yanked from the soil to slowly expire, right here, on the mountain of doom."

Skye blinked. "Mountain…of…doom. Wow. You take your venting seriously." They held a gaze, then broke into simultaneous laughter. "Can I ask what you're frustrated about without ending up as a dead weed?"

"Sure. Pull up a patch of lawn." Emily patted the grass beside her, and Skye lowered herself to sit on her heel, while the other leg, knee pointing up, supported her folded arms and chin. Emily raked her eyes up and down Skye's jeans, her T-shirt peeking out from under another rugby top, and the dark blue sneakers. Skye really liked the low hum that was the result of that appraisal. She doubted that Emily realised the sound had been audible.

"So, shoot. I'm all ears," Skye said.

"Well," Emily sighed. "The *Cascade* townhouses?" She raised her eyebrows at Skye, who nodded. "Right. The domino pieces aren't falling down as they should be. It's supposed to go developer, then architect, then developer, then construction, then developer, and leave the architect the hell alone." She grit her teeth. "But!" Emily plucked up her small garden fork and shoved it under the roots of another weed. "The developer keeps changing the plans *verbally*!" She twisted the handle. "And that means the site manager needs to keep checking in with us to make sure the plans still make sense." She flicked the tool and tossed the weed onto her mountain of doom. "Which means that the very clear sequence I had planned for *Cascades* isn't being followed at all. And that," she stabbed the fork into the ground and stared at Skye, "is a situation I find challenging. I like things to follow one behind the other." Emily decided that she was someone who installed strip lighting in a previous life.

Skye rolled her head so her cheek sat on her forearms. "Right. Okay. What else? Because that's not enough to create the," she flicked her chin at the weeds, "mountain of doom there." Emily's cheeks had flushed with her exertions, from both the weeding and the retelling. Her eyes sparkled with energy, with very faint gold highlights shining in that incredible dark brown. Skye held her breath for a moment, then released it quietly. God, Emily was so pretty.

"You're right. I have a client who is fighting with the *Heritage Council* about a heritage overlay that they didn't know was on their land but now everything is stopped because they need to sort that out which means we've been put on pause as well." Emily stared towards the front fence. "Which means who knows if we're building new or rebuilding old, and all this weeding is doing wonders for my lawn, but not sorting out my head at all." She let out an enormous sigh, and Skye rolled her lips together to hold the goofy grin at bay. The adorable factor had kicked up a notch, and grinning goofily, like a besotted idiot, was not a particularly great idea when Emily was in venting mode.

"When I get frustrated, I climb a tree. Want to go climb one of my favourites?" Skye suggested.

Emily tilted her head and looked quizzically at Skye. There was a beat, and their breathing seemed to synchronise. Then she nodded contemplatively. "Okay. Yes. I'll climb a tree with you." A slow smile pulled her lips.

A whisper of excitement, like someone had puffed thrill into her lungs, galvanised Skye, and she leapt up, and held out her hand, pulling Emily to her feet. While the conversations and the back and forth of dialogue were fabulous, the moments, like right now with Emily standing so close, where they didn't speak but said so much with their eyes were becoming Skye's favourite things ever. Emily seemed to register their proximity, and stepped back slightly, releasing Skye's hand.

"I should change," she said in consternation, looking down at the paint splatters.

"No, you're fine. Perfect for tree climbing. Besides, the tree I have in mind is just at the park down the end of your street." Skye frowned in mock concern. "Unless you have a terribly important role as the chairperson of the Neighbourhood Reputation and Upkeeping of Standards Committee and they'll vote you out for daring to wear renovation clothing."

Emily giggled delightedly, and lightly smacked Skye's flat stomach. "As of today, I officially resign my position and will walk proudly along the footpath in…" she waved her hand up and down her torso. Then she raised her finger, turned and trotted up to her front door, went inside, then returned to the porch, where she locked her door, shoved the keys into her pocket, and joined Skye, tucking her hand into Skye's elbow. Which was an action that sent an army of scintillating goosebumps marching across Skye's skin.

The walk to the park was brisk in light of the cool breeze that had picked up. Emily commented on the architectural styles of each house that they passed, and Skye regaled Emily with some of the more unusual deliveries she'd had that week. She chose not to share the news about Yvette and Rhiannon's troublesome situation. This moment was Emily's, Skye decided.

Eventually, they arrived at the enormous Moreton Bay fig tree at the high point in the park. Skye waved her hand, like a shopping channel presenter. "My thinking tree. One of many in the city, but this one's my favourite. Don't tell the others." She bumped Emily's shoulder, who laughed.

"It's a beautiful tree. I've always thought so. I haven't ever climbed it, though. I should commemorate this moment." She whipped out her phone, then flicked her fingers at Skye. "Come on. You're making me do this. Jump in."

Skye stepped up behind Emily, leaned her head very gently against the wool beanie, and smiled. The screen reflected the tree, Emily's windblown cheeks, and her smile which was full of spark and fun. It also reflected Skye's expression of unbridled attraction, which she tried to rein in to one of general happiness, but she wasn't sure she managed it in time, because the screen flashed.

"Hang on. One without the beanie," Emily insisted, whipping the hat off and aiming the phone again. Skye held her grin for the photo, then stepped away and looked at the package of adorable that was standing in front of her.

"What?" Emily said, head tilted.

"How do you get your hair to look like that?" Skye asked, waving a finger at Emily's short strands.

"Look like what?"

"All, you know…" Skye circled her finger.

"Messy?" Emily laughed, then shoved the beanie back on, and slid her phone away.

"No, more like professionally dishevelled. Like you've woken up after a—"

Emily's eyebrows lifted as Skye blushed. "After a…?"

"A long, undisturbed sleep all by yourself in a bed. Independently. By yourself." Skye smiled winningly and pointed to the tree. "So… tree climbing?"

Emily's eyes danced with mirth. "Okay, where do we start?"

Skye grinned again, then grabbed Emily's hand.

"Let's go."

She led Emily around to the other side of the trunk and pointed out the branches that could be used to clamber up. Emily went first and Skye forced her eyes not to stare at her backside because she was supposed to be assisting, not ogling. She followed Emily up until they reached a large, fairly horizontal branch.

"Hang on. We stop here. This is the meditation sorting-things-out branch," Skye said, and Emily twisted to position herself on the wide limb, scooting over slightly so Skye could fit into the space between her body and the trunk. Then Emily warmed Skye's arm and thigh when she shuffled sideways again so she could use Skye as a brace. The mechanics of breathing became Skye's focus for a moment.

They sat in silence for a while.

"I like this," Emily whispered.

"What part?"

"All of it. The silence. The not-quite silence. It feels like the tree is holding my thoughts for me."

"It does. Sometimes it's nice to pass them off for a bit so your head can relax."

Emily hummed. "True."

Skye's eyes grew round as Emily's fingers walked across to land on Skye's thigh. Then those fingers flattened, not holding, not caressing, just sitting there, little lines of heat. Skye didn't say a word. She kept her hands curled around the branch. It seemed safer that way. But she couldn't stop, wouldn't stop, the look she gave Emily when she raised her head. Skye let her eyelids drop slightly, hooding them. Knowing exactly what she was doing, because Emily did too, right? With her hand and thigh manoeuvre? Skye was elated to watch the result of her weighted, intimate gaze. Emily swallowed, her face so close that when she exhaled ever so slowly her breath drifted across Skye's skin. They held still, their eyes searching. Skye's lips parted, and Emily blinked, an indecipherable expression whisked across her face, and she casually pulled away, turning her head to the open parkland that was visible through the leaves. Swiping her tongue across her bottom lip, Skye swung her gaze as well.

"Have you always been a courier?" Emily asked, her voice husky with intimacy, as though the significance of the previous moment hadn't quite dissipated.

Skye glanced down at Emily's hand resting on her thigh and smiled. "No. It was a leap of faith a year ago. In my previous life, I was an office-bound slave." A small single laugh popped out. "But the leap has paid off so far. I mean, I don't make enough money to save heaps yet. Not at all. But my expenses are paid, including rent." She bumped her shoulder to Emily's, who chuckled.

"Where were you bonded to slavery?"

Skye hesitated. "Ah...*Traverse Energy*." She waited for the inevitable reaction.

The quick inhalation came right on cue. "Oh no!"

Skye dropped her shoulders. "Yeah. That's how most people respond." The fingers on her thigh tensed in a sympathetic squeeze.

"Were you there long?"

"Not really." Skye sorted through details in her mind. "I graduated from Uni at twenty-three, which is a little late, but I wasn't sure what I wanted to be when I left high school, so I did jobs here and there." A tiny shrug. "But then I figured marketing would be okay. I wanted to tell people about all the good that companies could do. You know, environmental initiatives, social strategies that help people, that sort of thing." A glance at Emily earned her a nod and an encouraging smile.

"So anyway, I got a job at *Traverse*, which I thought was amazing. I was just a lowly marketing assistant to a manager who had his own manager." She pointed to the end of their branch. "I was that twig. Right there." Emily chuckled.

Skye let a small silence pass, then clenched her jaw. "It didn't matter, though. It was *Traverse Energy*, the company that was taking Melbourne and Australia by storm," she said, the sarcasm dripping off her words.

Emily reached between them, found Skye's hand, and brought it up to her thigh. Her fingers wrapped around Skye's palm, and the gesture produced a golden light in Skye's heart.

"Anyway, for three years I slogged away at my desk, promoting and championing the company philosophy of crossing over from traditional energy to clean energy." She couldn't dodge the sarcasm again. "I was so convinced of the environmental forward-thinking vitality surrounding me that I invested all my savings in *Traverse* shares during my second year."

"Oh, Skye," Emily breathed.

A grunt, humourless like a scoff, fell out of Skye's mouth. "Yeah. It paid off for twelve months until, six weeks after my twenty-sixth birthday, the news broke that *Traverse Energy* had blown up a 40,000-year-old, 500-acre Aboriginal heritage site in the Outback of Australia in preparation for a new coal mine funded by overseas investors."

Even the birds must have found the information devastating because silence dominated their little tree space. Emily tentatively leaned into Skye's shoulder, the pom-pom brushing Skye's cheek. "I remember the news," she said sadly.

"Mm. Yeah, the sheer devastation to the Aboriginal community, the public outcry, the high profile court case brought about by the Lands Department and *Heritage Council*, the guilty verdict and the financial repatriations bankrupted *Traverse,* so by the end of the year," Skye breathed deeply, "I was twenty-six years old, unemployed, had virtually no money, and possessed an overwhelming need to blame myself for my blind faith in corporate persuasiveness."

"Do you...do you want to go back into marketing?"

This time Skye did laugh. A singular, short noise that did nothing to suggest humour. "I tried. Every time human resources managers spotted the *Traverse* name on my CV, they couldn't show me the door fast enough."

"That's incredibly unfair!" Emily's hand tightened again.

"Tell me about it." Skye squeezed Emily's hand in return. "Eventually, after a year of working in mind-numbing jobs, I chanced upon a random website for cargo bikes. It went on about their health benefits and their value to a sustainable future. I'm big on environmental stuff."

"Environmental stuff?" She heard Emily's note of mischief and turned to check. Yes, there was a cheeky smile on those soft lips, and yummy swirls developed in Skye's stomach.

"That's serious marketing jargon there, Fitzsimmons." She winked. "Anyway, by the end of that week, I decided to leap in feet first again, even though that is a behaviour I'm really trying hard to curb, and I had a marketing plan, I'd sourced two cargo bikes, phoned Seb and convinced him to work for me, and quit the job I had at the time."

"What were you doing?" Emily asked.

"Selling ceiling fans to people who generally didn't need them."

A loud bark of laughter filled their intimate space. "Oh, dear," Emily said through another laugh.

"Uh-huh. So, *Quick Cargo* was born a year ago," Skye finished, lifting their joined hands a little then letting them fall, as if to punctuate the end of the story. The little niggly voice still whispered, even a year later, that maybe she had thrown herself into yet another venture, but she ignored it because she didn't need that interrupting what was a very intimate moment right now. Doubt had no place when she was sitting in a tree, holding Emily's hand, and feeling like her skin was on fire and her heart was beating out of her chest.

"Well, I think you're brave," Emily leaned into Skye's shoulder again, but this time, she stayed there. "I can't imagine my adult life being completely upended like that and then having to create a brand new plan from scratch. That would be impossibly frightening."

"Yes. But no?" Skye moved a little and Emily pulled away, her eyes questioning. "My life plan got nuked, but I didn't. I knew I'd be okay. Sure, the year afterwards wasn't great. But I made a new plan, and it's working so far. And I ended up in a sweet studio with a pretty nice landlord." She smiled mischievously at Emily who laughed.

Then her laugh softened to a smile and Skye fell into the dark pools of Emily's eyes.

"I ended up with a pretty nice tenant, too," Emily responded. "Thank you for telling me that. Thank you for letting me climb your tree." And it seemed to Skye that if she'd given a small affirmative gesture or quietly murmured, "Yes," then Emily would have kissed her. She teetered on the edge for a moment, then another, until all the moments had expired.

The walk home was quiet, much like the car ride back from *Utopia*. Friendly, but contemplative. Particularly Emily. Skye wondered what she was thinking about, but something held her back from asking.

Chapter Twelve

Emily caught the movement out of the corner of her eye, as she twirled her stylus about the screen, blocking in shapes and fitting lines to the required scale. The last little touches on the 3D modelling software for the Jameson home were fiddly, and she wanted to present the finished, error-free product to them next week.

She paused her stylus again, as Jas spun balletically on her chair. It was her gesture of triumph and usually meant that she'd successfully inserted data into a complicated spreadsheet, or found the name of an obscure paint colour for Nic. Dimitri looked up from the drafting board across the room.

"You do that so gracefully. If I tried it, I'd fall off my chair," he said, his smooth voice sliding through a smile.

Jas grinned evilly. "Please try."

Dimitri made eye contact with Emily and pointed at Jas. "That's workplace harassment, right?"

Jas laughed, and Emily immersed herself in the good-natured moment as she placed her stylus on the desk.

"As your boss, my only response is…I'm not getting involved."

Dimitri joined in her laughter, and it was at that moment that Nic strolled through the door. Jas leapt up, grabbed his hand, and dragged him to her monitor.

"*Lauren's surprise!*" she exclaimed, gesturing energetically at the screen. Nic's eyebrow lifted.

"Who is Lauren and why does she need a surprise?" His hand flipped palm up and the wrinkles gathered on his forehead.

Jas tsked. "The colour," she stated like it was obvious. "It's called *Lauren's Surprise*. It's that blue-green-grey one you wanted. I found it!" She beamed.

Nic lifted their joined hands in celebration. "Yay, you! Firstly, thank you. It's been bugging me. But also? What the hell type of name is *Lauren's Surprise* for a weird blue that resembles a pair of denims that got accidentally soaked in bleach?" He turned to the room. "How are we all?"

Emily grinned at her friend. "Excellent. I was just in the process of negotiating new reporting procedures for workplace harassment at *Fitzsimmons*." Her pointed finger collected Dimitri and Jas. "But you two can work it out. I'm ducking out to get some drinks from…" she tilted her head to indicate the little grocery store about fifty metres down the road. "Anyone want anything?" There was a general shaking of heads and a murmured, "No thanks", but then Jas picked up her bag as if to leave as well.

Emily held up her hand. "You can't come," she said quickly. "I need time to think about what to get you for your birthday tomorrow and you know I talk my ideas aloud. You'd find out what you were getting." Emily laughed at Jas's aggrieved expression.

Nic gave Emily a narrow-eyed look, then spun back to the door. "I'll come. I need to mull over my gift ideas, too."

Jas huffed. "I don't know whether to be touched by your thoughtfulness or offended that you've left it until the day before my party to get me anything."

Nic reduced his stride a little to compensate for Emily's smaller version, as they walked along the footpath, after leaving Jas to her lighthearted sulk.

"So, you really don't have Jas's gift?"

"Of course I do," Emily scoffed.

"Okay. So, are we actually walking to the shops to buy a can of carbonated sugar or did you just need to get out and stomp around a bit?"

Emily stopped abruptly in the middle of the footpath, stretched her arms out, rolled her shoulders, then tipped her face to the sky. Nic adjusted his position slightly so his heels didn't become impaled on the grating that dropped over the curb and stared.

"What's up?"

Emily pressed her palms into her forehead, then dragged her fingers through her hair. "I like her, Nic," she said, her voice just loud enough for him to catch the words before the breeze whisked them away.

"I'm going with Skye as the pronoun-haver there," he said, ducking his head to catch Emily's eyes.

"Yes. Skye." She looked despairingly into Nic's understanding face. "I keep looking for reasons to be near her. It's irrational. We sat in a tree last weekend. And talked and I was so close to kissing her. So close." She delivered a hand toss. Nic's eyebrows rose, and he opened his mouth, probably to ask about the tree kissing, but Emily ploughed on. "We text. That's a thing now. On Tuesday, I texted her —my tenant who lives just metres away in my backyard—I texted Skye, and we got into a long chat which was kind of flirty." She pondered that for a moment. "Rather flirty, and then!" She raised a finger. "Then, I told her that, though not simultaneously, Agatha Christie lived on the same street as the man who introduced fingerprinting to British policing."

Emily clutched at Nic's shoulders. "*Why?*" she breathed into his face in dismay. He rolled his lips, holding a smile at bay. Emily ground her palms into her forehead again. "Last night, she sent me a photo of her cup of tea, all artfully arranged, with the message that she wanted to send me calming vibes." She clutched his shoulders again. "I'm not my mother! Do I look like someone who needs calming vibes?" She removed a hand to point at his face. "Don't answer that. And the scariest thing is, Nic, I loved it. I love that my phone now has a photo of a random cup of tea and that Skye wants me to have vibes."

Nic snorted.

Emily rolled her eyes and growled. "Not those kind of vibes. Behave."

Finally, Nic laughed and grabbed her hand, holding it in both of his. "It's all incredibly sweet to tell you the truth," he said.

Emily huffed and withdrew her hand. "It…is." She flicked her fingers sideways. "And! She delivered to Jas last Monday and it was the. Most. Awkward. Interaction I have ever experienced. But she clearly wanted to say more and I certainly did. It's driving me crazy, Nic. I like her so much. But now my frustratingly chatty, overly cautious head is leaping onboard, which is just," she tossed her hands, "*super*."

"You want more moments with her." Nic looked thoughtful.

"Yes!" She widened her eyes in frustration. "Lots more."

He shrugged elegantly, his bespoke suit jacket rolling with the movement. "Invite her to Jas's party tomorrow."

Emily recoiled. "No!"

"Why not?" he demanded.

"Because, well, she's got that courier race on Sunday, so maybe she won't want to come and besides, my idiotic head is very busy making plans about…her—and doing its thing—you know why I can't invite her."

"Yes. But…" He peered into her face. "You're clearly attracted to Skye. It seems she's attracted to you." A beautifully outlined eyebrow was raised. "So?"

"But…I…it's all very," she waved her hands erratically in the air like a first year drama student asked to interpret a tree blowing in the wind.

"What does *that* mean?"

Emily's arms dropped. "This…her…it's…the idea of her is quick and uncomfortable and scary and tingly and—" She yanked her phone from her pocket, swiped to the photos to pull up the one of her and Skye at the tree and waved it in front of Nic. "And she's sexy. Look at the sexy." Nic held her hand to keep the phone still and raised an eyebrow. Emily made a face that said, *See?* and slid the phone away.

"Em, I know this is outside the postcode of your comfort zone, but you're not asking Skye to sign a life contract, hon. Seriously. Just invite her." It was Nic's turn to toss hands about.

Emily sighed.

Nic continued. "Tell her…" he paused. "Tell her to bring a plus one, then it's like you're inviting her because—"

"I want a threesome?"

Nic dropped his head back on his neck and barked out a laugh.

"Sure. Tell her that. I dare you."

"You're chicken, that's what it is. You clearly like her, so what's stopping you?" Emily glared at herself in the harsh fluorescent light of her bathroom. Friday night had come and gone, and somehow she'd expected the courage to ask Skye to Jas's party to arrive like a welcome pizza delivery. Which, of course, it hadn't, because she hadn't made that metaphorical phone call in the first place. Now here she was on Saturday morning, arms braced on the vanity top, oddly enjoying the way the bathroom acoustics handled her self-recrimination. It hadn't helped that she'd flicked open her photos in her phone and stared at the tree photo a hundred times this week. Skye's look of warmth—maybe desire—was aimed squarely at Emily, not the camera, and it filled her with all the difficult to decipher feelings.

The doorbell rang, halting her staring competition, and she walked down the hall.

The opened door revealed Skye, casually dressed, hair down, wide smile, hands tucked under her armpits to maintain their warmth.

"Hi. Good morning," she said brightly.

Emily took a full second to appreciate the sizzle of attraction that set up residence in her stomach—again—then her manners kicked in.

"Hi. God, come inside. It's cold today." Having stated the obvious, Emily moved to the side and waved Skye in. "Would you like some tea?" she asked as she closed the door, and turned to find Skye, smile still planted on her lips, standing not a metre away. Emily found herself returning the gesture, and the way her heart flipped over slightly was a very pleasant feeling.

"No, thanks, I've had a pot already. I'm actually here to pick your brain," Skye said, dissolving the tension. Emily breathed.

"Okay? In architecture, or handmade lasagne sheets?" She grinned cheekily, because cheeky grins felt appropriate somehow, like Skye might appreciate them. Welcome them.

Skye laughed. "Neither of those, although that second one sounds excellent. But," she rubbed her palms together. "Luke, a florist *Quick*

Cargo works with, wants to try out Ikebana and he's been on various sites to find out all he can, but I said that I knew someone who actually does it, and therefore that's much more relevant intel than random research on the internet."

Emily tipped her head. "Right. And this someone is me."

"Yep. And I didn't just want to chuck your phone number about. So, I thought I'd drop by to see you, and, like I said, pick your brains, which," she squinted, "kinda sounds like a ghoulish thing to do."

Emily gave a weak smile. "Pick my brains means checking out my craft room?" She twisted her fingers together in front of her body, and Skye studied her for a moment.

Then, with a flash of awareness that made Emily's heart squeeze, Skye said, "We can just talk out here if you like. I have the feeling just by looking at you that your craft room is very private and special." Her voice was soft, her eyes holding Emily's in a gentle caress.

It took all of a second for Emily to come to decision. "No. I'd like to show you. It's a much better way to explain the art form than the cut and dried words of a conversation," she said, then grinned as Skye registered the pun.

"Flower joke. I like it."

A warmth created by understanding, of being seen, of care, filled her body and it was felt right to reach over and grasp Skye's hand and lead her to the second bedroom door. Inviting Skye into this space felt right. She pushed open the door.

"So, here it is," she said, drawing Skye into the room. She watched her execute a very slow arc, taking in the crafting tables against two walls, the bookcases filled with tools in neatly labelled boxes, the aligned cutting mats, the vases of all shapes, designs and finishes, and the three completed presentations that were displayed on a tiered stand in the corner.

"Oh! Emily, this is amazing." She spun back and looked into Emily's eyes. "I love them." She indicated a black walnut burl vase on the nearest table which was highly polished, squat and seemed entirely aware of its beauty. "May I?"

Emily nodded and smiled as Skye reverently cradled the empty vase, smoothing her thumbs along the surface. Skye quirked an eyebrow at the small well in the centre. "That looks dangerous."

Emily giggled. "It's called a frog, and yes, there are spikes inside, but it's to support the stems. Ikebana is about structure more than anything, so it's necessary to have a stable foundation."

Skye replaced the vase, then stepped over to the display stand. Her movements were careful, like she appreciated the shrine-like atmosphere of the space. "This takes a lot of patience," Skye murmured, bending to look closely at the second arrangement.

Emily leaned against the door frame. "It does. My therapist put me onto it," she said, then blinked at how easily that admission had fallen out of her mouth. "Um…it's the whole planning ahead but living in the moment thing. Floral therapy for the over-planning thing I do, which I blurted out to you during CurtainGate."

Skye gave a low chuckle, eyed Emily, then winked. "CurtainGate." They held eye contact, then she turned back to the arrangements. "These would make incredible gifts. I could imagine giving a relative one of these for their birthday instead of some random whatever I'd bought at the shopping centre."

"Yes, I take one to my mother every time I visit her." Then Emily realised that the metaphorical delivery of courage had arrived. She hummed, and Skye straightened to look at her. "Speaking of birthdays, would you like to come to Jas's birthday party tonight?"

Skye took a long moment to contemplate Emily, then her forehead wrinkled. "Really? Is Jas okay with that?"

Emily flapped her hand. "Oh, totally. It's Jas. She's invited everyone she knows, which I'm sure is half of Melbourne." She breathed in. "Besides, I'd like you to come."

Skye's lips quirked, then she nodded. "Okay. That would be—"

Despite Skye having already accepted the invitation, Emily added the silly get-out-of-jail excuse she'd mentioned to Nic.

"I know you've got *Rush* tomorrow, so going out tonight might not be something you want to do." Emily then mentally suggested that she might like to shut up because Skye's lips were very slowly curling into a delighted smile. Her internal and external monologues were having a joint conversation and she wondered if she left the room that they'd carry on without her. "You can bring someone if you like. If there's someone else…" Finally, she trailed off. The existence of a potential girlfriend tightened every muscle in her body.

With her grin still firmly in place, Skye held the eye contact. "Hmm," she said. "That's really cool. I'll bring Seb."

That immediately killed Emily's weird jealous-not-jealous reaction. "Seb?"

"Yeah. He lives with his parents and two sisters and they're always telling him to get out more and meet people. Half of Melbourne sounds like the perfect opportunity."

Emily rubbed at her hair. "Okay. Good," she said, then blew out a breath. "Can I drive you? It's at *Gary's*."

"No, it's fine. Thanks. I'll get a taxi to Seb's and we'll go from there."

They stared at each other again for a moment; Emily now using the doorframe to maintain her outward nonchalance, while butterflies rampaged through her stomach. She couldn't focus on anything. That was a lie. She was very much focused on Skye's lips. Emily wrenched her attention back.

"Would you—"

"Do you think—"

Skye gestured for Emily to go ahead.

"I know this is a little odd, and you might not want to, and you're bringing Seb and…ah…do you think you could wear what you wore to *Utopia*?" Emily said softly, the butterflies increasing the more she babbled. Her face flushed.

Another slow smile drifted onto Skye's lips. "I was just about to ask you the same thing. We didn't get to appreciate what true fashion plates we were last time." She grinned and Emily disagreed. She'd appreciated every minute of Skye's fashion statement that Saturday.

"That would be really nice." A mutual blush touched their cheeks, and Emily needed to nip this whole moment in the bud because it was suddenly galloping out of control and she couldn't have that. There was stepping back to do with analysis and evaluating of options and checking of forward movements about what this…crush was.

She moved into the room and opened one of the drawers. "So this is a sabitoru, which is a whetstone for cleaning the small scissors." The next thirty minutes, holding the tools, the materials, feeling their textures, and explaining their function and purpose to Skye, were the equivalent of having a nap under a weighted blanket. Very calming. So much breathing. In and out. Then, Skye announced that she had to leave.

"Thanks for showing me this.' She gestured at the room, then stepped closer. The gold-brown of her eyes glowed. "This was a big deal to show me this room, and your craft."

Emily delivered a little shrug-hum combination, mainly to deflect how laser-like Skye's perception was and how close she was standing. "You're welcome. You can pick my brains about anything you like. Pasta, architecture, Agatha Christie trivia…"

Skye smiled, her eyes lighting up. "Noted." She'd taken a step to move towards the door, but that brought her even closer to Emily, who inhaled and wasn't sure if she'd be able to release the air back into the wild. "Thanks for the invitation as well. I'll see you tonight at…?" she murmured, the only volume necessary in the quiet of the house.

There was a moment. An important one. One that stood up and smacked Emily in the arm. *Pay attention.*

"*Gary's*. Eight o'clock," Emily finished, then laughed and rolled her eyes. "Or thereabouts. It's Jas, so anytime is fine."

They said their goodbyes at the door, and it was a few minutes later when Emily realised that she was developing a habit of springing invitations on Skye at the last minute. Yet Skye had accepted readily on both occasions. Perhaps the readiness meant that Skye was as equally attracted. Did Skye have a crush as well? Not possible. Emily's was out of control, which was delicious and frightening all at once. Then another thought occurred to her. If the situations had been reversed, would she have accepted the spontaneous invitations so readily? Probably not. But she would have wanted to.

Maybe, just maybe, it was time to unpick some of the tight knots around her heart and see where it went. But without a plan. That horrifying idea created a sudden, panicky increase in her heart rate and the swirly, twisty, yummy tightening low in her belly.

***

Gary's, the venue of choice, seemed to suffer an identity crisis every five metres. It was part restaurant, part pub, part club, but it all gelled seamlessly into a highly successful venue. The guests for Jas's party had commandeered the section that straddled the imaginary line between restaurant and club, filling the couch seating and bar tables. Emily was in the process of slipping onto a stool when she spotted Skye entering the restaurant. She was accompanied by Seb, who looked very handsome with his pitch-black hair and chiselled features that all athletic people seemed to possess. A wide smile split his face, as Skye bent her head to say something to him.

Emily abandoned the stool, but before she could step away, her elbow was grabbed and she was pulled sideways and spun around. Nic's face was priceless.

"Oh my God, I've only seen her in hi-vis and a helmet, but she is spectacular," he whispered frantically into her face.

"I am completely aware of that fact, Nic," Emily groaned. "I have eyes. Leather pants?"

Nic nodded emphatically, the skin of his shaved head catching the artificial lights.

Emily shook her head. "But I should only be looking and not touching."

"Oh!" he gasped. "Has there been more touching?" His eyes sparkled, the extraordinary makeup around them adding to his glee.

"No! And it's not—"

Nic clutched her upper arms. "Do you think you're not good enough?" He didn't give her time to answer. "Because that's ridiculous. You are utterly beautiful and a good person and kind and smart as a whip and while Bec was a stunner, she didn't come with all those add-on features." He took a breath. "That woman?" He tipped his chin in the direction of the door. "V8 engine hot, and she's loaded with an extras package."

"The car analogy is awful," Emily stated flatly.

Nic winced. "I know but I'm making a point. She likes you, you like her, and most importantly, you deserve her. You deserve the potential. I don't want you thinking about the future. In fact, I don't want you thinking at all. And!" He thrust his face at her and glared. "If you don't do something about this tonight, I will make you sing karaoke with me."

Emily's eyes widened. "You wouldn't!"

Nic bared his teeth in an evil grin. "Try me. Now, let's go." He linked his arm through Emily's and walked them through the crowd towards Skye and Seb.

Chapter Thirteen

Skye watched Emily and Nic make their way through the throng, and spent a good second or two travelling up the length of Emily's legs from the low boots to the hem of the short skirt. The swirls that this enjoyable moment produced in her stomach were entirely delicious. Emily was a beautiful, intriguing woman who'd invited Skye to another woman's birthday party. Emily was a beautiful, intriguing woman who sometimes looked at Skye as if she could devour her whole, yet the next second she seemed to want to run a mile in the opposite direction. The puzzle that was Emily Fitzsimmons.

Emily stopped short just inside the invisible line where newish friends crossed over to rather friendly friends. Skye bit her lip.

"Hi," she said. Should she hug? Graze the air near Emily's ear? A micro-second of indecision passed, then Emily stepped forward and before Skye could react, briefly embraced Skye's shoulders, brushing the softest of kisses onto her cheek. Decision made. Excellent.

"Hi," Emily said, blushing, which was adorable. Her eyes drifted to Seb, and she delivered another fleeting hug-kiss combination, which Skye decided, in an irrationally territorial manner, was definitely in the acquaintance category and therefore fine. "Hi, Seb. I'm glad you could make it tonight."

Seb grinned. "Thanks for the invitation."

Nic joined the small group. The plum plaid-patterned jeans and black silk shirt were a combination that worked incredibly well, and Skye knew that he was completely aware of that fact.

"Well, if hugging is à la mode, then count me in," he stated flamboyantly, then flung his arms about Skye, who completed the embrace, then he disentangled himself and draped his arm across Seb's shoulders in a gesture that was pure class. It meant that Seb could lean in, or take the option to shift away, and Skye adored the consideration.

Seb chose to lean in and Nic smiled, quick and charming. "Were you at a loose end tonight, Seb, or did someone get the 'sorry can't make it' phone call?"

"No." Seb shook his head. "I was free, and I'm really not the kind of guy to chuck someone for something else. I'm not into that."

"What *are* you into?" Nic purred. Emily reached across and smacked his shoulder.

"Nic! Don't tease," she admonished, as the other three laughed.

Seb turned his laugh to a smirk. "That's fine. I have two sisters. I can handle anything."

"Ooh. That sounds like a challenge." Jas's voice cut through their conversational bubble, and she arrived as a vision in pink dye-tipped hair, and a fitted dress bearing a print that looked like Piet Mondrian had been resurrected and used the fabric as a canvas. It was all...a lot. But like Nic, Jas owned it and it worked.

Skye watched as Seb very slowly, and not at all subtly, decided that the moon and stars were now contained wholly in the woman in front of him. A glance at Emily told Skye that she'd also spotted Seb's reaction and they shared a delighted grin.

"Hey, Skye. So glad you came." Jas leaned up and pressed their cheeks together, then turned to Seb. "Hi. I'm Jas." She held out her hand, which Seb cradled in his.

"Seb. I'm," he tipped his chin sideways, "Skye's friend. Happy birthday, by the way." There was a pause, then Nic announced, with a grin and a roll of his eyes, that he was off to get a drink. Then Seb released Jas's hand and dug into his pocket. "I couldn't come to a party, especially a birthday party, without bringing a gift. My mum would kill me," he chuckled, then brought out a small package wrapped in tissue paper and handed it to Jas. "So, happy birthday," he repeated.

Jas blushed. "Oh! Thank you." And while Seb watched Jas peel away the tape, Skye took the opportunity to sneak another look at Emily's outfit, from her toes and ending at her eyes. She pointed to Emily's clothes, and mouthed, "Nice," which produced a wonderful eyebrow lift, then an echoed finger point, with, "Same," mouthed in reply. Skye hoped fervently that Emily was experiencing just as many delightful twists deep in her own body.

"Oh my God! This is beautiful! Thank you." Jas's exclamation returned their attention, and Skye looked with admiration at one of Seb's sister's handmade Filipina bracelets, the colourful design sparkling in the lights of the restaurant. Seb shrugged shyly.

"My sister makes them. It's for friendship." He helped Jas twist the loop around her wrist, and Skye shifted closer to Emily.

"This is so sweet. It's like watching a romantic movie," she whispered. Emily turned and at her slight blush, Skye realised that the same thing could be said about their unfolding situation if they decided to let it grow. She delved into her pocket and pulled out her gift.

"Happy birthday as well," she said through a grin, and Jas quickly opened the little parcel to reveal a miniature ceramic cat. She squeaked.

"This is perfect, thank you. I have a collection on my desk at work," she gushed.

"I know. That's why I thought..." Skye trailed off, mimicked Seb's self-deprecating shrug, then caught Emily's gaze, which was contemplative and encompassing. And warm.

"Well, this is amazing." Jas's voice jerked Skye and Emily from their reverie. Jas's grin was much too knowing, as she whipped out her phone. "I want selfies with everyone before we all get sweaty and I can't filter out the shine."

Arm length limitations meant that they had to squash together, with Seb crouching slightly next to Jas, which seemed to please him no end. Skye found herself tucked behind Emily, leaning against her body, and her hand resting on Emily's waist. She didn't breathe the entire time. It was perfect.

Then it became even more perfect. Jas waggled her finger at Emily and Skye.

"You two," she demanded and waved her hands, one clutching the phone, in a gesture that indicated for them to stand close together. Jas wasn't a person to argue with, so Skye stepped into Emily's space, held her lightly around the waist, and turned her head to Jas, who looked thrilled. The picture was taken, Jas swiped at her phone, and pointed to Emily which seemed to mean that she'd just forwarded the photo. Then Jas took control of the entire situation again, and with Seb—her brand new friend—in tow, they were absorbed into the horde of revellers and conversation spilled into all corners of the room.

Somehow, after she lost Seb somewhere in the crowd, but assumed he was still attached to Jas, Skye ended up at a bar table, perched on a stool, with Emily beside her. The woman opposite them, who was maybe early twenties, was shredding her beer bottle label and creating a miniature paper mountain in the middle of the table.

She looked up, flicking her eyes between Skye and Emily. A minute smile lifted her mouth, and Skye had the distinct impression that shredding labels from bottles was a coping mechanism for anxiety, rather than an actual creative endeavour. She was about to leap into some introductions when the woman straightened her shoulders, and a little determined frown appeared between her eyebrows. Then she leaned over, raising her voice above the sudden increase in volume from the speakers as comparisons between Michelle Pfeiffer and white gold poured out, while Bruno Mars announced his astounding degree of hotness.

"I'm Hope. How do you know Jas?" It was blunt, without preamble, and Skye would have bet that Hope spoke like that to anyone she encountered.

She watched as Emily swallowed a mouthful of her blackcurrant club soda, then grinned. "Jas is a colleague. I'm Emily." She replaced the glass, then gestured softly with her hand at Skye. "This is my friend, Skye."

It was an instant dunk tank of happiness. The deliberate identification of Jas as an equal, not an employee. The friend label delivered so very casually. Skye stood under the metaphorical Emily-is-a-really-ly-good-person shower for another second before she stuck out her hand. Hope ignored it, and Skye smoothly turned the movement into one where she picked up her glass, sipping on her own blackcurrant club soda.

"Cool. I'm her cousin. Are you going to dance?"

It wasn't something Skye had actively thought about, but when she turned and watched the lights chasing each other over Emily's skin, her clothes, her hair, suddenly dancing seemed like an essential activity on the evening's agenda.

Emily shrugged. "Sure." Then she tilted her head, raised an eyebrow and Skye's breath lodged in her throat. These random, emboldened, overtly flirtatious moments were breathtaking and Skye was right there for it, thanks very much.

"How are your dancing skills?" Emily asked, sending a smoky look over the top of her glass.

Skye's stomach clenched. There! Another one. The confusing, toe-curling, entirely delightful flirting that appeared from nowhere. Jesus.

"Ah. Well, I think I'm dreadful, but other people might be less biased. My ratings generally depend on their alcohol consumption."

They held eye contact for a moment. Then Hope leaned on her elbows and tipped her head to peer under the wooden top. "You look like you could dance, I guess. You have dancing boots on," she stated loudly. Skye chuckled.

Emily bumped her shoulder into Skye's. "Would you like an unbiased and entirely sober opinion of your dancing ability?"

"Yours?"

"Yes," Emily said, and then looked at Hope. "Do you want to come dance?"

Hope's sharp, single laugh cut through the noise. "No," she answered, her eyebrows wrinkled in confusion.

"Okay," Emily said easily, and she slid off her chair, grabbed Skye's hand, and dragged her onto the dance floor, snaking between people until she'd found a spot near the far wall. Then Skye watched as Emily's bath of confident spontaneity dried up because suddenly she froze, looking for all the world like the next step, such as moving her body to the beat, was completely beyond her. Skye's heart lurched as she stared into those gorgeous dark brown eyes which bore a tiny speck of panic. So, she stepped closer and rested her hands on Emily's waist. It must have been exactly the right thing to do because Emily's eyes darkened, the panic blew away, and the whole situation felt exactly right.

David Guetta's 'Titanium' slipped smoothly into the end of 'Uptown Funk', filling their section of the venue with the heavy base that built walls around the lyrics as they fired away, fired away. Entirely appropriate. It was like a shot of liquid courage and Skye pulled Emily's hips forward, delighting in the way her lips parted, and their bodies moved with the rhythm. The suede of Emily's skirt was soft under Skye's fingers—she knew it would be—and Emily lifted her hands to cup Skye's shoulders. Small movements became bigger and their bodies swayed from side to side, undulating away from each other, then coming back together, all the while, throughout that song, then the next, the eye contact was anchored. And heated. Emily's eyes were impossibly dark, and Skye imagined hers weren't far behind.

They mouthed the words of the songs, laughing quickly when the lyrics were misheard and misspoken and misremembered. The bass reverberated through the soles of her boots. She felt it in her chest, as her heartbeat picked up speed because Emily ran her tongue across her bottom lip. The seductive bass line of Jennifer Lopez's 'On The Floor' crept up her legs and Skye grinned, because the song was a bigger throwback than one of her rugby passes at Uni. She felt so good; not just this moment but everything. She and Seb were prepped and ready for *Rush* tomorrow, her living situation was working out well, and she was dancing with Emily Fitzsimmons, who looked stunning and gorgeous and happy, even though it was possible that she'd freaked herself out with how bold she'd been. Their faces drew closer as their bodies undulated with the beat. It would be simple to nudge forward that last little bit and kiss her. Then Emily's lips parted as if on cue and Skye couldn't unsee that image, unfeel that touch, undo that want.

The beat swung their bodies away, then back, Emily's hands tightened on Skye's biceps, and it seemed that the speakers had malfunctioned because Skye's ears felt like they'd been stuffed with cotton wool. Emily's eyes, so very close, sparkled with a sudden delight, a resurgence of intent and confidence. And despite the rhythm keeping its steady pace, their movements slowed to half the beat, and the air became thick. Emily dragged her thumbs over the muscle that led to Skye's neck, and dancing became a simple sway on each beat, then no beat at all. Emily hooded her eyes, Skye froze, and with a tiny nod, like she'd confirmed a decision, Emily tipped her chin, and gently touched her bottom lip to Skye's, holding, breathing, softening the gesture, but not quite closing her lips. It was the sexiest not-quite-a-kiss that Skye had ever experienced in her life. She felt the jolt right to her core. Emily pulled sideways slightly so she could lean into Skye's ear.

"My unbiased opinion is that you're actually a very good dancer," she said huskily. Skye laughed unsteadily, and Emily drew back, grinning with delight, then with an eyebrow lift that spoke volumes about how much she was enjoying the moment, slid her hands around the back of Skye's neck and brought their hips up to speed with the song. The cotton wool cleared from Skye's ears and she let out a breath. Leaning in to repeat the kiss, enhance the kiss, to kiss Emily for hours, or a combination of all three were all solid choices. Really solid choices. But Skye ignored them. Emily's tides of confidence that had drifted in and out throughout the evening didn't need a tsunami of desire dropped on them from above from a thrilled, blonde bike courier who wanted more, and lots, and yes, please. Emily would probably run a mile, so with the gentlest of movements, she drew Emily to her chest and they continued to sway to the rhythm that filled the space. Not leaping in boots and all was such a responsible, very difficult, sometimes not fun thing to do. But right then it seemed like the right thing to do.

It was only ever meant to be a brief night out, what with the race tomorrow, so after dancing to one more set, and sharing soft looks, and gentle smiles over another drink, Skye announced that she had to leave. Emily nodded, in a kind of business-like manner, like Skye imagined she would when signing a new contract. Utterly adorable. Holding hands, they navigated their way across the restaurant to retrieve Seb, who apparently hadn't left Jas's orbit for the entire evening.

"Hey, mate. We've got to get going," Skye leaned over the back of the couch, inserting her head into the limited space between Jas and Seb and laughed at the instant scowl that filled her friend's face. She pulled back and threw her hands up in defence. "I'm just the messenger! You can race around the city with late-night head-haze if you want."

Emily laughed. "That sounds dangerous," she said, then bit her lip as Skye winked at her.

"See?" She patted Seb's shoulder. "Emily gets it." Then she grinned at Jas who had extracted herself from Seb's side, stood, and was flirtatiously crooking a finger at him.

"Come on," Jas said, her red-painted lips smiling widely. "You've talked enough about this race for me to know how important it is." Then when he'd stood, she held the sides of his face, and kissed his cheek down low near his mouth, pulling away after a moment to say, "Thank you for coming tonight. The present is beautiful and—" she moved closer to his ear. Skye couldn't make out the words, but Seb's back stiffened, his shoulders squared, and his hands fluttered like he suddenly had a desperate need to clutch at Jas's waist. Skye and Emily sharing a knowing look and laughed.

Then, Emily shifted sideways and held Skye's hand. "Thank you for coming tonight. This has been fun," she said, leaning close to Skye's ear.

Skye beaming smile said she felt the same. "Yes, it has." Then, after a beat, she delivered a soft hug, kissing Emily's cheek on the way, and held Emily to her chest. This new development could be discussed later, but for now, it existed as a not-quite-a-kiss and the indescribable feeling of Emily in her arms.

"I'll text you…tomorrow?"

Emily's mouthed "Yes" and her smile created euphoric shivers under Skye's skin.

Then, while absorbing Seb's long look and evil grin, which held the threat of an interrogation, she reached over to hug Jas, accepted everyone's good luck wishes for the following day, and dragged a reluctant Seb out to the taxi rank.

Chapter Fourteen

Having a crush was always irrational. Having a crush on her tenant was pure madness. Emily changed lanes to veer around a panel van that was travelling twenty kilometres under the speed limit on the highway out of the city. The only thing that could make her crush more logical would be if there was a plan in place for the future. Which there wasn't so therefore she was back to pure madness.

"I kissed her, which doesn't help the logic part at all," she informed the blue station wagon in front of her. The drive to her mum's place was the perfect time to analyse last night's moment of delicious madness. Kissing Skye—sort of—the brush of her skin, sharing breath, feeling the strength of Skye's body against hers; all of it made her insides tingle. But poor Skye; Emily's stepping forward then stepping backward business last night must have confused her to no end. She probably had no idea what Emily wanted.

"I sure wish I knew," she muttered, as she zipped past a delivery truck. She'd stepped forward again that morning, flicking a quick text to Skye that wished her good luck, and that she'd found out what a fixie bike was and it sounded dreadfully difficult to ride and therefore to be safe today in the race and did she mention good luck? The thumbs-up, smiley face, bicycle, sunglasses smiley, party hat with streamers combination that appeared on her screen in reply made her smile. She flicked a glance at the digital clock. Midday. *Rush* would be starting soon.

Then, her phone, cradled in the holder near the steering wheel, rang, as if it knew it was the item of the moment. The tinny music reverberated through the car's speakers, so she pressed the answer button on her steering wheel.

"Emily Fitzsimmons speaking."

"Hello, Emily Fitzsimmons. This is Nic, the Thoroughly Abandoned. Why didn't I get a goodbye, or a vague wave-like gesture, or even an 'oi' across the room last night?" Nic was teasing, but there was a thread of hurt running through his question.

Emily sighed. "I'm sorry, Nic. I was a bit discombobulated and I forgot my manners."

Nic gave an abrupt laugh. "Discombobulated?"

Another station wagon, the roof racks laden with planks of wood that looked remarkably unstable, cut in front of her. She growled and changed lanes. At this rate, she'd run out of road if any more Sunday drivers accessed the highway.

"I'm going to assume that animalistic noise is not for me," Nic said, his voice infused with laughter.

"No. Drivers. Anyway, discombobulated. I kissed Skye," Emily stated matter-of-factly, and gripped the steering wheel in preparation for Nic's response.

"Really?" He stretched the word. She could feel the waves of glee pouring from the phone.

"Well, yes. Sort of." Emily glared at the dashboard, noticing her speed was increasing in direct correlation to her anxiety. She softened her foot on the accelerator. "It was more a touching of a lip."

Nic snorted. "One?"

"Yes. Like my mouth had heart failure right at the critical moment..." she faded away as Nic's deep laugh rolled through the car's interior.

"Still qualifies as a kiss," he said finally. "Sounds quite sexy, actually."

"I'm flying in clouds, Nic. Not in the good way, and I can't see where I'm going and it's freaking me out. I'm wildly attracted to her."

"It's okay, you know."

"Not really," she disagreed.

"It is. Bec was not the one for you. You were flying in low-level clouds with her the whole time, by the way," he said seriously.

"No, I wasn't. I had a plan."

"Okay. Sure," he agreed. "But it was a pretty bad plan."

Emily sighed and flicked her indicator to take the turn-off to her mum's, whizzing up the off-ramp, then slowing to navigate the side streets into the suburb.

Nic continued. "Bec was a blind date who sounded perfect because your bad-advice-giving mutual friend said she was. Maybe Bec *was* exactly right when you got together, and so your plan made sense, even though it didn't because seriously, hon, plans that early are scary." He paused. "Then, suddenly Bec wasn't perfect, and so you ended up flying through crap planning clouds. But you never thought about landing and changing those plans, Em. So she did it for you." He delivered a low hum of displeasure. "In a really shitty way."

"Tell me about it," Emily said, swinging into the road that led to her mum's street.

"You need to land your plane, hon. Bec jumped out of it with her own parachute but thoughtfully didn't leave one for you."

Emily grunted, pausing at the give-way sign. "Yeah." She checked both directions for traffic, waiting for Nic to continue speaking.

"Are you loading Skye into the plane when you take off again?" he said softly. Emily crawled to a stop outside her mum's house, pulled on the handbrake, then leaned her head back into the headrest, staring at the safety instructions sticker on the inside of the sun visor.

"Probably. Maybe. I don't know, which is appalling. I know I shouldn't load any planes at all. Just let things happen blah blah blah. What am I doing, Nic?"

There was a long moment of silence. "Do you reckon Skye is a parachute-chucker?"

Emily barked out a laugh. "No, Skye is not a parachute-chucker."

"Then listen to that advice. Maybe don't plan. Don't load planes. But if you do," he paused, "let her know, because if she's not on board, then I have a feeling she'll walk away." There was another tiny pause. "Say hi to your Mum for me. And Leanne. Bye." He hung up abruptly, which was fairly standard. Emily turned off the car and continued to read the safety warnings, attempting to match the English words with their German and Spanish translations as best she could. A conversation with Skye was next. Tonight. Or tomorrow. She couldn't pretend that last night's kiss and the flirting and the stomach-swirling proximity was imaginary. She couldn't ignore her overwhelming desire to kiss Skye senseless, and then run a mile the other way. So mature. Finally, she grabbed her phone, bag, and the Ikebana sculpture, and desperately hoped her mother was actually home, and not still checking the ripeness of the tomatoes at the farmer's market.

***

Skye hadn't stopped fizzing with distracted energy since last night. Having a crush was always irrational. Having a crush on her landlord was pure madness. The only thing that could improve the situation would be to give herself a serious talking-to about not rescuing or leaping in without checking first or taking her time or some other sensible advice. Which didn't look like it was happening in the immediate future so therefore she was back to pure madness. And with all of Skye's stepping forward stepping backward palaver last night, Emily probably didn't have a clue what was going on in Skye's brain. Skye didn't know either and that—

"—buy some of the cool gear at the stalls." Seb's voice cut through her thoughts.

"What?" She looked sideways, blinking in confusion, and Seb rolled his eyes.

"Bloody hell, Skye. You need to get your head straight. So what if Emily's the angel appearing on earth to shine in everlasting brightness, which I know you think because I saw you two last night. But, you've got a race starting soon." He leaned across his bike and thumped her shoulder. His eyes sparkled with mischief and excitement under the shadow of his helmet.

Skye chuckled. "Yeah, yeah. Okay. We're good to go. I've handed all the waivers and legal paperwork in, so if you stack it," she grinned and Seb scoffed, "then the organisers will send you a get-well-soon card and that's it." They shared a laugh and a nod of acknowledgement. The action behind the scenes of a race like *Rush* was incredibly complicated, and the organisers had done an amazing job. Every courier carried a mini-sports video camera attached to the top of their helmet, their phones were held in race-approved cradles on the handlebars of their fixie bikes, the markers located all over the city were stickers with QR codes that uploaded the courier's ID to *Rush*'s server as soon as the marker was logged. Then the next marker location was immediately pushed to the courier's phone. It was incredible. Every competitor started with a different location marker, then the sixty racers were directed all over the city to find as many of the sixty tags as they could in ninety minutes. It was frantic and full-on. And worth every cent of the five-hundred-dollar entry fee for that twenty-five thousand dollar prize. Skye grinned at Seb again, as she adjusted her small backpack. Water bottle racks were forbidden on fixie bikes, so her little bag contained a bottle and a basic tyre repair kit.

"App ready?"

Seb rolled his eyes again. "Yes, Mum."

She laughed as they shuffled, duck-walking their bikes between their thighs, with all the competitors who moved to the far end of Kellior Lane, where it joined onto Graham Street, the major thoroughfare through Melbourne. The volume of traffic in the city at twelve-thirty on a Sunday afternoon was pretty low, but it was still dangerous to take idiotic risks. Wearing the helmet cam meant that all competitors had to stick to the road rules and not disappear on 'creative' detours to make up time. It had happened before, so this year they'd clamped down hard. Good. A race should be about speed, experience, and knowledge. And talent.

The council had given the *Rush* organisers permission to hold up traffic on Graham Street for the start of the race, but only for five minutes. So when the yell came through on the squawking walkie-talkies Skye tightened her muscles, and sensed Seb's tension rising beside her. Scanning over the helmets in front, Skye saw that Graham Street was clear of all traffic, so she rolled her fingertips under the hem of her lycra shorts, then flattened the fabric against her skin. A nervous tic.

"Here we go," she breathed. The air tasted like success, because she could do this. They could do this. Goosebumps travelled across her skin. And sitting in the back seat of her confidence, cheering her on, was the text from Emily that morning wishing her good luck, with a smiley face, a fingers crossed emoji, a hilariously inaccurate description of a fixie bike, and a GIF of Barack Obama, with accompanying finger guns, letting her know that he had the faith. It was cute, sweet, and Skye had immediately screenshot the entire message in case she accidentally erased it.

"Good luck, mate," Seb said, bumping his fist—encased in his lucky red fingerless glove—to hers. They held eye contact, then her phone screen lit up, and she glanced at the little flashing dot. Skye grinned. Yes. She knew where 36 Hawkers Road was.

Skye braced her foot on her up pedal, then pushed off with the rest of the pack, and swung into Graham Street. Everyone scattered like fireworks, pumping their legs, their hi-vis flashing in the muted winter sunlight, and Skye let her instincts take over.

***

Pride was the overwhelming emotion on her mum's face when she turned Emily to face the dwarf cherry tree in the middle of the backyard. Emily took in the circle of rocks elegantly placed around the base, and the stout little branches jutting out from the trunk. Considering the tree—and some of the other backyard inhabitants—had looked like scenery from a horror movie last year, her mum had done a marvellous job at plant triage and critical care.

"It's doing really well," Emily said, wrapping an arm around her mum's shoulders and drawing her in. They were the same height, with Jane Fitzsimmons a more sturdy version of Emily's slight frame.

"Thank you, sweetheart. I made sure to follow through on my moon healing rituals with a good dose of fertiliser and severe pruning." Emily squinted at her mum's expression. A large amount of self-deprecation was underlying that statement, and she laughed.

"Whatever works, hey?" she said, and her mum nodded.

"A philosophy for life."

Being married to Gareth Fitzsimmons had been a traumatic rollercoaster, yet despite her coping strategy of airy-faerieness, her mum still maintained a solid grasp of 'taking-the-piss'. They shared a smile.

"Are you going to see him today?" Emily asked quietly, staring at the proud little tree for a moment.

"Yes."

Emily slipped her hand into her mum's elbow and blew out a breath.

"Can I come?"

A pair of wide eyes stared at her. "Honey, of course you can."

"Well, I didn't want to…" She shrugged. "I didn't want to intrude on your conversation with my own stuff."

Jane wrapped her other hand over Emily's, pulling her closer. "It's both of our stuff."

Emily's aunt, Leanne, arrived home as they were walking back inside from the garden, and hugged her niece.

"Em, sweetie. You look so *well*!" she exclaimed, emphasising the final word, then wrapped her arms about Emily, swaddling her in a copious amount of bosom, brown curls, and *Elizabeth Arden Red Door* perfume. Then Leanne pushed Emily away, holding her shoulders. "Have you eaten? What about some lunch? How about I make something? Let me have a hunt around in the fridge for some of that cheese we bought at the market last weekend." She looked at her sister. "Jane, have we still got some of that? I can't remember. Did we eat it?"

Emily let it all flow over her. If for some horrible reason, she was ever made to live with her aunt and her mum, Emily knew she'd go completely spare within five minutes. But visiting this soft chaos was like travelling to one of those amusement parks where everything was topsy-turvy but somehow it all seemed to work. Inexplicable.

After an investigation, they discovered that the cheese had not been consumed—good news—and when combined with the exciting discovery of fresh tomatoes, a new jar of spiced pear chutney, and half a baguette, which was sliced and toasted, lunch became quite a gourmet event.

Leanne decided on a nap after lunch, so it was only the two of them walking from the carpark an hour later, and along the pathway that cut through the manicured lawns. Emily pulled in a deep breath, held it for as long as she could, then exhaled. Very slowly. It was one of the first strategies that Kristen had insisted that Emily master before they moved on in their patient/therapist relationship.

Her mum gave an involuntary shiver.

"Cold?" Emily didn't wait for the answer and tucked her mum's arm into hers.

"No. Not really. Just…I don't know. Contemplative," she said quietly. Conversations could be quiet here. Her dad probably found it maddening. The quiet. He hadn't ever been quiet. Not exactly. The quiet always meant the inevitable arrival of the loud.

They stopped at the long, low wooden benches, artistic with their Jarrah wood slats and metalwork frames, which were arranged to mirror the arc of the gardens. At a chin tilt from Jane to indicate the second bench, they stopped and sank into the curve of the seat, facing a low cream brick wall, small brass rectangles spaced in rows regularly along the length.

Emily crossed her legs, her jeans riding up at her raised ankle so the red bootlaces flashed. An incongruous colour amongst the cream and green of their setting. The silence was substantial and both mother and daughter seemed to be waiting for the other to speak.

"Thanks for the new Ikebana," her mum said.

"That's okay." Right. Small talk it was.

"How's your new tenant?"

Emily's smile was involuntary, and she let it play about her lips. "She's great. She's…really great." A happy nod joined the smile. She may as well have leased space on a billboard announcing her massive crush.

Jane shifted so she could gaze at her daughter properly.

"That smile looks good on you, sweetie." She covered Emily's hand with hers, and they contemplated the slats of wood where their hands rested.

Then, her mother's voice was tentative. "You haven't been to visit here for a while, have you?"

Emily stared vacantly at the plaque on the middle row two metres in front of her. "No," she replied. "I think I was avoiding coming because, in a way, if I didn't come then I could pretend things never happened." It sounded stupid saying it out loud, and her mum gave a soft grunt, which sounded very much like she agreed with that assessment.

"So, why today?"

Emily turned square on. "You know what? I have no idea. I just decided on the spur of the moment. It felt right suddenly." She blinked at how stupendous that thought was. Her mum smiled and plucked up Emily's hand to hold it both of her own.

"That's a first."

"Gotta start somewhere," Emily said dryly and leaned her shoulder into her mother's solid shape. "Eleven years, Mum." The words were more a statement to fill the air than to acknowledge the passing of time.

"I know," her mum replied, adding to the air as well.

"Do you think Dad knew?" Emily stared diagonally at the crematorium wall of sealed and commemorated ashes.

"About what?"

"About his highs and lows. About his bipolar. About how his mind locked him away from the outside world." She swallowed heavily.

Her mum inhaled, the movement jostling Emily's head. It was a collecting-thoughts kind of breath. "We've talked about this, sweetie. I don't think he did. I've always wondered but I haven't done nearly as much reading about it as you have, but I do know that many people with undiagnosed bipolar just ride the waves until they can't anymore."

"Yeah." She unglued herself from the comfort of her mother's side. "I've forgiven him for all the turbulence he put us through. I've taken ages to find that forgiveness even though I still go to therapy and I still do my crazy planning thing. But I do forgive him, mostly because of how he struggled to know."

Her mum squeezed the hand she hadn't relinquished. "I'm glad, sweetie. For that aspect of his life, I have, too." She carefully lifted her other hand and cupped Emily's cheek. "I haven't forgiven him for deciding to die in a place where he knew you'd find him."

Muscles in Emily's jaw jumped around as the images of that day flashed before her. The garage. The car. Turning on the light switch and then denial and realisation co-existing in her throat until the scream forced them out. "He didn't kill himself with the intention of me finding him. I'm sure of it. I just don't think it occurred to him." That particular trauma was one that she and Kristen would be working on for years to come.

"Yes. I wish that I'd noticed—"

"Don't. You can't do this each time, Mum. No one was really aware, not even Dad. The years of Swiss cheese-like foundations, the upheavals, then the suicide. You can't keep analysing it or thinking that somehow you could have changed his plans."

"You need to start listening to your own advice, honey," her mum said quietly. "Yes, you have a coping mechanism, which is valid. But perhaps it's time to start chipping away at it. Just a little bit."

Emily pulled her lips sideways, then bit the inside of her cheek as it dragged across her teeth. "I think I might be."

"Really? Is it the tenant?" Suddenly her mum was a bottle of champagne, all fizzed up with excitement.

"Skye. Her name's Skye." The involuntary smile was back, which earned her a raised eyebrow. "I'm doing a few spontaneous things, and Skye has been a part of those things."

"Hmm." The sound was quintessentially her mother. A thoughtful tone, usually followed by a word of approval. "Good." There it was.

"I think so," Emily agreed.

"Bec wasn't the one for you," her mother elaborated. "She always came across like one of those disco balls, like her focus changed according to where the light was shining."

Emily looked at her mum. "Really?"

"Oh, yes. You were the one in the relationship that kept it going. Kept it on track. And I'm pretty sure that you weren't at the 'I love you' stage, even after more than a year. Even with a plan."

"Huh." It was always interesting when people looked into the fishbowl of your life, then shared their opinions, because generally their thoughts never matched the reality or were so brutally truthful that it was like walking naked down Graham Street. And Emily felt so very naked after her mum's collection of sentences.

"Well," she began, simply to gain some time and traction. "You're on the money there, Mum." Absolutely no need to share cheating, and dining tables, and the lack of 'I love you' statements. No need at all.

They looked at the plaques on the wall.

"Did you love Dad despite how much chaos he caused?"

"Oh, sweetheart. That's such a complicated question. Yes, I did. I loved him and held him and supported him while we sailed together over enormous waves in tempestuous seas," her mum said, her voice thin with emotion. "I loved him when we could calmly contemplate the horizon. That was the hardest part because the horizon always became lost when the waves rode too high. I loved him even when he went so far away that I couldn't see him any more. He always came back." She paused. "Until he didn't." She shook her head. "He can hear me saying this, you know."

Emily nodded. "I know."

"I couldn't stand not seeing the horizon. I loved him, but, oh gosh, I hated that." Another head shake. "This is why your planning fixation is so very easy to understand. You need your horizon."

"What about your horizon?"

"Oh, sweetie, I have my horizon. It's right here. I just moved it, that's all. I realised after—no, probably before, Gareth died, that it was much too hard to keep the horizon out in front of me. Always aiming for it. But having it here," she pressed her hand flat to her chest, "means that I can constantly change my horizon line. Change my plan."

Emily gave a slight shudder, and her mum threw her head back and laughed, the sound rolling away over the manicured grass. "I'm telling you, you'll move your horizon line one day. Or you'll make your plan nice and fuzzy so it's not difficult to change it on your way to that imaginary line."

Emily looked at her sceptically.

"You'll get there, but what you do now is perfectly fine as well." Her mother raised her eyebrow. "But, you could blur your road a little when you're ready."

They stayed for a while longer, not saying much more. Sitting together in the ornamental gardens, and having an internal monologue with her father was more than enough. Emily didn't have a great deal to say to him. She'd said most of her words to him via Kristen, and in the letter she wrote when she was twenty-six. A letter she'd read aloud, sobbing violently through all four pages of tightly squeezed handwriting, and then burnt in the backyard.

Later, as she was sliding into her car, she paused and sent a quick text to Skye.

Hey there. How did you go? Em xx

She thought about adding something along the lines of 'Hope your muscles aren't too sore' or 'I bet you're looking forward to a hot shower' but figured that could be misconstrued. Or not.

There was no immediate reply, and Emily checked the clock on her screen. The race had finished at two o'clock, an hour and a half ago. With a shrug and the assumption that Skye and Seb were out celebrating somewhere, she started the car and prepared for another sixty minute battle with the returning Sunday drivers on the highway.

***

There is a strange sensation that people have described when they're about to be involved in an awful event. They talk about time slowing down and that they leave their body to watch in fascination as the awful event plays out, totally objectively, without a need to create an emotional attachment to it. Then with a whoosh, the person is vacuumed back into their body and time catches up to reality and the awful event is real and subjective, and there are so many emotions, and noise, and action.

Skye was well-placed. She knew it, without knowing that fact at all because the course was individualised and random. But she *felt* it. The next tag was located at an office building on the second floor, which meant leaping off her bike just outside the foyer, racing across the open space, galloping up two flights of stairs because who was going to wait for an elevator? Then capturing the QR image outside suite three and galloping back downstairs again.

She rocketed out from the laneway, and hopped the bike, in a well-practised move, up onto the footpath, and then up the two steps to the forecourt. The grey concrete pavers were damp. Someone had watered large Banksia shrubs in their enormous squat pots near the entrance, so she dropped her bike near the closest one, danced over the more voluminous puddles, and bolted into the building. Making quick work of the stairs, she crashed through the fire door, located suite three, aimed her phone at the symbol, making sure to keep her hand steady—they'd been warned that adrenalin-blurred photos were invalid—then pumped her legs as she reversed her course back to her bike.

The puddles were camouflaged from the opposite direction. Absolutely flat with zero reflection, so that they became a chameleon in the urban landscape.

The edge of Skye's sneaker sliced through the puddle's surface, time slowed down, and Skye left her body to watch in objective fascination as her torso languidly rotated, and her feet escaped very deliberately from under her. She watched with emotional detachment as the point of her left shoulder connected quietly, firmly, with the concrete paver, and her head rolled on her neck so that the back of the helmet clattered, the sound distant, into the remaining water, splashing it about like a kindergartener. Then whoosh. The vacuum grabbed hold and pulled her back into noise and action and pain.

Skye screamed, her right hand instantly grabbing her shoulder, as she writhed on the concrete in the forecourt. Bile rose in her throat and she quickly turned her head to vomit onto the ground. Blinding pain—the worst she'd ever known—filled her head with white noise. Yet, the only logical thought she had, before she succumbed to irrational fear, was that her race was finished and that, again, putting all her eggs in one basket had resulted in failure. Tears of pain, of fear, of defeat, tracked down her temples as she howled into the square of blue sky created by the office tower fingers reaching towards the heavens.

It was sudden but not sudden, like time was fluid, when a face filled her vision, speaking earnestly, the words tumbled about in her rinse cycle of agony.

"—with *Ambulance Victoria*. Can you tell me your name, please?"

Skye swallowed the salty taste in her mouth. "Skye Reynolds," she gasped. "I'm in a bike race and I think I've dislocated my shoulder and I know what that's like because I played rugby at Uni and I've seen it happen and…" she trailed off, unable to supply further details but the opportunity to ramble was like verbal paracetamol. Somehow it took the edge off.

The head, the blurry outline now sharp, belonged to a clean-shaven man about Skye's age, his face relaxed and focused; one of those calmly competent people who manage these situations on a daily basis.

"My name's Jimmy, Skye. I'm going to do a few things here, but meanwhile, are you allergic to any medications?"

Skye licked her lips again. They seemed dry but she wasn't sure because they'd gone numb. "No," she panted.

"Great. Can you suck on this? It's pain relief." He inserted what could only be described as a plastic green whistle into her mouth, eased her right hand away from her shoulder, and helped her hold the device at her lips. "It'll kick in soon. Probably in the next minute or so."

Magic words. Skye inhaled like she was sucking a thick shake through a needle because the opportunity to dull the pain became all-consuming. Jimmy's head disappeared and another took his place. Keenan, the race organiser, his blue eyes wide with concern peered over her prone form.

"Skye! I'm so sorry. Jesus. I saw the whole thing through your helmet cam. I couldn't do anything from our base, except ring the ambos." The skin on his forehead concertinaed into his eyebrows.

Skye pulled the whistle away a little. The medication was working, because it felt like her shoulder wasn't actually being ripped from her body now. More like a pack of wild horses had run her over. Much better.

"That's…" she pulled in another lungful of the inhalant. "That's good. Thank you."

"Can I do anything? I can look after your bike and helmet if you like. Maybe I could hand them off to your teammate, Seb. No, I know. I'll stick them in the van and drop them around to your house. Your address is on the entry form." He was babbling in that manner people have at accidents or emergencies; offering all the solutions as one giant buffet, hoping you'll pick something.

"Home. Please," Skye panted. Giving the bike and helmet to Seb was pointless. He didn't have a car. Oh, shit. Seb.

"Right. Gotcha. Okay. So," he looked up, and Skye stared at the underside of his chin. "Is her helmet staying on or are you taking it off?" This was clearly aimed at Jimmy or the shadowy figure that Skye assumed was Jimmy's colleague.

The answer was immediate. Soft hands unclipped the strap and Skye felt the helmet being slid away, as fingers adjusted their support on her neck and cradled the back of her head. It was tempting to drift off to sleep, because she felt light, like out-of-body light. Maybe she was. Maybe the Earth's gravity was broken. Was it broken? She was. So broken. Like gravity. Maybe they'd call it grav now. Not gravity. Just grav. Because it was broken. The thought made her giggle.

"Okay. The Penthrox is working well, then." Jimmy was back.

"Heeyyyy, Jimmy," Skye slurred.

"Hey there, Skye. We're going to get you to the hospital, okay? Looks like you were right with your dislocated shoulder assessment. Good catch. But we'll get a doctor to check that, okay?"

Skye's mouth and lips didn't seem to be working properly so she couldn't confirm if she'd effectively delivered a smile in response to Jimmy's words. But the thought was there.

Then, in a Penthrox-induced haze, Skye found herself strapped onto an ambulance gurney, acknowledging her backpack and phone when they were held up by Jimmy's colleague—Shane—for her to identify, and after another mercurial stretch of time, Skye was wheeled into a curtained-off bay in Accident and Emergency.

"You're going to need another x-ray now to ensure your shoulder is in the correct position. Donna will take you to Radiology, and I'll see you when you return." Doctor Lowenstein, the Accident and Emergency doctor spoke rapidly, as if a frantic PA was yelling into an invisible Bluetooth telling her to get a move on. And yet, the time she'd taken with Skye before and after each step in the procedure indicated how truly professional she was.

The procedure—Skye's shoulder gave a painful twinge at the memory of an hour ago—had consisted of three stages; none of which Skye recalled very clearly. In the throes of agony as the painkiller wore off, she was bundled into x-ray, then straight back to the curtained triage bay, where Doctor Lowenstein had found her a few minutes later with the news that Skye had suffered a dislocated shoulder, but wasn't it good news about not having any fractures? Skye had made an inarticulate noise and delivered a sort of sick smile. Nothing about this whole situation was good news.

Then, she'd started to shiver uncontrollably, so after Doctor Lowenstein muttered something about "shock" and "vagal response" and "Are you doing a reduction?", the nurse dosed Skye with something heavy-duty but apparently short-lived, and the next thing she knew, the doctor and another nurse were rotating her arm and gently manipulating her shoulder back into its joint. It seemed to take only a minute, and a weird, probably drug-induced, thought zipped through Skye's mind that perhaps she'd somehow been short-changed. Surely the extreme level of pain and the hour or more of suffering shouldn't be fixed in just a single minute. But the instant relief was literally angels-singing-from-on-high. It was beautiful. As the pain haze dissolved, Skye became more aware of her surroundings, like how wet and sweaty and gross she was.

As she sat in the wheelchair being driven efficiently by Donna through people-shaped slalom poles towards the x-ray department, Skye inspected the cuts and scrapes on her right hand, the streaks of dirt up her arm. She couldn't see what her left arm looked like. It was tucked inside an industrial-strength sling, which had more velcro tabs on it than a pair of kid's shoes.

Her shoulder received a gold star via another clear x-ray and then Doctor Lowenstein was suddenly handing a prescription for painkillers to Skye, who was perched on the bed, the thin cotton fitted sheet doing nothing to stop the cold from the vinyl seeping into her damp lycra shorts. The doctor's eyebrows were raised as if she'd asked a question.

"What? I'm sorry," Skye said, trying to shake the clouds of despair that were gathering in the corners of her mind.

"You'll need to take these three times a day. You're going to be in a lot of pain still, and your everyday movements will be severely restricted for at least five days. You're very fortunate that you're so fit, otherwise the recovery could have taken longer. As it is, I expect it will take a month for you to be back to full capacity."

Skye couldn't breathe. Oh no. Her business. Her little company. Doctor Lowenstein wasn't finished. "You're going to have swelling, bruising, and weakness in your arm for a while. Plus that knock on your head was quite an impact. You'll have a headache for another day or so. Thank goodness for helmets, hey?" She tucked her hands into the pockets of her dark blue scrub pants like she had all the time in the world. "So, let Donna know who to call to take you home. And you'll need someone at home with you to help for a while, okay?"

Skye assessed the doctor's expression and knew that the very nice medical professional in front of her was not going to be thrilled at Skye's response.

"I don't need help. I'm fine. And there isn't anyone to call. I'll just take a taxi."

Doctor Lowenstein waited until Skye's gaze eventually stopped meandering around the room and met hers. No, not thrilled at all. "I do advise that you ask for assistance from someone. The shoulder is still unstable, and that sling is on for another two days, maybe three. You're going to need help showering and clothing yourself at the very least."

That did it. Skye grabbed the edge of the bed and pulled herself upright; a little wobbly with one arm incapacitated, but still with enough authority that she could pass as someone who actually didn't need assistance, thanks very much. She'd never received help in her life. Not from the people who mattered, anyway, so she sure wasn't going to ask for help now. It was hard enough when it was offered voluntarily.

"It's all good. My neighbour is available if I need a hand," she said, reaching for her little backpack on the seat. That was an awesome lie. Asking Emily to help her shower was a scenario she couldn't ever imagine.

Doctor Lowenstein delivered a sigh, which seemed well-practised. "Okay, well, as I said, Donna will take you out in the wheelchair—" she delivered a quick, intense look. "Hospital policy, and there's a taxi rank just to the side of the front entrance."

A heartfelt thank you, another efficient wheelchair adventure with Donna, and having the prescription filled at the in-hospital chemist counter, meant that in no time Skye was holding herself like a piece of glass in the back of a taxi. And gasping silently at the everything and the all and the entirety.

Chapter Fifteen

Emily carefully wiped down the expensive maple chopping board, which was already clean, but the need to continue the repetitive motion far outweighed the need to slide the board into its holder on the craft table. The conversation with her mother earlier in the day had been, quite frankly, enlightening. It wasn't new information, although Bec's resemblance to a disco ball was sudden. For years, they'd talked and talked about their combined trauma, but today had felt condensed. Succinct. Like she'd finally finished the literature review, collated all her notes, and now the final essay was due. It felt like she could breathe a little inside the restrictions she placed around herself. Kristen would be delirious with joy when Emily had her appointment next week.

Her hand stilled. It was five o'clock in the afternoon, and she'd been home half an hour already, still without a word from Skye. The first thing she'd done after she'd dropped her bag inside was fire off another text, asking how the race had gone. Not hearing from Skye was strange, because *Rush* was a major event.

Ensuring all the tools and equipment were correctly replaced, Emily wandered into the lounge, and stopped. Something felt wrong. She could sense it, which sounded like she'd spent far too long today with her mum and Aunty Leanne. But that's what it was. A sense.

***

Skye dropped her backpack, phone, chemist bag on the floor just inside the front door, too tired and sore to care. Opening the front door had been challenging and the last dose of painkillers was wearing off, so the bone-deep ache in her shoulder and literally everywhere in her body had started up again and even Seb's news shouted through the phone on her journey home, couldn't temper her distress.

"Skye! I've left you a thousand messages. Where have you been?" His voice had sounded shrill with concern and, strangely, excitement when she'd phoned him from the taxi.

"I stacked it at tag number thirty, and they chucked me into an ambulance. I ended up with a bit of dinged shoulder, but nothing serious, and a headache. All good. It sucks that I didn't get to finish, but how did you go?" No need to elaborate on what a 'bit of a dinged shoulder' actually entailed.

"I came first!" he yelled, and Skye moved the phone away from her ear in reaction to the volume.

"What?"

"I won the whole bloody thing, Skye. I won it!" The decibels were set at maximum, and the taxi driver had smiled into his mirror.

"Oh my God, Seb. That's so incredible. I'm…"

Suddenly, tears readied themselves in her eyes. He'd won *Rush*. He'd won the twenty-five-thousand dollars. *Quick Cargo* had locked in the *Gower's* contract.

"Skye? You there?"

"Yeah. Yeah, mate." She swallowed heavily. "I'm so happy for you. You must have flown through the city. What was your finishing time? Did you get all sixty tags?" Skye shifted uncomfortably as the taxi turned the corner, and she stifled the soft gasp of pain.

Seb's voice filled the car's interior. "I absolutely smashed it. Got all sixty, and in eighty minutes. Nearly got done when Yves from *Melbourne Couriers*—God, their name is boring—came for tag forty-five, which was my last one and his third last one. But I did that back tyre kick that's a little dirty but totally legal and besides, he was lining up to block me. But yay, cargo bikes, for the win, right?"

Skye grunted, which Seb seemed to interpret as a short laugh because his laugh rolled out of the speaker.

"Seb, I'm so proud of you. Go celebrate. Phone me tomorrow, because right now I need a shower as I'm still in my race gear and I'm feeling a bit like a wet tissue on the road." She made sure to inject an upbeat note in her voice because knowing the true nature of his boss's busted shoulder would be the last thing Seb needed to hear. Not when he was on such a high.

"No worries, Skye. Take care. I'll talk to you tomorrow." Then, just as she dropped her hand to end the call, she heard, "*Quick Cargo* rules. Yeah!" She laughed and then grimaced as the movement sent a spasm through her joint and down her arm.

"Shit," she whispered, and the tears fell over the edge, softly tracking down her cheeks.

It didn't take a genius to work out that some of the twenty-five thousand dollars was going to be eaten up in having to employ a temporary courier to replace her for the next month. Skye walked gingerly down the driveway and contemplated the injustice of that scenario. The tug of guilt was fierce, knowing that Seb had succeeded for their company, for himself, and there she was, sucking up the winnings because she hadn't been watching where she was going. A quick sob punched through her chest. Then another one when she saw her bike propped up against the rosemary hedge under her window, her battered helmet dangling from the handlebars.

She realised how cold she was, standing there in the middle of her studio. Thank God they'd taken off her bra at the hospital. Cut off, actually. It was only a cheap sports bra, and the idea of manoeuvring it over her shoulder and head had sounded excruciating, even without trying. Therefore, Donna, the efficient wheelchair driver became a scissor-wielding nurse. Now her shirt hung over her injured arm, her right arm through its correct hole. She'd started shivering in the taxi and desperately needed a hot shower, then to curl up and cry for a really long time.

"Oh, God," she whispered into the space. Another sob broke away as her body relived the feeling of falling, the hitting, the crashing of bone and concrete. Her fingers trembled as she attempted to curl them under the waist of her cycle shorts and drag them, one-handed, down her thighs. She didn't get very far, because the fabric rolled in that way that slightly damp clothing always does, and Skye jerked her hand in frustration. Her shaking body gave way and she sank much too quickly into the couch, the harsh change in direction jolting every nerve ending, and she howled, the soul-wrenching sobs spearing straight into the beautiful wooden floorboards.

***

"That's it. I'm going to check," Emily muttered, and before she could talk herself out of it, she pulled on a jacket, and marched down the driveway in the near-dark to the studio, coming to an abrupt halt when she confronted Skye's bike outside. Despite looking like it was missing most of the necessary functioning parts, she knew that the bike was worth a lot of money. And Skye would not leave it cuddled up to a hedge. The back of the helmet was scraped and broken, and prickles of anxiety scratched at her skin, so she stepped up to the door.

The howl, raw with sadness and pain, arrested her quick knock. Holding her breath, she listened, leaning closer in case she'd imagined the sound, which of course she hadn't. It had come from inside the studio and the person in pain was Skye. The decision was simple.

Emily tried the handle, and when it gave way, she pushed inside, conscious of walking on the cracked ice of emotional fragility that hung in the air.

"Skye?" she said tentatively,

Rhythmic sobs wracked Skye's body, and Emily rushed to the couch, dropping to her knees in front of the distraught woman.

"Skye! What happened?" The lopsided T-shirt and the bulge of the sling instantly set off alarm bells, so Emily cupped Skye's cheek. "Skye, sweetie. Please tell me what happened."

The soft touch brought Skye's eyes up. "I slipped," she hiccoughed, "during," another hiccough, "the race." Fresh tears fell at the admission.

"Oh, hon. Where are you hurt?" Emily left her hand on Skye's cheek but raked her eyes across as much of Skye as she could see. It looked like she was protecting her shoulder the most.

Skye breathed deeply in an attempt to stop the crying. "I dislocated my shoulder. It's back in and everything, but it's in this sling for a couple of days and then I've got exercises and stuff. But I can't go to work, Em." Her face crumpled, and Emily scooted forward so she could cradle Skye's face with both hands. The fact that Skye had shortened her name and how good it had sounded whizzed through her brain. But that was for later. A dislocated shoulder? That was for now.

Then her fingers registered the chill of Skye's skin. "Jesus, Skye. You're freezing. I don't know much about cycling injuries, but I do know that a dislocated shoulder means you can't move that arm properly." She stood and looked around. "Come up to the house. You can have a shower there because the studio shower is really small. You'll bump yourself."

Skye's gaze hadn't followed Emily's movement, and she spoke to the floor. "It's okay. You don't need to offer any help."

Emily growled which surprised both of them, and Skye lifted her head.

"It wasn't a suggestion," Emily stated. "Have you got a bag that you can put some clothes into? Toiletries? You're staying with me for a few days, so I actually can help."

"No." Skye eased herself off the couch and straightened, her face set, her breath whistling through clenched teeth.

If they were going to compete in the Obstinate Olympics, Emily was determined to win.

"Skye! You're hurt. You need—" She glared and pointed her finger. "You need someone to help you for a few days. Just accept it, for heaven's sakes!"

The intense eye contact lasted for a long moment, and it looked like Skye was having an entire conversation with herself. Finally, she nodded briefly, a soft sigh finishing off the gesture.

"Okay." She looked at Emily in resignation. "Thank you."

"Of course," Emily said briskly. "Right. Can you handle being in those," she indicated to the cycle pants and shirt, "for a little bit longer?"

A little smile flickered on Skye's lips. "Sure. I've been gross all afternoon. What's another ten minutes or so?"

With strict instructions for Skye not to move, and to only answer questions about locations of a bag, then clothes—

"Oh gees, Em. I'm not fussed about the colour of my undies. More like the fact that you're actually in my underwear drawer."

With toiletries collected as well, Emily held Skye's hand as they walked up the driveway and into the house.

Emily dropped the bag in her bedroom.

"You're sleeping here." Her statement left no room for argument, but Skye attempted one, anyway.

"But this is your bedroom."

"Yes. You need a larger bed. You're taller, broader and your shoulder can't be bumped. The little bed in the spare room will just be a horizontal hazard for you."

Skye smiled briefly. "Where are you sleeping then?"

"In the horizontal hazard."

Skye laughed, then hissed. "Oh, shit that hurts." Her eyes dulled with the pain.

"Come on. You need a shower, more painkillers I imagine, and sleep." Emily tipped her head. "And food. When did you last eat?"

"Before the race."

"Which was hours ago." Emily bustled to the linen cupboard, pulled out a couple of towels, then zipped open Skye's bag and found a pair of soft track pants and a heavy cotton t-shirt that looked misshapen and loose from years of love. She gestured with her chin for Skye to follow. "It's this way."

In the bathroom, Emily raised an eyebrow as Skye's good hand hesitated at the top of her bike shorts.

"I…uh…"

Emily's heart flipped over. She understood the need for independence, and how very difficult this situation would be for someone as proud as Skye.

"I won't look," she said.

"It's okay."

Emily disagreed. At any other time, it would be more than okay to stare at Skye's body, let her eyes languidly trace the muscles and lines in that athletic form. But right now? Not okay. She knelt and pulled off the sneakers and socks, then wriggled the shorts down, keeping her eyes averted, all the while acutely aware of how her fingers grazed Skye's legs. Then she stood to angle the shirt over Skye's head, then manoeuvred it off her arm. Never mind Skye's skin; Emily's was crackling like fire. Finally, she swung her gaze, which had been firmly aimed at the tiles, back to Skye.

"You'll need to take the sling off, so you can de-gross that arm, too." They held eye contact, as the sling was detached. Then, with a practised move that emphasised the muscles in her right arm and neck, Skye reached up, yanked out the elastic tie in her ponytail, and her blonde hair fell, hanging damp and limp about her shoulders.

"Thanks," Skye said.

"Okay, well," Emily was back to talking to the wall because she'd caught a glance of that torso; the expanse of skin, the lines, the small breasts, topped with dark pink nipples, and gosh, those tiles were pretty. "Yell out if you need me. Be careful with that arm."

With that, she scurried out of the bathroom, closing the door behind her, and made her way to the kitchen to pop two slices of bread into the toaster. Vegemite toast was probably all that Skye could cope with, and two squares of wheat, salt and yeast sounded fabulously medicinal. She buttered the warm bread when it leapt from its slots and analysed her strongest impulse. The need to embrace Skye, hold her against her chest, smooth circles into her back, kiss the top of her head, was overwhelming. It had certainly been comforting when Skye had done those very things when Emily fell apart after the curtain attacked her, then unloaded all sorts of unnecessary personal details. She closed her eyes briefly, rolling her head to the side, then round in a semicircle.

"Thanks for doing this," the soft voice floated into her ear. Emily turned and absorbed the fatigued, slightly defeated yet still proud, adorable version of Skye, bundled into warm clothing, albeit with the shirt askew—asking for help might have been an option there—and swaying slightly next to the kitchen bench. That overwhelming impulse to protect, to hold, nearly engulfed her. She reached for Skye's hand, the one outside the shirt, and squeezed.

"Of course. You were there for me. Although, I'm not sure the two equate."

Skye lifted the corner of her mouth, like her lips were beyond exhausted and had given up entirely. Emily guided her to the stool. "So, Vegemite toast if you want."

"Thanks," Skye said, taking a small bite off each corner, like a child. The adorable factor drifted into delightful, which meant that sexy was just around the corner. Uh oh. "I need to phone Seb. Let him know that I'm off work." Her words were losing their ends, and Emily calculated that Skye probably had another ten minutes of vertical left in her before the medication completely kicked in.

"I can call him if you don't mind me using your phone. What should I tell him?"

The relief was palpable. "That would be good. The passcode's one, two, three, four."

"Really?" Emily let the absurdity of that slide.

"Yeah. Uh…tell him I dislocated my shoulder. I haven't told him that yet. Tell him just to do what he can and that we'll have to reject some jobs. It's just how it goes." Then tears filled her eyes. "He won, you know." Her throat worked, swallowing the tears that looked close to falling.

"That's wonderful!" She reached across to hold Skye's cheek. "And I get how bittersweet that is for you." Skye let out a shaky breath and leaned into Emily's hand.

"Yeah." She looked like she'd happily fall asleep against Emily's palm.

"Come on. Bed." Emily commandeered Skye's hand and led her down to the bedroom, settling her into the bed under a blanket. "The quilt is too heavy to fling off if you need the toilet in the night so a blanket it is," she explained. Then, as she brushed Skye's hair from her forehead, their eyes connected for a while, then Skye's eyelids fluttered, and sleep pulled her under.

Emily stayed for another moment, then wandered back into the kitchen with Skye's phone and its ridiculous passcode, rang a dismayed Seb who accepted Emily's congratulations momentarily, then promised to drop by tomorrow afternoon to check in.

Another call, this time from her phone, was made to Jas because she needed to know that Emily wouldn't be in tomorrow, as she'd be caring for Skye. Jas didn't even pause.

"Absolutely, boss. She'll need a couple of days of looking after. It's good that you're there." And despite the fact that Jas seemed to exist on Earth simply to create innuendo and ribald commentary, *not* mentioning that Emily would see a lot more of Skye than she'd ever expected to was testament to Jas's innate understanding of moments. And in this moment, Jas got it.

It really was good that Emily was there.

Chapter Sixteen

Skye decided that if she didn't move, not even to blink, then nothing would hurt. But it did. A lot. She conducted an inventory of the various locations in her body where pain was having a frat party. Left shoulder. That was a given. There was a throbbing conga line all the way to her fingertips. The same pain party had spilled out across her shoulder blade, taking the sound system with it, danced up her neck and settled in her head. Drop the bass, indeed.

"Hey." A soft voice drifted into her ear, accompanied by a touch on her forehead, brushing back strands of hair. It was deliciously tempting to fake sleep, just so those touches would continue. But the desire to see won out.

Emily's face swam into focus, and those dark eyes scanned across Skye's hair, face, neck, and then returned.

"Hi," Skye croaked, then cleared her throat to try again. "Hi." She blinked quickly. "So…ow."

Emily giggled, and sat on the edge of the bed, her thigh snuggled into Skye's. She indicated to her leg. "Is this okay? Am I too close?"

An easy question to answer. "No. You're fine. Thank you for letting me sleep here last night. And use your bathroom. And—"

"And nothing. There was absolutely no way you would have been able to deal with everything last night." Emily frowned. "You needed help and so I helped."

Skye gazed up at Emily's serious expression, a tiny line appearing between her eyebrows, as if to emphasise just how important her words were. It was adorable.

"Well, thank you again. I do need to get out of bed, though." She made a movement, and Emily leapt up.

"You don't seriously think that you're going to work?" Emily's hands had parked themselves on her slim hips.

Skye eased herself to a sitting position, her left arm braced against her chest. She gestured vaguely at the ensuite with her chin. "Not unless I'm conducting deliveries from the bathroom." She grinned. "I need to pee."

"Oh," Emily said, then blushed. "Of course. I'll be in the kitchen. Any requests for breakfast?"

Skye stood gingerly, then grunted in surprise as the world decided to stay in one place. How nice. "No, I'm easy. Whatever takes your fancy," she answered. Emily's eyes briefly flashed darker, and Skye suddenly wished that she were in Emily's bedroom for a completely different reason, particularly if there were fancies being taken.

Later, after painkillers had been washed down with a strawberry and yoghurt smoothie, Skye leaned back into the couch with a cold pack tucked under the strap of the sling. Emily sat beside her, pouring over the dos and don'ts in the 'So You've Dislocated Your Shoulder; What Next?' pamphlet the nurse had slid into Skye's backpack. What next indeed.

"You're allowed to sleep without a sling tonight." Emily tapped the paper, and Skye chuckled.

"There's no quiz, Em. You don't have to memorise it."

Emily rolled her finger into her thumb, then flicked it against Skye's leg. "I'm helping." A smile played about her lips, and Skye breathed carefully as her gaze took in the soft jeans, slippers, fuzzy jumper, and that disorganised hair. Dislocated shoulders sucked.

"Yes. You are."

The next few hours continued in very much the same manner. Skye rested, iced her shoulder some more, and listened with increasing amounts of affection as Emily pointed out the flow chart of rehabilitation that started with "gentle exercises not outside the shoulder's range of motion".

"Good to know," Skye agreed.

"You're being flippant."

"You don't know me that well," Skye laughed, then the pause after that statement was long enough that the words "not yet" could have been added by either one of them.

Emily blushed. "No, I don't. Okay. I'm going to be in my craft room if you need anything."

Skye must have slept, because she woke to find her legs stretched out along the couch, and a pillow under her head. Emily was sitting cross-legged on the chair opposite, tapping away at her laptop.

"Hey. I dozed off," Skye said, then delivered a self-deprecating laugh. "Obviously." She lifted her upper body and dropped her feet to the floor, then stretched awkwardly, trying not to aggravate anything, but of course, it did. "Oh. Ow."

Emily snapped the laptop closed and made to move towards her.

"No," Skye said. "It's nothing." The sheer frustration of it all was threatening to consume her.

"It's not nothing," Emily insisted. "You're injured."

Frustration won. "You've done enough, Em. Stop helping." Her voice was strained.

"Stop pushing back on my wanting to help," Emily snapped. The tension stretched.

"You're fussing over me," Skye said quietly.

"I'm looking after you, Skye. That's all. I care about you."

"Well, you can stop."

"No."

Skye glared, tightening her hands into fists on her thighs. "Yes!"

Standing abruptly, Emily marched over to the couch and sat next to Skye. Then she held Skye's hand. Well, the fist that was Skye's hand, and without Skye having any say in it, her fingers unclenched and they slid into Emily's palm.

"Skye, you're injured and you need help, so I'm helping. Why are you so bloody stubborn?"

It was hard to be angry at someone as gorgeous as Emily, who was as lovely as Emily, who was simply Emily. Skye slumped back into the couch.

"I'm not used to it," she said. "People helping."

"Have you ever tried asking for help?" When Skye turned her head, Emily's eyes shone with mischief.

"Fine," Skye grumped. She turned away and stared blankly ahead, while Emily held her hand.

After a minute, Skye asked, "Why did you kiss me?" Emily squeezed her hand, then released it, which was a shame, Skye thought. But this conversation probably needed some space. She tipped her head and watched as Emily's face danced through a choreography of emotions.

"Well, it wasn't really a kiss—"

"Emily."

Emily tucked her lips into each other, flicked her eyes about for a second, then looked at Skye. "I'm attracted to you." Then she breathed out, like the words had gone on a journey without their air tanks, and she'd had to chase after them.

This time, Skye collected Emily's hand and brushed her thumb over the skin. "I'm glad you said that. I'd wondered."

"You had?"

"Well, more like hoped."

"Really?" Emily said, her confusion evident.

"Yeah. Because it means that my attraction isn't all lopsided," she gestured slightly with her sling, "like the rest of me." She brought Emily's hand to her lips and gently kissed a knuckle. "I'm attracted to you, too."

It was like watching the slow-motion artistry in the *Matrix*. The frisson of panic that rolled through Emily's eyes was breathtaking, and Skye tightened her grip before Emily could yank her hand away.

"Hey," Skye said softly. "Both of us admitting an attraction doesn't mean any more than what it is." She caught Emily's gaze. "Seriously. We can have an almost kiss, declare an attraction, I can kiss your knuckle, and," she paused, "and that's all, if we want." The part of Skye that liked to bungee-jump into situations suddenly asked all the questions, like *Do you want more?* and *Gosh, could we try for a relationship based on those tiny moments?* and *Would you mind if I tasted your skin?* She sent that part of herself back to its room.

Emily nodded slowly. She hadn't let go of Skye's hand, which was wonderful, because it felt warm and oh so right. "Okay." Then, to Skye's delight, she brought their joined hands to her lips, and kissed Skye's knuckle. "There. You're not lopsided anymore."

Their mutual grin was wide, open, and just a tiny bit goofy. And it was just as well that a notification pinged on Skye's phone, because she would have sat there for another minute, or five-hundred, staring into Emily's lovely face.

Can't get to yours. Want a video chat?

Skye leaned her phone against her water bottle on the table, and sent through the request, as Emily stood and made her way into the kitchen.

Seb's face filled the screen, then he pulled back and grinned.

"Hey, Skye. How're you doing, mate?"

Skye eased back into the couch. "Stuffed shoulder. Dislocated, but you know that. How was today?"

"Yeah. Good. I had to turn down three new deliveries." He hissed a "Sorry" through bared teeth.

"It's fine. You're in charge, mate, so do what you can do. You've got all the *Gowers* orders now, so I did a phone around to the other companies earlier today, in the odd moments I was awake, to see if they've got a casual who wants some extra work."

"Oh, yeah? Any luck?"

"Marta at *Melbourne Couriers*—" she held up a palm. "I know you're not a fan but she's got Hayley—a Uni student—who's busting for extra work, and Marta said she's happy for Hayley to work with us for a month."

Seb delivered a non-committal shrug. "Sounds good. God, I can't believe you've done your shoulder."

"And on the same day you won *Rush*," Skye said, tossing the hand that was not in the sling. "I hope you're still riding high on that. Pun completely intended."

They shared a grin.

"I won't let you down, you know," Seb said seriously.

Skye inclined her head slightly. "I know that. You're incredibly reliable. In the whole year we've been operating, you've never been late for a job. And you've always delivered that job on time, as well. I trust you."

It was like she'd inflated his chest with helium. "You know? Not only did I win *Rush*, I'm gonna win the weirdest delivery this month." He grinned widely.

"Why?"

"Cat box delivery today," he said.

"So? We've delivered pets before."

"Yeah, nah. No cat. Just the cat box."

Skye laughed. "That is a weird one, although you still win with January's."

Laughter poured out of the phone. "Yep. A breast pump takes the prize."

A snort of laughter joined in from the kitchen, and Skye looked over to find Emily's eyes sparkling over her hand as it covered her mouth.

"You at Emily's?" Seb's voice suddenly became very innocent.

"Yes. Yes, I am. She's helping…" It was interesting, in the way that a train wreck is interesting, how Skye's imagination created all types of ways that Emily could be helping, and that Seb knew Skye well enough to dissolve into a coughing fit that sounded too much like glee.

"So, I'm hanging up now," she growled, and Seb's smile couldn't be wider.

"Take care, boss. Get well soon." Then he leaned his face closer to the screen and shouted, "Bye, Emily. Look after her!"

Skye poked the red hang-up button to silence his chuckle. Then she wandered into the kitchen to where Emily was stirring a saucepan of something that smelled like Thai red curry. Skye's mouth watered.

"You don't have to cook for two. I can go back to the studio and —"

"Shut up, and taste this," Emily said witheringly, a small smile playing at her lips, then held the wooden spoon out, one hand cupped underneath. Skye grasped the handle, covering Emily's fingers, expecting her to release the spoon into Skye's hand. But she didn't, and with wide eyes, Skye followed the spoon's slow journey to her lips, their hands joined. She sucked the sauce from the end of the spoon, swallowed, then licked her top lip. Their gaze locked, and a soft flush rose up Emily's neck and into her cheeks. Skye melted where she stood.

"What do you think?" Emily asked quietly. Her eyes were set at the darkness of midnight, but when the stars were the brightest.

Skye's breath hitched. "Really good. Am I allowed to have another taste?"

A long pause. Then Emily gave a single nod, and Skye stepped forward, encroaching on Emily's space. Her eyes roamed across Emily's elfin face, her parted lips. Then they settled on those impossibly dark eyes. She leaned her face closer, and the sizzle of fireworks ignited her skin as Emily sighed, angling her head slightly so when their lips touched, they fit perfectly. Her eyes closed for the brief touch, and when she pulled away, Emily's opened as well. Their faces were so close, a millimetre, then with another soft sigh, more a breathy "Yes", Emily captured Skye's lips. Slow. So slow, and gentle. Lips caressing. Skye felt Emily's shudder of pleasure pass through her body like a waterfall. Then, Emily pulled away with a gasp.

"Oh! Your shoulder!" Her eyes were round with concern.

A lazy smile filled Skye's lips, and she raised an eyebrow. "I'm not kissing you with my shoulder, Em," she said huskily.

Emily's eyes didn't quite roll, but they swung in preparation as she indulged the quip, then her gaze levelled and she lifted her hand to touch Skye's cheek. "What is this?"

"It's called kissing. People do it when—" Skye's words were cut off when Emily softly pressed their lips together again, then withdrew, narrowing her eyes. "Smart arse," she whispered. Their smiles were gentle.

"Do you want to…?" Skye trailed off.

"Have dinner? Yes. I think that's a really good idea," Emily said decisively, looking almost relieved at the interruption.

There weren't any more kisses for the remainder of the evening, but Skye was quivering with the potential, with all the possibilities, like when they touched hands and cheeks, like during dinner with the sensuality of eating, while they tidied up and drank tea with desire in their eyes, and as they said goodnight with the very long, heated look that went with that wish.

Eventually, the house stilled, and Skye lay under the quilt, sling abandoned on the bedside table and stared blankly at the ceiling. Quivering.

Chapter Seventeen

Emily decided that Skye was clearly someone not accustomed to being inactive or restricted physically because when Emily left for work the next day, Skye was already up, somehow dressed, breakfasted, and rolling her shoulder around in the lounge room as she followed the prescribed exercises in the aftercare pamphlet. After a brief hesitation at the door, they'd shared a shy smile, then Emily had leaned up and kissed Skye. Not for long. Just enough to let her know that the kissing was welcome. Just enough to ask for more.

Which meant that she was highly distracted at work, nodding vaguely as Rach enthused about their application for the *Browning Federal* townhouse development and that she'd heard positive things about it through the real estate development and architecture grapevine—

"There's a grapevine?" Emily refocused.

"Yes. It's called the 'Jas Conway Dated A Guy Who Works For *Browning Federal'* grapevine." Rach grinned, then pointed at the reception desk. Emily turned to Jas whose grin was even wider.

"That particular juicy grape was," Jas paused and looked at the ceiling, "a Bordeaux blend."

Emily laughed and shook her head. "You are never allowed to resign."

She called it a day at three o'clock, informing her colleagues that she was going home to check on Skye.

"You know…to make sure she's comfortable, and not overdoing it," she said earnestly, nodding at the same time to add strength to her flimsy excuse. Dimitri, Jas, and Rach stared at her as she continued to nod, while walking backwards to the door. Literally moonwalking.

Skye was on the phone—another video call—when Emily arrived home, so she closed the door quietly, and made her way to the kitchen to get a drink. The emotional intensity from the other room was a wave rolling from wall to wall, and even with her head stuck in the fridge, Emily could hear the tension in the words.

"—didn't expect you to answer, darling."

"That's because I'm normally at work, Mum. And you only ever call when I'm working."

"Are you not working anymore? Is it like last time?"

Emily heard the disapproving tone and wanted to march out with —she scanned the interior of the fridge—the bunch of celery and defend Skye rather assertively. She grabbed a water bottle instead, closed the fridge door, and hovered in the middle of the tiled space, feeling awkward and curious.

"No, it's not like last time. I dislocated my shoulder on Sunday in the race I told you about in my email. Did you read it?"

"No, darling. You know what the internet connection is like here. The local villagers have more important things to be concerned about than access to Facebook."

A sigh wafted into the kitchen. "Yes, I know. Anyway, that's all my news. My friend, Emily, is looking after me, Seb won *Rush*, and I've dislocated my shoulder, which means there goes some of the prize money," Skye said wryly. Emily's skin warmed at the 'friend' label.

"Well, you'll make it work, I'm sure." The dismissal was a virtual slap.

"I always do, Mum. I don't expect help."

"Well, of course not!" Skye's mother sounded incredulous. "You're living in a country with free healthcare and access to services that people in other countries can only dream of. The locals here in Cambodia would never be able to attend a modern public hospital like you did, I'm sure. It's why the work your father and I do is so important. You'll be fine."

Emily flicked her eyes about like people do when they're waiting out a long silence. Then Skye spoke sadly.

"I know that, Mum, but my business might not be."

Skye's mum tsked. "There are services in Australia that can assist you, Skye. Government payments and the like. Although, you shouldn't access those, of course. You have privilege!" The voice rose. "Those services are for people who've lost their way."

Emily's mouth fell open. Wow. The lack of awareness was breathtaking.

"I know I have privilege, Mum. I've always known it. And I've asked you not to refer to people on assistance as lost. It's rude."

"Oh, tosh. You know what I mean."

"Sure."

"Well, if that's all your news?"

"Yeah, Mum. I thought that you might be concerned that your daughter was injured," Skye said bitterly. She sounded defeated. Resigned.

"Well, of course I am, but you'll make a full recovery. Now, it was lovely to catch up with you, darling. Such a surprise. Keep sending your emails, and I'll let your father know we spoke."

There was a mutual murmur, a goodbye. Then silence. Emily's heart broke, and she began to understand why Skye was reluctant to ask for help. It seemed that she never received any when she did.

Emily walked into the lounge and sat next to Skye, then leaned her elbow on the back of the couch and the leather huffed and dipped. Skye mimicked her posture, leaning on her right elbow.

"Hi there," Skye said, her eyes warm. Emily's stomach muscles tumbled.

"Hi," she replied and grabbed her bottom lip with her teeth. Skye's eyelids hooded and she rolled her cheek across her hand, bringing her face close to Emily's. The conversation with her mum seemed to be forgotten, or at least shelved for the moment.

"Are we kissing again? We should, you know, considering that we find each other attractive," Skye said cheekily, her eyes sparkling.

Emily's smile was automatic, and she moved to cover the distance, pressing her lips to Skye's. She pushed a little, opening her mouth, and swallowed a gasp as Skye tentatively licked across her bottom lip, then dipped into her mouth to slide briefly against her tongue.

They pulled away at the same time, breathing heavily.

"Oh," Emily said shakily, resting her fingertips on her bottom lip. Skye looked equally as flustered.

"Yeah."

Fabulous kisses seemed to produce a loss of vocabulary, so Emily blinked, straightened her shoulders, and pointed to the silent phone on the coffee table. "I…um…I couldn't help overhearing. I'm sorry. Your mum?"

"Oh yes. My mother." Skye's smile was forced, as she sank further into the couch.

Emily searched Skye's face. "Your reluctance to ask for help. Is it because of…"

The sigh was loud. "Mm-hmm," Skye rumbled through closed lips. She took her hand from under her cheek and ran her finger down Emily's forearm, tracing the lines in the sweater, then running it back up to Emily's fingers, along the line of her jaw. Emily nearly missed the question.

"—want the whole story?"

"Please," she said, looking into brown eyes filled with trust and friendship and more, if she wanted.

"Well, my parents have always believed, right from when I was little, that I don't need help because I was born into a privileged position," she pointed to her chest, "white and middle-class. They said I should learn to cope for myself." She angled her head. "Cope for myself in any situation."

"Any situation?" Surely not.

"Yep. I had to learn to do everything on my own. It's their philosophy. Apparently, it's the only way you learn, if you're privileged. Because you have means." She fluttered her eyelashes in a gesture that Emily took to represent sarcasm. "They run environmental tourism ventures and charities in what they call third world countries to provide help to the locals. Tourists—their guests," the snark was a sharp blade, "help build, set up or create some type of environmental infrastructure or system, like forestry management, or irrigation, in a village and feel virtuous about giving their time and money to local businesses while saving the planet. But then the infrastructure fails because Mum and Dad and those people, with their white, middle-class knowledge, have marched into a village in a foreign country that is not white and middle-class, and instead of giving the locals a set of skills to build their own system, they've imposed theirs. And it never works, so my parents go, "Oh look! You can't help yourselves, you poor people. We'll stay and help."

Emily stared, and said quietly, "White saviours."

"Bingo."

"Oh, Skye." Emily scooted closer, snuggling into Skye's uninjured shoulder.

"It's not like my parents don't care about me. They simply care more about other things. Other people who they feel need saving, because those people can't do it on their own, apparently. Kind of a weird compliment to me, I guess." She paused. "Or not."

Emily listened to Skye's breathing.

"What did your parents do when you lost your job at *Traverse*?"

Skye barked a laugh, making Emily's head jostle.

"They basically washed their hands and said that it was karma for getting involved in a toxic capitalist energy company in the first place."

Emily jerked back, her eyes round with outrage.

"They did not!"

Skye shrugged, then winced at the movement. "Yeah, they did. It didn't surprise me, Em." Her hand crept across to entwine their fingers. "Some people have fundamental Christian parents. I have fundamental, environmentalist, white-saviour parents, and even though I love them and I know they love me, their response two years ago to my newly-acquired dreadful life situation really hurt."

Bringing their joined hands to her lips and kissing Skye's knuckles, Emily then shook her head. "I'm so sorry that happened." Another kiss. "So, you've had to solve everything in your life by yourself. No wonder you don't ask for help." She raised an eyebrow. "Or get grumpy accepting it." Skye's lips quirked in response.

Emily snuggled in again, enjoying the shiver she felt from Skye's body, feeling the corresponding flutter herself. What a remarkable woman. Skye was strong; not just physically. Emily shifted slightly and felt the muscles of Skye's arm and torso tense and slide under her cheek. Yes, physically strong, and the acknowledgement of that was delicious. But Skye was resilient, and resourceful, and—Emily's mind spasmed at how quickly Skye had crept under her skin, how quickly her humour, and presence, and certainty had insinuated themselves into Emily's awareness of each day. Then the word flew into Emily's agitated mind. Safe. Skye felt safe. All the strategies she'd developed to cope with uncertainty, and insecurity, and the absence of guarantees now viewed Skye as a retirement home. The very idea was unimaginable. Emily needed those strategies. The planning. The focus. The dismissal of sudden, and spontaneous. She *needed* them. For Skye to be sitting there on Emily's couch, being all safe and spectacular, full of *Maybe-I'm-A-Great-Choice* was too much for her brain to handle.

But not her heart, apparently.

Dinner was Skye's decision, which ended up being a creamy miso Brussels sprout fettuccine, which Emily swooned over. Insisting that she could cope with all the cooking one-handed—Emily raised an eyebrow as if to say, "You could ask for help, you know"—Skye made herself at home in the kitchen. Then, during dinner and afterwards, while sharing long looks, smiles, touches of hands and cheeks and forearms, Skye filled Emily in on her exciting day of shoulder rehabilitation exercises, social media scrolling, and *Quick Cargo* organisation.

"I'm simply exhausted now," she stated dryly, cupping Emily's cheek, who giggled and went about angling the plates into the dishwasher later in the night.

"I can tell," Emily said, appraising her track pants, the misshapen t-shirt that was so large it hung lopsided. Skye sighed dramatically and slumped into the bench, but then straightened as her eyes, animated and interested, watched Emily walk towards her, breaching the invisible barrier of personal space, to stop just before Skye's body halted any further movement. "Poor Skye. You should have made a ta-da list." She ran her finger along Skye's forearm.

"A what?" Skye's eyes had glazed a little.

"A ta-da list," Emily said, overjoyed at how her proximity was disrupting Skye's concentration. "It's a to-do list, but you write things on it that you've already done, so you can immediately cross them off, therefore...ta-da!" She twinkled her fingers next to Skye's temple. "It makes you feel very accomplished. You should listen to me, you know; I'm an expert list-maker."

Skye laughed, closing her eyes as her smile filled her face, and Emily felt emboldened. So, she stepped even closer, and Skye's eyes flew open.

"So, we've established that we have a mutual attraction," Emily whispered, and catalogued her bodily responses; her caught breath, her tight muscles. What the hell was she doing?

"Yes," Skye whispered in return.

"And the kissing is beyond delicious, and makes my stomach flutter."

"That's kinda nice." Skye brought her hands to Emily's waist, relaxing her fingers into the curve. "Me too," she added.

"I want to discover what it's like to hold you," Emily said, then Skye's eyes blew wide. "Oh! Just for a hug. You're flat out just getting your clothes on. Besides, I'm not sure either of us is ready for anything other than kisses and hugs right now," she said, which was truly an outrageous lie from her perspective but then again, not. So complicated.

Skye huffed a breath. "Hmm. Hugs are on my rehabilitation chart." Emily gazed into those melted caramel eyes, then she curved her arms around Skye's body, tucking her head into that amazing place where her cheek fitted with Skye's collarbone and her forehead skimmed her neck.

"Good, because this is rather nice," Emily mumbled into the fabric at the collar.

Skye folded Emily in, holding her body fast to her own. Then the soft, subtle adjustments of two people unfamiliar with each other's shape began. The relaxing, the letting go, and the reducing of air between. Then they stayed joined in their new space. Emily inhaled Skye's scent; a combination of vanilla and sunshine. She trailed her fingers across Skye's upper back; the soft cotton hinting at the firmness underneath, then shivered as Skye's fingers created patterns across the back of her shirt.

"Skye," she breathed.

"Yeah, I know."

Emily pulled away, leaving her hands on Skye's waist, and fell into an uninhibited, utterly sensual gaze.

"I'm going to head off to bed. I like to read for a while," she said, and Skye quirked a smile.

"Sounds good. I'll see you in the morning." The promise sent goosebumps up and down Emily's spine, as did the follow-up kiss.

The sound of the water in the pipes ceased and Emily allowed her Kindle to flop onto the quilt over her chest. The little third bedroom was half-filled with random objects that people put somewhere in their house when they don't have a garage. Like luggage, Emily thought, as her eyes landed on the bright red suitcase in the corner. A floorboard creaked, and Emily recognised it as the one between the ensuite and main bedroom. Skye was probably anxious to get back to the studio, but she was still very fragile and sore, despite her determination to do things like take her own clothes on and off, and cook, and complete all the exercises, and wrap her arms about Emily's body. Emily blinked at the ceiling, conscious of the smile that curved her lips. Anyway—she rolled her eyes—according to the pamphlet, Skye would need help with—

The cry of pain had her flinging off the quilt and racing to the main bedroom. She found Skye leaning against the ensuite doorway, shirt askew, and tears in her eyes. Her face had paled.

Not really knowing how to help, Emily wrapped her arm around Skye's waist and raised the other to place her hand on Skye's cheek.

"What happened?"

Skye swallowed, and grit her teeth. "I lifted my shoulder without thinking. Just stupid. And I think I did too much with the rehab today." She hissed. "Ah, crap."

"Okay, let's get you into bed, and I'll grab your painkillers. An icepack as well."

Once installed in bed, painkillers swallowed, and the cloth-wrapped icepack situated correctly, Skye groaned. Emily sat; her thigh nestled against Skye's hip where it lay under the blanket.

"You should be right now. The meds will kick in soon," she said and brushed a lock of hair from Skye's forehead. Then Skye caught Emily's hand.

"Would you sleep here tonight?" Her eyes pleaded, and Emily's head and heart were in total agreement.

"Of course." She walked around to the other side of the bed, shuffled under the blanket and lay on her back next to Skye. They held hands as their breathing synchronised and filled the silent room.

"Why does it still hurt?" Skye asked softly into the darkness. Emily knew without a doubt that Skye wasn't referring to her shoulder.

"I don't know," she answered, under her breath. Skye hummed, nearly asleep.

But Emily did know. She knew about the hurt, because it never went away.

***

"I visited Dad on the weekend."

"Right." Kristen's eyebrows rose and dropped in time with the word.

"I didn't say a great deal. There's not a lot to say now, but I'm not floundering as much." Emily stopped scratching at the arm of the chair and lifted her gaze to her therapist.

Kristen crossed her legs. "You have a sense of coherence?"

"Yeah, that. I'm starting to see that my default sense of coherence, not this new one, but the over-planning business, is restrictive and creates more chaos than sense." She scoffed. "I have no idea. But," she pointed vaguely towards Kristen, "your immersion therapy suggestion has been helpful."

"Oh, good. Yes, you leased your studio. That was a major step," Kristen said, then smiled encouragingly.

"To a woman named Skye, who is a bike courier, and she's a really lovely person." Emily pressed her fingertips together so that the knuckles went white. "Um, so I spontaneously invited her to Nic's show, and then Jas's birthday, and we sat in a tree and talked, and…" she let her head flop back. "We have become quite close," she told the ceiling. Then she dropped her head down at the silence.

"I thought you were just taking in a tenant."

"Yes, but I've done all this other stuff."

"Why?"

Emily flipped her hands over, then back. "I…I don't know. I'm overachieving a bit, aren't I?"

Kristen laughed. "Sounds like the tenancy was the immersion therapy part, but everything else happened organically."

That was a thought. Would kisses and hugs, organic or otherwise, have occurred if Skye wasn't living in her studio? Wasn't injured? If Bec hadn't cheated?

Resentment suddenly flashed hot through her mind.

"I feel like I've got delayed anger," she said in frustration.

"Okay." Kristen wore her 'tell me more' face.

"The cheating. The derailing. The realisation that I didn't love her, which I feel guilty about, which makes me feel angry." She poked herself in the chest. "At myself."

"Misplaced, but we'll chat about that later. So what does love look like for you?" Kristen asked calmly, like she was asking Emily to describe a coffee table.

Easy. "Impossibly chaotic, mutually forged, wonderfully true." The sudden clarity was deafening, and she stared at Kristen, who raised an eyebrow, nodding slowly.

"Hmm," she said. "Have you ever experienced that? We've not really discussed your relationships before. Our time has been spent working through other topics."

Emily laughed. "Yep. Lots of those topics. But in answer to your question, I don't think so. My other relationships have been calm and all involved forward thinking and, oh God, that's so desperately dreary." She pinched the skin between her eyes.

"Why did those relationships end?" Kristen sounded genuinely curious.

"Well, I've really only had three, because I couldn't even contemplate being with someone for years after Dad died."

Kristen lifted a shoulder in a shrug of understanding.

"I just focused on Uni and my mentorship with Lorraine and work. But then there was Monique, and we lasted eight months." Emily's mind came to rest randomly on the black, almost blue, hair of the woman who became her first real girlfriend.

"Why did that relationship finish?" Kristen asked.

It was Emily's turn to shrug. "Not sure. We just sort of drifted apart. Like a mutual ghosting."

"Had you put a plan in place with Monique? Did you see a future with her?"

"Yes, but it hadn't set itself in concrete. Probably best for both of us then," Emily said, then grunted at the honesty of that statement. "Then there was Keira who was terrific but was into weed and while I didn't judge or anything, I couldn't handle it after a while."

Kristen recrossed her legs. "What couldn't you handle?"

"The highs and lows." Emily waved her hand to give physicality to the words. "It was too much like my childhood." She gave Kristen a look. "I know we've talked about Keira because the being-too-much-like-my-childhood point was brought up."

The special psychologist smile, as Emily labelled it, lifted Kristen's lips. "Yes, we did, but here's a question. Did you love her? I don't think I've asked you that before."

Emily let the silence sit for a beat. She'd found that Kristen liked silence. It allowed information to float gently to the floor after having been hurled into the air in a psychological ticker-tape parade.

"I...I don't know? If you'd asked me at about the three-month mark, I would have said yes. But reflecting on that, I think I would have been wrong. I wasn't in love with Keira. I was in love with the idea of a future with Keira, even if Keira was completely the wrong person."

It was a wonder that Emily wasn't bruised from all the revelations hitting her this week.

Emily continued, amazement colouring her words. "That's what happened with Bec. I didn't love Bec, yet I loved the plan we—" she stopped at Kristen's pointed finger. "The plan *I* had in place, and Bec cheating and leaving was destructive but highlighted so much."

Kristen delivered a hum along with her enigmatic smile. "And now you have Skye."

Emily frowned. "No. I don't really have Skye, to be completely accurate."

Kristen sat in silence for a beat. "And now you have Skye," she repeated in an infuriatingly logical tone.

"Fine," Emily huffed.

"So tell me about this relationship."

"I…" It wasn't a relationship. That was absurd. Wasn't it?

"Have you created a plan for the future?"

"No, I—"

"Why not?" The questions were speeding up and Emily knew exactly what Kristen was doing. She'd used the same strategy many times to get Emily to finally admit to truths, to embrace epiphanies.

"Because—"

"Do you love her?"

Emily's stomach rolled. "I can't possibly even answer that. It's too soon to—"

"Do you think you could?"

"I don't—"

"But why do you want to be with her?"

"Because she makes me feel safe!" Emily shouted, her hands curled into fists, her elbows dug into her ribs.

Her breath shuddered in the boundless silence, which stretched across the carpet and up the walls.

After another breath, and in a much more appropriate volume for an inner-city office, Emily continued. "She makes me feel safe, where I don't have to plan, and if I want to, if I'm ready, and much later, I could say the 'I love you' words, and I would trust myself because I'd trust her."

"Trust," Kristen said blandly, but Emily knew it was pretence because her therapist didn't do bland. Particularly with rainbow-striped socks, like today's.

"Yes. I haven't trusted before. Not Bec. Not Monique. Not Keira. And not my father. I couldn't trust them. I couldn't depend on them. But," she paused as yet another moment of clarity delivered a wallop, "I trust Skye."

"Despite knowing her for a month."

"Yes." Emily lifted her hands helplessly. "Yes."

"Maybe with Skye, you don't need to shoehorn her into one of your designs."

Emily contemplated the idea of having no plan at all. The untamed bush land with no destination. The utter vulnerability of that. The concept scared her beyond all reasonable thought. Then, very deliberately, her mind introduced an image of Skye into the scenario and suddenly the terror abated.

The understanding smile on Kristen's face was like opening a window in a stuffy room, and Emily nearly burst into tears. It wouldn't have been the first time. She let out another breath. The plants in the corner were certainly receiving a great dose of carbon dioxide today. No wonder they were thriving.

"Maybe I don't," she agreed.

Chapter Eighteen

Kissing Emily was probably the nicest thing that Skye had done in a very, very long time. It was currently featuring as number one on her list of all that was wonderful, and she intended on keeping it there by repeating that nice and wonderful thing as many times as possible.

She'd asked Emily to stay with her each night after Tuesday, just talking and holding hands and sleeping. And stealing kisses as goodnights and good mornings and for no reason whatsoever. All that nice and wonderful. She sighed happily as she stared out the kitchen window of the little studio mid-morning on Saturday and pedalled, the back wheel of her bike propped up on the triangle-shaped exercise trainer stand that Emily had brought home on Thursday night.

"It was a gift from a client," she'd stated, which confused Skye no end.

"Who gives their architect a bike trainer stand?" Her brow wrinkled.

Emily laughed loudly and shrugged. "You'd be amazed at the gifts we get. Champagne, chocolate, flowers," she listed. "But occasionally, the odd random thing." She pointed to the stand at Skye's feet. "Like that. But that wasn't for me. Dimitri received it from a commercial property we did. The owners thought that he was into cycling."

"Is he?"

"Not at all," Emily said quickly, then laughed again at the bemused expression on Skye's face. "Dimitri has an amazing ability to blend into situations, and clearly his client was a fan of cycling, therefore Dimitri was, too." She stepped into Skye's space, and Skye's skin tingled with goosebumps.

Emily ran her finger along Skye's collar, which exploded the population of tingles exponentially, and Skye pushed that sensation further up the list of wonderful.

"I figured that you can't steer a bike, but you might be missing it," Emily said shyly. "The feeling of riding. The wind in your hair. Perhaps it could go in your place if there's no room here." Her fingers played with the loose strands of Skye's blonde hair that she hadn't been able to tie up because of her shoulder. Skye reckoned she was five seconds away from spontaneous combustion, the light touches on her skin like Skye was made of glass. Talk about a lit fuse. Emily had been thinking of her and wanted to do something nice for her, like a friend would, like a friend who kissed her would. Oh, watch that fuse burn. Skye swallowed.

"Thank you. I am missing those things. I miss the exercise, too. General muscle movement. I don't want to lose conditioning," Skye said, smiling into those dark eyes.

Emily delivered a slow scan of Skye's body, which only stoked the fire. Then she smiled playfully.

"Your condition looks completely fine from where I'm standing." Her eyes darkened even further.

The fire inside Skye burned bright. She wanted to throw herself in, let Emily consume her, but that had happened too many times before. Allowing the relationship, the woman, to wholly devour who Skye was. Nope, from now on Skye's new person had to come to her. If that was Emily, then excellent.

Meanwhile, though, there was kissing. In that moment, their lips savoured and tantalised, and then Skye couldn't help it. She pushed her tongue into Emily's mouth, her hands moved of their own volition, skating up Emily's sides, and the lightning flash of desire was staggering. Emily whimpered, and Skye's list of wonderful collected a new addition.

It had been the same on Friday.

After more *Quick Cargo* organisation—emails and calls back and forth to *Gowers* to confirm the final details of their new contract, checking in with Seb who was so on top of everything that it seemed like Skye was completely unnecessary—she'd started planning ideas for dinner.

Emily had bounced—it really was the only word for it—into the house not ten minutes later, with the news that her firm had signed a new contract with *Browning Federal*, which meant nothing to Skye, but she was thrilled for Emily because…well, because that's what friends did. They were thrilled when their friend was thrilled. And Skye regarded a thrilled Emily with an emotion that had shuffled a toe over the consumed-by-a-special-person line. Uh oh.

Having delivered the news, Emily dropped her bag, and marched up to Skye and planted an exuberant kiss on her lips.

"Pizza," she declared.

Skye blinked. "I might need more information than just the noun."

Emily grinned, then leaned in for a hug. Skye's heart jumped about chaotically, like an enthusiastic toddler experiencing bubbles for the first time.

"Pizza. We're having pizza tonight because *Fitzsimmons* scored the *Browning Federal* townhouses, and you're on the mend, and because…I like where this—us is going," she finished quietly, and held Skye's hand, walking her to the couch.

So, by noon on Saturday, as Skye climbed off the bike and dragged a towel across her neck and face, she decided that they needed another date.

"Not that anything else we've done has been a date," she muttered, wandering up the driveway. "Liar," she whispered, stretching the word into a long, windswept note, like a crowd at a football match.

She found Emily hunched over her crafting mat, the intoxicating strains of *Deep Forest*; the field recordings mixed with New Age electronica by French duo Eric Mouquet and Michel Sanchez, drifting from the little speaker squatting on the corner of the desk. She lingered in the doorway until Emily finished carefully splicing the stems of three bamboo grasses.

"Hi. That's looking incredible," Skye said, indicating the half-completed display on the other table. Emily placed her knife in its holder, silenced the music, then stood and stretched, linking her hands behind her back.

"Thanks. Yes, I'm happy with how it's going." Emily wandered over to the piece and smoothed one of the leaves. "I've probably got a day left to have it done, otherwise it starts to lose its form." Then she turned, crossed one arm over her stomach and rested the elbow of the other arm on top, cupping her chin with her hand. "How was your bike ride today? Roads busy?" she said cheekily, one eyebrow raised.

Skye grinned. "Yeah. Traffic everywhere. The journey back was awful. Gravel all over the place. Nice view, though."

Emily tipped her head as her palm continued to claim her chin. It was a flirty gesture. Then she added another eyebrow raise, which nearly sent Skye's skin into meltdown.

Delicious.

Tension.

"I'll go have a shower, and then do you want to go to the *Food Truck Festival* later?" Skye said, after slowly exhaling.

"Oh! Yes, I love that festival. Excellent, that's lunch sorted. Probably dinner as well," Emily enthused.

The United Nations of twenty-five food trucks filled the carpark of the *Victorian Arts Centre*. Each truck, with its individual menu, created invisible aroma clouds, so browsing for their late lunch/early dinner choice was like teleporting to a new country every few metres.

Skye, her left arm back in its sling, simply to remind herself not to wave it around, and to let the crowd know she was injured, drew Emily's hand into the crook of her right arm as they wandered past the bright red truck calling itself, '*No Fries On Me, Mate*'. They giggled at the Australian-ness of it, and Skye sighed. How could this…this thing be so new, yet be so perfect? It was tempting to leap in. She could hear the little voice in her head saying, "Do it. Dooooooo iiiiiit", like a bad horror movie.

Tossing up between burgers—

"The fundamental dilemma is that burgers are a readily available comfort food versus the fact that here they're from a food truck and therefore awesome and exotic," Skye explained seriously, which dissolved Emily into gales of laughter.

—and dumplings,

"They're like little presents, filled with surprises," Emily said, and because that was probably the most adorable thing Skye had ever heard, they chose dumplings.

They found a table, and conversation came easily. As they ate their own dumpling selection and sampled each other's, Skye discovered all sorts of information about Emily, such as the fact that they both didn't drink alcohol, the contract finalised yesterday for the double townhouse development was a bit of a coup, and that Emily knew nearly as much random trivia as Skye.

"Did you know that architecture was once an Olympic sport?"

"Really?" Skye was incredulous.

"Uh huh," Emily said, swallowing quickly. "Pierre De Coubertin stated that the arts had to be included in the Games, and it actually was for the first four decades." Her eyes flashed with interest, and she ran her hands through her short hair. "Can you imagine? Emily Fitzsimmons, gold medal winner for designing the new Melbourne velodrome." She grinned.

"I would love to cycle in a gold-medal-winning Fitzsimmons velodrome," Skye said softly, then they held eye contact for a long while.

Dessert was of the walk-and-eat variety because Skye insisted that the dessert rules for food truck festivals meant that you could have more than one. Therefore, they stuffed themselves with a shared donut, a shared maple syrup crepe, and a shared toffee-crusted, raspberry-topped crème brûlée, which forced Skye to moan in delight, and made Emily stutter-step, blushing in the late afternoon light.

At the car, Emily's blush bloomed again, and she dropped her hands into her coat pockets. Skye stepped closer, pushed her right hand into the pocket closest, and pulled Emily's hand out, linking their fingers together.

"Hey. You okay?" she asked, rocking their hands lightly. Emily breathed in and gave Skye a considered look.

"I'm enjoying you," she said, her expression one of bemusement.

A smile slowly filled Skye's face. "I'm glad. I like being enjoyed." She angled in to brush her lips to Emily's cheek, back near her ear. "I'm enjoying you, too," she whispered and indulged in Emily's shiver. She nuzzled her cheek, sliding away so her parted lips brushed against Emily's mouth. The soft gasp was exquisite.

Emily's fingers tightened around Skye's, and her other hand reached up to cup the side of Skye's neck, her thumb slipping along the skin.

"You know?" Skye whispered. "If this was a movie right now, and your hair was longer, I'd tuck a bit of it behind your ear and stroke your cheek as I took my hand away."

Emily's eyes were a solar system; a million lights of desire in the night sky. She breathed out carefully, then bit her bottom lip.

"Like this?" Emily suggested, and shifted her hand to tuck a lock of Skye's blonde hair behind her ear bringing their bodies together, then ran her index finger along Skye's jaw. A perfect shudder rocketed down Skye's spine.

"Yeah."

"And if this was a movie," Emily whispered, holding Skye's gaze, "I'd step closer and stare into your eyes, while my lips nearly touch yours."

Skye's tongue slid along her bottom lip, very quickly, then she angled her head, and brought her mouth close to Emily's.

"Like this?" Skye husked.

"Yes."

The brief touch was a firecracker through her body, and Skye pushed forward, taking Emily's mouth with hers, pulling back, letting Emily take the lead, then eagerly advancing once more. She eased her tongue into the warmth of Emily's mouth and her heart raced. A familiar heavenly ache began low in her pelvis as her centre twitched and sent out a high priority alert.

"Oh, Em," Skye breathed, her hand trembling in Emily's, and the dark eyes gazing back at her mirrored a similar wish, a want.

"I know. Me too," Emily breathed unsteadily. She untangled their fingers, then held each side of Skye's face. "You kiss like a goddess, and I want more of those, please. But," she glanced down at the sling, "I'm not sure your shoulder is up to anything else."

"You'd be amazed at how good it feels right now," Skye said, eyes wide with innocence, and Emily's reaction was perfect. A long laugh, then a total body embrace, her head tucked into Skye's neck.

Later that night, after her shower, after cleaning her teeth, after struggling into her sloppy t-shirt, and panties, Skye battled with her hair, swearing in her attempt to brush out the tangles one-handed.

"Ow! This is so bloody difficult!" she growled through clenched teeth, then gave up, threw the hairbrush onto the bed, and wandered into the kitchen.

"I heard exclamations of pain and swearing," Emily stated matter-of-factly, looking up from the tablet screen. Skye leaned against the doorframe and watched Emily's eyes rake down her body, over the hint of nipples, and settle on the hem of the sleep shirt, which stopped mid-thigh.

"The swearing was to assist in the hair brushing situation. Didn't help at all. So," Skye wrinkled her forehead plaintively. "Em, I need a favour. It hurts to brush my hair because I need two hands, but I haven't brushed it for days and I'm worried I have wildlife."

Emily giggled, then swiped the screen closed. "Come on."

Having worked out the logistics, Emily then shuffled around on top of the bed to kneel behind a seated Skye, whose feet were braced on the floor.

"Let me know if I yank too hard or something. My hair has been super short for years, so I've forgotten what to do with the long ver-sion," Emily said into Skye's ear, a location which seemed a little unnecessary because she could have said the same thing further away. Skye wasn't complaining, though.

Then, Skye instantly liquified. Strokes, bold and smooth, scorched through her strands, scraping just enough on her scalp to raise goosebumps. Her hair was held in a loose ponytail and it felt like each length was smoothed and straightened, then placed carefully back into position. Smooth, straighten, repeat. She purred.

Apparently quite loudly, because Emily chuckled.

"That's a lovely sound to hear," she said huskily.

"You're doing an amazing job, Em. Thank you." Skye swallowed and made an 'o' with her lips to steady her breath.

"You're welcome." Emily continued to work. "Your hair is so soft. It's beautiful." Then Emily's voice whispered in her ear. "This is quite a sensual thing to do."

This was not at all new information as far as Skye was concerned.

"Uh huh," Skye muttered, her nerve endings stretched to their limit. Then the bed dipped as Emily rearranged her body so she was sitting tucked in behind, her legs hugging Skye's, whose centre sprang to attention, the pressure expanding into her legs and lower stomach.

So good.

So frustrating.

So good.

"Em," Skye whispered.

"Mm?" Emily continued brushing the ends of Skye's hair.

"Do you know what you're doing?"

The brushing paused. "Not really," Emily admitted in a shaky breath. The brush must have been placed to the side, because Emily's arms snaked around Skye's middle and she leaned her face into Skye's back between her shoulder blades. "Am I hurting you?"

"Not at all." Skye alleviated her worries by embracing Emily's arms. "In fact, I feel fantastic," Skye said to the wall in front of her, relishing the feel of firm breasts against her back.

Emily breathed deeply, then slid her hands out from under Skye's. Her fingers, one by one, slowly bunched the fabric of Skye's shirt, lifting it higher and higher. Skye's breath grew ragged. Then those searching fingers slipped under the shirt and skated across Skye's stomach. Her muscles tensed and hollowed.

"Is this okay?" Emily breathed into Skye's neck, following the request with a soft kiss.

"Jesus. Yes," Skye panted, then swallowed very deliberately. Her mouth was dry. It was incomprehensible how aroused she'd become just from having her hair brushed and fingers trickling over her body like raindrops.

"I'd like to feel more." Emily's fingers paused.

"Yes," Skye groaned.

Languidly, yet steadily climbing in roundabout randomness, Emily finally reached Skye's nipples.

"Oh! Oh God," Skye gasped. Then gave another gasp as those talented fingers became more purposeful, twisting, tugging, rubbing her nipples so that pleasure shot straight to her core. "Em!" Skye's hands gripped her own thighs, collecting the bottom of her shirt so that it pulled away from her body, giving Emily even more room. A familiar pressure hummed low in her pelvis.

Emily's torso pressed into the length of Skye's back, her heat moulding to Skye's bum.

"Jesus!"

Skye's heartbeat pulsed in time with the twitching in her centre, as Emily worked her magic, drifting away from the nipples to caress the curve of Skye's small breasts, then returning to pluck at the tight buds, then lingering on her abdomen, tracing the line in her muscles down the centre, then back again to her nipples.

Emily's rapid breath tickled the fine hairs on the back of her neck. She sounded like she was struggling to contain herself, struggling within the overwhelming eroticism of the moment. Skye whimpered. Emily could obviously feel Skye's growing excitement, her need, but suddenly she stopped, her fingers splayed across Skye's breasts.

"Skye," Emily whispered, and Skye nearly combusted. Her name had never sounded so electrifying.

"Ah," she grunted, the exhalation cut off when she clamped her jaw.

"I can stop." Emily's fingers were trembling.

"Don't you dare," Skye commanded.

"What do you need?"

Emily hadn't even finished the question before Skye slid her right hand up under her shirt, captured Emily's, and brought it down to the waistband of her panties.

"Please," she moaned, and Emily didn't delay. She shifted her fingertips under the elastic, and curled into Skye's sex. "Oh! Shit. Jesus. Yes," Skye uttered in quick succession, as her climax cleared a faraway hill and came charging towards her. Emily explored Skye's heat, the wet folds, finally settling at Skye's centre, purposefully rolling, circling the tight bundle of nerves. All while fondling Skye's breast.

"Oh. My. God." Skye's head felt like it was about to explode. Her hands gripped her trembling thighs, and her abdomen shivered in preparation. Then Emily laid her hand over Skye's sternum, holding her fast against her chest, ready to ride the wave of contractions that were nearly upon Skye. The other hand quickened. Rolling. Circling.

"Please come for me," Emily whispered. There was no way that she couldn't feel Skye's accelerated heartbeat.

Skye grunted. Whimpered. The sound stretched with tension.

"Please, Skye."

With a cry that cracked as it left her throat, Skye came, shaking in Emily's arms as the orgasm radiated chaotically through her entire body. She shook again as Emily pressed her whole hand to Skye's centre. Then, after a moment or two, as she took her first full breath, Skye heard Emily say quietly,

"I've got you."

It took another full minute or two for her heartbeat to slow, but in that time, Skye realised that, yes, Emily did have her.

That revelation was galvanising, and she held Emily's hand, stood, then twisted and pulled Emily up flush against her body. Then it was the most natural thing in the world to bring their lips together, opening to slide tongues, slow and strong. Skye felt Emily gasp silently, then smile against her mouth, as delight had overtaken her. She pulled back to check. Yes. That was an entirely delighted smile.

Emily leaned in and kissed the skin under Skye's ear. "So, is that how you brush long hair? I'm not sure."

Skye laughed. "You are a," she paused, hunting for the word. "A revelation," she finished, and Emily bit her lip, lust shimmering in those dark brown eyes.

"And you are remarkable," she breathed, and another delighted smile, this time bearing a hint of disbelief—at Skye? at the moment? at herself?—consumed her.

"I want to—is it okay if I touch you as well?" Skye asked tentatively.

The delighted smile slowly lifted higher on one side, drifting into a smirk, which sent various sparks and lightning and other fiery entities rampaging through Skye's system.

"I'd like that, but I'm not sure about your shoulder," Emily said in concern.

"Ohhhhh. I'm fine," Skye replied, holding Emily close, their thighs touching.

Emily chuckled softly. "I can imagine. Well, I think we need to take our clothes off for this."

Yes, they did. Absolutely. Skye was a big fan of that idea.

"I agree, although it did take me half an hour to get this shirt on," she said sadly, and Emily laughed.

"How about some motivation?" She proceeded to remove her shirt, whipping it over her head, revealing firm breasts, and lovely curves, and the surprising appearance of a small butterfly tattoo on her right side, the translucent watercolours held in strong black foundations. Skye's heart stopped. Then Emily removed her track pants, taking her panties with them, kicking away her slippers until her body was gloriously naked. Her nipples instantly puckered. Magnificent.

"I'm jumping into bed because," she pointed to her tight nipples, "cold." She paused. "And aroused, but take your time."

Skye blinked. There would be no time-taking. She awkwardly slid her panties off, tossing them towards the ensuite, then carefully, aware of Emily's intense observation, manoeuvred her shirt one-handed over her head and slithered her arms out of the holes. It joined the panties on the floor.

"Stop," Emily commanded, and Skye froze, then grinned as Emily raked her gaze up and down Skye's body. "You are…" Emily faded off. She looked lost for words. "Come in here." Skye obeyed immediately, slipping under the covers, ensuring her good arm took her weight as she faced Emily. She trailed her fingers from Emily's neck across her collarbone, around the swell of her breast, dipping under it, then travelling over the top of the other one. A sexy figure eight. She repeated the action, reducing her circles until her fingernail skated across the top of the pronounced buds and Emily gasped, her skin a landscape of goosebumps.

"Lie back," Skye instructed, holding eye contact. "I'm going to do this left-handed so it might not be as effective but—"

"I doubt that," Emily said huskily. "I imagine you can do quite a few things left-handed." Skye raised an eyebrow and flicked a nipple. Emily's eyes blazed.

"I found out some lovely things about you today. But I think I'd like to discover hidden secrets before you," she said, then breathed the next word. "Come." Skye grinned at the gasp that fell out, leaned in to kiss her mouth, her neck, then trailed her fingertips along the skin of Emily's stomach, which trembled. She traced the outline of the butterfly tattoo before skimming lower again.

"What's the brand of lip gloss you use?" Skye asked, like she was enquiring about the next train from Melbourne Central. She brought her lips to Emily's and made contact, not quite a kiss but Emily moaned all the same. Meanwhile, Skye's fingertips continued to meander.

"Uh, God. Um, it's *Lifestyle Strawberry*," Emily stuttered.

Skye grazed Emily's pubic hair as she continued her light touches. "Mm. It's delicious when I kiss it off your lips." She cupped Emily's breast and thumbed her nipple, which caused Emily's hand to flutter, and head towards Skye's hips. "Uh uh," Skye said, placing Emily's hand back on the mattress. "I'm a terribly injured woman with special rehabilitation needs, one of which is you," she tweaked a nipple, "not touching." She grinned evilly. Emily's heated gaze swallowed her whole. So good.

"Skye, please," Emily breathed.

"Another question." Another nipple tweak produced a low moan, and Skye fizzed inside, thrilled with Emily's responsiveness. "What's your favourite cheese?"

Emily made a sound that started as a laugh but ended as a grunt of pleasure as Skye's fingers ran up the inside of her thighs. "Brie and G-Gouda," she choked out, trembling, fingers digging into the mattress.

The flushed cheeks, the eyes wild with desire, the hair in disarray; Skye couldn't get enough of Emily in the throes of pre-orgasmic bliss. "Jesus, Em. You are incredibly sexy." She pushed the covers off properly, revealing Emily in all her glory. Then she dipped into Emily's folds and brushed the hard centre.

"Yes!" Emily hissed, lifting her hips to chase Skye's hand, which had resumed its delicate tracing along Emily's thighs, across her stomach, around the swell of her breasts in ever-decreasing circles so that her nipples were teased, and played, and worked, until Emily was writhing on the bed.

"Milkshakes or thick shakes?" Skye whispered into Emily's ear, licking along her neck, trailing after the tremulous swallow that worked the muscles in Emily's throat.

"Oh!" Emily's grip on the mattress tightened.

"Answer the question." Skye's hand drifted lower, and into Emily's folds again, slipping across her centre.

"Oh God. Um…uh…God…milkshake!" Emily fell over her words, consumed with lust, and pleasure.

Increasing the pressure and speed of her fingers, Skye leaned in, to kiss Emily's soft lips, sweeping her tongue inside her mouth. They whimpered in stereo. Emily broke the kiss to arch her neck in response to the pleasure Skye was drawing out.

"Last question," Skye whispered into Emily's ear again, elated at how the whispers seemed to further reduce Emily to a writhing mess.

"Thank Christ," Emily gasped. "Oh God! Please."

"So, the question is," Skye held the pause for longer than necessary. "The question is…will you come for me?" Emily's eyes were wide with unbridled want.

"Yes." She was nearly hyperventilating. "Yes, please."

"Look at me." Skye increased her speed. "Look at me, Em, then come for me."

And as much as Emily tried to maintain eye contact, as her body tensed, as her orgasm tugged her over the edge, and as she uttered an extraordinarily erotic, low groan, she broke Skye's gaze, her eyelids closed, and the shocks, the aftershocks, then the soft trembling overtook her, sending her flying. Skye stared in wonder. Emily was stunning.

Finally, Emily opened her eyes and smiled. It was the most beautiful smile, filling her entire face with joy. Skye's heart flipped over. She brought her hand up to touch Emily's lips, then leaned over, and they kissed. They kissed like they'd kissed for years. They kissed with purpose, then paused to smile against each other's lips.

"Well, I didn't find out that much, except that you're the sexiest person alive," Skye said against Emily's mouth. She felt the lips curve in reply. "Although, you did cheat by answering with two cheese varieties."

Emily laughed loudly, rolling her head away. Skye grinned, then shuffled onto her back as she realised her shoulder had started to ache. Emily turned so she rested on her side next to Skye.

"I have a lot more to share, you know. You may have to interrogate me again," Emily said, her voice sultry, and she raised an eyebrow.

"Another interrogation?" Skye quirked a smile. "I'm a terribly injured woman, remember?"

Emily hummed, then narrowed her eyes. "I'm not."

Chapter Nineteen

All mornings should be this lovely. Emily considered who in the government she should write to so that they could pass that statement into law.

"Good morning," Skye murmured sleepily and rolled her head sideways, the turn slow and lazy. Her blonde hair fanned out on the pillow.

"Oh, it is," Emily agreed, adding her smile to Skye's. "Good morning right back. How's your shoulder feeling?"

"What shoulder? I have no bones."

Emily dissolved into laughter, burying her head in her pillow. God, this was nice. Yes, Skye was physically impressive, but she hadn't lied to Kristen when she'd said that Skye was safe, because that was everything right at this moment. Why else would Emily have spontaneously pleasured Skye if she wasn't a safe person? Spontaneous sex hadn't really featured in Emily's relationship resume prior to this moment. So what on earth was she doing? Emily felt like she was the entirety of Skye's attention when they were together. It was intoxicating and very comforting, and it dawned on her that Skye was exactly who she'd been looking for. Had she? Had she been looking?

She lifted her head to catch Skye's playful little grin. "It's," she bit her lip and Skye's brown eyes, tinged with amber, darkened. "It's not a good thing, but it's weirdly good that you dislocated your shoulder, because I've liked getting to know you before we got all naked last night." She rolled her eyes. "That wasn't worded well."

"I get what you mean," Skye laughed. "Although, I could have done without hurling myself onto the forecourt of the *City Finance* building."

Emily grimaced, then a thought occurred to her. "Do you think you'll stay for another week?" She propped up on her elbow.

Skye smiled warmly. "I'd like to. For a couple of reasons."

Emily placed her fingertips on Skye's injured shoulder.

"That's one of them," Skye whispered.

Then Emily dragged her fingers across Skye's chest, up her neck, over her jawline, coming to rest on her lips.

"That's the other one," Skye murmured, the vibrations chasing the whorls in Emily's fingerprints, and then, because how could she not, Emily bent her head and kissed Skye with everything she had.

***

Via a collection of emojis and dramatic punctuation, Nic announced that he was coming over for a late lunch at two o'clock, so Emily and Skye quickly sorted themselves out with showers, and general let's-not-look-like-we've-had-sex-all-night tidying.

Nic wasn't aware of the new development in Emily and Skye's relationship, because Emily felt like it needed to be hers for a while. However, his 'energy' radar was finely tuned, so it wouldn't be long until he cornered Emily, probably in her office tomorrow, and dragged out the whole story.

He arrived in a flurry of exuberance and was soon ensconced in a chair in the lounge, as Emily put together grazing platters from the eclectic food parcels he'd thrust into her hands after he'd kissed her cheek.

She listened in on the conversation happening in the lounge.

"How's the shoulder holding up, Skye?"

"It's on the mend. Emily's been great letting me stay here."

"She's a good one, that's for sure. Is Seb doing well holding the fort?"

"Totally! It's like he was born to run the business. Has he dropped by *Fitzsimmons*?"

Nic laughed. "Yes. He's popped by to flirt with Jas." He coughed. "Oh, my apologies. To *deliver* to Jas."

In the kitchen, Emily rolled her eyes, scooping the capsicum dip into a little bowl. She could hear the sass, which was probably hovering over him like secondhand cigarette smoke.

"The temporary courier, Hayley, is doing well," Skye said enthusiastically. "If we keep on growing, I could buy another bike and take her on permanently. Who knows? Meanwhile, I'm here being looked after by Em."

There was silence. Then, "Oh, I can ima—that's terrific. Yes. I'm sure—"

"Here we go," Emily announced loudly, marching out of the kitchen. She narrowed her eyes at the mischievous glint in Nic's gaze and arranged the two platters on the coffee table.

With the availability of food, the conversation, as it does, eased to news of the world, various celebrity scandals, and who'd flung open their closet lately. Emily sat on the couch, further away from Skye than she wanted and again questioned her motives. Nic was her best friend and a confidante. But it was pointless trying to articulate to him when she couldn't really explain it to herself. However, it didn't stop her bringing the platters to Skye so Skye didn't have to lean forward, then staring at her mouth as she chewed, itching to take Skye's fingers in her mouth after they'd been licked clean. The compulsion to be near Skye, to breathe the air near Skye, was staggering.

Nic leaned over to spear a piece of roast pork and pear onto his plate and caught Emily and Skye's unbidden soft smile. Then Emily watched in surrender as he flicked his gaze between the two of them, and his eyes widened. The speech bubble over his head literally screamed, "Oh, hello!"

Skye left to visit the bathroom, and Nic immediately crossed his legs, then folded his hands over his knee, and slapped a smirk on his face. "So. Tell all."

"There's nothing to—"

"Oh. No, no, no." He wiggled a finger at her. "I saw that look. That's the look of two people who haven't had their clothes on while they're in the same room," he said definitely.

Emily had to laugh at that. "That's quite specific."

He nodded, confirming his theory. "So…go."

"We're friends."

"Mm-hmm. And?"

"Friends…I don't know, with benefits? I hope more?" Emily furrowed her brow and lifted her hands briefly from her thighs.

"Good." Nic gentled his wicked grin. "I was worried you wouldn't bounce back after the Bec thing."

"Well," Emily rocked her head from side to side, "the Bec thing was sort of the catalyst for Skye."

"Oh? How?"

"When I had my next session after Bec left, my therapist suggested I try immersion therapy. You know, to break the cycle of my over-planning business. Immerse myself in spontaneity," Emily explained.

"Okay? Which meant…" Nic left the unfinished sentence hanging.

"Which meant that I rented out the studio as immersive therapy. It was a spontaneous decision. I was corralled into a conversation by Lorraine Hudson at her retirement dinner and the next minute I had a tenant."

Nic cocked his head. "I imagine your therapist didn't have you and Skye's friends arrangement in mind when she suggested your strategy."

"Kristen said as much, but it's not like that. Yes, Skye's here spontaneously, but the rest of it, being with her, isn't part of the spontaneity strategy. That happened by itself."

Nic fixed her with a long look. "Did it?"

"Yes!" Emily thumbed through a highlights reel of the last month, which was definitely entitled, "Look At All This Impulsiveness".

Skye chose that moment to return and sat one seat away from where she'd been sitting previously. Her smile was polite.

Emily gave her a puzzled look, then asked if anyone needed a fresh drink, but Nic lifted a hand to decline, and Skye met Emily's offer with an even stare.

"I'm fine. Thanks," she said quietly.

Nic squinted one eye, as if analysing a moment, then clasped his hands together, and stood.

"I have to go, lovelies. Marco asked me to pick up a bottle of *Grand Marnier* for his latest cupcake creations. *Baked Alaska Saint Pierre* or something fabulous. Apparently, he sets the gorgeous creation on fire once it's done, so I imagine we'll be a meme, announcing that everything is fine while the apartment burns."

Emily chuckled, then cast a worried glance at Skye, because her normal vibrant laugh was missing. Nic departed with hugs for both, and Emily turned to find Skye standing in the middle of the lounge seemingly conducting an internal debate.

"Are you okay? Is your shoulder hurting?" Emily hurried over.

"No," Skye answered sadly. "No, it's not. But my heart is a bit."

Emily felt her face lose all colour. It was like sinking into a cold pool.

After a deliberate swallow, Skye rubbed at her mouth with her hand. "I heard what you said. The immersion therapy thing. And, uh —"

"It's not like that," Emily said anxiously. "You aren't…"

"What am I, Em? Tell me what is it like?" Skye folded onto the couch, and Emily, her stomach roiling with distress, sat beside her, albeit with a decent amount of space between them. It gave her room to take a breath.

"You're wonderful." Emily grit her teeth. "You're unexpected."

"I still don't get it. Enlighten me, please, because I'm confused. I heard that renting the studio was a strategy suggested by your therapist, so good for you." Sarcasm dripped from Skye's words and Emily cringed. "But really? Everything else that came from that is part of the therapy, isn't it? All the 'jump in and live the moment' stuff we've done, including last night? Skye Reynolds Therapy." She shook her head and stared emotionlessly into Emily's eyes, her mouth a straight line.

"No! Stop it." This was awful. She scrubbed her fingers into her hair, then clutched the strands. "Yes, Kristen suggested immersion therapy. And you know why?" She made the question rhetorical. "I have issues with over-planning and being the antithesis of spontaneous, as you know, but I've only told you a tiny bit of the reason. But," she repeated. "But I'm going to tell you this now, not to justify anything, not to defend anything, but to explain why you have literally turned me inside out and how incredibly safe I feel with you and how none, *none*, of what we've done together is based on what Kristen suggested." She let out a breath, and Skye leaned forward to drink from her glass of water.

"Okay," Skye said, turning slightly. "I'll keep an open mind."

Emily entwined her fingers in a tight clasp and brought her hands to her mouth, biting at the knuckle to halt the wave of big. The wave of huge. The wave that only Kristen and Nic had experienced, and now Emily was letting it out. For Skye.

"My dad died by suicide," she said quickly behind her hands, and then it was Skye's turn to ride a wave. Shock, dismay, then sorrow, perhaps regret, and finally sympathy. Chasing each other across her face.

"Oh, God. Em, I'm so sorry." Her eyes were round as she processed Emily's announcement.

Despite the rawness of her revelation, Emily wanted to reach across and cuddle into her, because Skye hadn't asked how her father's death related to immersion at all. She'd just let it be what it was; a piece of tragic information.

"Mm." Tears pricked at Emily's eyes, and she crushed her lips together to stop them trembling. When she'd composed herself, words poured out like an open faucet. "He killed himself when I was twenty and I promise I'm getting to the point in all of this. I'm sorry that you overheard what you did, but oh my God, I want to tell you everything." She was rambling. Then Skye shifted over and held Emily's hand, which gave all the tears permission to fall.

"It's okay. Keep going," Skye said tenderly, watching Emily's face intently.

"So…so we're—Mum and I—we're positive that he had bipolar disorder. He wasn't ever diagnosed but all signs pointed that way. Of course, that meant he was unmedicated. And I know! I know he couldn't help how he was. I know that his impulsive, financially-damaging, live-in-the-moment, high-as-a-kite, dangerous, claustrophobic behaviour was a symptom of bipolar, as were his remorseful, devastating lows. We think he knew, as well, but he always said his impulsive periods were when he was the most creative." Emily looked at Skye. "He was a metal artist. But for twenty years, his behaviour dominated my world." She let out a shaky breath. "Kristen calls it trauma, which seems a tad dramatic."

Skye squeezed her hand and rubbed the knuckles with her thumb.

"By twenty-one, I'd shifted into a sort of protective mode. I'd lived for twenty years with this wavering, trembling ball of chaos hanging over my head, ready to smash right through any consistency and normality that I'd carefully created." Her tears increased. "Never knowing what the day would bring, like if we were suddenly going cage-diving with sharks, or in an hour buying a vineyard in Italy. It was a fear of the unknown, so I swore I'd never have that uncertainty again." Her words caught in her throat and she clenched her teeth, breathing through the tiny spaces between the gaps.

"Em," Skye whispered, reaching up to hold Emily's cheek, swiping her thumb across to catch the tears. Emily smiled wetly.

"Ah…so I was the one who found him, and…um…anyway just after that, probably brought on by the shock and everything else, the planning behaviour started. Life stuff, like relationships, my business, that sort of thing. But I was constantly planning little things as well, like meals on certain days, or driving certain routes to work. Crazy stuff but necessary, because I needed to know that my life would never be chaotic again. Ever." She checked Skye's face for derision but found empathy. "But I knew it was all too much, so I started seeing Kristen who has worked a lot with me on curbing my planning of the little things. The Ikebana has helped. And now we're working on the big things because she said I was ready. Renting out the studio was about combating my big stuff over-planning. I figured leasing my space is a giant tick in the immersion therapy column."

Skye shuffled even closer, pressing her thigh to Emily's. "It is. I'm sorry I got all defensive," she said.

"You don't need to be sorry at all!" Emily replied forcefully, her eyes flashing. "I'm the one who made you feel dreadful."

"I jumped to conclusions, which was very on-brand for me. I tend to do a lot of leaping without looking," Skye grumbled and Emily squeezed her hand.

"I didn't tell you about my dad for any other reason except that it explains a lot about how I am, about how my head works now because of my life before. But," she huffed a breath, "I did tell you because I trust you. You're safe spontaneity, Skye. You feel safe, like I could—"

"Go paragliding tomorrow without a booking?" Skye's expression, which had been full of sincerity and understanding, suddenly flashed with mischief. Emily poked her solid thigh.

"No! That's not safe. That's bonkers." Even Skye's teasing felt safe, like malice had no place in her words.

Skye laughed, then scanned Emily's face. "Thank you for telling me."

"Thanks for listening. I really didn't mean for you to overhear that, so I am going to apologise for a few more hours this afternoon, if that's okay."

"You don't need to," Skye said, smiling. They sat in silence for a moment.

"His illness and death shattered my world," Emily told their clasped hands.

"Yeah," Skye murmured. "Suicide is a unique, complicated grief, isn't it?"

Emily nodded. "As illustrated not ten minutes ago, I'm still affected by it." She released Skye's hand, so she could grind the heels of her palms into her eyes, now itchy from the tears.

"Grief is always hanging around, Em. It might play hide and seek for a while or wear a different coat but it's always there. Sometimes it turns up without a disguise at all and it knocks you sideways."

Emily turned at Skye's contemplative words.

"Thank you. When I do get a visit from my grief, my need to plan amps up. Then, after a while, it drops back a bit, which means I'm quite the work in progress." Then the heat from Skye's leg, her shoulder, the parts of her pressed into Emily's body registered properly, and when combined with Skye's instant non-judgemental compassion, it felt like a perfect package had been delivered. Emily could wallow in her bath of indecision, opening the perfect package occasionally to demonstrate how predictably unpredictable she could be. Or she could step out properly, dry off, and launch herself at all that perfect.

She leaned over and briefly, like butterfly wings, brushed her lips over Skye's.

Skye growled seductively. "Oh no, that's not nearly enough. Come back here, missy."

Emily bit her lip, then pushed up to straddle Skye. "Missy?" She raised an eyebrow.

"Would you prefer Mistress?"

Emily shivered in delight at the connotations related to that particular title, then, mindful of Skye's shoulder, kissed her hard, fully, lips tugging and sliding. She smiled against Skye's mouth. "I'm not sure I could live up to Mistress," she murmured. The brown eyes gazing back at her crackled with heat.

"Oh, I think you could, but we'll table that for another time."

Emily grinned, then braced her hand on Skye's right shoulder, and crept the other under Skye's shirt. She began to slowly rock, backward and forward, rolling over Skye's lap.

"Oh, God. You're determined to—oh Jesus!—divest me of all my —Shit, Em!—shirts," Skye gasped, as Emily worked her nipples into tight buds. Emily's gaze scorched a fiery trail across Skye's face, and they held eye contact, as Emily continued to rock, and play, and their magnetic energies were loud in the air.

"You scare me," Emily said sincerely, her fingers purposeful and urgent, her other hand gripping Skye's shoulder. Her brain threw her a look. Why was right then an appropriate time to blurt out that admission? Perhaps she felt safe to share such vulnerability while sitting in the sexy driver's seat.

"Yes, oh God," Skye said shakily, then, "What? Me?"

"Not you personally as such. The idea of you," Emily mused, then changed to cradling Skye's compact breast and strumming the nipple, which produced a gasp.

"Me—oh!—me, too." Skye's breathing was becoming quite ragged, and Emily revelled in how responsive she was as she ran her thumbnail over the nipple, then swapped to the other one.

Then she paused as she registered what Skye said. "You're scared?"

Skye caught her breath, blinking away her lust.

"Em, I want to tumble into you." Skye exhaled deeply. "But I've fallen too quickly before and jumping in that quickly has only ever got me hurt, and I'm scared I'll get hurt again," she said, still breathing carefully. "It feels weirdly like we've reversed our psychologies here, with our prudence-not-prudence quirks." Another deep breath. "Anyway, I'm scared too."

Despite how much her skin was aflame, and despite wanting to continue teasing Skye into a hurricane of directionless pleasure, Emily leaned forward and kissed Skye with an all-encompassing passion. Then she tucked her face into Skye's neck and wound her arms around her back.

"I don't want to hurt you, sweetheart. It would be devastating if I did," she mumbled into the shirt. "This, this *us*, feels important. I feel like we should give it our attention, and time."

"Yes, please. Both of those."

Chapter Twenty

Emily tossed her stylus onto the desk and pushed her tablet away. Her skin held the memory of Skye's lips, which had kissed and nibbled delectable paths for an hour that morning and therefore, four hours later, attempting to join sensible lines and calculate measurements on an electronic screen was impossible.

Her mind strayed to—stayed on, more like it—their goodbye at the front door.

"Sometimes I want to kiss you so badly that I forget to give you any warning, or even ask," Skye had whispered at Emily' mouth.

Emily breathed in Skye's scent. Vanilla. Sunshine. "Don't ask," she replied and kissed her soundly. Skye's hand rested on Emily's hip, but Emily reached down and slid Skye's hand up her side, so the heel of her hand skimmed the outside of her breast. Then she released it, placing her hand around Skye's neck, while Skye continued her journey to settle her hand between Emily's shoulder blades—a perfect spot—bracing their bodies together. They complemented each other beautifully and Emily marvelled at the series of events that had occurred to bring Skye into her life.

Knuckles rapped on the laminate of her drafting table and she jerked her head up to find Rach's knowing grin dominating most of her face.

"I did try coughing, clearing my throat, taking my clothes off…" she said, shaking her head. "Nothing. Nada."

"Smart arse," Emily said, highly embarrassed at being caught mooning over Skye in the main office. Rach pulled up another high work stool and laid her tablet on the desk.

"It's adorable. You were never like this with Bec. I'm really happy for you, Em."

"It's all new and a lot," Emily admitted.

Rach scoffed. "It always is. You didn't invent that particular feeling. Now," she tapped the table, "I've got news. 45 Anders Road."

"Please tell me it's good news. I have been onto the *Heritage Council* to check on our paperwork." The red tape hoops that architects and developers had to jump through to make the *Heritage Council* happy were ten metres in the air and on fire. It meant that the integrity of the city buildings was maintained but the rigmarole to prove the renovation or redevelopment was extreme.

"Well, mighty leader, you will be thrilled to know that as of ten minutes ago, we have been absolved of our overlay problem, because the owners of 45 Anders Road got a very sizeable slap in the form of an infringement."

"Oh! Okay, so what about..." Emily fixed on Rach's grimace. "What?"

"The owners have withdrawn their plans for the site," Rach answered, staring into Emily's frustrated gaze.

"And yet, I can tell there's more."

"Yeah. They're refusing to pay for the time we've spent on those plans, claiming that the overlay fine cancels their requirement for payment." Rach vacuumed air through her gritted teeth.

Emily fumed. "Like hell it does!"

"Yeah, that's pretty much what I said."

Emily ground her index finger into the desktop in harsh circles. "I'll send a letter to them, via our lawyers. That'll fix it hopefully. Far out! Why do people—"

"Suck?" Rach interjected.

"Generally, yes."

"One of the mysteries of the Universe." Rach flicked a look at her watch. "Want me to come with you to the site meeting with Jacinta and Philip from *Browning Federal*?"

Emily checked her watch and slid from her stool. "No. I'll go solo. Thanks, though." She collected her tablet and stylus, waiting for Rach to move from her own stool.

"No problem," Rach said, then threw Emily a smirk, her eyes glittering with amusement. "Will we see you back in the office or will you be done for the day so you can head home to—?"

Emily narrowed her eyes and pointed her stylus. "You. Behave, or else I'll let Darryl know about your secret desktop folder of Chris Hemsworth."

Rach cackled and wandered back to the larger desk on the other side of the office. "Oh Em, babe. He knows and enables."

***

After conducting a slow cruise past Lorraine's old place, like an architectural undercover detective, and confirming that it was being cared for in a manner in which Lorraine would have approved, even snapping a couple of photos which she sent off to her mentor immediately, Emily pulled up at the site of the new townhouse development. The dreadful cinder block masonry work, the cube of sand-coloured bricks, the tiled roof which was more tiling grout than tile. All of it was incredibly depressing, and Emily was appalled to acknowledge that, if she was honest, it was the first time she'd properly thought about the people who lived in such poor conditions. Theoretically, she knew people lived in social housing. Of course she did. Looking at buildings was her business. But this was her first *Browning Federal* government purchase, and the nitty-gritty details of that were now staring her in the face. The building was neglected, overcoming the embarrassment of its situation with a facade of bland and boring. Anger sparked in her chest. How could the government let these places fall into such disrepair? Yes, they relocated the tenants into new housing, but while those new places were under construction, those people had to live in conditions that bordered on squalor.

"At least the government actually relocates them into modern homes. Tossing people out is unconscionable," she muttered, hating the system that created the situation in front of her. Hating that the system and situation in front of her benefitted her company. It felt the same as when there's an annoying stone in a shoe but no place to stop and remove it, so better just accept the stone and carry on.

The staccato slam of two car doors sounded, and she turned to see a man and a woman in business wear walking towards her.

"Emily Fitzsimmons?" the man asked, and Emily smiled.

"Yes. Philip from *Browning Federal*?" She stuck out her hand at the nod.

"Yes, this is Jacinta from our marketing department," he continued, and Emily received a handshake and a bright smile from the stocky woman. "So," he pointed vaguely at the unit block, "the demo crew will be here to knock all this down in a month. Meanwhile, if you look towards the back of the building from this angle…" Philip began detailing *Browning Federal*'s vision for the site, which she already knew since the brief had listed everything they were looking for. So she tuned him out, plucked out her tablet and pulled up the council site plans and the allotment's official measurements. She'd been over these a number of times, but seeing the actual site was always much better for envisioning the big ideas.

She swiped the documents aside and clicked open the camera and *ArchiMeasure*—the virtual measurement tool that worked nearly as well as a surveyor's instrument—then synced them together. Emily could hear Philip's voice behind her as he followed in her wake, up the cracked concrete path, and over to the property's edge. She held the tablet up and took a number of photos, watching them stay on the screen for a second, then minimise into the measurement app, ready for downloading at the office.

"We're looking forward to the pitch night in two weeks," Jacinta piped up, and Emily lowered the tablet.

"Yes. Actually, I wanted to ask about that," she replied. Pitch night, as it was known in real estate circles, was the unveiling of the full plans, with three-dimensional models of the development, a flashy speech from the project's marketing manager, a verbal walkthrough by the lead architect, giveaways, swag, food, and alcohol. It was an invitation-only event for the high-flying realtors and the buyer's advocates who already had cash to toss about. It was glitzy, and monied and slightly tawdry as far as Emily was concerned. But she'd been to enough of them to know how necessary a successful pitch night was for any new development.

"Oh? How can I help?" Jacinta seemed eager to please.

"We're a boutique firm. It's me, two junior architects, and my designer. I'd like all of us to be present on the night so that the buyers and agents recognise the team approach that we'll be utilising for this build." Emily tipped her chin at the group of units, huddled in their block, looking for all the world like they were trying to make themselves invisible.

Jacinta beamed. "Absolutely! I love that. That plays so well. I can see the four of you presenting as a team—" she paused, then splayed her fingers as if an idea had burst from her palms. "Oh! Why don't you have your 3-D walkthroughs up on the large screen and then add layers to them when each of your team speaks?" She nodded, as though Emily had already agreed. "Yes, that's...Oh! I can see it. The guests will be led on a journey as the building grows."

Jacinta was giving off serious Aunt Leanne energy.

Emily chuckled. "That sounds amazing, Jacinta. I'll get the team to work up their parts." She turned to Philip, and her gaze captured the cement footpath with its crinkled texture, raised and lowered, like a miniature representation of shifting tectonic plates. "Philip, the tenants in these four units have new homes, modern homes to go to, don't they? The demo day is coming up very quickly."

Philip frowned, not in consternation, more like he was confused about why on earth Emily was even asking the question. "Yeah, of course. We do these city improvement purchases all the time, and the social services department relocates everyone. I've never heard any different, and believe me, we'd hear about it if the department forgot someone! The media would have a field day," he chuckled, shaking his head at the absurd idea of a government department forgetting about people. Emily sighed. Philip was right. All the dominoes were falling into place, despite the strangest little feeling sitting in the pit of her stomach. Maybe she'd eaten something off at lunch.

***

Passion. That was the only word to describe Emily's life. Passion for her work. Passion for the new projects, particularly the *Browning Federal* one. Passion for Skye.

It had been a contentious topic of discussion in Kristen's office last year.

"I hate how other people make that infuriating assumption that over-planners, people who need a map for life, people like me, aren't passionate about things. It's like passion is only available for the special spontaneous folk, like a VIP line."

Kristen had smiled quietly. "Of course you have passion, Emily."

"Right?" Emily waved her hands about her head as she strode small circles across Kristen's carpet. "The assumption is that I'm boring because I plan. I'm not boring! And I'm passionate about so much. Sometimes it teases at my fingertips, Kristen." She pressed her fingers together, then pushed them apart, to demonstrate how much passion was actually contained in that body part.

"What does?"

"Passion. Life. That revving I get in my body when something new and right is going to travel along my road and I can get it to stick it into the lane I've made for it. That," Emily had exclaimed, registering but not really taking in the slightly concerned look that her therapist had sent her way after that final sentence.

But as Emily lay in Skye's arms on Friday morning, she realised that this passion she had for Skye—the flirting, overt sexiness, sultry behaviour, wanting, needing, enjoying, basking in her space—had disappeared quite early from her repertoire in the relationship with Bec. Certainly, Bec had been flirty and overtly sexual on occasion towards Emily and it had been flattering to be desired, but when had Emily lost her passion in return? Had it actually arrived? When had she stopped desiring?

She blinked away the thoughts because those thoughts had no business being in her head when she was lying next to Skye Reynolds, a gorgeous warrior Goddess, and current lover who was not being shoehorned onto a pathway. She grinned as that sentence ran through her head.

The phone on the bedside table buzzed repeatedly and Emily rolled carefully out of Skye's arms. The screen announced Lorraine Hudson.

"Hello, Lorraine?"

"Emily, darling. How are you?" Lorraine sounded like she had been up for two hours, drunk two cups of coffee, checked her share prices, and completed a full yoga session. Emily squinted at the screen to check the time, then slapped the phone back to her ear.

"I'm well, Lorraine. And you?"

"Fabulous! Now, I know it's preposterously early," Emily blinked in acknowledgement, "but I wanted to catch you before we both got on with our days."

"That's fine, Lorraine. I'm awake, and it's lovely that you called." It was simply a fact of life that Lorraine Hudson did whatever the hell she liked, so it was better to roll with it. If Lorraine chose to phone her at stupid o'clock in the morning instead of texting like a normal person, then that's what happened.

"Excellent. I'm in the city tomorrow. My hairdresser is the one person I couldn't replicate when I moved up the coast, but Faye can only fit me in on Saturdays. But I'd love to catch up with you. I feel dreadful that it's been nearly seven weeks since we last saw each other and that's simply too long. I thought lunch tomorrow?"

Seven weeks? It was inconceivable how much time had passed and how much had taken place during that period.

"That sounds great, Lorraine. I'd love to." She felt Skye stir beside her, and angled her head so she could watch the languid stretch and twist of muscles, and torso, and thighs, and—

"—time?"

"Sorry? What time tomorrow?"

"Yes. Let's say one o'clock at *Kiln*?"

Emily recognised the name of the inner-city cafe. It was a clever mix of trendy and classy. Very Lorraine.

"That's perfect," she replied, her eyes now fixed on Skye's sexy, sleepy gaze and just-woken-up hair. The phone call needed to end very quickly.

"Done! Oh, and Emily?" The question dragged her attention back. "Yes?"

"Please extend the lunch invitation to Skye when you next see her. It would be such a treat to catch up with her as well."

The world's best eraser of prudence is lust, which would explain why Emily's brain sailed ahead and said, "I can ask her now. She's right...here..." Prudence arrived half a second too late as Emily heard the last syllable fall into the phone, and then Lorraine's joyful hum confirming the dot-connecting she was performing in her brain.

They probably wouldn't have time to eat actual food at lunch tomorrow, what with all the catching up they had to do.

***

Lorraine had limited capacity to be anything other than authentic, so when she saw Emily and Skye walking into the cafe the next day, her smile was entirely genuine. But Skye caught the gleam in her previous landlord's eye and chuckled. It was going to be an entertaining afternoon.

"Skye! Emily! I am so happy to see you," Lorraine enthused, leaning in to kiss both of Emily's cheeks and squeeze her shoulders, then repeating the same gesture to Skye, who very subtly dipped her arm so Lorraine's hand wouldn't touch down too heavily. Lorraine, of course, spotted the movement.

"You're hurt," she stated authoritatively, then sat, flapping her hands at both of them both to sit as well.

"Yeah, I dislocated my shoulder during *Rush*," Skye said, sighing at how pathetic that sentence sounded. Lorraine gasped and clutched at Skye's hand on the table.

"Oh! I told you not to go rearranging your limbs." Her frown lines meshed themselves with the general wrinkles on her forehead. "That's such a shame, Skye. You really wanted that *Gower's* contract."

Skye grinned. "We did get the contract, Lorraine. Seb won."

Lorraine pressed her hand flat against her chest. "Excellent news! I'm so pleased. And how is your shoulder now?"

"Heaps better," Skye confirmed, flicking a glance at Emily, which redirected Lorraine's gaze. And then Skye watched in amusement as Lorraine subtly probed for more information, coaxing from both Emily and Skye all sorts of revealing tidbits about text messages, and Nic's show, and Jas's party, and Skye staying at Emily's to rehabilitate. The expression on Lorraine's face was one of utter satisfaction.

Skye sipped at her tea. "How's your new place?"

"It's delightful. I'm thinking of writing a book about the historic homes in the area," Lorraine enthused, folding her hands together to beam into their faces.

"That sounds wonderful," Emily said, pushing her coffee cup away. "It looks like retirement is agreeing with you."

"It is! I keep my hand in with *Architects Australia*, of course—I simply can't let go completely—but I'm looking to purchase a couple more properties and do something interesting with them."

Skye wondered what Lorraine's version of 'doing something interesting' was. Casually dropping into the conversation that she had a very large sum of money to wave about to purchase properties—plural—in an expensive place like Melbourne and its surrounds wasn't to show disrespect to her table guests. Skye knew that Lorraine didn't function that way. No, that was just Lorraine imparting information. Even still, Skye smiled wryly to herself at the unconscious lack of awareness and privilege showing, even from someone as open-minded as Lorraine.

Their conversation ebbed and flowed around all sorts of topics, in that enjoyable manner where three people interested in the world share and diverge their thoughts.

"Oh, Emily, darling. I heard you picked up the *Browning Federal* contract!" Lorraine plonked her tea cup onto its saucer.

"I know! It's such a coup. I'm hoping they'll showcase our designs for the marketing of the next developments as well. That would be fabulous for our reputation, and my plan for the firm."

Skye beamed at Emily's enthusiasm, the way her dark eyes lit up, and her face radiated excitement. She wanted to lay her cheek in the palm of her hand and gaze at Emily while she spoke. The embodiment of a heart eyes emoji.

Lorraine smiled, then reached across and held Emily's wrist. "And, I must thank you again for those photos you texted me, even if you could only capture the front of her."

"What photos?" Skye asked. "Photos of who?" Her face must have looked hilariously befuddled because Emily and Lorraine fell apart with laughter. Then Emily slid her hand onto Skye's leg.

"Her. The building," she said. Skye still had no idea. "Lorraine's old place. I was in the neighbourhood doing the site visit for the *Browning Federal* project and I snapped a couple of photos to show Lorraine how it was being looked after." Emily smiled into Skye's face.

The heavy sound of pieces falling into place filled Skye's mind, and her stomach dropped. It couldn't be.

"Emily," she said carefully. "Where is the site for your *Browning Federal* contract?"

"Well, it's on Solon Street, basically down the road and around the corner from Lorraine's," Emily said, then her smile faltered, and finally dissolved like hot day ice cream as she took in Skye's appalled expression.

"Is it the housing commission site?"

Emily frowned. "Yes. That's what *Browning Federal* do. When the government have their big land sales, *Browning Federal* swoop in. They're known for it." She laid her hand over Skye's. "Why?"

"That's where Yvette and Rhiannon live," Skye said, looking at both Emily and Lorraine's faces as understanding slowly dawned.

"Oh my!" Lorraine gasped, and Emily's face paled.

"Oh!" She blinked furiously. "But it's okay. Honestly. I checked. They're being relocated to a brand new home."

Skye's shoulders stiffened, and she pulled her hand away. "It's not about how new it is, Em. Their new place is on the other side of the city, which means that Yvette can't accept it."

"Why not?"

"Really?" Skye was stunned. "I can't believe you're that naive." Skye felt rather than saw Lorraine sit back in her seat, as Emily's eyes widened. "Being rehoused all the way over there means that she'll lose her job at the hospital. There's nothing over that side of the city *except* new housing. No infrastructure, no proper public transport yet, it's too new, which means she'd have to buy a car. The department doesn't think about things like that. It's all about moving a case number around. That's all they think about. And money. Plus they give in to pressure from owners of houses near the flats to demolish the building because it brings the real estate price down in the area." Skye breathed deeply

"I…I had no idea," Emily whispered.

Skye knew that was true, but it still didn't stop her eyes flicking about the table in agitation, then landing back at Emily's stricken gaze. "I can't believe you're working with those vultures."

Emily jerked. "Who? The social services department?"

"No. They're the original arseholes. I'm talking about *Browning Federal.* Like you said, they swoop in and feed off the dead houses that the government has left neglected, while they wave a shiny toy at the tenants to keep them distracted," Skye said scathingly.

"Skye, the land has already been sold and the building is due for demolishment soon." Emily stared helplessly at Skye. "So it's happening, and I can't back out of the contract."

"Why not?" Skye scowled, knowing she was being unreasonable, but the tide of powerlessness was threatening to consume her.

"Because I can't!" Emily stated firmly. "It's binding and besides, this contract, this build, will keep *Fitzsimmons* on track. I have a direction for the firm, and this is part of it."

There it was. Skye had wondered when more planning behaviour would manifest itself. This was Business Emily and her plan, so it wouldn't be too long before Personal Life Emily arrived with her plan. Skye felt nauseous. She looked over at Lorraine who hadn't spoken a word. Her face was impassive, carefully arranged to not give away any thoughts about the matter at all, but when her eyes held Skye's, the sympathy was apparent. Skye shook her head.

"I'm so sorry, Lorraine. It was nice to catch up with you, but I'm not hungry anymore and I think I need to go home." She pushed her chair back, lifted her napkin from her lap, then tossed it on her plate. Emily was on her feet instantly.

"Skye!" Her hands fluttered in distress. "Let me drive you."

"No," Skye said, sadly, holding Emily's gaze. Then after another moment of contemplation, she tipped her head and shrugged. "I can catch a tram. I'd like to be alone for a while." Skye smiled tightly at Lorraine, then looked at Emily who seemed close to tears.

Then she turned and walked out of the cafe.

Chapter Twenty-One

During the remainder of the lunch with Lorraine, which had been more a counselling session than an actual eating event, and then on the drive home, Emily stewed on everything that Skye had said. How was she supposed to know that the new houses were inappropriate? How was she supposed to know that there wasn't any infrastructure over that side of the city? Actually, she probably should know that, but that wasn't the point! And, she mentally waved her finger in the air as she stopped the car in the driveway, how dare Skye call her naive?

Skye had obviously spent her time stewing as well, because when Emily stomped down the gravel to the studio, knowing full well that Skye wouldn't be in the house, and knocked on the door, Skye looked ready to take on any argument.

"I'd like to talk, please," Emily began and squared her shoulders in preparation. Skye gave her a long look, then stepped aside to allow entry. But as soon as the door closed, Skye was the first to start.

"I can't believe you're going ahead with that contract. You should withdraw," Skye said evenly. Emily flipped her hands over and back in disbelief, then deposited them on her hips.

"Why?" she asked.

"Because I thought you were more ethical!" Skye shot back, her face tight with tension.

"Oh, you did not—of course I'm ethical. But my ethics are only as strong as the knowledge I have at hand. I didn't know that Yvette's new place was so inappropriate for her needs, and I'm sorry that this situation is messing with her life plan." Emily curled her hands into fists.

Skye delivered an incoherent noise. "Plans! That's all you think about! You need to pull your head out of your arse, Em. Nothing in life goes to plan. Nothing! And now Yvette's life is going down the toilet again because of Social Services. But now that you know that, are you going to withdraw?"

"No!" Emily's voice lifted in both pitch and volume, and she breathed deeply to control her emotional turmoil. "I can't do that. It's not that easy. The building is still going to be demolished, and the townhouses will still be constructed, no matter what. That part is a done deal. And if *Fitzsimmons* pulls out, another architecture firm will simply step in. So, I may as well be the architect that gets to complete the design." Her eyes felt like they were filled with angry fire.

"It's just wrong."

Now there was a statement based on naivety, Emily thought. "I understand that and I'm sorry, but I can't fix this."

Skye chopped the air with an open hand and Emily flinched. The frustration, the sadness, the anger, the pain was literally pouring off Skye.

Those anguished eyes settled on Emily. "Yvette is stuck. If she accepts the new place, she has to look for a job in a dreadful employment market, which means she might not be able to make payments, despite the rent not being a great amount. But if she doesn't accept the new place, she keeps her job and tries to find a place privately, which as we know," Skye poked herself in the chest, "is next to impossible and so she and Rhi will be homeless."

"And asking me to do something about it is unreasonable," Emily countered, which was probably the wrong thing to say because it seemed to inflame Skye even further.

"Yvette and Rhiannon don't mean anything to you, do they?" she yelled. "You're exactly like the department! People are just Lego pieces to put in and out of your buildings." Skye's voice was tense and strung tight, like an elastic band struggling to contain too many rolled posters.

Emily choked on a breath. "Ow! That's bullshit. I need that contract because...because," she flapped her hands away from her body. "Because *Fitzsimmons* is a business, Skye. And this situation is something you just can't fix. You're making this about you because you can't gallop in on a white horse and save everyone."

Emotions rippled across Skye's strong face. "I'm not trying to, for God's sake. I used to but I only got a 'thanks very much' and then they left. I'm not trying to save Yvette and Rhiannon. I want to help, but I can't even do that with any extra money because I went and stuffed my shoulder and I had to use the prize money to pay for another courier instead of investing it in the business."

"You are rescuing, though, because you're trying to fix this," Emily said quietly.

Skye jerked. "Fine! But can't you see? If people have the capacity to make things better for other people, then shouldn't they do that?"

"Isn't that what your parents do?"

"God, you're infuriating. That's a...I am not my parents!"

"I know that! But you're acting like it." Emily wiped her hands down her face and took a deep breath. "I'm not deviating from my plan for my company just because you don't like one contract. I can't deviate from big plans like that, because that's how business works, and I know you know that. You're being ridiculous."

Emily knew instinctively that this whole situation was more than trying to help Yvette and Rhiannon. Skye's next sentence confirmed it.

"Jesus, Em! It's hard to reconcile the two of you."

"Two?"

"Yes. The Emily Fitzsimmons business owner who sees the collateral damage but keeps forging ahead, and this," she gestured at Emily, "woman who I've been sleeping with. Are you even the same person?"

"Of course we...I am."

"I wouldn't know. The Business Plan Emily isn't who I thought you were. I need to step back. I need to reassess."

"Reassess what?"

"Reassess how far I've leapt. Maybe I've gone too far. Maybe you've already shoved me into a Skye and Emily plan that I don't even know about."

Emily gasped around the lump in her throat. "I haven't. In fact, I have been the most spontaneous I've ever been with someone when I'm with you. I've told you that. You're the one who jumped into my life, boots and all, like bloody Tigger." This entire interaction was becoming ludicrous and unkind and she'd started to unravel a little.

Skye slowly nodded, then changed the gesture so she was shaking her head in disbelief. "Okay, then I don't know who you are."

Emily deflated at Skye's response. Not that she had much air in the first place. Then she lost all air completely when Skye continued.

"I'm going to take some time out, okay? I can't talk to you right now. I need to be here in my own space. I've got all my stuff from the house, so you don't have to worry about that."

Emily felt marooned in the middle of the lounge, while the air crackled about her, then, with a sort of grunt through closed lips, she turned on her heel and wrenched open the door. Halfway up the driveway, the tears started, and her shoulders shook with sadness and hurt, and the awful feelings of paralysis and foreboding when a solution cannot be found, and safe plans suddenly were anything but.

***

"And then, after all that, she said that she needed time out," Emily said, the weight of the sentence crushing her heart.

Nic wrapped his arm around her shoulders. She'd arrived at his apartment an hour ago and immediately fallen into his chest, sobbing spectacularly, which immediately sent Marco into the kitchen to create comfort cupcakes and Nic to lead Emily over to the soft lounge suite so she could hug a box of tissues.

Emily blew her nose. "I can't believe I'm still like this even a day later." She tossed the balled-up tissue onto the seat next to her.

"Hon, you're allowed to be upset."

Emily gasped, as the realisation crashed into her mind, like an Instagram influencer at a party. "Nic! I'm more upset about Skye calling a time-out than I was about Bec destroying our relationship."

They held eye contact. Then Marco's soft Italian-accented voice travelled from the kitchen.

"This Skye? She lives in your heart more than your head. This was not so much your Bec. The strength of our reaction will always match the location of our pain, si?"

The look of adoration that Nic sent Marco was palpable, and Marco's day-old stubble couldn't hide his blush. He ducked his head and bent over the last batch of cupcakes.

"Marco's right," Nic said.

"I know," Emily sighed.

"You've certainly shown everyone around you how much she's in your heart," Nic stated, removing his arm and crossing his legs. Emily assumed a proper conversation was about to happen, rather than the series of scattered sentences that she'd shared so far through the ocean of sobbing.

"Have I?" Emily grabbed another tissue.

"Oh yes. You've been less cautious." He poked out a finger in preparation of a list. "Less reserved." Another finger. "More fun."

Emily spluttered. "I've always been fun!"

Marco appeared with a tray bearing a plate of orange-iced cupcakes, and three lattes. Nic beamed at him. "Thank you, gorgeous man of mine." Then he turned to Emily.

"Yes, you've always been fun, but your fun is like a slow cooker, sweetie. It takes a while for people to see it, for you to let people in. You keep people in a holding pattern until you've worked out where they fit onto the blueprint in there."

He pointed at Emily's head.

"But Skye?" he continued. "You just made room for her and I'm not sure if you remembered you even had a blueprint. And you're having fun being—"

"Being me," Emily interjected. "I'm having fun being me. And I'm flirty, Nic. Oh my God, I've been so forward and overt. It's exciting." She shredded the tissue, littering her crossed legs with a snowstorm of tiny pieces.

"It is, isn't it?" Nic reached over and tugged Emily's hand from the destruction in her lap. "It is exciting, so is that—"

"Being flirty and sexy and fun makes for a very vulnerable Emily, doesn't it, cara mia?" Marco interrupted, as he passed over Emily's coffee. Emily completed the difficult task of smiling her thanks, nodding sadly, taking the cup, then turning slightly to widen her eyes at Nic.

"See? Marco gets it. I've made myself incredibly vulnerable with her and it's felt so right and now she wants a time-out because I'm unable to fix something that she wants fixed and I can't see a way to do that without throwing a nuclear bomb at the blueprints in my head."

Nic sipped at his cup. "Mm-hmm."

"She said such unreasonable and hurtful things," Emily said, the tears creeping up again as she cycled through the argument in her head, then she deposited her cup onto the table. "But, you know what? For all the stupid hurtful things, I really believe I saw something in her eyes. Like when you wave your arms about in frustration and stuff gets whacked without you meaning to. That. Like she didn't mean it but did?" She looked up and Marco and Nic nodded in encouragement. "What she said was hurtful; that's a given. But it must be difficult being a highly efficient and competent person who has always fixed things and rescued herself and been thoroughly independent, then suddenly watching a situation unfold where you can't fix or save anything at all. I don't know. I think I'm too tired to think straight."

Emily scrubbed at her chest with her fist.

"Still hurts so much," she whispered.

"I know, tesoro. What are you going to do?" Marco asked, patting his mouth with a napkin.

"She asked for a time out, so I guess I respect that."

***

The tree photo shook slightly. Probably because the screen displaying it was trembling. Emily tightened her grip so she could hold the phone still, and Skye's face, her undeniable look of desire and unbridled passion, came into focus.

"Oh, Skye," she whispered to the screen, then flipped her phone over, and rubbed at her chest as tension rode close to the surface. It was a wonder she didn't have bruising there since the gesture had been a constant companion for the last two days. It was only Monday and she'd already told herself possibly two-hundred times not to text Skye. Time-outs needed to be respected, even if the time-out caller had said awful things. Emily itched to bang on Skye's door, yell "I'm not naive and you're beautiful and you were mean, and you can't save everyone and I'm not a horrible person if I plan stuff and I feel beautiful with you and I really like you a whole lot," then run away up the driveway. So mature.

Skye was right, though. It shouldn't be part of Emily's world knowledge to know how social housing worked. But now she did know. Emily assumed that Yvette didn't actually want to live in social housing, which was a completely baseless assumption. But she figured that having to rely on the whims of the government and bureaucrats must be continuously exhausting and stressful, then add a child into that mix and—

"And she'd never be able to think ahead for Rhiannon's future, or her own," Emily said to her laptop. She stared unblinkingly at its silver case and drummed her fingers on the desk. Skye's mother had labelled those receiving government assistance as people who'd lost their way, but that definition was divisive and didn't sit well in Emily's head. Definitely not in her heart. She drummed her fingers some more, then chewed on her lip for extra contemplative power.

"They're not lost because what if they haven't got a map in the first place?" she muttered.

The government housing system was too convenient for those in charge to ever redesign. Why would they? It kept people under a thumb. And Emily certainly wasn't about to throw on a white saviour costume and fix something that needed years of structural change and societal rethinking to transform. But what if she created something that existed in parallel to the housing commission? What if—

She sprang from her chair and marched into the main office.

"Drop what you're doing, everyone. Team meeting in the corner," she announced, and pulled the chairs away from the coffee table, then sat, vibrating with energy, while Jas, Dimitri, Rach and Nic ambled over.

"Here's a hypothetical," she stated emphatically, once everyone was assembled.

"Ooh, I love those," Jas squeaked and clapped her hands.

Emily grinned, aware that lightning flashes of excitement were sparking from her eyes.

"So," she began, "let's say there's a block of units that is in reasonable shape. It just needs some gutsy reno."

There was a collective murmuring and nodding. She grinned again.

"The reno on this block of units can be completed within a normal timeline, but let's say that down the street there's a separate two-bedroom unit that needs doing up very quickly."

Dimitri sat forward. "How quickly?"

"Eight days," Emily said. He sat back and inhaled deeply, contemplating the speed of that.

"Eight days? To renovate a two-bedroom unit?" Rach pulled the corners of her mouth down in thought, then she shrugged. "I guess it could be done."

"It'd be like those renovation shows," Jas enthused.

"Which are not real, Jas darling," Nic said, resting his head on her shoulder. Emily waved her hands about.

"Back to the scenario, guys. If I said that this reno had to start," she rolled her hands in the air in search of a date, "at the end of next week, what materials and labour could you source for free?"

"Free?" Nic's eyebrows shot up.

"Yep. Free and eight days," Emily confirmed.

Everyone engaged in their personal thinking postures; Dimitri scratched at his chin, Rach stared at the ceiling, Jas jiggled her foot, and Nic sat quietly, staring at Emily.

Dimitri leaned forward again, his eyes bright with interest. "I'm talking with the plasterers, sparkies, plumbers, and other trades from *Cascades* all the time. Hypothetically, they could give up their time for a couple of days." He peered at Emily, and when she smiled in response, he nodded, like he'd scored an A+ on his assignment.

"If I get onto the suppliers from our last two projects, I might be able to persuade them to donate plasterboard, paint, and other materials if it's for a good cause?" Rach looked around the group and shrugged. Emily pointed to her.

"It's for a good cause," she confirmed. "And you are one of the most persuasive people I know. You'll be fine."

The group chuckled.

"Well," Nic said, stretching out the word. "I have a file of people, nay, a vault, to call upon, so no dramas there." He turned and lifted an eyebrow at Jas.

"What? I'm just the receptionist."

Unfettered laughter filled the room. "Oh, my God. If there's anyone who fits the brief for this hypothetical scenario, it's you, Jas," Rach cackled. "Come on."

Jas smiled cheekily. "Give me a list. There's bound to be someone I know who can tick the boxes. Be warned," she frowned at everyone, "that list will be retired soon."

Emily stared. "What? Why? Isn't your 'people Jas has been out with' list constantly updated like a new phone?"

Jas giggled. "Ha! No, I've been seeing the same person for two weeks now." She squared her shoulders and shook out her purple-tipped hair to emphasise this astonishing information. Rach clutched dramatically at her blouse, while Nic collapsed sideways in the opposite direction onto Dimitri's shoulder.

"This person wouldn't happen to be a hunky Filipino bike courier, would they?" Rach enquired.

Jas blushed. Another astonishing event.

"Right, everyone." Emily's voice returned their attention. She erased the sudden image of Skye in her lycra shorts that had appeared when Seb's name was mentioned. "That's the hypothetical, but I'm about to make some phone calls and see if this hypothetical can dip its toes into reality, so be ready to activate your contributions." She smiled at her team. Could this work? She had the best people around her, but she needed one more player. A very important player.

As everyone made movements to stand, Nic caught her eye.

"Go, you," he mouthed, and he pressed his hand to his chest, his eyes sparkling.

***

"Emily, darling!" Lorraine delivered the words like she was in the room, and Emily basked in their warmth.

"Hi, Lorraine. Have you got a few minutes to chat? I've got an idea to run by you."

"Ooh. Lovely. Firstly, though, how are you and Skye? I hope you were able to patch things up," Lorraine said, the worry clearly evident.

"Ah, not exactly, but I think we'll be okay. But strangely enough, that argument on Saturday relates to my phone call today."

"Oh? Do tell."

Emily chuckled to herself. She knew that whatever activity Lorraine had been doing would be instantly abandoned because a chat about a good idea with a good dose of gossip was basically oxygen for her mentor. And it was exactly the focus that Emily needed right now. She took a breath.

"I'd like to start a foundation with your help. A foundation or trust that provides homes for people just like Yvette and Rhiannon. I'm not sure of the details yet, and I was hoping you'd be able to guide me a little." Her fingers plucked up a pen and she began drawing circles into the notepad.

"Tell me more," Lorraine said, and Emily shivered with excitement at the change in Lorraine's voice. The frivolity and fluff had been booted by laser-sharp intensity, honed from fifty successful and lucrative years in business.

"I thought this trust could be for people who needed a home in a specific location because of their work, or because of their needs."

Emily gestured vaguely like Lorraine was seated in front of her. "The trust will own renovated properties—units and flats mainly. People apply to the trust and if successful, they can rent one of these renovated units for the same low rent that the social services department charges. But the rent never increases, and the tenant is never relocated unless their circumstances change for the better, which is unlike when the housing commission places are due to be demolished and they all get moved about whether they like it or not." Emily sat back and blew out a slow breath. "But I found out that to register a trust with the tax office takes forty days or more, which means we'd be out of time because the demolition of Yvette's unit is before that."

She scribbled a series of circles on the notepad. "So, what do you think? Is a housing trust something I should do? Where should I start?"

There was silence on the other end of the phone.

"Well, Emily darling, that is a simply marvellous idea, and I do believe I have some answers for you," Lorraine declared. "*Architects Australia* already has a trust registered with the tax office."

"But…" Emily furrowed her brow. "That's *Architects Australia's* trust."

"Of course," Lorraine said like it was obvious. Emily blinked.

"I don't—"

"The *Architects Australia* trust only has one program under its banner. A scholarship programme, which I founded when I became CEO." The pride was clearly evident.

"Okay?"

"But the trust has an open registration, which means that other programmes can be created under its auspices," Lorraine explained, and lights, bright and shiny, began firing in Emily's mind.

"Oh!"

Lorraine chuckled. "Exactly. So, your housing programme simply needs a rationale written out, the application process for prospective recipients finalised, and then it just needs authorising."

Emily contemplated the simplicity of those steps. This was amazing. "Who authorises it?" she asked.

"Me," Lorraine replied. "I'm still on the board, Emily, and my purview happens to be the trust."

Blinking away tears, Emily smiled shakily into the phone. "Oh, Lorraine. That would be incredible. I've…" she swallowed, "I've got my team ready to go. We just needed the programme set up, but it sounds like it can happen really quickly."

"Of course it can. I didn't get to where I am today by driving in the slow lane, for heaven's sakes! Now, we've got some work to do, you and I, but I imagine we can get this programme up and running within a week. Oh!" Lorraine stopped short.

"What?" Her heart in her mouth, Emily stared wide-eyed at the wall. What now?

"What are you going to call the programme? The scholarship one is called *Strive*, which is rather pertinent. Did you have a name in mind?"

Tears filled Emily's eyes again. "*Home*. I'd like to call it the *Home Programme*."

"Oh, well done. I do like that. Now, the next step, obviously, is to purchase properties, so let's keep our ears to the ground. Hmm. Vacant blocks of units are not readily available in Melbourne at the moment. Single units, however," she let the word hang in the air.

Emily hummed. "Yes. I'd like to quickly find a place for Yvette and Rhiannon and fix it up as our initial *Home Programme* unit."

"Yvette's already approved? Do you have the application criteria already?"

"She's approved. Yvette can apply retrospectively, because I'm going to ask her to help me write the application package. Nobody knows better about the needs of those in social housing than someone who needs social housing."

"I'm very impressed, darling. Look, I must run. Pop all the details into an email and we can make a start. Well done," she repeated, then rang off.

Emily breathed in slowly. Lorraine Hudson had always been a force of nature as a mentor, but now she was the person in charge of a housing programme that had appeared in Emily's mind not three hours ago. Inconceivable.

The metaphorical wrecking ball hanging overhead swung ominously, and Emily realised that time had started ticking on the surreal juxtaposition of designing townhouses for *Browning Federal* to sell to rich people and purchasing properties for a housing programme designed to get people away from *Browning Federal* and the rich people.

Chapter Twenty-Two

A full two weeks and a day after the Stupid Argument—in Skye's head it was capitalised whenever she thought of it—Skye found herself scrounging around in the fridge for the ingredients of a Monday night salad. It really was a stupid argument. She knew she'd been unfair to Emily.

"Downright horrible," she muttered at the lettuce. But she felt so impotent, and that was blocking any sort of apology.

"I can almost," she chopped into a cucumber, not caring if the pieces had any uniformity, "*almost* understand Mum and Dad's motivation now." Which was an admission of such magnitude that she paused, knife in the air, and stared vacantly at the cutting board. Then she shoved those thoughts aside, which meant that all the other thoughts crowded in. She had rushed headlong into...*something*... with Emily. That's all it was so far. A something. But they had a spark, a potential, and her heart gave a disappointed lurch, like when you travel over a speed bump too quickly. It served her right. She'd chucked romance for self-pity and recrimination.

The tomatoes met a similar fate to the cucumber.

At least she had work to occupy her mind, along with an aching shoulder. Pushing herself with non-stop deliveries for eight hours was actually one of the dumbest decisions she could have made, because, for each of the ten days she'd worked so far, she'd enjoyed the company of an ice pack every night.

"There's that leaping into things again," she admonished, tossing the ingredients aggressively into the bowl.

Despite not apologising and insisting on the time out, she'd paid attention to Emily's comings and goings, and noticed that she was working very long days, and Skye assumed that Emily had buried herself in work just as much as she had. The two times when they had crossed paths, they'd hardly spoken. The interactions had been about the rain—"It's raining"—or next door's car parked over half the driveway—"I'll get him to move it." All so frosty and impersonal. Skye poured olive oil over the vegetables. At least they were talking. She scoffed. They weren't talking. They were passing words across a giant void, with most of them landing in the deep valley below, which made Skye feel like last week's rubbish.

"Bin day!" she exclaimed and dropped her fork with a clatter. Monday night. Shit.

Tugging the red wheelie bin behind her, Skye strode up the driveway in the dark, the plastic wheels scrabbling on the gravel, but just as she passed the front door of the main house, it opened and Emily stepped out. Skye froze, because really, Emily didn't step out. She floated. The electric-blue cocktail dress, the heels, the shawl shot through with something sparkly, the short hair styled so the beautiful, dishevelled-but-not, elfin effect that was utterly Emily was intensified. She looked fragile and sexy at the same time, which should have been impossible but it wasn't because there it was, embodied in her landlord. Skye swallowed very deliberately.

"Um. I'm just putting the bin out," she finally managed to say.

"Okay."

Skye nodded at that because it really was the only reply necessary. But then, suddenly, desperate to continue the exchange, such as it was, she said, "Going out?"

"Yes. I have a function."

Emily walked down the few steps and made her way to her car, and Skye trundled the bin a few more metres, then stopped.

"Okay then," she said, flailing, knowing what she should be saying, but wondering if it was too late.

Standing with her car door open, the interior light illuminating her features, Emily's eyes, wide and gorgeous, held Skye's for a long moment, saying more than their actual conversation. Then she got into the car, backed it out of the driveway, and drove away.

The hot feeling that comes before tears rose in Skye's chest. She should have said how sorry she was. She should have asked to cancel the time-out. She should have told Emily how beautiful she looked. All of it would have been the truth.

***

Browning Federal's pitch night was located in one of the smaller function rooms of the *Horizons Hotel,* and as Emily had expected, the atmosphere reeked of wealth. A string trio was perched in the corner; their instruments the musical version of the three bears. On the other side of the room, a small bar was doing a roaring trade with the fifty or so guests drawn in by the free drinks. Emily decided to leave her drink until later. It was only going to be a mojito mocktail and hopefully the bartender wouldn't be overly troubled by syrup, lime and mint.

She couldn't see any of her team, which meant she had a minute or two to allow thoughts of Skye to drift into her mind. The last two and a bit weeks had been one of the most stressful fortnights in her life. Well, that was being melodramatic. Her father's death and the aftermath would qualify first in the Stress Olympics, but Skye's reticence, her clear reluctance to meet Emily halfway, or even a third of the way, to resume their relationship stabbed at Emily's heart. Skye had looked lost tonight, like she had no idea what to do, but Emily refused to dive in and save her. Although it had been touch-and-go, because Skye, with her hair loose about her shoulders, standing in the middle of the driveway in her track pants and misshapen sweater, and clutching the bin, looked like she needed saving. Needed to be swept up and embraced. Needed to be held. Emily bunched her fists and felt the nails dig into her palms. No, Skye needed to sort herself out, but it didn't stop Emily missing her terribly.

"Hello, lovely. You look all levels of fabulous," Nic said silkily at her shoulder, and she turned to smile into her friend's face. She leaned back and pointed.

"And same to you," she acknowledged, then gestured to his eyes. "No enhancement tonight?"

"Well, *Browning Federal* and the money they attract is so very right-wing that I'm surprised this room isn't listing to starboard, and besides, we're a team, sweetie; if we want more of these contracts, peacock feathers painted over my eyeballs is not going to help."

Emily swallowed thickly. "Oh, Nic." Then she flung her arms about him, burying her face in his neck, his cologne filling her senses.

"Hey, it's okay, hon," he whispered. "Time-outs don't last forever, and Skye will get bored sitting on the bench, believe me."

She pulled away to breathe deeply, and Nic shook his head. "And that is the last sport metaphor I will ever make. Thank you for putting me through that experience," he said sarcastically.

Emily laughed, which relieved some of her tension.

"Bloody hell, these events are superficial. They're like cheap one-ply you accidentally put your finger through." Rach's growly voice landed between them, followed by the woman herself, resplendent in a red wrap blouse and black silk pants. Nic snorted and buried his chin in his chest, and Emily widened her eyes at her junior architect who looked completely unrepentant.

"Rach," she hissed.

"Psh, no-one heard. Oh!" she exclaimed. "Whenever you're ready to go ahead with your unit, I've got all the suppliers lined up like shopping trolleys. Just say the word."

"Oh my God, that's awesome. I've got a couple of leads but nothing's quite right. I need to get a move on, though, because demolition is in eleven days."

"Nah. You'll be right. Buy a vacant place tomorrow, twenty-four-hour settlement, send in Dimitri's sexy contractors with all the materials, Nic works his magic, then bing bang boom, you've got your first recipient in and you're up and running." Rach brushed her hands together and winked. "Right. I hate these things, so I'm off to grab—" She spotted an elegantly dressed Dimitri making his way over, and reached out to hook his elbow, spinning him in a turn worthy of an international dance competition. "Dimitri, help me with the drinks," she instructed, and they headed to the bar.

Their presentation was very well received, judging by the applause and appreciative murmuring when each element appeared on the screen that filled the wall at the far end of the room. During Nic's design stage, she scanned across the nodding and smiling crowd and suddenly locked eyes with Bec. Her brain spasmed. Of course Bec would be in attendance. This type of high-level event had Rebecca Deans' name written all over it. Emily swiftly averted her gaze, but couldn't avoid her ex-girlfriend when she cornered Emily not ten minutes after the last speech.

"Em! Hi. When I found out that *Fitzsimmons* got the contract, I knew you'd be here tonight," Bec gushed, and Emily marvelled at what a waste of oxygen that sentence was. "How are you?"

Emily blinked. "Um. I'm good, thanks. You?" This was uncomfortable. She took in Bec's beautiful dress, her heels, her perfectly coiffed hair, her model good-looks, and felt...nothing. Then, unbidden, images of Skye popped into her mind and she felt...everything.

"I'm fabulous. Would you like to have a drink in the pub next door? We could catch up," Bec suggested.

"Why?" Emily asked immediately.

Bec looked contrite. "I feel like I should..." She seemed to be struggling to get the words out. "I feel like I owe you an explanation." Emily waited, holding fast eye contact. "I feel like I owe you an apology," Bec finished eventually, and they let out a mutual breath.

If apologies were being bandied about, then Emily was all for it. "Why not. Let me just say bye to my team and I'll meet you out the front."

After reassuring three worried colleagues that she'd be fine, Emily found herself sitting up at the bar in the upmarket pub beside the hotel. She crossed her legs and shuffled slightly on the high seat. Then, sipping her second mojito mocktail of the night, which was far superior than the free much-too-sweet version earlier, Emily looked expectantly at Bec.

"Your presentation was terrific," Bec began.

"Thanks." Emily decided that she wasn't going to give an inch, so she took another sip, as did Bec. Of course, the silence was awful. "How's Theresa?" Emily asked, eventually.

Bec placed her wine glass carefully on the little white napkin. "We broke up," she said and shrugged. Emily rolled her lips together to ensure that idiotic words didn't fall out.

"That's too bad," she said, carefully screening that sentence before allowing it into the air.

Bec widened her eyes and alarmingly leaned right into Emily's space. "I miss you, Em," she said beseechingly, then she continued quickly as Emily's eyes widened, mostly in horror. "We were good together. I loved how reliable our relationship was, you know?" Bec opened her hands, a gesture perhaps meant to indicate how obvious it was or perhaps she had sweaty palms. Who knew?

Forcibly closing her mouth, Emily felt a confused, maybe appalled, expression take up uncomfortable residence on her face. "Bec," she began. "We never really loved each other."

Bec placed her hand over Emily's, which set her teeth on edge.

"We could learn to, though," Bec simpered.

Like curriculum?

"No, I really don't think we could."

Sliding her hand out from under Bec's, Emily pressed her thumb into her eyebrow and dragged it along the arch. She was so tired of her own ongoing emotional merry-go-round regarding Bec, about how Bec had flipped the table of Emily's life and left her to deal with everything. Much like what her dad used to do. Flip Emily's table and leave her to put things back on top, but never in the same position. Bec had certainly flipped Emily's table and Emily had been putting objects back on top ever since. But she'd come to a place of acceptance with her dad; at least that's what she'd told her mum and Kristen.

Then it struck her. She'd reset her table, and Bec did not belong there.

Emily held Bec's blue eyes. "I don't hate you," she said, fascinated at the simplicity of the statement.

Bec sat back in astonishment. "Really?"

"Yes. I realised that fact just now, and I forgive you."

Her words seemed to stun both of them. Certainly, Bec looked shaken, because she blinked quickly, then skittered her gaze away.

"That's...that's nice. Thanks. I mean, I know what I did wasn't the right thing to do," she told Emily's right shoulder, then brought her eyes back.

Emily nodded, letting the not-really-an-apology slide. "Yep, absolutely. But I'm serious; I no longer hate you." She gave a single mirthless laugh. "I did, that's for sure, but not now."

"Well, good." Bec sipped her cocktail, and Emily waited for the apology that Bec had promised upstairs, but it didn't look like it was going to arrive any time soon, so she continued with her section of the conversation.

"What you've said to me privately and publicly since we broke up hurt dreadfully, though." She held eye contact to make sure Bec really understood the amount of suffering.

"I know. That was pretty shitty, I guess," she murmured, and Emily had the distinct impression that Bec felt more remorse for the unkind words than for the actual cheating.

There was another silence. "I don't condone the cheating, but I think I understand." Emily was carrying the conversation and it was not making for a fun experience.

"Really?" Bec's eyebrows shot up.

"I think you felt that you were locked into one of my plans and that created a sense of claustrophobia for you," Emily mused, rolling the idea out of her head and onto the wooden top of the bar.

Bec exhaled like an enormous weight had been lifted from her shoulders. "Thank you! Yes! You have no idea!" she gushed.

Emily sipped and gave her a long look over the top of her glass. "Actually, Bec, I do," she said flatly, and Bec's subsequent head bob suggested that she knew her response had contained a bit too much relief.

Draining her glass, Emily turned square on. "I do wish you well, Bec. I really do, but we're not getting back together."

Bec laughed humourlessly. "No. That's been established." Then, inexplicably, her expression became sultry and Emily wanted to remind her of the very last sentence in the conversation, for God's sake. "Are you still with tall, blonde and athletic? The one you were with at *Utopia*?"

Emily wished she could say yes, if only to slap a massive grin onto her face and drive in another nail. But she couldn't because right then, she wasn't with tall, blonde and athletic. Right then, Skye wasn't hers, so she contemplated her glass.

Bec hummed, seeming to gain more meaning from the non-answer than any verbal response Emily could have given, which was irritating. The irritation activated her desire to leave because there really wasn't any reason to stay at the pub now. Emily had forgiven Bec, Bec hadn't apologised, they'd established that they weren't ever getting back together, and Bec was still Bec. Then inspiration struck. Bec was still Bec who was a realtor.

She flashed a bright smile, and Bec's smirk disappeared as her eyebrows wrinkled in confusion.

"Bec, I have a cashed-up friend who wants to buy a block of vacant units with a quick settlement. Do you have any on your books? They need to be vacant."

The real estate agent veneer slid across Bec's face like silk and Emily watched in fascination as the cogs rolled about in Bec's head, engaging happily with the concept of Emily's cashed-up friend and how much commission that meant. Then Bec grunted in disappointment.

"No, but Travis does," she said testily. "He's got one listing in Haverton, which he can't shift, even though he's tried because the price is completely unreasonable. And!" She tossed her hand in a dismissive gesture. "The owner wants the block refurbished, not demolished." She tossed her hand again, adding a scoff.

"Why?"

"He doesn't want to see another part of the city destroyed or some such rubbish." Bec was very much a fan of the government and

Browning Federal's skyline rearrangement philosophy, therefore, Emily decided, Travis was getting a phone call first thing tomorrow. Despite forgiving her ex, Emily was not feeling generous enough for Bec to pounce on this sale, tearing the listing from Travis simply to grab a sizeable commission. Benevolence only stretched so far.

They said their goodbyes and Emily watched as a satellite in her life drifted from her orbit. And that was okay.

The intoxicating feeling of a project coming together had Emily smiling for the majority of the drive home. This programme was her baby and she wanted it to succeed, simply because it meant that people could be helped. One of her annoying doubtful voices whispered snarkily that she was doing it to solve Skye's dilemma and win her back.

"Fuck that!" she muttered, in one of her rare moments of swearing. She turned into her driveway. What an outlandish thought. The two were distinctly separate situations. If Skye wanted to walk away —Emily's heart flipped—then she did. But the *Home Programme*? It was about Emily recognising her privilege, knowing she'd had a head start in life to actually create her roads. So many people didn't even have a starting line from which to see ahead, but when they did, that's when plans could be made and horizon lines were seen.

"That's when plans are okay," she said, contemplating the darkness filling the interior of the car as the soft ticks from the cooling engine joined her thoughts. "Plans come *from* a foundation. They're not *the* foundation." Astonishing.

Surely Kristen gave out a certificate of achievement when a client's brain burst through a metaphorical door and yelled, "Oh my God! So that's what normal looks like!"

***

Skye scrubbed sweat away from across her forehead and down the sides of her cheeks, then guided the cargo bike into the storage garage. Seb had texted that he'd be another fifteen minutes so she decided to wait to catch up in person. They still only had the two bikes, which meant that Hayley's casual work hours had been knocked back to zero. Luckily, she'd been philosophical about it, even though Skye had said the extra hours would be for a month.

"It should have been a month," Skye grumbled as she massaged her shoulder. A fortnight for rehabilitation was like taking a vitamin for pneumonia. Completely useless.

She wondered how long she could do this job. The doctor had said that once a shoulder was dislocated, it would forever be unstable, and the thought made her want to sit in the corner of the bike lock-up and cry. Her annoyance at her physical injury was sliding into self-pity, where it joined the situation with Emily pit of self-pity.

Last night, Emily had been a vision, stunning in her blue dress, illuminated by the porch light, and clearly waiting for Skye to do something. Anything.

Seb rolled to a stop as self-pity continued to tumble through Skye's stomach. He dismounted, took one look at her, and said, "Right. What's in your head?"

Skye gave a huge sigh. "I'm really sore, and I miss Emily, and I'm worried that I've wasted company money because I got injured, and I'm annoyed that I entered both of us into *Rush* especially since we're the only employees of *Quick Cargo* and I didn't think of the consequences and I suck because I can't fix…things." She rolled her eyes. "How did I get to this—"

"Shut it!" Seb said, fiercely. "Just stop. You're being sad and pathetic."

"I am sad and pathetic."

Seb guided the bike into the garage. "Skye," he growled, then grabbed his road bike, and wheeled it out into the alley. He fixed her with a glare. "Look, I know you had a childhood with parents who are—"

"Nut jobs," Skye supplied.

"Your words, not mine. And I know that they made and still make you solve everything yourself, but," he pointed forcefully towards her chest, "I want you to look at all the things you have achieved by yourself. Look!" He cast his arm towards both cargo bikes, the storage shed, then waved a hand between them. "You've got a successful company." He pointed again. "It is successful! You picked yourself up from nothing and built *Quick Cargo*. And…" he paused. "And your shoulder was an accident and it simply needs rest. And the Emily thing? You'll work it out. I know you will. You really like each other, and you're both sensible people." Then he laughed. "No, you're both workaholics, actually."

"What?" Skye leaned back against the garage door.

"Emily's really pushing herself lately."

Skye knew this from her surreptitious observations.

"How do you know?" she asked.

Seb straddled his bike, then leaned against the opposite steel upright of the garage. "Jas told me. I told her you were working too hard as well."

"And you said this because…" Skye squinted.

He shrugged. "Because she asked."

Skye hung her head. "Oh gees, mate. Emily and I shouldn't be part of your conversations. You and Jas should be finding out things about each other at this stage."

"Oh, we are, don't worry." He grinned lasciviously. "But when two of our favourite people are hurting, we talk about that, too."

Skye tilted her head and smiled gratefully. But then groaned. She could imagine one of Jas and Seb's entertaining conversations. "God, I hate to imagine what that conversation would sound like."

Seb rubbed his hands together, grinned widely, then inhaled.

"Like this." He placed his hands on his hips. "Hi Jas, so Skye is pushing herself too hard and shouldn't have come back to work so soon but she's incredibly stubborn." He pitched his voice higher. "Oh, that's too bad, but that's like Emily, too. She's stubborn as well. They really need to sort out their shit." He lowered his voice. "I reckon." His voice went higher again. "Emily's really down even though she's working on an amazing project. She misses Skye." Down he went again. "What a massive coincidence. Skye totally misses Emily as well. So, wanna get naked on the couch?" He pointed at Skye to punctuate the monologue.

Skye spluttered a laugh. "You're such a bloody shit, Seb. That didn't happen."

He chuckled. "Not exactly, but it could have, so pull your head out of your arse, mate."

***

Later that night, with her new best friend the Ice Pack cradling her shoulder, Skye realised that head removal from arses was a challenge. She had a conversation with her porcelain teapot as it squatted on its trivet in the middle of the kitchen bench.

"For someone so rigid, Emily certainly leapt into our relationship with great abandon."

She created a new voice. "That's because of you, Skye, you idiot. She leapt because of you."

Skye reclaimed her voice. "And I really miss her."

"But why do you miss her?" Teapot Skye asked.

"Because she's fabulous and fun, and hot."

"And what have you always done with women?"

Skye growled. "Saved, rescued, lost myself."

The teapot raised an eyebrow. "Done any of that with Emily?"

"No."

"Why not?"

Skye grabbed the pot's handle and poured the liquid into her cup. "Because I didn't need to. Emily doesn't need saving or rescuing or anything. She's someone I could fall for. I think I already have. She's her own person, which is why she's probably moved—" Skye jerked her head. "I'm talking to a teapot."

But her odd conversation germinated an idea for how the idiotic time-out could be resolved, how she could fix this situation because fixing stuff is what she did. It was what she'd always done. And, of course, ending the mess with a very large, heartfelt apology, because forgiveness from Emily was the most important thing ever.

Skye marched over to her bookshelves, pulling out every copy of the *Guinness Book of Records*, then dropped them on the coffee table. She opened the latest version to the index and ran her finger up and down the page. "Architecture, architecture," she muttered. "Architecture!" She poked the page number, then flipped the pages back until she found the entry for the *Maraya Concert Hall*.

"Saudi Arabia's architectural wonder, the *Maraya Concert Hall*, has been declared the world's largest mirror-clad building," she read aloud. "That's a good one."

Skye grabbed a pen and note paper.

Dear Em,

Did you know that the Maraya Concert Hall in Saudi Arabia has been declared the world's largest mirror-clad building? It captures and reflects the goodness and wonder that exists around it.

Just like you.

I'd like to revoke my time-out, please. I'd also like to apologise, but not in this note. I'd like to do it in person. I'm going to need a lot of time to give my apology because I have a lot to say sorry for. Could I drop by on Saturday afternoon?

Skye

When she pedalled down the driveway on Wednesday night, she noticed that the note was gone from where she'd wedged it behind the metal ironwork on Emily's front door. Skye's Thursday note was just as heartfelt.

Dear Em

Did you know that the largest flower arrangement is located in Dubai and measures 72.95 metres by 78.34 metres by 21.98 metres?

But I'd give anything to see one of your beautiful Ikebana displays again.

I still want to revoke my time-out and I still want to apologise on Saturday afternoon. Could I drop by, please?

Skye

It had also disappeared by that evening.

She knew the notes were cheesy, particularly the trivia and the sentence underneath, but Skye hoped they'd help rekindle at least some of the fire that was simmering between them. And then attached to her door on Thursday night was a small envelope, with a folded—exact to the corners—piece of paper. It contained a single word.

Yes.

So, Friday's note was simple.

Dear Em,
I miss you so much. I'll see you tomorrow.
Skye

After work on Friday afternoon, Skye slipped in behind a frozen goods truck as she whizzed down the main thoroughfare that led to Solon Street and Yvette and Rhiannon's block of units. The slipstream pulled her along for a minute, allowing her to slow her pedalling. Besides starting with the obvious sentence of "I'm sorry for being a complete wanker", Skye had spent most of the day formulating an apology for tomorrow's conversation. It needed to be pretty damn good.

Veering away from the traffic and turning left, Skye sat up, lifting her hands from the handlebars, and steered comfortably down the tree-lined street, purely by the motion and angle of her legs. A year of daily bike riding meant that she was just as comfortable on two wheels as two feet.

The housing block came into view, and again she questioned her reasons for visiting. Was it to torture herself knowing that she was unable to help? That was spectacularly self-absorbed. No, this visit was to say goodbye, because she probably wouldn't be seeing Yvette and Rhiannon again.

Skye jumped the bike up onto the footpath, braking near a collection of boxes that two burly men were busily loading into a rental truck.

"Skye!" Either Rhiannon was in possession of a portable amplifier and microphone in the front yard, or she was beyond excited because Skye leapt sideways as the yell, followed by Rhiannon, plunged over the low wall. Her thin arms and legs were a confusion of limbs as she bounced up and down on the footpath. "We're moving!" The grin split Rhiannon's face.

"Hey, Rhi." Skye grinned back at the girl, then scanned the windows of the four units. The lack of curtains on the other three units indicated that Miles and Lydia had already relocated, which calmed her anxiety a little, because a glance at the government's notice of sale sign had reminded her that demolition on the site was in seven days. Cutting it fine. She ducked her head to look into Rhiannon's face. "I'm assuming this truck is for you. Where are you off to? The place over the other side of the city?" God, she hoped not. Yvette's life would become even more difficult if that was happening.

"Nope! We're moving closer to the hospital to a brand new place!" The bouncing resumed.

"Not brand new, but close enough, Rhi sweetie." Yvette's soft voice interrupted her daughter's impromptu workout. Skye raised her eyebrows. If she had met Yvette for the first time right then, she would have assumed that the woman didn't have a care in the world, because this Yvette was relaxed and refreshed, and Skye immediately wanted to know why.

"Hi. Moving day, hey? And to a brand-new-but-not-quite place," Skye grinned. "Can I ask where?"

Yvette smiled broadly, and Skye realised that it was the first time she'd ever seen the facial gesture fully unleashed on Yvette's face. It was pure radiance.

"To Plover Road, down the hospital end."

"Oh my God, that's brilliant. So the department listened to you finally?" Skye couldn't believe it.

Yvette laughed wryly. "Oh no. They were being awful right up until I told them to," she cut a look at Rhiannon, "insert their automated placement system where sunlight should never be found."

Skye gaped. "Wow, that's telling them in no uncertain terms!"

Yvette lifted her eyebrows. "Mm-hmm. So we're no longer in social housing which is a sentence I never thought I'd be able to say. I mean, I thought I'd be in one of those," she tossed her thumb over her shoulder, "concrete boxes forever because I had absolutely nothing when I needed to quickly leave our family and home situation—" She subtly indicated Rhiannon, and Skye nodded, realising that Yvette's circumstances had arisen due to a number of dangerous events earlier in Rhiannon's life. The cramping feeling that preceded her need to save and fix hit Skye's stomach. She'd give anything to travel back in time and tell that—she shook her head and blinked away the pointless thought.

"I'm really excited for you, Yvette. What happened?"

"It was the most amazing thing, and I'm still somewhat in disbelief. I had a lovely woman contact me to pick my brains about a new housing program." Yvette smiled. "I thought she had the wrong person, but apparently she wanted to know what my thoughts were about the application criteria for the programme, like how people should apply, who should be selected, how they'll be selected, that sort of thing. I was blown away, Skye. She used nearly all of my suggestions because she wanted this programme to be for people who needed—oh, what did she say?" Yvette paused. "Oh, that's right, for people who needed a solid foundation to set up their scaffolding. It was a sweet sentiment. And then we had a good old chat about what should be in the units in this housing program." Yvette let out a bark of laughter. "You should have seen her face when I listed just a few essentials like working power points, flooring that didn't have holes in it, a functioning oven, windows that actually closed, and no leaks or mould. She thought I was pulling her leg." Then Yvette rested her hand on Rhiannon's shoulder, calming the vibrating girl. "I said people just want a place that's safe, secure and liveable, which made her a bit teary, then she held my hand and apologised, as though it was her fault! Poor love."

"That's fantastic," Skye enthused, thrilled at Yvette's good fortune. "Are you moving in today?"

"No. We're the founding tenants, if you want to call us something. The unit's not ready yet, because it was only bought earlier this week, so the foundation's programme is paying for our belongings to go into storage and they're putting us up in a motel for a few days."

"That's really generous. I'm so happy for you two," Skye said. Then, a small glow, like a tiny lantern in the dark, shone into her muddled thoughts.

There was no way. But maybe? Surely not.

"What's the programme called?" Skye asked casually.

"The *Home Programme*. Isn't that the nicest name? It's part of a trust that's organised by *Architects Australia*."

Instantly, the bell from Big Ben in London teleported itself to the inside of Skye's brain, and struck twelve, because understanding crashed through her confusion.

"And the woman's name?" She held her breath.

"Emily Fitzsimmons. She's such a delightful person, and I can't thank her enough for this."

Skye's mouth opened and closed silently. Oh my God.

Then she ruffled Rhiannon's hair, but her thoughts had already hopped on her bike and ridden away.

"I'm so stoked. It means I get to swing by and shoot targets with you, kiddo."

Rhiannon beamed. "Yes!"

With a last wave, Skye angled her bike towards the road and chased her thoughts. Tomorrow or tonight? That was the question. The tsunami of emotion surged inside and made the decision for her.

Chapter Twenty-Three

Emily reattached that morning's note with the others in the magnetised clip and hung it on the refrigerator door. The notes made her smile, simply because the cheese-factor coupled with the adorability made the studio audience in her head respond with an "awwwww".

Although, the message in today's note had tugged at her heart. Tugged. Really? The message had lassoed her beating organ and hurled it from her chest. Thank God she had until tomorrow afternoon to gather her thoughts. Imagine if Skye walked through the door right then and started apologising. Skye would spit out the word "I'm" and half of the word "sorry" before Emily would cut her off to babble something inane and unhelpful, like "Oh, it's fine...don't worry about it...let's carry on...sex?" As far as plans for building a healthy relationship, that was frankly awful.

"See? I can dispose of plans. Look at me go," she muttered.

The update that morning from the renovation crew working on Yvette's unit—sourced, bought, and signed in the whirlwind that was Travis's excitement and Lorraine's efficiency—had been incredibly upbeat. The final touches were being completed on Monday and Tuesday, then Yvette could move in on Wednesday afternoon, exactly two days before the demolition. Emily had nearly rubbed a hole in her sternum worrying about how close they'd come, but Rach had been correct; they'd been fine, particularly with everyone offering up their contributions like a giant potluck.

A small Ikebana piece sat half-finished in her craft room. It was to be a gift for Yvette, and Emily quite liked the idea of the floral display taking pride of place in the programme's initial home. Ikebana not only embodied focus and structure, but the arrangements also highlighted the inner qualities of materials to express external emotion and beauty.

Kind of like people. Help folks find their structure, their plan, and all their inner qualities had the chance to shine.

"Something like that," Emily said and squeezed her hands together in joy. It was working—the programme and all the bazillion facets that Lorraine had identified and taken on board, like the purchase of the block of units from an even more excited Travis—all of it was working, and now Emily could metaphorically stick it on a shelf for a little while, as she prepared for tomorrow.

A rapid knocking at the door startled her.

A sweaty, wind-blown, manic-eyed, lycra-clad Skye stood on her front porch, and Emily looked at her in incomprehension. Her long blonde hair was only just held together in a ponytail and it had that slightly squashed look created by a day of helmet-wearing. She looked incredible

"You're early," Emily stated dimly, as her thoughts scattered and her body reacted to the woman in front of her, who was vibrating with an emotion that had escaped from under the umbrella of calm. Then it occurred to her how dark it was outside and since Skye was still in her courier clothes, she must have had a busy day indeed.

Skye gestured abruptly. "You bought them a house?" she spluttered.

"Excuse me?" Emily blinked.

"You bought Yvette and Rhi a flat, like, a whole flat!" Skye crossed her arms, emphasising her biceps and her strong chest, which was very unfair, and it felt like Skye was playing dirty.

Emily frowned. "No I didn't, but if you know that Yvette and Rhiannon are moving into a unit soon, then you've spoken to them, which means that you also know about the housing programme, which means you're being dramatic." She glared, then moved aside. "Come in. You're sweaty and it's cold, and your shoulder doesn't need to get a cramp."

Skye pulled her head into her neck, gave her whole body a sort of shrug, then walked inside the house. Emily closed the door behind her and congratulated herself on that small speech. It was assertive and strong. And she had no idea where to go next.

She turned to find Skye rubbing at her shoulder and walked over.

"Two weeks rest, then back to work, hey?" Emily rolled her eyes to let Skye know what she thought of that decision.

Skye grimaced.

"Do you have frozen peas or any other small, very cold vegetable?" She squinted as a sharp pain seemed to shoot through her. Emily pursed her lips, marched to the kitchen, yanked the freezer drawer open, and rummaged around for the bag of peas she knew was in there. Skye's footsteps sounded behind her, and without a word, Emily whipped the tea towel from the handle of the oven, wrapped it around the bag, pulled open the third drawer under the kitchen counter where everything lost ended up, found masking tape, and leaned into Skye's space to tape the temporary cold pack to her shoulder. Emily held her breath because the proximity to Skye was doing odd things to her thoughts, which were further frazzled when she gently ripped the roll away from her handiwork and slowly looked up, right into soft brown eyes.

"Thanks," Skye whispered.

Emily stepped back in self-preservation and tossed the roll of tape onto the bench. "You're welcome. So," she gestured to the lounge, "do you want to know the whole story or are you happy assuming I'm some sort of real estate tycoon?"

With a sheepish look, Skye trailed after Emily and they sat on opposite ends of the couch. They'd never sat so far away. Skye stared down at her limp hands in her lap.

"I'm sorry," she breathed. Emily heard the words but knew they were the sounding note before the full version, so she waited.

Skye lifted her head and turned. "I'm sorry," she said with more conviction. "God, Em. I shouldn't have said what I did. I just wanted to fix things, because it looked like everything was falling apart for Yvette and all I could do was stand there and watch, and…and stupidly, because I couldn't do anything, I wanted you to do it." She wiped her palm across her mouth and chin and looked briefly at the ceiling. "That wasn't fair." She dropped her head to regain eye contact. "I made assumptions again, and I hurt you. And I knew, *I knew*, you couldn't pull out of that contract, but it didn't stop me from be-

ing an arsehole about it. Being an arsehole to you. I'm so sorry, Em."
Her eyes glistened, and she swallowed deliberately as if the action
would suck the tears back inside her body.

"Mm," Emily began because there was more to say, but the hum
helped prepare her words. "You made me cry, you know. The sort
where my breath had to stay at the bottom of my throat because I had
tears in my eyes, and I was loathe to let them mingle." The sort that
seemed to be happening right then, except these were good tears,
relieved tears.

Skye inhaled sharply. "I know. Well, I don't know, because I
didn't see you because of my stupid time-out. But I can imagine because why wouldn't you cry? I was shitty and idiotic, and I hurt you.
I really hope you can forgive me." The body language, the expression in her eyes; everything about Skye screamed utter remorse and
a certain amount of resignation, that she'd rolled her dice. It had
been a pretty good roll, but Emily needed to say her piece before she
collected the dice, slid them back into Skye's pocket and whispered,
"Of course" into her ear.

"I didn't do this for you, or because of what you said," Emily said
carefully, and Skye's head shot up.

"Of course," she replied emphatically.

"Good. I wanted to make sure you knew. The *Home Programme*
is for Yvette and people in similar situations. It's about giving people
a starting line." Suddenly, overwhelmed by Skye's apology, and the
high-flying philanthropy she'd instigated, and the speed of the last
two weeks and the sheer impromptu nature of everything, Emily's
voice caught around a lump in her throat. "It's so unfair, Skye," she
whispered. "And it needs to be fair for them."

Skye rubbed her hands down her thighs, looking for all the world
like she was trying to come to an important decision. Then she gave
a definitive nod, stood, and took the single step on her long legs to
sit quietly beside Emily. She laid her hand, palm up, in the small
space between them, just like she'd done two months ago during
CurtainGate, and waited for a response.

Emily glanced at Skye's hand, then up into her eyes, and very deliberately twisted their fingers together, and felt, like a punch in the heart, the empathy shimmering in Skye's gaze.

"The social services department is like a bureaucratic version of my dad. Making decisions without thinking of the consequences, and Yvette and the others end up being collateral damage, like Mum and I were. I'm not trying to impose my coping strategies onto people, because those strategies are mine, but oh my God, these people need somewhere to start. A starting point that is stable and theirs; a place where they don't have to hold their breath." She looked directly into Skye's eyes. "Because when you're not fearfully holding your breath, you can lift your gaze and see where you need to go."

Skye squeezed her hand. "You've created something brilliant, Em."

"Yes, I did." She exhaled deeply. "I did, and while there's so much work to do to fix the system, this was something I could do. This was one thing I could fix" she said, then laughed quickly. "I'm not even fixing, really, in the true sense of the word. This programme provides assistance so people can fix their...I don't know...direction?" She shrugged. "It doesn't infantilise people. They can get on with fixing what they need to themselves."

"I need to work on that; the fixing things for others, even though they might not ask for it. Saving folks tends to infantilise them, and people can do things for themselves, can't they? We can give someone a leg up, and not swoop in and take over and solve their dilemma." She smiled wryly. "I'm stepping too close to the I-am-my-parents line. Jesus." She widened her eyes at their joined hands, and Emily focused on the light brushes from Skye's thumb across the back of her hand. Then Skye whispered, "Em?"

"Yes?"

Emily slowly lifted their hands, then Skye's gaze followed their journey until they held eye contact and Emily pressed Skye's hand to her chest.

"One of the many reasons that I like you so very much is that you don't need rescuing, because you're you. You own your life and the way your childhood has impacted on you, and then all your strategies, but you don't need saving or fixing or rescuing, because if you think you do, you look after it yourself." Skye quirked a smile. "It's a really attractive quality." Skye raised her eyebrows hopefully. "Among other attractive qualities."

Emily's eyes twinkled and she shifted their hands up to her lips to kiss Skye's knuckles, one by one, maintaining eye contact.

Then, Emily bit her lip, and said, "Want to know one of the reasons why I find you so very attractive? I threw myself into your space, into you, and you met me halfway or more. I jumped, Skye, and you were there. It was wonderful. It *is* wonderful. It's because you're there." She delivered more kisses as if they helped her to think of the words. The knuckle kisses had darkened the brown in Skye's eyes, so Emily kept going with her explanation before she lost all sense of herself and attacked Skye's mouth.

"I have no idea how you do it, but I get somewhat carried away with you. I'm ripping up any semblance of plans and structure, and it's completely fabulous. With you...with you, I feel like I'm letting go of everything I should actually be holding in place right here." Emily rubbed her temple with her free hand. "So no, I don't need saving, but..." She gave herself permission to lean into Skye's space, and brushed their lips together. Then again, just so she could hear Skye's soft whimper.

"But?" Skye breathed, their heads close.

"I think I'd like a defender, which is very different from saving, isn't it? Someone who stands with me on a path or goes on a journey, but fights dragons if necessary, side by side, with me, not for me."

Skye lifted her left arm, wincing with the movement, but was obviously determined to cup Emily's face in both hands.

"A defender sounds really good. Everyone should have one, but a defender can lead you off the path into the underbrush without a compass sometimes," she stated earnestly.

Their eyes roamed each other's face.

"I think I could handle that," Emily said, smiling into Skye's face, then she inhaled carefully. "I'd have to forgive you first."

Skye pulled away, dropping her hands. "Oh! Oh, right. Um…do you?" She carefully studied Emily's expression.

At Emily's crooked finger, Skye drew closer.

"I forgive you." Emily touched her cheek. "I forgave you when you said sorry. I think I forgave you when you sent me Wednesday's note." Her last word, rounded from the 'o', skimmed Skye's mouth, and without any decision being made, their lips came together, softly sliding, then pushing and nibbling, and then opening a little so tongues, tired from talking, renewed their energy as they tasted each other's mouths.

Breaking the kiss, Emily sank into Skye's body, tucking her face into Skye's neck. Skye smelled earthy; a consequence of a day's exercise, but the aroma wasn't unpleasant. More like powerful, if she was really honest, because the effect it was having on her heart rate was extraordinary.

After a silent minute, punctuated with breathing, and heartbeats, and an overwhelming sense of perfect, the damp patch on the back of the couch made itself known.

"You're leaking all over the couch," Emily mumbled.

Skye detached herself from their embrace and looked over her shoulder. "Oh, crap. Sorry. I'll grab another tea towel."

"Let me," Emily said, then stood and walked into the kitchen. Then, as she plucked the extra tea towel from the drawer, Skye pressed into her back, placing her hot mouth against Emily's neck and delivered a slow kiss. Then another. Then a lick. Then another. Emily's body rioted, and she experienced the exquisite shudder down to her toes, which curled in desire.

"Hey Em?"

Skye's whispered words catapulted an electric shock straight down Emily's spine, and her hand, clutching the tea towel, dropped loosely at her side. What was that list in her head? Apology, forgiveness, chat, chat, chat, okay that's enough, sex.

"Yes?" she replied croakily, staring at the cupboards, trembling with heat and want because Skye's body was pressed tightly against her back.

Skye chuckled, the vibrations delicious and enticing. "Thank you for forgiving me. Maybe we could start again?" Hope and desire were the loudest words in the request.

Emily's smile sparked, and she turned in Skye's arms, draping the tea towel over the wet shoulder, then placed her hands on Skye's hips.

"I'd rather," she said, looking right into those gorgeous brown eyes, "not start again, to be perfectly truthful. I'd rather pick up from the moment where we paused." A sultry look hooded Skye's gaze, then she added a smirk, which exploded the sexiness chart. Emily swallowed.

"That moment? Hmm." Skye frowned in mock seriousness. "I think we paused," she tapped her lip and a devilish smile appeared, "on a Saturday morning. I believe you were naked on the bed, and I was worshipping your body. Yes, that's right. It's all coming back to me."

Emily giggled, her heart expanded as tides of happiness surged within, then with great care, and a bit of body adjustment to avoid defrosting legumes, she hugged Skye and exhaled.

"Does that mean you're my girlfriend now?" Skye's voice rumbled across the top of Emily's head.

Emily gave a contemplative hum. "That's a very boots-and-all type of word." She expected Skye to tense at the definition, but Skye simply laughed.

"I guess it is, although I actually thought it was a very planning-road-building kind of word," she replied, still resting her cheek on Emily's head.

"Oh. Well, I guess if we're engaging in all this planning and leaping, we should have a name for our thing." She snuggled further into Skye's body. "Girlfriend works very well. I like it. A lot."

Skye squeezed her tight, which made her smile into the lycra collar.

"I didn't plan on finding you," Emily mused quietly, continuing her train of thought.

Skye breathed into her hair, holding her fast. "Me neither. I guess we both needed a change of plans."

Epilogue

Three months later

The loud double-bang on the front door alerted Skye to Seb's arrival. He seemed to make it his mission in life to strength-test all inanimate objects.

"Movers are here," he announced as soon as Skye opened the door.

"Great. I was just checking to make sure I haven't left any last-minute items, particularly of the embarrassing variety," she sassed, and they shared a grin. Skye walked out onto the driveway to find Angel and Carmen, Seb's sisters, Datu, his father, and Jas, who had decided that Seb was perfect, deleting her profile on the dating app within a week of their relationship becoming a confirmed entity. Each of them was bearing a box or a large bag or a pile of objects.

"Skye, this is a whole box of Seb's cycling manuals and magazines," Angel, the youngest Arturo sibling at twenty-two, moaned. "Please convince him to purchase online subscriptions because, seriously."

Skye raised her hands. "Nope. Not getting involved in that argument."

"Angel, if I do that, and then drool all over the pictures of the gear," Seb paused, then tapped the box, "it'll mess with the electronics."

"Ugh, you're gross. Thank God, you're moving in here."

Skye laughed. "Thank God, I'm moving out. Can you imagine both of us flatting together?"

That produced general laughter.

They trooped in with their loads, Datu Arturo indicating for Jas to go ahead of him. Seb's father had been exceedingly happy that Seb had not only found a delightful girlfriend but one named Jasmine, which was the national flower of the Philippines. Skye felt it prudent not to tell him that Jas was not at all a delicate, shy flower and that Seb regularly appeared at work some mornings with a stunned, mostly euphoric expression on his face.

Everyone deposited their boxes and bundles of Seb's possessions and trailed back up the driveway for more. As Seb walked past, Skye touched his shoulder to stop him.

"Hey, come up to the main house. I've got something for you," she said.

He laughed, then fell into step. "Ooh, the main house," he teased.

"Shut up. I know it's Emily's house, but it's home now because I live there as of today."

Seb scoffed. "You've lived there since *Rush,* mate. I'm beginning to think the dislocated shoulder was all a ploy to—"

The hip check knocked him sideways. "Don't say it!" she threatened.

"What?" He held his hands away from his body innocently. "I was going to say it was a ploy to get access to a bigger kitchen."

That earned him a softer nudge and a laugh.

"Where's Emily today?" Seb asked.

"Finishing an Ikebana piece inside," Skye said, walking up the steps to the front door, and holding it open.

"Cool. Hey, I'm really grateful that you suggested the studio and that Emily said yes. I love my family, mate. But you know…I'm a manly man with man needs." He nodded and narrowed his eyes menacingly as he made his way into the lounge.

Skye collapsed in laughter, leaning on the closed door. Seb pretended to look offended, and Skye felt a sea of affection for her best friend. He was right when he said that Skye had technically been living with Emily since they'd restarted their relationship. She hoped the mechanism on the sofa bed in the studio still worked because it hadn't been pulled out since the night she'd apologised. Her chest expanded with heat and joy at what today meant. It meant love. They hadn't said 'I love you' yet, but Skye had wanted to for a while. Truth be told, Skye knew she'd fallen in love with Emily ages ago, but there was a fragility to those three words. Skye was very aware that Emily had never said the words to Bec in that relationship. But Skye wasn't Bec and Emily wasn't Bec's Emily anymore. Today felt like a great day for Skye to say 'I love you' to her Emily, particularly as they were now officially living under one roof.

***

Emily's suggestion for Skye to move in permanently had preceded the astonishing information that Skye's rental payments hadn't been going to Emily at all.

"What?" Skye turned away from the stove as Emily slid around the bench and stopped in front of her.

"No, they go somewhere else. I know it distressed you when you couldn't help Yvette and Rhiannon, but you have been helping."

"How?" Skye wrinkled her eyebrows, laying the spatula on the counter.

Emily ran her hands up and down Skye's biceps. "I never needed the money from leasing the studio. You know I did it for another reason. So, I kept the rent money in a separate account, and it sat there, not doing anything, and then when the *Home Programme* was placed into the *Architects Australia* trust, the programme was instantly granted charitable status."

"Right…" Skye rested her hands on Emily's waist.

"Well, that's where your rent goes, sweetheart. It supports people in the programme, so you do help because the money never went to me. I was just the…" she made a gesture with her hands that seemed to indicate that she was simply the holding bay for the funds as they were transferred but she must have thought it looked vaguely sexual—it did—so she stopped and blushed. Skye's heart expanded and she held Emily's pink cheeks.

"You are incredible. I wish I'd found you earlier in my life, because you get me, Em."

Emily beamed. "I do get you. But while it would have been amazing to find you earlier, as well, I'm glad I didn't. I wasn't ready for you, because I would have shoved you into a plan and then you would have probably left. Or I would have. So, right now? Right now you're perfect."

***

Skye joined Seb in the lounge, sitting opposite, with the coffee table separating their chairs.

"Hi, Seb," Emily said, her greeting preceding her into the room. "How's the moving going?" She perched on the arm of Skye's chair and leaned in, acknowledging the one-arm embrace Skye gave her with a kiss on the head.

Seb's spine straightened. He still regarded Emily as one of the Elven straight out of a Peter Jackson movie. It was completely understandable, as Emily had an ethereal beauty that dropped Skye to her knees.

"It's going well. Dad, Angel, Carmen, and Jas are bringing in my stuff, so I should be helping," he said guiltily. "But Skye wanted to give me something?"

"We'll let you get back to them in a few minutes," Skye assured him, then pointed to the large business envelope on the table. "That's your birthday present for next Sunday. I know I'm early but it felt right to give it to you today." She held up a palm as he opened his mouth to add to the conversation. "Hang on. Now, I had a phone call the other night from Lorraine Hudson, my old landlord."

"Yeah?"

"Lorraine is the former CEO of *Architects Australia* and when she retired, she continued to oversee their charitable trust that Emily's programme—"

"It's not my programme, sweetheart," Emily murmured, and Skye gazed up at her adoringly.

"Yeah, it is." She hugged Emily quickly, then returned to Seb. "That the *Home Programme* is part of. Anyway, Lorraine's nearly seventy-one, which she reckons is too old to be doing anything sensible, and she's decided to," she paused deliberately, "and this is a direct quote, 'study Ayurvedic medicine and keep myself stimulated because I'm not yet ready for the drafting board in the sky'."

Their chuckles acknowledged the bittersweet aspect of that statement.

"Anyway, in our phone call, she said that it would be nice to have someone replace her who had a handle on business, not just in architecture, who was younger, who could bring in sponsorship and donations, who could market the programmes and look after the applications."

Seb caught on immediately, and his face dropped. "You're leaving. What does that mean for *Quick Cargo*? What's—"

"Woah, woah, mate. Only two things are going to happen. One, I'm taking over the reins of the trust. I can't keep courier riding, not with my shoulder. My physio was really cranky last time I visited, so, yes, I'm not going to work for *Quick Cargo* anymore." Skye watched potential responses race through Seb's brain, then she leaned forward and picked up the envelope, shaking out the business documents. "I'm not working for *Quick Cargo* anymore, which means I'd like you to accept my resignation, boss." Seb's head shot up, and then he snatched the paperwork, frantically reading through the pages, then he froze in stunned silence.

"Oh, fuck me," he whispered, then glanced apologetically at Emily. "Sorry." His hand holding the documents fell. "Are you serious? You're just signing it over? Just like that?"

Skye nodded, her eyes hot with unshed tears, and Emily rubbed soft circles in her back. "Yeah, just like that. Seb, you were there for me, offering a couch to sleep on, offering everything that was intangible as well, when I was so lost. You were there in a flash when I was finally able to ask for help. You were the *only* person I knew who I *could* ask for help. You've worked as hard as I have on our little courier company, if not more. And," she swallowed, "and you're my best friend and so," she gestured at the papers, "I'd like you to have it. I mean—" The thought occurred to her that Seb might not want the company at all. "Uh. Perhaps accepting…" she trailed off.

Seb, the muscles in his jaw clenching and releasing, tossed the paperwork to the side and stood, then strode quickly around the table, hauled Skye from her chair, and wrapped her in a strong hug.

"You bugger! You amazing good, good person," he grouched into her ear, and they broke apart, laughing, both of them shedding tears.

"Does this mean you'll accept?" Skye peered carefully into his eyes.

"I accept. Thank you. This is amazing, Skye." Then he jerked, as a thought struck. "So when do you take up your new job?"

Skye grinned. "I'm still a courier for another two weeks, or until you get Hayley up and running. She's anxious to start, by the way."

Seb grabbed the paperwork, skimmed his eyes over the front page, where his name and *Quick Cargo* appeared together, and he grinned. "We've got heaps to talk about still, but I really better go help." He turned to Emily. "You've scored a good human, Emily."

Emily laughed. "Oh, I'm very aware of that." Then delivered such a sexy scorching look at Skye that Skye wondered if she'd spontaneously combust.

Seb cleared his throat. "Are you sure that my family can storm your house for lunch?"

***

Emily collected herself. The overt, forward sensuality that Skye produced in her was astounding. She raised an eyebrow at Seb. "They better be storming in. There's a huge amount of food in that kitchen and we're going to need a lot of help to eat it."

Seb nodded, his grin so wide that it filled his entire face. Then he disappeared through the door, clutching his new company.

Emily was thrilled at his reaction to Skye's gift. Her heart had exploded with happiness and love when Skye had explained what she was going to do. There was that word; Love. She could feel the word filling her chest, bursting to come out. Maybe today, the day they officially combined their spaces, their lives, would be the day they combined their hearts.

Emily stood and gathered Skye in. Their bodies fit so well. Their philosophies on life worked together. They felt real, and Emily knew how silly that sounded but it was the only way to describe it. She drifted her hand up and down Skye's back.

"Are you okay with all the changes?" she asked tentatively, her head tucked in so the words sent tiny puffs of air across Skye's neck. The goosebumps on Skye's skin threw a party, and she smiled to herself because she hadn't meant to cause that reaction but unravelling Skye, even accidentally, was a lot of fun.

The 'Are you okay?' question was clearly meant for herself as well as Skye because checking on her okay-ness remained part of her therapy. Kristen asked the question. Nic asked the question, and now Skye did as well, which made the tension in Emily's chest ease. Skye was wonderfully, exactly, completely who she needed in her life. Who she *wanted* in her life.

"Sweetheart, I am very okay with the changes," Skye said. "I'm starting a new job which I think I'm going to love, my best friend is happy, and I'm living with the woman I love." A giant stop sign seemed to appear at the top of Skye's lungs because Emily felt Skye's breath stop. A waterfall of joy ran through her body. Skye loved her. Perhaps she'd been waiting for Skye to say it first, because that meant it was safe for Emily to say it. Who knew? It didn't matter, because right then the words that she'd wanted to say pushed up and revved their engines in her heart.

She drew back. "Say it again," she whispered, acknowledging the fragility of the three-word phrase.

"I love you, Em," Skye said, her eyes beautifully brown, and filled with love. In fact, her whole face radiated joy and desire and… love.

Emily's eyes glistened, then she held Skye's face, her thumbs sliding on her cheekbones. "I love you, too, sweetheart." Then she exhaled because that was the best, most enormous three-word sentence she'd ever uttered. Even if it had technically been five words. A spontaneous smile pushed up her cheeks and she shook her head in wonder. "I love you," she repeated, and her smile widened, then, because she'd heard the sentence Skye had used, she said, "You'll be happy to know that I am also living with the woman I love."

A wicked look passed over Skye's face.

"Do I know her?" she said, devilishly.

Emily narrowed her eyes. "Sassiness like that might prompt me to inform Jas, Seb and his family that lunch is off."

Skye's eyes widened with eagerness. "Really?"

Emily collapsed with laughter. "No! You are incorrigible. As if I could cope with changing plans on them like that, and I wouldn't do it anyway." Then she ran a finger along Skye's bottom lip. "Later, however…"

The End

I sincerely hope you enjoyed reading *Change of Plans*. If you did, I would greatly appreciate a review on your favourite book website. Or even a recommendation in your favourite Facebook lesbian fiction group. Reviews and recommendations are crucial for any author, and even just a line or two can make a huge difference. Thanks!

About the author

Best-selling author KJ lives in Melbourne, Australia with her wife, their son, three cats and a dog. Her novel, Coming Home, was a Goldie finalist. Her other best-selling novels include Learning To Swim, and Kick Back.

Twitter at @propertyofkj
Instagram at kjlesfic
Facebook at https://www.facebook.com/kj.lesfic.7/

Made in the USA
Las Vegas, NV
02 May 2022